C000303073

AUTUMN'S CHAOS

AUTUMN TRENT SERIES: BOOK FIVE

MARY STONE

To my husband.
Thank you for taking care of our home and its many inhabitants
while I follow this dream of mine.

DESCRIPTION

Guilt is a powerful motivator...

Less than twenty-four hours after yet another near-death experience, forensic and criminal psychologist Dr. Autumn Trent should be resting and recovering, not back at work. But she has no choice. Her best friend, Special Agent Winter Black, is missing.

So is Winter's baby brother, Justin...a brutal serial killer.

To make matters worse, Autumn feels responsible for Winter's disappearance. Plagued by guilt and haunted by the memory of her little brother before he was kidnapped and groomed by The Preacher, Autumn knows that Winter would do anything for Justin. She should have stopped Winter from visiting her brother in the maximum-security treatment program for the criminally insane so soon after his capture.

Could Winter have helped him escape? Or is she his next victim?

Now, Autumn must put aside her guilt to focus on the only thing that matters. They have to find Winter...before it's too late.

Autumn's Chaos, the bone-chilling fifth book in Mary Stone's Autumn Trent Series, is a breakneck race for survival, where forgiveness is deadly and timing is everything.

1

Special Agent Winter Black flipped her credentials back into her jacket pocket and nodded to the stony-faced guard standing at the entrance of Virginia State Hospital. There were a few perks and privileges to being an FBI agent. Visiting her brother after standard visitation hours had quickly become an important one.

If asked the reason for her late arrival, she could simply claim the visit pertained to a case. Information gathering. Fed stuff. Though the explanation lacked detail, none of those statements would be lies. Not exactly. And Winter was seldom interrogated by the staff regardless, which was a blessing because each of these visits sent her anxiety levels shooting through the roof.

Winter paused inside the lobby to inhale and exhale in a slow, steady rhythm, battling the desolate wave that assailed her each time she entered these premises. The battle was ongoing.

She wasn't crossing the threshold of an ordinary hospital. The sheer volume of deviant minds locked away in this edifice created an almost palpable cloud of malevolence.

In contrast to the eroded bricks that lent a russet-infused warmth to the structure's outer walls, the hospital's interior was colorless and sterile. Every hallway was a monotony of white concrete blocks. Every room a lifeless, soul-stealing enclosure.

The disparity was unnerving.

Though Winter understood that the neutral color scheme was chosen to prevent overstimulation of the criminally insane patients held in the state's only Adult Maximum Security Treatment Program, the net effect was disorienting. Stepping inside the front doors was like entering a ghost world where time no longer mattered nor existed.

Was that her little brother's experience each morning upon waking within these walls? Did Justin find himself in an undefinable vacuum where time lost all meaning...no today, no tomorrow, and no escape?

A doctor in a white coat squeaked along the tile floor as he hurried past, jolting Winter from her brooding. Great, she'd allowed her mind to lead her down the pity path yet again. Standing in the lobby and feeling sorry for her brother wasn't helping anyone.

She exhaled one last time and headed through yet another set of security doors, tossing her keys into the tray for the harried looking guard to x-ray. They were the only thing she brought inside with her. No gun and not even an ink pen. She felt exposed without her weapon, but she understood the necessary steps it took to get inside these halls.

"You working alone tonight?" she asked the guard. There were normally at least two guards at this checkpoint. Maybe the other was on a break?

The grim shake of his head told Winter otherwise. "The entire place is short-staffed. Guards...nurses...orderlies... every damn place. You sure you want to go inside? Might not be the best night for visiting."

Did she want to visit Justin?

No, she didn't.

And that immediate answer brought on a fresh wave of guilt. It was that guilt that forced her forward. "I won't stay long but thanks for the warning."

The guard shrugged and had her sign the book. She did so with a flourish she didn't feel before facing the maximum-security hallway. Patients were screaming and pounding on doors while nurses and other staff rushed around, their faces tight masks.

This was where her brother lived.

No.

This is where Justin *belonged*.

He may very well never leave. You can love him, but you cannot pity him. Not after the terrible crimes he committed.

Justin was a serial killer, plain and simple. He'd murdered his victims with gory, ruthless abandon, following in the unrepentant footsteps of the man who had raised him... Douglas Kilroy, The Preacher.

Kilroy showcased his nontraditional views of "family" when he'd kidnapped six-year-old Justin from Winter's childhood home. Before disappearing with her brother, The Preacher murdered their parents and left Winter for dead.

Life as she knew it had altered irrevocably when she was just thirteen years old. Her brother's life had mutated when he was less than half that age.

Winter often wondered if Justin would have been better off had Kilroy killed him alongside their parents rather than sucking him into a depraved, demented abyss. Instead, Kilroy had raised her once sweet and innocent younger sibling as his protégé, molding him like clay into a fresh devil to unleash on the next generation.

Justin Black had sat in the kiln, endured the fire, and emerged from the flame hardened.

Brutal.

A serial killer created by a serial killer.

Thanks to Kilroy, her brother grew up believing his calling was to carry on The Preacher's brutal legacy of torture and slaughter. Justin had already made considerable strides in his efforts to prove himself as a worthy disciple before the FBI apprehended him and locked him away. Due to his questionable competency to stand trial for reasons of mental illness, he'd ended up in a state mental hospital instead of prison.

For now.

There was help—hope, even—for Justin at Virginia State Hospital. The building bustled with psychiatrists, psychologists, counselors, and nurses, all trained to find the humanity lying dormant beneath layers of trauma and violence.

Here, Justin had access to proper medication, education, and numerous forms of therapy...talk, group, art, music. He had the opportunity to *heal*.

He could get better. Nothing is impossible.

No one else seemed to believe recovery for Justin was probable, though. Even Winter clung to hope by a very fragile thread. But she refused to release that strand, feeble as it was.

Justin was still alive. Where there was life, there was hope.

The elevator doors slid open as she approached, exposing a paunchy midsection first before widening to reveal the passenger as Victor Goren. Despite his substantial girth, the public defender moved quickly, speeding between the steel doors as soon as space allowed.

Winter studied Goren's expression as he emerged. Her brother's lawyer appeared frazzled. His wispy hair was messier than usual, jutting from his scalp in all different directions, and sweat dotted his forehead and cheeks like fine beads.

Her internal alarms flared.

Had Goren just finished a visit with Justin? If so, his harried demeanor didn't bode well.

"Hello, Mr. Goren. How are you this evening?"

She hated the feigned nonchalance in her voice. Like she and the lawyer were run-of-the-mill acquaintances, stopping for a chat in a normal hospital after checking up on a mutual friend.

Victor met her gaze and offered a tenuous smile. "I'm good, Agent Black. Fine. Your brother, however," he growled low in his throat, "I couldn't say the same for him."

"What's wrong with Justin?" She blurted the words without thinking, panic cloaking her mind and sabotaging any attempts at finesse.

Victor dabbed at his forehead with his purple paisley silk tie. "*Wrong* isn't the word I'd use, Agent Black. More along the lines of distracted. Very distracted. I'm not sure how much he was able to take in from our meeting this evening. He seemed to be…somewhere else."

Winter digested the statement, her brain formulating and spewing a number of possible explanations for Justin's behavior. "Maybe meetings this late in the evening are a mistake? Concentrating at this hour might be too difficult for him. He seems much more lucid during the day."

She hadn't intended the statement as a criticism, but Victor apparently received it as such. He dropped his tie and reared back, the extra flesh beneath his chin wobbling with indignation. "And yet, here you are? The time of day doesn't seem to deter *you* in the least."

Good job, Winter, insulting the one man who's trying to keep your brother out of a prison cell.

She held up an apologetic hand. "I'm sorry, Victor. That

came out wrong. I know you're doing your best given the… given Justin's condition. I appreciate the time and effort you've put into helping my brother. I really do."

To his credit, Victor seemed to forgive as swiftly as he'd taken umbrage. "You're a tough woman, Agent Black. I imagine it's very difficult to walk in your shoes, and I applaud you for attempting to balance family matters with your law enforcement duties."

Winter's throat constricted, but she retained composure. "Thank you. That's incredibly kind."

And wrong. So wrong. I'm not balancing shit. It's more like failing in every aspect of my life. I'm worrying and disappointing the people I care most ab—

"Have a nice evening, Agent Black. Give my regards to Justin."

Goren retreated with noticeable haste. Politeness and civility aside, Winter knew the lawyer couldn't wait to escape the time-warp hellhole that was Virginia State Hospital.

Not that she blamed him. Once she finished her visit with Justin, she planned to haul butt out of this dismal place too.

"I will. You have a nice evening as well."

It was a meaningless tiding offered more from obligation than anything else, but it was the best Winter could do. The monumental effort of playacting like an unaffected individual in a world full of madness was wearing her down, slowly but surely.

Pretending. Everyone was pretending because that was easier.

No, not only easier…*expected.*

Over the past months, Winter had learned the hard way that most people preferred to avoid ugly, inconvenient realities. And when it came to frequenting a maximum-security hospital to visit your baby brother, who'd happened to commit so many murders that no one could pinpoint the exact number? Few realities got uglier or more inconvenient than that.

Instead, most of Winter's friends and acquaintances preferred that she gloss over her personal nightmare for the sake of their own peace of mind.

Yes, my brother's a killer. Should we pick up Chinese for dinner?

No, he's not remorseful. Not at all. Did you catch last night's game?

I'll never be happy or normal or okay because someone I can't stop loving is sick. Demented. Lost. Does this sweater make me look fat?

Sometimes, Winter wanted to drive deep into the woods and scream at the top of her lungs. But what would that change? She'd simply be venting her own craziness out into the world with only the trees as witnesses.

Meanwhile, Justin would still be Justin.

Slouching against the elevator wall, she closed her eyes and attempted to gather her strength. Steel her mind. Brace herself.

That task was proving more difficult with each and every trip into this godforsaken building. Brother or not, Justin Black was taking a toll on her psyche.

Winter had barely spent an ounce of energy focusing on the new case the Special Agent in Charge had assigned her. As a federal agent in the Richmond Field Office, she was by no means basking in free time. Eventually, SAC Max Osbourne would notice her lagging attention and call her out. The Violent Crimes Division couldn't afford slackers.

The sad truth was, Winter struggled to care about the case at all.

A money-hungry woman named Camilla had dated a man who Winter guessed was more apt to follow his dick than his brains, assuming he ever possessed any of the latter.

The happy couple had wed in Vegas, the hall of fame for train-wreck vows.

In less than a month, the husband was dead, and his widow was suspected of burning down their home to cover up his murder. Oh, and coincidentally, the newlywed had taken out a million-dollar life insurance policy on the man right before his "accidental" death.

That case would basically solve itself as soon as they found Camilla. And if or when that day arrived, Winter would deserve none of the credit.

Deep down, she realized her apathy was a problem. She *should* care about the FBI job she'd worked so hard to achieve. But even though the shame of being a piece of shit slacker had settled into her chest like cement, she found the motivation to dive into her FBI duties as elusive as ever.

Lucky girl that she was, the screw-up train didn't stop there.

Her relationship with Special Agent Noah Dalton also rested on shaky, sometimes turbulent ground. Not that she'd ever considered herself a romantic expert, but lately, Winter was proving to be a particularly craptastic girlfriend.

Their main source of contention? Justin.

The same went for her friendship with Dr. Autumn Trent. Autumn was a gifted criminal and forensic psychologist who'd teamed up with the FBI's Behavioral Analysis Unit on numerous cases. More than that, she was Winter's best friend.

At Winter's urging, Autumn had been tasked with determining Justin's competency to stand trial for all his heinous crimes. An admitted gray area—having a close friend evaluate her brother—that had taken a few dark turns.

They didn't butt heads on much.

Except for Justin.

Well, Sherlock, I'm not sure if you've noticed a pattern here...

All of Winter's turmoil seemed to be connected with direct lines to her mentally unstable little brother. Bold, brazen lines that flashed bright red like a neon warning.

The problem was, whenever Winter looked at Justin, she saw a six-year-old boy with silky black hair and blue eyes wearing SpongeBob pajamas, who just wanted to cuddle with his big sis.

Try as she might, she just couldn't make that image disappear.

The elevator dinged, and Winter exited onto Justin's floor, drawing the immediate attention of the male nurse on duty. Dale Miller had seen her enough times to know who she was and why she'd shown up at such an hour.

"Follow me, Agent Black." The order was filled with more than a little annoyance as he took off down the hall at a fast clip.

Winter trailed behind him and kept her mouth shut. Except for the moment when he passed her brother's door.

"Um...where are we going?"

Dale didn't break stride. "He got moved this morning."

Winter frowned at Dale's back. "Why?"

The agitated nurse threw his hands in the air. "Why does anything happen around this shit place?"

Winter was sorrier than ever for coming here this late. None of the hospital employees appreciated after-hour visits, but some were better at hiding their resentment than others.

Dale fell more into the "what you see is what you get" category, and Winter didn't mind the attitude. She could handle blatant irritation.

On the other hand, one more fake smile might trigger a profuse stream of vomit.

When they reached Justin's room, Dale moved aside, leaving the observation window clear. Mustering her courage, Winter stepped forward, tapped on the glass, and peeked inside.

Within the small enclosure, her brother paced from wall to wall, eating up the floor with rapid steps that struck her as aggressive for reasons she couldn't formulate. Justin's mouth moved just as quickly, muttering what she guessed was an intense torrent of thought.

Winter's heart sank over the clear signs of her brother's distress. Victor's assessment had been spot-on. Justin's body was here, but his mind was elsewhere. And there was no way to know which kind of reality he'd traveled to this evening.

Maybe you should follow your own advice and come back later. Meetings this late in the day are a mistake.

She'd already taken a step back when Justin's head whipped up. Blazing blue eyes locked onto her own, and he actually jumped in surprise, as though he couldn't believe she'd come.

Winter froze in her tracks. Her baby brother had sensed her presence just as she was preparing to leave and abandon him *yet again.*

Her actions on that last evening before Justin had been stolen came flooding back, swamping Winter with ever-lasting shame. While she could shoulder the limitless remorse—she deserved that burden and worse—what she could never accept were the consequences of her thoughtless behavior on that fateful night.

Sweet, pudgy-faced Justin had only wanted to snuggle with his older sister. Like any other six-year-old, he'd sought comfort and warmth from a person dear to him.

A person he'd trusted.

The horrible truth was that Winter had been too concerned about her sleepover plans that evening to spare him any attention. Too distracted by important stuff like the upcoming movie marathon. Boy talk. Popcorn.

Justin would never forget that she'd left him, and neither would she. The horror of his present-day reality was her fault.

Her. Fault.

She ignored the guilt hammering in her chest, offering him a grin and a wave. Justin focused in on her, the startled look he'd first displayed narrowing into something calculating for a split-second before a wide, toothy smile emerged.

She didn't have time to register his expression completely before he was gesturing her to come in.

A sudden stab of pain pulsed through her temples, nearly stopping her in her tracks. Ignoring the discomfort, Winter retained her smile even as the shot of agony hit and faded.

Now was no time for one of her headaches.

Or blackouts.

Winter hesitated outside the door, wanting to ensure the episode had passed before she risked entering. She sniffed and touched the area under her nose to make sure it hadn't started to bleed.

Yet another remnant of The Preacher's brutal legacy.

When Douglas Kilroy disappeared with her brother, he'd assumed Winter was dead. Instead of killing her, though, The Preacher had gifted her with a severe brain injury. The emergency surgery that followed left Winter forever changed. As a result, objects or areas in her visual field would sometimes glow red, a silent alert to turn her attention toward the light.

More powerful and considerably more debilitating were the blinding headaches, most of which caused a loss of consciousness. The fainting spells were always preceded by a nosebleed.

While blacked out, Winter experienced visions related to current events in her life. Sometimes, the imagery coincided so well with a real-time issue that she was able to uncover advantageous pieces of information. Those types of visions had helped her solve many a case for the FBI.

Other times, the visions produced jumbled reels of footage that were impossible to decode. Her "special ability" felt like both a blessing and a curse in turn, leading to unpredictable, stress-inducing pivots that she had grown to resent.

"Oh, Jesus Christ. Straddling the fence, are we?" Dale stalked past her and jabbed the key into the lock with an angry twist of his hand. He glanced at Winter, shedding disgust and sarcasm in spades. "He's still batshit crazy if that's what you were wondering."

Winter disregarded the man's mood altogether. Anyone who worked in this building day in, day out was entitled to a few bouts of crankiness.

"Thank you." She stepped into Justin's room with a firm resolve to make the best of this visit. That was all she could do. Garner as much good from the time with her brother as possible.

"Nighttime meds in ten minutes. Don't give me any crap tonight."

Dale barked the order over his shoulder and started to close the door.

Surprise had Winter reaching for the heavy metal. "You're leaving?" She very nearly added "me alone with him" but managed to keep the words from escaping.

The nurse whirled on her. "In case you haven't noticed, this place is a shitstorm of understaffing. You don't feel comfortable alone, then you'll need to reschedule. I'll check through the window every five minutes, but it's the best I can do."

Winter glanced at her brother. Honest to god tears welled in his eyes, and the very tip of his nose had turned pink.

She forced a smile. "I'm happy to stay. Thank you."

The nurse slammed the door without another word, the key grating in the lock, echoing through the room.

Winter flinched but didn't take offense. She assumed Justin's interactions with the staff were often deplorable and that he'd more than likely earned the harsh treatment. She turned to face him straight on, bracing at the ice-cold chill that coasted down her spine as their eyes met.

He was staring at her in a way that...

Fresh bolts of pain spiked her temples, nearly bending her over with their intensity.

"Grandpa had a hard-on for you, big sister. I do too."

Her stomach lurched as the vile words sifted into her head. He'd said them just that morning, turning feral right before her eyes not even twenty-four hours ago.

Yet here she stood in a private room alone with him.

Am I crazy too? Or maybe I've become suicidal without realizing it?

But even as she second-guessed herself, she knew that neither explanation fit.

She was just a sister who had lost too much and had a list of regrets a mile long. The thought of adding more regrets to that list was unbearable.

"Dale's an asshole." Justin aimed a one-finger salute at the door.

Ignoring her throbbing temples, Winter tilted her head. She was skeptical but attempted to keep an open mind. "And there isn't a reason he's like that?"

Justin studied her as though he were preparing a rebuttal in court. "Dale is an asshole because Dale is an asshole. He threatens to quit every damn day. And he's always a jerk to the other nurses. They fight all the time out there."

Winter didn't doubt that the staff of Virginia State Hospital was on edge. Earlier that day, the team had caught the mysterious killer who'd terrorized the premises, but not before he'd killed two nurses.

The perpetrator had turned out to be Albert Rice, an orderly of the same hospital his victims had worked for. Hiding in plain sight throughout the FBI's frantic search.

Albert's sister had committed suicide while under the psychiatric care of Dr. Philip Baldwin. Albert blamed the doctor for her death and plotted revenge, waiting until Baldwin was hired as Virginia State Hospital's medical director to spring his trap. After accepting a job as an orderly, Albert strangled two hospital employees and tried to frame Baldwin for the murders.

The grief-stricken brother's attempt to ruin Dr. Baldwin's life had resulted in chaos. Amidst that mayhem, they'd come close to losing Autumn. *Too* close.

"Spacin' out on me there, Sis. Catching Rice was hard on you, huh?" Justin's blue eyes met Winter's identical ones, and for a moment, she believed he might actually care about her mental state.

Her mind drifted, and once again, images of Autumn tied to a chair with a plastic bag clinging to her face like a second skin blazed through Winter's psyche. If they'd arrived even a minute later...

Too close.

"Wow. You're *crazy* distracted. You don't have to be here if you—"

Because he looked so hurt, Winter grabbed Justin's hand and squeezed. "I want to be here. I do. How is your head feeling after," she licked her lips, "after—"

"After your jerk ass boyfriend shoved me into a concrete wall?" Justin ripped his hand away.

"Justin. You grabbed...you grabbed his..." Winter didn't want to finish the sentence or relive the moment.

"I grabbed his stupid dick. So what? He can't take a little

joke? Has to hurt people half his size to make himself feel better?" Justin wiped a hand across his eyes and slumped, shifting moods in an instant. "It was just a cut. Didn't even need stitches. Maybe I deserved it."

"No one deserves physical violence." Winter was aware that she'd once again fallen into an invisible trap...consoling the penitent serial killer she doubted was truly sorry for his actions. Not yet. Maybe never.

A harsh truth Winter had only just acknowledged earlier that day.

Justin shrugged. "I deserve it for what I said to *you*. I'm sorry. I don't understand why my brain goes all *screwy* sometimes. I hate it."

Winter's headache had eased to the point that she was sure the episode was over. She allowed herself to relax and sank into the room's only hard plastic chair. Justin followed suit and plopped on his cot like a little boy, causing an instantaneous warmth to blanket her heart.

Just two sibs hanging out. This is kind of like that. This is almost what life would have been like if...

"Tell me one of your favorite memories from when we were kids. Anything." She grinned at him, interested in his genuine response. Assuming he gave her one. He might not remember much from those earlier days, but surely, he'd stored a few moments somewhere deep down inside, in a heart she prayed he still possessed.

Justin appeared suspicious, angling his body away from her as though she'd requested an internal organ. In a way, Winter supposed she had.

"I don't remember a lot. I was younger than you." Justin stared out the barred window before turning back to her with a grin. "But I guess I sometimes think about when you'd take me 'fishing.'" He air quoted the word. "Took me a while to figure that one out."

Winter laughed, the sound rising from her belly like a volcano of happiness. Memories assailed her of Justin, maybe four at the time, sitting beside her and carefully lowering his stick into the deep, rain-filled ditch in front of their home.

"You were *so patient*. Determined you were gonna catch a big one before the sun went down." Her shoulders shook as she sputtered out the words.

"You told me there were fish in that damn water. I was four. A little too young to call bullshit, but I figured it out later." Justin snickered, unable to keep a straight face. The levity softened his expression, returning an almost childlike quality to his handsome features.

Winter's breath caught in her throat. She wished she could freeze the moment. Stay in it forever. She could see him in there, the piece of her baby brother that was alive and well. Buried deep under layers of trauma and brainwashing.

It wasn't fair.

If she could figure out a way to bring Kilroy back to life just to kill him again, and again, and again, she'd perform necromancy in a heartbeat. The man would never pay enough for what he'd stolen from them.

Never.

"How about jet fighter battles?" Justin lowered his voice to a cockpit-worthy drone. "Approaching hostiles. Prepare to fire. Over."

"Roger that," Winter replied with equally sober emphasis before a second round of chuckles overtook them both. "We were going to save the galaxy."

Justin snorted. "Sitting at our kitchen table with the chairs turned backward, flying through the cosmos. You always let me lead the missions, though," he mused, nodding his approval at the past gesture.

Winter grinned. "You were much better equipped to save the world." She grew somber as a gut-punch of melancholy brought their present reality into focus. The stark contrast between then and now was undeniable. She hated it.

"Guess that kinda flew out the window, huh?" Justin's thoughts seemed to match hers perfectly.

Too perfect. He's doing it again. He's saying what you want to hear...mimicking your mood. Manipulating, manipulating, manipulating...

"Was every day awful? With him? With Kilroy? Were you ever even...did you ever feel happy? Have good days?" She wished she hadn't asked as soon as the words left her mouth.

Justin stiffened with the same indignant hostility she'd witnessed earlier that morning, his eyes flaming with a similar hellish fire. "Grandpa taught me *important lessons*. He opened my eyes to the way things *are*. Life isn't about being 'happy.' That's the mistake you all make because humans are selfish idiots."

Winter hated that Justin considered the evil bastard to be his grandfather. Kilroy was Justin's second cousin at best.

"I'm sorry, Justin. I didn't mean—"

"I know exactly what you meant." Sneering, he pulled his knees to his chest. "You couldn't possibly understand. Grandpa warned me almost no one would. He said that was okay, though, that it meant he was on the right track. He was a hero. Brave."

The ache in Winter's chest throbbed as she stared at him, realizing he'd transitioned yet again. That he was still in Kilroy's thrall somehow.

"But the crimes he committed...surely you can see how wrong they were. Brutal and heartless. He could have 'spread his message' in a way that didn't hurt, or torture, or kill innocent human beings." She was desperate for just one small sign that her brother could separate himself from Kilroy's depravity.

Justin's eyes narrowed, reminding her of the hateful

monster he'd become when Noah had interrupted their visit. He didn't speak. Instead, he studied her with unnerving intent.

Winter leaned forward, desperate to make him understand. "Don't you see how he changed you? Made you his puppet? How the actions you took were wrong too?"

She realized she was pushing too hard, but she couldn't help it. He was drifting away in front of her eyes again, and she was powerless to reel him back in.

Her brother's nostrils flared. She caught the flex of his jaw before he schooled his features into an indifferent, if not quite pleasant, mask.

A second later, he crumpled, as if a heavy blanket of guilt fell upon his body and weighed him down.

"I do know the things that I did weren't...right. I've had a lot of time to think about all of that."

His shoulders slumped. His tone was penitent.

But Winter wasn't buying it. Every movement, every tiny change to Justin's facial expressions occurred with perfectly executed calculation. His moods didn't flow naturally, changing from one to the next in response to his shifting emotions.

Justin simply morphed, in the blink of an eye, into whatever role he predicted was most advantageous to him at any given time.

She'd experienced enough training on body language through the course of her career to notice these microscopic modifications and see them for what they truly were. Justin was lying to her. Sailing through hoops as he seamlessly adjusted to the version of himself he'd perceived would best garner her sympathy.

She could push. Call his bluff and prod until her brother's own emotions shattered his self-control. Prove to herself once again that he was always just a flash away from the feral, demented animal he'd become this morning.

But what was the point? She knew the truth and understood that her brother may, or may not, ever change. That the odds were in favor of the latter. For now, what was the harm in preserving the moment? In reminiscing about ditch fishing and kitchen-chair-jet-fighter flying?

"What are your dreams, Justin? You have to imagine a life outside of this hospital room..." Winter slouched against the back of her chair, exhausted from the never-ending "damned if you do, damned if you don't" dilemma that presented itself each and every time she interacted with her brother.

He raised an eyebrow, staring at her as though she must have also lost her mind. Not even a second passed before a warm smile spread across his face. "Everyone always wants to talk about my *past*. No one has ever asked me about my dreams...my future. Not that my dreams matter much now."

A tear—that she prayed was real—slid down his cheek.

Winter persisted, intent on dragging a genuine response from her brother's mouth. She didn't need nor want the act. She wanted *him*. "But if the situation was different. If you were a free man right now. Today."

He met her gaze, his eyes exuding an evil that she'd only ever seen in one other person. Pain rippled, merciless and sharp, through her head as she imagined that these weren't Justin's eyes at all, but Kilroy's.

Kilroy alive and well...and sitting right in front of her.

The telltale trickle of warm liquid dripped from her nose to her lip. Justin jumped off the cot, appearing alarmed as she grabbed the ever-present tissue from her pocket and pressed it to her nose.

The door swung open, and Dale Miller entered unannounced. "What's going on here?" he practically roared.

Winter swiveled to assure him that she was okay,

knowing what the situation must look like. But the nurse had already made his assumptions.

"On your cot." Dale pointed to the small bed, his face an angry mask. "Now. Sit."

Justin instantly obeyed, and Dale made a swift grab for a gauze roll sitting on the medicine cart he'd been pushing.

"Dale—" Another burst of pain skewered her skull, and Winter broke off with a moan.

She needed to inform Dale that this wasn't Justin's fault. If only her head would stop pounding like a watermelon whacked with a sledgehammer.

"Always this one with the troublemaking. Hurts his own damn sister. Probably the only person that cares whether or not he's even alive." Dale's low mutter was all too audible. "I'm not even supposed to *be* here right now."

"Dale—" The piercing pain in her temples intensified as she glanced at her brother, who was watching the scene play out with naked interest.

"I'm working a godforsaken double shift because this hospital can't keep a full staff with or without nurses dropping dead left and right. *No one* wants to work in this psycho-filled hellhole. Me included." Dale stomped toward her, wielding a white square. Gauze.

The pain was pulsating now. Intense, steady beats of unforgiving agony. "No," she mumbled. "This wasn't his fault. You're mistaken."

She attempted to peer Justin's way again, pain slamming into her brain as their gazes locked.

"Don't do that. Don't defend a criminal, even if he's your brother. He's a sick little nutjob, and the sooner you..." Dale's voice faded away as Winter's vision blurred with the debilitating strokes of her headache.

Through the pain-streaked fog, she glimpsed her brother's form rise from his cot, grasping something in his hand that she couldn't make out...couldn't focus in on. He approached them, raising the object he held overhead.

Look out!

Winter grabbed Dale's hand. Desperate to warn him, but her tongue was too clumsy, her coordination slow and muddled by the haze of pain.

In the next breath, Justin pounced, slamming his weapon into the back of Dale's neck. Without a sound, the nurse collapsed into Winter's lap.

Pinned to the chair by his weight, her hand instinctively reached for the gun holstered snug against her body.

Not there.

Panic was an icy knife to her chest as she remembered that weapons weren't welcome inside the walls of Virginia State Hospital. Her gun was locked in her car.

Useless.

Just like she was right now.

Pushing through the blinding, skull-crushing pain, Winter struggled to wiggle out from beneath the dead weight of Dale's body. Relentless throbs kept perfect time with the frantic beating of her heart.

You cannot pass out now. You cannot pass out now.

Even as she ordered herself to stay awake, her vision grayed around the edges.

Her last conscious image was of a shadowy Justin, grinning...grinning *so wide* that for a wild, nightmare moment, she feared that yawning mouth would devour her in a single bite.

When his arm swung a second time, the motion was nothing more than a blur. Something cold and sharp pricked Winter's skin.

After that, the pain mercifully faded until Winter felt nothing at all.

2

Autumn Trent screamed and thrashed, desperate to escape the plastic bag that imprisoned her head. Nearby, her mother stood as still as a black-and-white statue next to her father, who glowed red as he glared at Autumn.

His angry shout was deafening.

"Take off that bag! Do you hear me? Take off the stupid bag and stop causing such a fuss! What's wrong with you? Why do you insist on breaking the rules? Why are you always trying to get attention?"

Sarah peeked out from behind their mother, gleaming yellow and bright. Too bright. The intensity of the glare burned her eyes, and the fire spread through Autumn's veins until she was convinced she'd been lit like a candle.

"Stop competing with your sister! She's dead! You've gone too far this time!"

Autumn choked on plastic and braced for her father's cruel hands. He'd rip the bag off her head. Hurt her. But she'd be able to breathe again. She'd be able to inhale...maybe escape.

Only he didn't even take a step toward her. He bellowed and turned deeper shades of red until he morphed into a giant drop of blood, splashing against the ground and drowning her mother and sister in a massive tidal wave.

Autumn couldn't help. Couldn't scream. Couldn't do anything but watch as the crimson currents swept Sarah's yellow glow farther and farther away in the crimson currents until her sister was just a dim, fading light.

"Mom?"

The bag smothered Autumn's cry. It didn't matter. Her mother wasn't there, had never been alive at all except as a statue.

She'd always been a statue.

There was no one to help Autumn. This bag was her life, her death, her eternity. Punishment for being a bad little girl who caused a fuss. She had it coming.

Suddenly, strong arms picked her up, throwing her body across broad shoulders.

"You killed my sister."

Albert Rice was hauling her away, his muscled grip unbreakable. Philip Baldwin lay behind them on the leaf-covered ground, his eyes open but vacant. Dead. Albert had ended his life. Just as he'd end hers very soon.

Philip's blank stare shifted to hers. Not a muscle of his body twitched except for his lips. "You're going in the closet. That's where bad little girls go. What did you do to earn yourself this punishment, Dr. Trent?"

Autumn sobbed, her ankles and wrists bound together, the bag melding to her skin. Her lungs burned.

No air.

Can't breathe.

Can't. Breathe.

Albert threw her into the hatch of a station wagon. "You killed your sister. I'm going to make it right."

His green eyes turned reptilian as his body mutated.

Scales broke through his skin, gradually coating the man until *he was no longer human, but instead a crocodilian beast. Giant fangs protruded from his slimy, blood-covered snout.*

Autumn begged for mercy, but her words were silenced. Trapped by the plastic clinging to her face like a second skin.

"I hope you can swim, Pippi."

The scene shifted, and they were in the ocean. Giant waves tossed her like she was an abandoned soda bottle. She needed to swim, but her arms and legs were too tightly bound to tread water. She gasped to breathe, but the bag wouldn't allow it.

No fair. Why didn't anyone ever fight fair in this world?

The backdrop morphed again. Rough hands yanked her from the water. Winter, Noah, and Aiden stood above her, their expressions grim. Winter knelt and tapped at Autumn's cheek, which had hardened like clay. The bag had sealed to her face...had become her face.

"She's plastic now. Like a doll." Winter sneered as Noah and Aiden approached, disgust dripping from their eyes.

"We don't have time for this, Agents. This isn't a daycare. Stop playing with toys." Aiden barked at the others, turning his back on her without another word.

Noah shook his head and knelt beside Winter. "Why did you kill your sister, Dr. Trent? Why are you always making such a fuss?"

The pair rolled her body off the wooden dock she lay on, and the sea swallowed her whole, pulling her down, down, down...but she wasn't alone. Jaws chomped somewhere close...too close.

"I hope you can swim, Pippi."

Beautiful woodland pictures in elaborate frames with cracked glass floated and sank all around her.

They calmed her. Mesmerizing.

"Isn't this better, Pippi? Would you rather die in a forest all alone? Slow and painful and cruel? You have friends here." Albert swam past her, his gargantuan tail leaving a powerful wake that caused the pictures to bob uncontrolled.

A body dropped upside down into the water, mere inches from her face. Evelyn Walker, the nurse who'd plunged into Autumn's elevator car. Still just as dead and unblinking, though she was waterlogged and rotting. "You shit yourself after you die." The stiff lips cackled. "Isn't that funny? You're dead, but you can still shit!"

The woman sank into the inky blue depths, but her voice carried from below. "Why did you kill your sister, Dr. Trent? Why are you always making such a fuss?"

Autumn's screams resumed, but no one was coming. She was a plastic doll now, drowning in the ocean. They couldn't hear her scr—

Autumn shot up straight in her bed, her heart threatening to take over her entire chest. Her tiny Pomeranian mix was on her with immediate licks to the chin, presumably trying to rid his beloved owner of the terror that had found her. While Toad's excessive underbite may not have been the most comforting sight for anyone else to wake up to, she loved her dog's silly little face.

Peach, her ginger tabby cat, remained a safe distance away on the dresser top, surveying her owner's plight with disdain. Her feline stare conveyed a clear message. *Have you gone insane?*

Autumn pressed a clammy hand to her damp forehead. Her digital alarm clock glowed 6:11 in the morning. Technically, she still had another nineteen minutes of sleep to indulge in, but the idea of falling right back into that nightmare was enough to keep her awake.

It's been less than a day. Not even twenty-four hours. You went through a lot. Your psyche is processing. That's all that was. Your brain processing random bits of information.

The clinical assessment helped Autumn's pulse return to a normal rate. Albert Rice had attempted to smother her to death with a plastic bag less than twenty-four hours ago. Only a few days before that, Evelyn Walker's cold, dead body dropped through the ceiling of her elevator car along with the nurse's leaking postmortem defecation.

Autumn collapsed back onto the pillow and threw a hand over her eyes, making Toad yelp in surprise. Was she seriously going back to work today? The doctors had told her to rest for seventy-two hours, but here she was.

Maybe she *was* insane.

Except, work was her sanctuary. Or at least, it had been, up until she'd started teaming up with the FBI. She supposed the danger level was a bit too high now to qualify her current job as a refuge. But even with the diminished sense of safety, Autumn enjoyed immersing herself in her new duties.

There was an excitement unique to this job that she craved. And though she'd never deny the assignments came with great risk, they were equally balanced with substantial reward.

She just needed to figure out how to stop ending up at the epicenter of every dangerous situation her team encountered. To start, perhaps she could avoid cabins where a psychopath had trapped multiple hostages. Or be certain to decline any and all invites to speed-dating events since history proved those could go horribly wrong. And jumping out of helicopters into the effing Atlantic Ocean?

Not her best decision ever. Although, in her defense, the alternative to the helicopter escapade had been letting what she'd thought was a baby drown. She gave herself a pass for that one.

However, absolutely no more unplanned visits to the prime suspect in a double homicide case...even if she believed the suspect to be innocent.

She was almost positive she could manage that.

After a hot shower and a fresh change of clothes, Autumn felt like a revamped version of herself. She'd opted for a sleek, black turtleneck to hide the angry red line on her neck, a parting gift from Albert Rice, and the plastic bag he'd used to strangle her. No other visible signs of yesterday's disturbance, thank goodness.

She was ready to save the world once again.

But first, Toad needed a short walk to release some of his own pent-up burdens.

When the walk was finished and both pets were settled with bowls of fresh food and water, Autumn took a deep breath and checked the time. Seven o'clock was just now approaching, giving her plenty of time to pay an early morning visit to a patient she knew was waiting for her.

Her past two attempts to meet with Justin Black had been thwarted by unforeseen circumstances, like elevator-spelunking corpses and murderous orderlies. Not her fault. Still, Autumn harbored a pang of deep guilt for abandoning a patient with severe abandonment issues. Going to see him this morning would ease some of the self-reproach eating away at her mind.

Aside from all of that, she had a great deal of work left to do with Justin. His case was complicated, his traumas deep-set.

Autumn drove her Camry toward Virginia State Hospital, determined to attack Justin's demons and assist his recovery in every way she could. She parked in the front lot, checked the rearview mirror to make sure the turtleneck was doing its job of concealing her wounds, and exited her vehicle.

Partway across the parking lot, her long strides faltered, slowing until she stopped altogether. The gargantuan brick building loomed before her. Though always large and foreboding, the facility seemed to have acquired a more sinister air after the Albert Rice case.

A shiver skimmed down her spine.

Nothing good happens in this place.

She checked herself as she started walking again,

rejecting the thought outright. Good could happen, and good *would* happen, because she wasn't giving up. Not on Justin's case or any others.

After showing her badge at the front door and passing the various security checks, Autumn headed toward the patient wing.

The wild din of rage hit her the second she walked inside.

Autumn stopped mid-stride, her hand flying to her throat as she took in the scene.

What on earth?

Chaos. Philip Baldwin's tightly run ship had devolved into a madhouse, for lack of a better term.

Apparently, the hospital was not doing so well after the strangled nurse debacle.

Some patients were shouting. Others were shrieking. Maybe there were intelligible sentences in the midst of it all, but when combined, the mass of voices resembled a crazed lion's roar. Impossible to understand…and unsettling at best.

The staff might not have been screaming like the patients, but their faces conveyed competitive levels of hysteria.

"Watch out!"

Autumn leapt back just in time to avoid wheel marks on her toes when a medical cart flew by at breakneck speed. The red-faced nurse who'd issued the warning raced the cart down the hall, narrowly missing a collision with yet another frantic nurse.

Everywhere Autumn looked, staff members hurried from room to room with agitated haste, the stress evident on their harried faces.

Employees darted around, doling out meds and calming nerves, and there simply wasn't enough staff to keep pace with the demand. Orderlies rushed to assist with sedation shots where needed, and phones seemed to be ringing from every direction and wing of the hospital.

As Autumn absorbed the chaos, she clutched her bag to her chest like a shield.

She was really going to have to rethink that whole "work as a sanctuary" thing.

After double-checking the hall for speeding objects, Autumn hurried to the nurses' station and attempted a genuine smile. "Just here to sign in for a meeting with Justin Black."

She recognized the nurse, Joan Singleton. They'd interacted on several occasions, and a familiar face amidst the din flooded Autumn with instant relief.

Joan nudged a clipboard toward her, attempting her own smile but not quite getting there.

"What exactly is going on? I've never seen this place so..." Autumn struggled to find an accurate description.

"Crazy? Ha. Well. Goes with the territory, I suppose." Joan shoved stray strands of brown hair back from her face. "We had one of our nurses, Dale Miller, up and quit. Just walked off the damn job last night without saying a word to anyone. Takes a special asshole to pull that kind of stunt."

Autumn scribbled her signature and twirled the pen in a circle, indicating the entire facility. "Maybe it's on account of the lovely atmosphere."

"He's half to blame for this 'atmosphere.' We were already short-staffed, and he walks out." Joan collapsed onto her rolling desk chair. "Some of the patients on his rounds didn't even get their evening dosage. But I'm sure that fact is evident."

"Had he mentioned quitting to anyone?" Autumn rubbed her temples, which had started to throb with the beginnings of a headache.

The noise in this place.

"He'd been grumbling all evening about being forced to work a double. Several employees claim he threatened to walk out the door. Repeatedly. But that's par for the course here. No one thought he was serious." Joan leaned closer to the counter. "And they think Dale took a med cart with him."

Autumn balked. "An entire med cart?"

Joan lifted a shoulder. "I think it's more likely that he hid the damn thing out of sheer meanness. Dale's always been an ass, but he wasn't a druggie."

The nurse had to raise her voice in order to be heard over the incessant pounding that joined the caterwauling of Virginia State Hospital's discontented residents. It took Autumn a moment to identify the source of the new commotion.

The doors. The patients were pummeling their doors.

Amidst the banging, Autumn made out irate demands for breakfast and aggrieved cries for freedom. The hospital was clearly in lockdown mode until some semblance of order straightened out the mayhem.

"Is there any way I can help?" Autumn's compassion and sense of duty overrode any discomfort from the unabated racket.

Visible relief slid across Joan's features. "We do have some temp staff coming in to assist, but what we *need* is for the temporary medical director to arrive. If you could stay until then?"

Autumn was aware that Virginia State Hospital's actual medical director was currently in a bed at the medical hospital nearby, recovering from several broken ribs and a severe concussion. Dr. Philip Baldwin had been reinstated as the official medical director of this facility upon proof of his innocence involving the recent strangulations, but he would have to spend some time healing before he could return to full duty.

She knew Philip was peeved by the delay. He wasn't used to being the patient. And even after Albert Rice had severely injured and nearly killed him, recuperating from his wounds wasn't an appealing way for the doctor to spend his passing hours.

Given her training and current ongoing work with an inpatient at Virginia State, Autumn enjoyed medical privileges at the hospital. Her professional credentials were more than sufficient to grant her the authority to make certain calls regarding patient treatment that the nurses and orderlies could not. She couldn't prescribe medication, but she could do just about everything else.

This was one of those instances where Autumn's drive to pursue multiple degrees paid off. In addition to her undergrad degree, Autumn had earned a Ph.D. in forensic psychology with a minor in criminal justice *and* been awarded a Juris Doctorate in addition.

A special ability that she kept much quieter was an aftereffect from a childhood injury. Her father, an abusive drunk, had gifted her with a massive brain injury, the result of a blunt force trauma from the table corner she'd struck when he'd hit her. She'd only been ten years old.

After the subsequent brain surgery required to save her young life, Autumn's reality was forever changed. She'd somehow developed the ability to read another human's thoughts and emotions with just a simple touch of her hand.

Overwhelming as the currents of information were, they'd proven useful in her chosen career path. She'd allowed herself to reframe the unrequested "superpower," eventually growing to appreciate the assistance it provided.

Especially when working with the FBI's Behavioral Analysis Unit out of the Richmond, Virginia, Field Office. Having a sixth sense of sorts often proved an amazing asset in the types of cases she'd encountered with the team.

Autumn believed her calling and duty was to help the troubled minds of this world. And regardless of the incredibly recent events connected to the Albert Rice case, she was primed and ready for action.

Why should today be any different than all the others?

"What can I do first, Joan?" She was one-hundred-percent decided and resigned to this task.

"Well, the most important feat we have to tackle is getting medications ready." Joan's words dripped with fatigue and exasperation. "The problem being some of them were on that missing cart. We're having issues knowing exactly who took what without Dale's chart. Many of the patients detest taking the pills to begin with, so we can't just ask them and trust they'll give an honest answer."

"Got it. I'll search for the cart." Autumn raised her hand to give Joan's arm a reassuring pat, opted against the contact, and took off down the halls.

She decided to start with the third floor—Justin's floor—and work her way back down. If Dale walked out based on anger and exhaustion, he surely hadn't dragged the bulky metal contraption too far.

There was no way to prevent the shudder that rippled through her body as she approached the elevators, which were fully functioning and ready to go. Everything appeared back to normal, as if Evelyn's corpse had never plunged through the ceiling of a Virginia State Hospital elevator car.

Autumn eyed the stairs before stepping into the car and hitting the button. She refused to let fear make decisions for her. Instead, she clasped her hands together, channeling inner calm and composure as the doors slid shut.

The car shuddered as it started to ascend. Autumn flinched, her gaze inadvertently drawn to the ceiling. Nothing to see there. No liquid feces dripping between the tiles. No dead nurse toppling through.

She let out a shaky breath. The memory of Evelyn Walker's dead body dropping through the ceiling was still a vivid memory, one she wasn't likely to forget any time soon.

But she would work through the aftershocks. Their Richter scale magnitude would decline over time. That was how the human brain operated, and she was grateful for the fact.

She was *more* grateful to step out of the damn elevator.

Autumn made her way down the hall, pausing to check maintenance closets, linen closets, bathrooms, and any other space large enough to contain a med cart. The noise level on Justin's floor was every bit as loud as it'd been on the first floor.

Ignoring the inmates licking the glass of their observational windows was second nature. The vulgar comments being shouted at her as she passed melded together in one mass of depraved white noise.

"The redhead doc is back!"

"My dick's ready and waiting!"

"I'm gonna bite those perky tits right off your body, Doc!"

She hesitated outside Justin Black's room. It was empty.

An orderly passed, and Autumn grabbed his arm. "Where's Justin Black?"

The red-faced man nodded toward the end of the hall. "Last door on the right. Got moved yesterday."

She was confused. "Why?"

"Hell if I know."

Shrugging, she headed toward the door the man had indicated and peered inside the window. She exhaled a sigh of relief. Justin lay still on his bed, his body turned toward the wall, and a blanket pulled over his head. She couldn't blame him.

The noise throughout the establishment boomed like thunder.

Autumn finished her inspection of the floor without any

sign of the missing cart. The minutes were ticking by, and she decided to waste no time tackling the next floor down.

As the dreaded elevators came into view once again, her phone buzzed. An acute sense of anxiety awakened in her stomach.

Just nerves. One day, her elevator fears would fade.

She grabbed the device from her bag and swiped to view a text from Noah.

Have you seen Winter? I don't think she came home last night.

3

"Y ou have reached the voicemail of 'Winter Black.' The person you are trying—"

"*Dammit*! Where in the hell *are* you?" Noah gripped his phone, fighting the urge to heave it at the living room wall.

Two hours. He'd been trying to reach Winter for two hours.

So far, all he'd communicated with was her voicemail. She wasn't even viewing his texts. Not one single read receipt.

Big shot federal agent who doesn't even know where his girlfriend is. Impressive.

Noah prowled the apartment that he and Winter shared, commanding himself to get a grip. Slow down.

Think.

Yesterday had been rough. He could admit that. The last twenty-four hours had been a veritable disaster where his and Winter's relationship was concerned.

He shouldn't have pushed her freakshow little brother so hard. That had been a mistake. But Justin had whispered something while locking her in a death grip, and whatever the little asshole said had altered Winter's expression into a stricken mask of despair.

Noah's rage had exploded, and before he could think straight, Justin was bouncing off the concrete block wall, bleeding from the head.

And laughing. The evil shit had been laughing.

He regretted physically harming Justin, but that didn't mean the psycho hadn't deserved it. As far as what Noah had *said* to him…in hindsight, he didn't regret his brutal honesty at all.

The truth was, Justin would never be a part of Winter's real life, the one she experienced outside of Virginia State Hospital's walls. And the kid *was* a twisted psychopath.

Noah stood firm behind that sentiment.

He just wished the altercation hadn't upset the woman he deeply loved.

She'd ordered him to leave after that, and they hadn't had a moment together to dive deep into the fight and discuss matters in a calm, rational manner before Autumn had gone missing and nearly been killed.

Late evening had arrived before he finished all his paperwork and visited Autumn in the hospital. He and Winter had returned home and heated up some lackluster TV dinners. She'd chosen the last fettuccini alfredo, even though she knew it was his favorite.

He'd settled for the reject meal of spaghetti and meatballs. Winter was also aware that that particular dish was his *least* favorite.

When their microwaved meals had all but disappeared, Noah was sure the time had come to discuss what had transpired in Justin's room. He'd figured they could stay up all night if necessary. Just as long as they cleared the air of pent-up, negative emotions.

Noah knew their love was solid, but he needed the relationship itself to recoup solid ground. They'd *both* feel better after that.

Instead, Winter had grabbed her purse and declared that she needed to go visit her brother. Again.

He'd stood there pissed and speechless as she walked out the door. No "I love you" or kiss or hug. Nada.

That was when Jack Daniels had become his date for the night. Two shots chased by three beers. He'd had every intention of waiting up for her return, but the alcohol outmanned him. He'd woken up on the couch the next morning with no recollection of seeing Winter come home.

His anger had grown while he busted his ass getting ready for work. Letting him stay on the couch in his work clothes like a dumbass drunk had been bad enough, but she hadn't even woken him for work before leaving this morning.

They didn't work at effing McDonald's. Their jobs were *serious*. Vital. Winter's passive-aggressive payback move of letting him oversleep and nearly arrive late to the field office was taking their fight too far.

His dark brown hair stuck out in weird spots, and the beginnings of stubble marked his face. He hadn't had time to shave. Or even tuck his damn shirt in.

For all Winter's preaching about keeping work and romance separate, she'd sure let the two overlap this time. And while he couldn't exactly blame his ill-advised spur of the moment drinking spree on her, he sure as hell wouldn't have been consulting anyone named Jack if Winter hadn't made the ridiculous decision to go see her lunatic brother at the end of an already horrible day.

But when Noah had stormed into the office...no Winter.

So, he'd called her.

Voicemail.

Shortly after he'd left a curt message, he'd been sucked into a meeting for a half hour.

When the meeting ended, Winter still hadn't shown. So, he'd called again.

Voicemail.

Scalp prickling, he'd swiped at his screen until he spotted the "Find My Phone" app. He and Winter shared their locations with each other at all times, for obvious reasons.

The app had indicated that her phone was turned off. Her last location was Virginia State Hospital. He'd immediately called the facility, but the conversation had gotten him nowhere.

"Virginia State Hospital. Can you hold, please?" The female voice had seethed with hostility.

"I'm sorry, I just really need to—"

"You know what I need, sir? I need you to stop talking and hold patiently while I do my job. Can you do that for me, sir?" Hostile and downright *mean*.

Noah had tolerated elevator music for a full twenty minutes before hanging up, his mind racing.

Maybe she'd returned to the apartment. Maybe she was experiencing some type of full-blown emotional breakdown due to the never-ending hell of dealing with her monster of a brother.

God knew he and the rest of the world would understand if that little jerk had become too much to handle.

There was just one problem with that scenario...Winter hated showing weakness. She'd probably turned off her phone, waited for him to leave, and crawled into their bed to sob in solitude.

Clinging to that hope, Noah had driven like a madman back to their place, but when he burst into the apartment calling her name, there'd been no reply.

Winter wasn't home.

As he'd searched each room, Noah realized that not only had he not spent a minute *worrying* about his girlfriend that morning, he'd also paid no attention whatsoever to her toiletries or clothes.

He couldn't even remember if the shower was wet when he'd stepped in.

Some FBI agent he was.

When his breathing grew ragged, Noah leaned his forehead against the bedroom wall until he regained control of his spiraling fears.

Slow down.

Think.

His pulse steadied. His mind sharpened.

Clothes. Check for Winter's dirty clothes.

Noah rushed to the fabric hamper in their bedroom and pawed through the top layer. Yesterday's outfit wasn't there. After a little more digging, he ascertained that it wasn't there at all. The rest of her clothing was either hanging in the closet or smashed deep into the hamper.

Neither of them had found two spare minutes to catch up on laundry in what seemed like months. If Winter had taken off for some unknown destination, she certainly hadn't packed a bag before leaving. And Winter always took a "go bag" when she traveled.

He ran to the bathroom and opened the drawer where she kept her birth control pills. Today's little white circle was still there.

Noah stared into the container, his hackles rising.

Winter didn't forget her pill. She was a freak about taking that thing. Same time every day, no exceptions.

This wasn't like her at all.

Noah called Virginia State Hospital again but was immediately placed on hold. He ended the call and took a deep breath, counting to ten as he blew the air back out.

Panicking never helped a situation, and it wouldn't help this one, either. Of course, that was assuming she needed help. *Did* she need help?

Where was she?

Not at home, that much was for sure.

Noah jumped into his truck and hauled ass to the field office, not giving two flying shits about the speed limit. He charged into the building like a bull into an arena, prepared to trample anyone and anything to get to the bottom of the situation.

The first person he encountered was Special Agent Sun Ming, who wasn't exactly the prime candidate for helping out her colleagues if the matter didn't involve a case. He approached her anyway. "Have you seen Winter today? I can't find her."

Sun rolled her dark eyes and turned back to her computer screen.

"Thanks a lot, Sun. I'll remember that." *Asshole.*

Noah whirled, already searching for someone more human to pester.

Overhearing his inquiry, Special Agent Bree Stafford lifted her head and frowned in genuine concern. "You haven't seen Winter today? Don't you two live together?"

Noah raked his hands through his hair and suppressed a groan. How did he explain last night's events in five seconds or less? "We do, but we must have missed each other this morning. I overslept."

There. That sounded decent-ish, right?

Bree raised a perceptive eyebrow. "I'll let you know if I hear from her, but I haven't seen her yet today. I'm working the new case we've been assigned, so I haven't exactly been paying attention to roll call."

Guilt punched Noah in the face. They were supposed to be homing in on an investigation into a suspicious series of deaths at a local nursing home. A shocking number of residents had passed within a week of each other, and foul play was suspected.

Local authorities had requested assistance from the FBI, but the agents first had to determine whether the case merited their involvement. Which meant digging. Research. Concentrating on the job.

Noah's shoulders slumped as he realized he hadn't given the case two seconds of his focus while his colleagues were already knee-deep in the assignment. "Bree, I'm sorry. I promise I'll be on it as soon as—"

Bree waved a smooth, ebony hand at him, shooing him away. "I'll be fine. You go find your girl."

Noah was grateful but had no time to express it. Even if Bree had dropped a ten-ton guilt trip on him, his unease concerning Winter overrode all else. He beelined for the hallway and nearly crashed into Special Supervisory Agent Aiden Parrish.

The last son of a bitch I'd ever want to get involved in my personal life...

Aiden halted and considered him with a cool blue stare. The man looked just as pulled together as always, despite the close call they'd all experienced in the last twenty-four hours.

Not a wrinkle in his expensively tailored suit. Not a strand of wavy light brown hair out of place. Aiden Parrish was impenetrable, and Noah disliked him all the more for that quality.

Sucking in his pride, Noah spit the words out. "Have you seen Winter today?"

The corners of Aiden's mouth curved upward ever so slightly. "Don't tell me you kids are having a lover's spat, Agent Dalton. Couples therapy isn't my specialty."

Noah's fists clenched with a barely controlled urge to punch Aiden in his smug face. "I haven't seen her today, and

I'm almost positive she never came home last night. *No one* seems to have seen her."

Aiden's grin dissipated. Beneath that cool exterior, the SSA cared a great deal about Winter and her well-being. All he needed was to realize the matter was serious and that Noah's current concerns extended far beyond those of a regular old boyfriend.

If Aiden was as damn good at his job as everyone professed to believe, he'd read the authentic panic on Noah's face, in his voice, and even the way he was standing. And he would have read it fast.

"I haven't seen her, Dalton. Have you checked with Osbourne?" No trace of humor emanated from Agent Parrish now.

Max Osbourne was both Noah and Winter's boss. If anyone would know for certain whether or not Winter had shown this morning or been whisked away on assignment, it was the Special Agent in Charge of the Richmond Violent Crimes Task Force.

"I was on my way to his office now. If I don't luck out there, I thought maybe I'd give Autumn a call. After her, I'm out of ideas. I don't know what else to do other than go to Cyber and see if we can track her."

Noah couldn't believe he was even having this conversation.

Yeah, so Winter disappeared. Guess we're gonna have to go hunt her down. No big deal. Normal, everyday stuff.

"I'll make some calls and see what I can find out," Aiden offered. The two parted ways with equal haste.

When he arrived at Max's office, the door stood slightly ajar. Noah rapped twice on the solid wood door before wiping his damp palms on his pants. Max would know. He kept dutiful track of his agents, whether they realized it or not.

"Come in." Osbourne's voice was more bark than bite.

Noah rushed across the threshold, deciding to cut right to the chase. "Have you seen Winter today?"

Max confirmed in two seconds what Noah had feared to be true. His gray eyes narrowed. "Winter Black hasn't set foot in the field office this morning."

Bad. Very, very bad.

"She's not out on some...special assignment or last-minute task?"

Noah's panic swelled as his mind raced to the next steps. Autumn. Cyber.

"No, Dalton." Max ran a weathered hand over his grayed buzz cut. "I haven't sent her anywhere. Is there any particular information you wanna share? Something I should be worried about?"

Noah wanted to display a brave front but knew anxiety was tweaking every muscle on his face. "I don't know yet, to be honest."

"Well, when you *do* know..." Max thumped his chest.

"Yes, sir." Noah was halfway out the door, his hand in a farewell wave. "I'll keep you informed."

He headed straight to the Cyber Division, texting Autumn as he walked.

Have you seen Winter? I don't think she came home last night.

Once he reached Cyber, he didn't waste time hunting down a familiar face. Anyone would do right now. Approaching the first tech in his direct line of vision, he jotted Winter's number on a sticky pad and slapped the page on the desktop.

A pair of wary brown eyes tracked his movements, conveying mild alarm at his abrupt mannerisms. Noah didn't know the girl, but that didn't matter. "I need to track this number. Special Agent Winter Black. Her phone is off, but you can still trace it, right?"

The girl glanced at the scribbled number and nodded. A few swift taps of the keys later, a dot flashed on the screen. "There she is."

Noah crowded the monitor, watching as the dot moved at a slow but steady pace straight north on the interstate. According to the screen, Winter was a good two hours away from Richmond already.

"What the *hell*, Winter?" He whirled away from the monitor and addressed the tech. "Keep that trace active. I'll send in an agent to take over."

Charging out of the room and back down the hallway, he whipped off a joint text to Aiden and Autumn.

She's heading north on I-95. Two hours out already. Absolutely no idea why. Cyber has her on an active trace. I'm going after her.

Noah couldn't think of one single reason why Winter would leave in such a way or where she could possibly be headed. None of this made any sense. This wasn't how his girlfriend operated.

Even if she'd succumbed to some wild, spur-of-the-moment urge to split town, she'd have provided Max with the basic details to say the least.

Winter Black didn't walk out on her responsibilities or the people she loved, and she certainly didn't drive off without so much as texting one word to anyone.

Distress pulsed in his chest, keeping time with his racing heartbeat. An adrenaline rush kicked in next, heightening his senses and infusing his muscles with taut energy.

When Noah jumped into the driver's seat of his truck, he had no idea what his plan was.

His goal, however, was simple.

He was going to find his damn girlfriend and bring her home.

4

As Autumn retraced her earlier path down the Virginia State Hospital's third-floor hallway, she was too distracted by Noah's message to be bothered by the patients pounding the windows with their fists.

According to Noah, Winter hadn't returned home to the apartment they shared last night.

Autumn bit her lip, reminding herself not to jump to any wild conclusions.

Winter was a smart, focused professional. If she was avoiding Noah, she probably had her reasons, and she wouldn't thank Autumn for jumping in the middle of a lover's quarrel.

Despite her logic and calm veneer, Autumn's stomach continued to writhe. She couldn't ignore the anxiety that burst to life when her phone first buzzed. That type of internal alarm bell didn't exactly fit into her set of sixth sense skills, but she'd learned to pay attention to all her instincts while working with the FBI.

Don't dismiss your gut.

With that in mind, Autumn approached Justin Black's

room. She knew for a fact that Winter had planned to visit her brother the previous evening. For once, he might be able to help someone else, and the ability to make positive contributions was paramount in reframing the way Justin viewed life.

He didn't have to be a killer. He didn't have to follow the ways of Kilroy. He could be whoever he wanted.

She'd just reached his door when another text from Noah came through.

She's heading north on I-95. Two hours out already. Absolutely no idea as to why. Cyber has her on an active trace. I'm going after her.

Autumn dissected her conversation with Winter at the hospital yesterday. No word of an out-of-town trip, and her friend had left the ER in high spirits.

What could have changed in such a short period of time?

Frowning, Autumn peeked through Justin's observational window. The lump under the covers was in the same position as the last time she'd checked. He hadn't moved at all. Maybe the racket from the other patients didn't disturb him, or else he was too worn out from all the chaos to care. That would be an understandable response.

Once she found an orderly to unlock the door, she could inquire about Winter and also make sure that Justin was doing okay. Holding steady, at least.

He couldn't afford any setbacks at this point.

Autumn raised a hand to flag down a nearby orderly when an altercation broke out down the hall. This time, the chaos wasn't instigated by patients. The *staff* was fighting.

"I've worked forty-eight hours in the last three days, asshole! You wanna tell me again just how slow I'm moving? Come on. Say it! I dare ya!" A beefy orderly towered over his colleague, who lay on the floor with a bloody nose.

"Sure, Sam! I'm gonna say it again so you can break my

damn nose. Screw you! You ain't worked no more hours than the rest of us, ya prick." The orderly on the floor was much smaller than Sam but appeared to be equally as fed up.

Autumn rushed down the hallway as nurses and orderlies gathered to pull the two apart. Sam appeared to resent the intrusion. When a middle-aged brunette nurse put her hand on his arm, he threw her off with so much force that she tripped backward into the wall.

"Jerk!" The stout woman rubbed the back of her skull, her teeth bared in disgust. "You push women now, Sam? I'm trying to help you keep your damn job!"

The smaller orderly sat up and glared at Sam in such a way that Autumn predicted he was only moments away from launching his own attack.

"Stop!" She shouted the word as loud as her lungs would allow, which after nearly suffocating to death less than twenty-four hours ago turned out to be a less-than-impressive volume.

Still, her command was effective. Shocked out of their argument by the presence of someone with the power to get them fired, Sam and the other staff members stared at Autumn in silence.

Even as "the redheaded doctor who didn't even work here," Autumn outranked them all because of the Ph.D. at the end of her name. They valued their jobs too much to continue the scuffle in front of her.

"Could you grab some gauze for this man's nose, please?" Autumn addressed the nearest nurse, who scuttled off without delay, before hurrying over to help the woman who'd been tossed against the wall. "Are you injured?"

"I'm fine. *I'm* not the one losing my *mind* like he's one of the damn patients." The nurse scowled at Sam, who stood nearly frozen and in obvious dread of the potential repercussions of his tantrum.

"Listen, everyone is on edge after this past week. That is completely understandable, but we're all professionals and we must act as such." Autumn focused in on Sam. "This is a hospital. That means there are people here who need *us* to take care of *them*. Physical violence is unacceptable."

"So, what, I'm fired by a doc who doesn't even work here? Are you serious?" Sam refused to concede so easily, puffing out his chest like a belligerent teenager.

Autumn gritted her teeth, wishing she could give them all a time-out. "I'm not firing anyone, but I will write up an official report on this. And I *am* dismissing you for the remainder of the day. I'll let the interim medical doctor handle the details from there."

Sam huffed and stomped past the gathering, giving Autumn a pointed sneer as he went.

The smaller, lankier man on the floor threw his blood-smeared hands in the air. "So he gets rewarded with a day off for making my damn face bleed? Unbelievable!"

Autumn knelt beside him. "He gets *reprimanded* and sent home to cool off so that your face can stay intact. Do you need your nose x-rayed? Are you in a great deal of pain?"

When he realized her concern was genuine, the man's anger dissipated. "I'm fine. He didn't break it. Not yet."

Autumn blew out a slow breath. "I'll need your name for the report."

"Orville Strachan."

"Will you be pressing charges, Orville? Or do you want some time to think about that?" She waited, giving him her full attention.

Orville sighed, pressing his fingers to the bridge of his nose again. "No, I'm not pressing any damn charges. Sam's not usually like that. Nobody is thinkin' straight right now."

Autumn stood as the nurse returned with the gauze and eyed the employees who were still milling around the hall in small clusters. "If we can all just try to understand that *everyone* is exhausted. You don't have to love your coworkers, but you must respect them. We're all only human."

She received a few nods and more than a few eye rolls, but the disaster had been averted. For now.

Autumn rubbed the back of her neck. The temp staff needed to arrive soon. Preferably yesterday.

She made her way through the wing to the nurses' station, knowing the report needed to be written as soon as possible for her words to hold much sway. As the hours passed, her account would be considered less of a record and more as "semi-accurate hearsay."

After finishing that bit of paperwork, she pulled out the patient charts to tackle. Joan had called up from the first floor while Autumn was writing her report, sounding desperate to get medications sorted and delivered.

They couldn't wait any longer to locate the damn medical cart. The patients' fury had escalated and would only continue to do so until they received their overdue prescriptions.

This entire scene was shameful. Politicians sure loved to mandate a good budget cut to the "ugly" places such as mental hospitals. She bet most of the men and women making those calls would change their tune if they were forced to spend a day working in a facility like this one.

Where's a damn soapbox when you need one...

Right now, calming the residents and restoring peace was more urgent than ruminating over the injustices of the system.

Autumn busied herself with the patient charts, digging for the appropriate information and sending out the corresponding orders. She wasn't sure how much time had passed before she was able to come up for air. She rose to grab a much-needed cup of coffee from the breakroom, checking her phone on the walk over for any messages she'd missed while knee-deep in someone else's job.

Her screen only showed one new message, and it wasn't from Noah. Relief stirred, easing the tension from her stiff neck. No text was a good sign. If something were wrong —*really* wrong—with the Winter situation, Noah would have blown up her phone by now. Hopefully, they'd located Winter already, and her disappearance was the result of a miscommunication.

Autumn did, however, have a message from Mike Shadley...her wonderful, kind, and *official* boss. Autumn cringed. In the past couple of months, she'd worked for everyone *but* Mike.

She reminded herself that the man didn't mind. Shadley and Latham received the enormous paycheck from the FBI for her services and would continue to do so until she was officially hired on with the bureau.

She still had no idea when that day would actually come, but that was all semantics.

For now, she was able to do the work she loved with the FBI and still get the substantially larger paycheck from Shadley. She'd milk that money tree for as long as possible. Deep down, though, she was eager to become an official federal agent. And whenever all the red tape had been sliced through, she would.

Once she was alone with a cup of questionable jet-black brew in the third-floor breakroom, Autumn called Mike back. Given the recent uptick in her life upheavals lately, who knew when she'd get another chance?

"Autumn Trent! When did you plan on telling me that you'd been *kidnapped*?"

Autumn flinched at Mike's question. Why hadn't she remembered to call him herself?

"Mike, I'm so sorry. I've been a little...overwhelmed. Not

quite firing on all cylinders yet." Her response seemed feeble. There wasn't a good excuse for not keeping her own boss up to date on matters as grave as her own abduction.

"Well, don't be too hard on yourself. How are you holding up? No serious injuries, I was told, thank god."

The compassion in Mike's voice reminded Autumn briefly of her adoptive father, sending a wave of homesickness through her chest.

She'd been lucky enough to escape the foster care system while still a young teen. An older couple had adopted her and given her the first experience of what a "happy home" was. The majority of foster children weren't so fortunate, and even though her adoptive father had passed, she felt honored to have known him.

"No serious injuries." She sank into a plastic chair and propped her feet on another. "My co-captive, Dr. Philip Baldwin, took most of the blows. He'll be recovering for a while before he can return to his position. He's the medical director at Virginia State Hospital, but you might have known that. I'm at the hospital right now, actually."

"I was informed that you were put through a bit of the ringer too. You should be at home resting. Didn't they tell you that?" Mike admonished her in such a concerned papa bear way that Autumn feared he might call the FBI and reprimand Aiden for allowing her to come into work.

She chuckled. "They did tell me that. But you know that you can't keep a good horse down." What would she be doing at home, anyway? Obsessing over the job? Berating herself for having neglected her meetings with Justin Black for this long?

Mike emitted a heavy sigh. "You're not a horse, Dr. Trent. You're a human. Doctors aren't impervious to trauma, not even in the psychology field." Autumn wondered how well he was standing up in the face of *his* struggles.

"The company doing okay, Mike?" She kept her tone light.

"Indeed, it is. I've decided on the new name and branding for Shadley and Latham. Insight Behavioral Analytics. Good?" Mike Shadley had made the tough decision to drop his own name from the company's title.

Shadley would naturally remind clients of Latham, and no one wanted to be reminded of Adam Latham.

"I like it. You chose well." Autumn was happy for Mike for dropping the dead weight from his business and moving forward with integrity.

"I'm working my ass off with these attorneys to get things transferred over as quickly as possible. Are you still willing to wait for the name change to be official before filing your suit against Adam?" Mike broached the subject in a calm manner, but Autumn noted the nervous energy in his voice.

While on a work assignment with Adam Latham, who at the time was her boss and supposed mentor, Autumn had received unwanted and inappropriate attention. After she'd rejected Adam's advances, he'd slapped her.

Her hand drifted to her cheek, as it often did when she thought of the horrible man. She'd determined that, though she wasn't his first victim—the assault prompted an internal investigation, which shed more light on Adam's true character and history with females—she *would* be the last.

She planned to take every action within her power to stop Adam from ever taking advantage of another woman. In layman's terms, she was filing a suit against him for sexual harassment and assault.

Mike was desperate to change the name of the firm before news broke of Adam's inappropriate conduct. He'd bought out his partner in quick form, determined to sever all ties with the deplorable man. But processing a full title modification for the company through the snail-paced legal system required more time.

"Remember that I only have one-hundred-and-eighty to three-hundred days to file a harassment suit. Longer for the assault." She hated to worry Mike and would assist him in any way necessary...so long as she was still able to give Adam what he deserved.

A lawsuit.

Allowing Adam Latham to walk away from his wrongdoings was unfathomable, the equivalent of her saying that what he'd done to her was no big deal. Standing up to such a high-profile man wasn't an undertaking she relished, but simply letting the incident fade away into the white noise of the past would be wrong.

How could Autumn expect the victims she counseled to stand up for themselves...for *justice*...if she allowed her own discomfort to call the shots and pushed Adam's abhorrent behavior under the rug?

She'd never save the world by staying silent. Victims' voices needed to be heard. In this world, speaking hard truths wasn't a luxury. It was a necessity.

"I would never want you to miss your window on my behalf." Mike's voice held all the sincerity Autumn knew he was feeling. He was such a good man. "Adam has to be held accountable for his actions, and I'm backing you all the way. If the rebranding isn't done when your deadline approaches, you absolutely have to file anyway. The company will recover."

"And I back the *firm's* mission one hundred percent." If Mike had been sitting next to her, Autumn would have hugged him. She adored Mike. Any time she could help him out, she would. "You're doing good work. That's why I wanted the job to begin with. I have no moral dilemma in waiting. Promise."

"Thank you, Autumn. I appreciate it. I do. I'll be checking in on you soon. Get some rest." The relief in Mike's voice, along with his thoughtfulness, was enough to cement her decision.

She crossed her fingers and promised to take some recuperation time before ending the call.

Recuperating while working with the Federal Bureau of Investigation didn't seem to be an option. Besides, she'd lose her mind sitting at home, knowing the team was out chasing down the next bad guy without her.

Autumn stood to pour herself another cup of coffee. She could use one last shot of caffeine before finally heading to Justin's room.

Better late than never.

As she crossed the short distance to the coffee pot, fresh guilt plucked at her conscience. Poor Justin. By this point, Autumn was positive that he believed the "never" part. Who could blame him? She'd been a no-show several times now. Whether or not that was within her control wouldn't matter to him.

He was her responsibility. He counted on her to keep her commitments.

While most people would run from the thought of having a serial killer depending on them for anything at all, Autumn truly wanted to help Justin. Earning his trust was vital if they were to make any progress.

Maybe he couldn't be "fixed," but he could improve. Justin Black could change, even if it was by one minuscule degree at a time.

She reached to grab the pot but stopped as her phone rang.

Noah.

Her belly knotted with a new wave of anxiety. Something was wrong.

Autumn stabbed the button and pressed the phone to her ear. "Everything okay?"

"She's gone. They found the phone, well, helped me find the phone. We found it, and she's gone. *Gone*, Autumn. She's just *gone*. How could this happen so quickly? What kind of a dumbass, idiot FBI agent boyfriend am I to just—"

"Whoooa…" Since Autumn didn't speak Texan auctioneer, she'd barely been able to process the majority of Noah's rant. "Deep breath. Take a deep breath and then explain to me from the beginning. 'They' found her phone. Who is 'they'?"

The hiss of Noah's inhale and extended exhale preceded his words. "The highway patrol. I was able to get their assistance in stopping the vehicle that Winter's phone was on. It was a tractor-trailer truck, and her phone was stuck behind the fifth wheel area. But *Winter* was nowhere to be seen."

Autumn absorbed the news, her muscles tensing. "So, her phone had been placed on the truck…" The gnawing in her stomach grew.

"Yes, but no Winter." Noah gulped, loud and hard enough for the sound to reach Autumn's ear. "The trucker said he'd stopped back in Richmond for breakfast at a gas station/diner combo. I'm headed there now. They might have some CCTV surveillance footage I can watch. I don't know what else to do."

A terrible idea surfaced in Autumn's mind. The anxiety ball expanded, growing until heavy pressure filled her entire chest. "Hold on, Noah. Don't hang up. I'm going to check something."

She paged Joan, requesting her immediate assistance. The nurse appeared in under a minute, chest heaving from her sprint up the stairwell.

Autumn waved for her to follow and rushed down the

hallway, her dread growing stronger with every step. She stopped at Justin Black's door and pressed her nose to the window.

He still hadn't moved. Not one inch.

Her pulse accelerated when she grabbed the doorknob. As she'd feared, the metal twisted easily beneath her hand.

The door was unlocked.

Heart hammering now, Autumn dashed inside and immediately spotted the missing medical cart on her left. Someone had pushed it far enough over to ensure the cart was out of view from the window.

"What's going on?" Joan whispered as Autumn approached Justin's cot.

She raised a trembling hand and reached for the blanket covering the figure on the mattress. One quick tug killed any remaining doubts.

Autumn stared at the unmoving form as Joan scooted closer. "Wait, that's not..." The nurse gasped. "Oh my god!"

An ear-splitting scream followed.

Dammit. Autumn had really wanted to be wrong about this.

When the nurse ran out of breath, Autumn could hear Noah yelling like a maniac through the phone speaker.

She needed to tell him what was going on, except her mouth refused to move, and her limbs were rooted to the spot. For now, all she could do was stare.

Dale Miller hadn't walked off the job last night. Dale Miller was dead.

The missing nurse was lying on the cot facing the wall, his body already stiff from the rigor mortis that had set in. At the base of his neck, dried blood encircled a puncture mark that didn't look like it'd come from a knife.

Once the shock wore off, adrenaline pumped through Autumn's veins, flooding her system with pulse-rocketing horror. In the midst of chaos within the building, Autumn's chaos began screaming and screaming in her mind.

Winter was no longer the only Black sibling missing.

Her little brother was also MIA.

Notorious serial killer Justin Black was *free*.

5

I opened my eyes and smiled with the enthusiasm that only a jailbroken prisoner could ever understand.

I'd done it. I'd escaped.

And my exit had been so *smooth*.

Grandpa must have been watching over me for every detail to have worked out so flawlessly. I couldn't have pulled that off better if I'd planned every single step for months.

After taking Winter's car, I'd found a substitute quickly enough. The owner, a Roger something-or-other hadn't even put up much of a fight when he realized that he'd stopped to "help" the wrong people.

While Roger's car wasn't quite as nice as Winter's, it hadn't given me a single problem as I drove most of the night to my temporary hideaway.

The dingy, cracked laminate ceiling of the RV was possibly the most beautiful sight I'd ever seen. It rivaled the seven wonders of the world.

Because it wasn't prison or the hospital.

Free. I was *free*. Released from that barren dungeon of a hospital room and back out into the big, wide world.

My greatest fan had really come through for me.

Well, mostly.

The RV he provided wasn't anywhere close to luxurious, but considering I'd given my fan only a few minutes notice regarding my needs, I was happy to have a secure hiding place.

Sure, we were currently inhabiting an effing dinosaur of a motorhome. Pieces of the faux wood paneling were hanging off in some places and missing altogether in others. More than one roach had scuttled out of the ancient cabinets suspended above the mini-sink and stove, both of which were long past being in working order.

The beast looked like hell, and the interior positively reeked of dog piss.

But I was free.

I turned my head and gazed at Winter, who lay bound and gagged on the other bed just a few feet away. My beautiful Sissy.

She was awake and giving me quite the stare-down. No, more like a glare-down. I waited for fear to shine from her sapphire eyes, but I couldn't detect any yet. That was fine.

She would soon enough.

Joy over her eventual capitulation bubbled through my body like a fizzy drink, and I leapt to my feet with a giant grin. "I'm so glad you're finally awake."

She tried to reply, but the gag caught each of the empty threats. I had to imagine the vulgarities being slung my way.

My grin widened. I loved gags. Such a simple, beautiful tool of control.

Look at her struggle. So animated, my sis. So hellbent on doing the right thing.

Her days of law-abiding nobility were over. She just didn't know it yet.

I bent and kissed her forehead, inhaling her heavenly

scent. Winter always smelled that way. Like flowers and candy and...

My mouth flooded with saliva, but there wasn't time for that right now. Focus.

Focus was key.

I grabbed the gag and pulled the cloth from her mouth with a slow, deliberate movement. My sister was a fighter, and I didn't feel like losing a damn finger this soon into our journey.

After lifting a cup of water to her lips, I tilted the container and watched her sip the trickling liquid. My god, she was gorgeous. I hoped Grandpa was seeing this.

But that was silly. I knew without a single doubt that he was viewing every single second. Grandpa had helped make this happen, after all.

"This is your first and only warning, Sissy. Stay quiet. No one will hear you anyway, not even if you scream. But there will be *no* second chances."

Maybe I was being a little harsh, considering I'd kinda just ruined her life, and there wasn't a soul around for miles to hear her whoop and holler about the fact. Better safe than sorry.

I'd driven us all the way into bumfuck Cherokee, North Carolina. Right into a campground that was, for obvious reasons, empty as hell. No one was stupid enough to go camping in January. Too cold. Duh.

Yet here we were, by necessity. I *needed* the privacy and seclusion.

The RV's main heater wouldn't work no matter what I tried, but there was a little space heater tucked away in the back that was churning out warmth. Enough at least to keep us from freezing to death.

Although watching Winter slowly turn as blue as her eyes would be a pretty fun way to spend the day...

I loosed a dejected sigh. For now, I supposed I'd let her live. I had all kinds of ideas as to how to end her pathetic, do-gooder life, and I hadn't decided which one was the best just yet.

The fact that I could only kill her once was aggravating.

Un-freaking-fair.

"I guess I should fill you in on how we managed to get away." I plopped down on the bed across from her, enjoying the way her eyes narrowed at my usage of the term "we."

My sister wasn't going to like the fact that we were a team now, not one tiny bit. She'd fight that idea tooth and nail. Given time, though, the human mind could come to terms with many off-putting realities.

I understood that better than anyone.

If *my* eyes could be opened, so could Winter's. Shared DNA and science backed that shit up.

I rested my elbows on my knees, giggling a little at the way Winter kept fighting the ties around her wrists. "So, you've been unconscious for like, fifteen hours. Or maybe fourteen. Whatever. But we've had quite the sibling adventure while you were out."

She was a lot of things. A slut, a sinner, a dumbass. A self-ish, abandoning bitch...but she wasn't a quitter. Not my sister.

"Your nose. Your nose started bleeding out of like, nowhere. It was kind of gross. And Dale, the asshole, thought he'd pretend to help you, when all he actually wanted to do was screw you. I guarantee you that." I hoped she was smart enough to realize this fact on her own, but all of that ridiculous belief in the good of humanity had probably clouded her vision.

I figured until one of those dicks actually proved to her, with their dick, what all men were thinking twenty-four seven, she'd continue to dismiss the idea that a noble-hearted whitecoat would ever harm her.

Disappointing, but not surprising.

I bounced on the cot, enjoying how the squeak of the ancient board made my sissy flinch. "Anyway, the perfect opportunity was basically dropped right in my lap. Ridiculous how easy stuff played out, and I knew that the old man had to have a hand in guiding our escape." I giggled at her sneer. She hated Grandpa, which made talking about him even more fun. "I guess I had other help too, though. I mean, the miracles Albert pulled off for me. He was a saint."

Winter's eyes widened. She hadn't known that Albert Rice was my accomplice in any way, shape, or form. She'd only seen the strangler in him...not the bigger and far more important picture.

A ten-year-old could strangle somebody if they wanted to. That crap was child's play. Laughable. Big, burly, tough-guy Albert had served a much more impressive purpose *behind* the scenes.

So had many others.

"I know. You're *shocked*. Oh goodness, gracious, *no*! You need to stop that stupid, Bambi-eyed bullshit." I curled my lip. "Wanting to believe people are good isn't the same thing as people actually being 'good.' The core of mankind is dark. Get over it."

A hateful protest flashed in her eyes, but that was good.

Feeling the hate was the first step to finding the truth.

"Anyway, Albert did an amazing job assisting me. He smuggled me in a phone, a tactical pen, and a few other handy-dandy objects. Dale turning his ogre back for two seconds was all the time I needed to grab my pen from its hiding place and take the effer down."

The sensation of the pointed end of the tactical pen

sinking between the vertebrae in that raging asshole's neck was one of my new favorite memories.

"You murdered an innocent man for no reason." Winter snarled the words at me, and though my first instinct was to smack her for speaking without permission, I realized I hadn't specified she couldn't talk. Only that she couldn't scream.

I fanned my face with my hands, beauty-pageant-winner style. "Oh, Jesus, Sis. I just feel so...so...*bad*. I've gotta find a *confessional*. A *priest*. Oh my god, I *killed an innocent man*."

Winter made some weird growly noise in her throat, reminding me of a junkyard dog on a chain. Not very attractive.

"And there *was* a reason. Duh." She was smarter than she was acting. Obnoxious. "We had to get out of there. I studied up pretty good, so I wouldn't screw up and make a blood fountain spring from Dale's ugly-ass neck. Did you know if you bring a tactical pen down *just right*, you can pierce the base of a skull and separate it from the spine in one blow? Crazy, right?" That neat little discovery had been my path to freedom.

"Yes. You *are* crazy," she muttered, obviously not impressed with my tactical pen knowledge. I guessed she'd learned that kind of weaponry crap in her bigshot Quantico training. Although, she'd apparently skipped the course that taught you not to trust a damn serial killer with your life.

Moron.

"Good one, Agent Black." I rolled my eyes and propped my feet up on my bed, which was really just a creaky bench with old as shit seat cushions attached to the top. "I managed to take Dale out with almost *no* mess and very little effort. That's impressive whether you want to admit it or not."

Winter's mouth tightened as she shook her head. God. Could we please skip to the part where she stopped being so damn unpleasant? This whole experience could be the *time of our lives* if she'd just quit with the moral high-and-mighty act and freaking get over herself.

"Anyway. You were pretty damn easy to handle too. Do you have a brain disorder or some other funky disease that causes seizures? Is it genetic? If so, I want to get tested just to make sure I never end up like you." I contorted my face and tensed my limbs at awkward, crooked angles, just to remind her of what she'd looked like.

There wasn't a way to recreate a random, wicked nose-bleed without punching her, and I didn't think the situation called for that quite yet.

"I've had the same concerns myself as far as genetics go." Winter's retort was a pretty decent burn, but an old and tired one. Kind of like her.

"I knocked you out in one hit. *One hit*. Who knew my federal agent sis had such a glass chin? One and done, ladies and gents!" I hadn't expected an ecstatic high five, but the whole dirty look approach she'd chosen was getting pretty annoying.

"Seems like kind of a weak move to me, Justin, considering I was on the verge of passing out anyway." Winter raised her eyebrow, defiant and hellbent on getting under my skin. "You're tougher than that. Why don't you untie me, and we can try a fair fight?"

Like I'd fall for such an obvious ploy. Even if I wanted to backhand the bitchiness right off her damn face, now wasn't the time. Things were going far too well.

"Serial killers don't give a whip about fair, Sissy." My voice sharpened with menace, a reminder that pushing too hard was a bad move, sister or not. There was no telling when my fuse would run out.

Even I couldn't predict that one.

"I'm the *only* person you have left. The only person who

really cared." Her voice cracked on the last word. That was good.

Emotions weakened people. All people. No exceptions.

"That's why this adventure is gonna be so great!" I was shouting now, which was fine. My motorhome, my rules. "I'm out on the open road with my actual sister who actually loves me. How much better could life get? We're gonna have a great time. A modern-day sibling version of Bonnie and Clyde."

"I'm not your fucking accomplice, Justin. You *kidnapped* me." Winter's jaw clenched so tight I was worried she'd bust a damn tooth, and I shuddered at the unappetizing image.

Gross. I didn't wanna be the *hillbilly* version of Bonnie and Clyde.

"Eh. Potato, potahto. We're together, and all I technically did was give you an armful of yummy knockout medicine before putting you on a gurney and rolling you to your car. Put you in nice and careful. Gentleman style." I flashed her a grin, which she, of course, refused to return.

Rude.

Winter shook her head, like that motion alone had the power to undo our getaway. "How in the hell did no one see you leave? That's...that's *impossible*."

"Easier than you think. The place was short-staffed as hell, and whatever staff *was* there was too stinkin' beat to care what was happening. And, you know, with the video cameras not yet operating, getting the hell out was basically a sure thing."

"Luck." She practically spat the word.

My eyes narrowed. Why was my sister having such a hard time believing I'd pulled this off? She knew exactly what I was capable of. She should, at least. What did I have to do to prove to her that I was just as smart and strong as she could ever be?

"Dale lent me his clothes, of course. And I returned the favor by tucking him into my cot, all nice and sweet. Probably just like his mommy used to do. Made sure he was all snuggly." I threw my arms around my waist and hugged myself to demonstrate.

"Great, you tucked him in." Winter let out a dry laugh. "That makes this all okay."

Of course, she was being sarcastic, but getting her humor back was a good sign. She needed to lighten the hell up.

"I even managed to rob the drug cart. Talk about a pot of gold. I've got enough sedatives to take down a horse." I snickered, lifting a shoulder. "Or keep an FBI agent knocked out for hours on end. Super useful haul."

Winter made that ludicrous growling noise again. "Where in the hell *are* we?"

"An RV campground. You did realize you're sitting in an RV, right? Crap, did I overmedicate you?" Not that I cared in the least, and my grin made sure she knew that.

"Camping. Okay. Of course." Her blue eyes glittered like icy sapphires before she glanced away. I was pretty sure she'd kill me right now if I let her loose.

Good.

Hate me. Get angry. Let it all go, Sissy. Open your eyes to the truth and experience the freedom.

"We are," I studied the invisible watch on my wrist, "approximately six hours and forty-five minutes away from your beloved River City and all your dumbass Fed buddies. You might want to give up hoping for a rescue now and save yourself some time and effort."

She didn't need to know our exact location. Not until I could trust her. And though I was confident she'd break at some point and finally see the world my way, that feat was going to take some serious time.

Sibling bonding time.

"How did you even know about this place? Why would you decide to come here?" She was trying for nonchalant now, hoping to fool me into sharing more info than I wanted her to have, but the switch was too abrupt. I saw right through her vain attempt.

You're gonna have to get up a lot earlier in the morning to fool a champion psychopath like me, Sis.

I laughed, enjoying the way the sound echoed off the shitty RV walls like the *ping* of a pinball machine. "I've got friends in high and low places, Agent Black. And something else you didn't know…I'm rich as heck. I've been growing my bitcoin accounts the whole time I've been in the *Looney Tunes* bin. I have fans who will get me anything I need, like our lovely accommodations here."

Her mouth fell open. "How? How is that even possible?"

I winked. "A favor here and there. Photo sales on the dark web. The big moneymaker is snuff films." This was fun. Educating my sister, who thought she knew everything about everything, though her knowledge of my world made her equal to a small dumb child.

"Snuff films?" She looked like she might throw up. "That seems like a stupid move. Someone will recognize you, and you'll get caught."

Her observations were so basic. So predictable.

With a theatrical sigh, I slid a grocery bag out from under my bed and pulled out the hair dye, scissors, glasses, fake mustaches, and hats I'd brought. There was more, but she'd get the general idea. She wasn't *that* slow.

What I didn't show her was my topnotch fake ID. And I wasn't about to divulge my most important accomplice. A sponsor of sorts who'd made all this possible. That information would be a fun surprise for later.

"Also, I *might* have killed a college student and *accidentally* stolen his car and clothes. And then one of my fans might have just left me the keys to RV. Oh, and your phone is tucked away on a pretty sweet eighteen-wheeler. You can thank Jim-Bob for that ride, not that he knows he's giving you one."

Although, I'd been tempted to kill Jim-Bob for the way his sweat ran down his face. Outside. In January.

Gross.

Winter remained quiet this time, which was nice for a change. I'd finally shocked her sassy trap into silence. Next, we'd see pigs flying, fat ladies singing, and—

The rumble of an engine snapped me straight out of my good-humored mental banter. I rushed to the nearest window and peered between the moldy orange, moth-eaten curtains.

A long, white-and-tan RV was pulling into a nearby campsite.

Crap crap crappity crap.

Apparently, we'd encountered our first obstacle. The first flaw in my plans.

Who in the hell goes camping this time of year?

I doubted this new RV was likewise occupied by a ridiculously handsome serial killer and his stupid, mouthy-ass sister, so it was best to take care of this problem right now.

Releasing a weary sigh, I pulled out the service weapon I'd snatched from Winter's car.

When she spotted the gun, she screamed, choosing this pivotal moment in our journey to betray her first promise to keep her damn mouth shut. But why was I surprised? All she'd ever done was betray me.

"Help! He's crazy! He'll k—"

Before she could finish, I slapped a hand over her mouth and used the other one to pinch her nose closed.

Bound as she was, all she could do was struggle for breath like an idiot fish out of water. I couldn't help the fascination that came over me as I stared into her oh-so-blue eyes and watched the fight fade away as quickly as her oxygen.

When her struggling grew so weak that it was nothing more than a flutter and she was on the verge of passing out, I let go. She gasped like an old woman with lung cancer. Another unimpressive moment for my big sis.

"Ssshhh." I put a finger to my mouth and did my best imitation of Elmer Fudd. "Be very, very quiet now. Be a good Sissy."

She was too busy gulping down air to respond or possibly even hear me. Oh well. I bent and kissed her forehead again before sinking a needle deep into her arm.

Winter's body jerked at the sting, but it was too late. She'd be sleeping for hours, assuming I didn't jolt her with a different drug to wake her up. I kind of liked having a state-of-the-art pharmacy at my fingertips.

When her body slumped and her head rolled forward, I peeked through the curtains again. A man, woman, girl, and boy were unpacking junk from their car, hauling crap around their RV like the damn Brady Bunch.

Sickening. And so inconvenient.

As I continued spying on them, though, my brain started to tingle.

Oh.

I was wrong. The arrival of this family wasn't a flaw at all. It was a gift.

I tilted my face up toward heaven, where I knew he was watching, and smiled.

"Thanks, Grandpa."

6

When Autumn ended the call with Noah, she was trembling all over, her mind still reeling over the recent discoveries.

Dead nurse. Empty medical cart. No Justin.

And no Winter.

She needed to call Aiden and fill him in on the gut-wrenching developments, but her devastation rendered her temporarily unable to function.

Justin had almost certainly murdered Dale, and now he was on the loose. And Winter...where the hell was Winter? Was she even still alive? Would Justin have killed his own sister so quickly?

Autumn dialed Aiden with shaky fingers and held the phone to her ear.

"Dr. Trent?" Aiden's curt tone crackled with stress.

"Justin Black is missing." She choked out the information with growing horror.

"What? *How?*" Through the line, papers rustled, and a briefcase slammed shut. Aiden was on the move.

"I don't know. I just found his nurse from last night dead

in Justin's cot. All the meds from the cart are gone, and so is Justin." Autumn braced a hand against the wall as nausea spun her stomach in double axels.

"And Winter?" Aiden was jogging now, his ragged breaths pulsing through the phone's speaker.

"Yes. And Winter." Autumn couldn't bring herself to add what they all had to be thinking.

What has he done to her?

"Sonofabitch. Close the door to Justin's room. Touch nothing, and do *not* let anyone else in until I arrive. Okay?"

Autumn swallowed and stared at Dale Miller's dead body. "Okay."

"I'll call Chief Lewton on my way and let her know what's happened. Hang tight, Autumn. The team and I are on our way." Aiden ended the call.

Autumn rushed to the door, exited the room, and pulled the knob. She waited for the telltale click that sealed those four walls away from the rest of the world and breathed easier at the sound. Even though the room was now free of Justin Black, his essence still lingered.

Justin had been locked up for a reason. He shouldn't be on this side of the click. Not yet. Maybe never.

But he is. He could have hopped a plane to Mexico. Or he could be standing right behind you, ready to take his—

The hair on the back of Autumn's neck prickled as she whirled, goose bumps racing across her arms.

Empty. The hall was empty.

She closed her eyes and counted to ten, giving her pulse a chance to return to normal. When she opened them again, a kind-faced woman in a doctor's coat stood before her.

"Dr. Trent? Are you okay?" The doctor approached, the skin of her hazelnut-colored forehead creased with concern. "Do you need to sit down?"

"Fine. I'm fine." Autumn bobbed her head up and down and hoped her vigor was convincing. "I promise. Fine."

"I'm Dr. Maeve Carpenter, the interim medical director. Joan Singleton said I would find you here. She told me to look for the flaming red hair."

Dr. Carpenter chuckled, which led Autumn to believe that Joan had failed to mention the cadaver lying on the other side of the door.

Poor Joan. The nurse had descended into an obvious state of shock upon viewing Dale's body. Autumn was surprised that the woman had been able to speak at all.

"That's me." Autumn straightened her posture into a more professional stance.

"Could we go to the conference room? I'd appreciate a briefing on all the chaos I just walked into."

"Sure. Of course. I'll be right there. Let me just grab a guard." Autumn searched the hallway for an appropriate candidate. When she located a stocky orderly, she stationed him at the door to Justin's room with strict orders to let no one enter until law enforcement arrived.

She speed-walked after Dr. Carpenter, and they both grabbed chairs just inside the conference room doors. As Autumn sank into the seat, her mind grew a little woozy, and her surroundings started to appear surreal, almost like she'd entered a dream.

This couldn't be happening. She'd just talked to Winter yester—

"I do apologize for arriving so late." Dr. Carpenter shook her head. "I was called into a board of directors meeting, and they don't take kindly to colleagues ditching out...since, as you know," sarcasm dripped from the words, "the most important part of health care happens in the head-honcho gatherings."

"Right. That *does* seem to be where the doctors are most

needed. Why free up their time to work with their patients? Ridiculous concept." Autumn snorted, trying not to dive too deep into the well of what was wrong with the medical field today. She was already shaky from the events of the day, and noon hadn't even arrived yet.

Maeve's throaty laugh echoed off the high ceilings. "I know. Such an outlandish idea."

Autumn liked Dr. Carpenter already. "I suppose you're ready for Dr. Baldwin to return now that you know what you're taking on."

Maeve pretended to check her watch. "Any minute now wouldn't be too soon."

Yes. She liked Dr. Carpenter a lot.

"Okay…a brief rundown. A male nurse, Dale Miller, disappeared on the job last night, and the staff assumed he'd walked out. His med cart went missing, patients missed their meds, and general hell broke loose by the time morning arrived." Autumn had no humor to soften the facts.

They sucked.

"And?"

"And I helped break up fights and attempted to find the missing med cart before going to check on Justin Black. He was the reason I came in this morning. I was going to meet with him." She braced her palms on the table, preparing herself to deliver the bad news. "But Justin is missing, and Dale Miller is lying dead in his room."

Dr. Carpenter stiffened. Her horror at learning a murdered corpse was in the room she'd stood outside of caused the near total dilation of her pupils. She coughed a few times and cleared her throat before regaining her voice. "Well, that explains your state of shock. But there's something more, isn't there?"

How does this woman know?

Autumn lifted reluctant eyes to meet the other doctor's

knowing gaze. "His older sister, Agent Winter Black, is also missing. She's a colleague of mine and...a very dear friend."

"You assume they're together?" Again with the gentle press. Dr. Carpenter was damn good at her job.

"I do. And I'm worried...so worried for her safety." Autumn realized her foot was drumming a rapid beat on the tile floor and crossed her ankles.

"How can I help you find your friend, Dr. Trent?" Maeve stood, her tone now serious.

Autumn didn't hesitate. "I'd like access to all of Baldwin's interviews with Justin as well as any recordings of other staff interactions with him."

A light knock paused the conversation. The door opened, and a woman poked her head in.

Autumn recognized her immediately. "Mia!"

"I'm sorry to interrupt. I was on this side of town when Aiden called..." Mia's instant apology warmed Autumn's heart.

"Don't be sorry at all. I'm *glad* you're here." Autumn stood and hugged Mia's tiny frame.

The petite FBI agent was also a member of the Behavioral Analysis Unit team. She had wavy dark hair and equally dark eyes, which contrasted with her creamy white skin.

The striking distinction reminded Autumn of the extreme polarity between Mia and her sometimes partner, Agent Chris Parker.

Autumn had witnessed Mia's patience and profession-alism regarding Chris on more than one occasion when she herself would have lost her mind...or at least her cool. Just thinking of the tall, broad-shouldered jerk with his super-fluous blond hairdo annoyed Autumn.

She had a deep respect for Mia's sweet, calm nature. Agent Logan was impervious to Agent Parker's shenanigans, and they all were thankful for that.

Autumn stepped back to perform the introductions. "Dr. Carpenter, this is Special Agent Mia Logan. Mia, this is Dr. Maeve Carpenter. She's the lucky chosen one filling in for Dr. Baldwin while he recovers."

Mia and Dr. Carpenter exchanged a polite handshake before the interim medical director headed for the door. "Follow me, ladies. Dr. Trent, I'll take you to an office where we can all listen to Justin's recordings."

Mia gave Autumn's shoulder a light squeeze as they hurried down the corridor. "I was made aware of this *crazy* rumor that you were supposed to be on bed rest." Mia flashed Autumn a mischievous smile.

Autumn returned the grin, relieved to have a familiar face on the scene. "That *is* a crazy rumor. Who makes this stuff up?"

They entered the office that Maeve had chosen and took seats around a large mahogany desk while Dr. Carpenter shuffled through some file drawers. She retrieved a small stack of tapes and grabbed the nearby player.

"Okay, Dr. Trent. Agent Logan. Sessions with Justin Black, patient under the care of Dr. Philip Baldwin." Maeve pressed play.

The recording began with two familiar voices greeting each other. Both Philip and Justin had unmistakable vocals. Dr. Baldwin promptly steered the subject into a resumed conversation from the last session.

"You were just beginning to tell me about your memories of your abduction. Would you like to continue, Justin?" Philip's baritone was smooth. Indifferent.

"I...I guess we could talk about that. Yeah. S-sure. That's fine." Justin's voice quavered like a twelve-year-old choir boy trying not to cry.

Autumn recognized his voice, but that *tone*. Justin was

outright playing Dr. Baldwin. She wondered if Philip had
known as much.

"Go ahead," Dr. Baldwin encouraged.

"Well, I always felt kind of guilty because...when Douglas
Kilroy kidnapped me, I was actually kinda relieved, you know?"
An exaggerated sniffle followed.

"Relieved how, Justin?"

"I guess...I guess I thought I might be getting a shot at a happy
life." More theatrical sniffling. "My parents were always so mean
to me. They hit me a lot and told me how worthless I was and how
I'd never amount to anything."

"So, you wanted to leave your family? Even your sister?" Philip
asked the questions as though they were sitting on a park
bench with ice cream cones. He'd definitely mastered the art
of speaking to residents of the adult maximum-security
hospital like they were acquaintances or friends rather than
patients.

Autumn applauded him in silence.

"My sister was worse than my parents. She used to pick me up
and throw me into the ditch in front of our house. It was a deep
ditch, Dr. Baldwin. I was so scared that I'd break a bone, and then
my parents would be mad at me for causing so much trouble."

Autumn glanced at Mia, whose jaw was hanging open in
disbelief. Had Justin actually tried to paint his family as
bullies? Villains? Abusers?

Unbelievable. Anger burned in her chest as the recording
continued.

"And how did that make you feel, Justin?"

A sob burst from the young man's throat. "I just felt like no
one would ever love me no matter what. Not ever."

Autumn's finger shot to the pause button.

"Bullshit. He's full of bullshit. I need to talk to Dr. Baldwin. Hold on." Autumn whipped her cell from her bag and
called Richmond Medical Center on speakerphone.

She doubted the man had bought any of Justin's nonsense, but they could at least compare notes and possibly shed additional light on the matter.

"Richmond Medical Center. How may I help you?" Polite and robotic. The female staff member who'd answered her call probably recited those lines in her sleep.

"Hi, yes. This is Dr. Autumn Trent calling. I'd like to be connected to Dr. Philip Baldwin, room number…"

Autumn spent the next couple minutes going through the HIPAA bullshit before the woman said, "I'm sorry, Dr. Trent, but Dr. Baldwin has been discharged."

Crap.

Discharged to where? Even if it wasn't still a crime scene, he wouldn't have gone back to his farmhouse so soon after Albert Rice had terrorized them inside those walls, and she'd learned through Aiden that his city townhouse was sublet to a young couple. Philip didn't even live there.

While Autumn's mind turned somersaults trying to find an answer, Mia jumped in to ask the next question. "Did he leave any word as to where he was going?"

"Let me check."

Autumn mouthed "Thank you" to Mia while they waited.

This turn of events was overwhelming. Winter *or* Justin missing would be bad enough. But both of them? Autumn's brain had set itself to a permanent tailspin. Mia's stabilizing force was more than appreciated. Her presence was *needed*.

"Thanks for holding. No one on staff knew anything other than Dr. Baldwin had called a taxi and left. I'm sorry, Dr. Trent."

Autumn thanked the woman and ended the call.

Nowhere. They'd gotten nowhere.

"We have to keep listening." Autumn grabbed at the tapes, checking their dates. A recent recording could provide a hint or hidden message from Justin, whether he'd meant to leave a clue or not.

Mia pulled a tablet from her bag. "I'll try to track Dr. Baldwin's movements. I can call the local cab companies, put a trace on his credit card..." She jumped right to work, bowing her head over the tablet and typing.

Agent Logan was indispensable.

Autumn returned to her own search, scouring the tapes until she came across a date from only a couple days ago. "Here. This one."

Dr. Carpenter popped in the recording, and they were instantly back in session with Justin and Philip. The same greeting and start-up, but a completely different Justin.

"Dr. Baldwin, I wanted to talk to you about Dr. Trent today, if that's okay." Now, Justin's voice was solemn. Urgent.

"Okay, Justin. What would you like to tell me?"

Autumn tensed. She hadn't expected her name to come up at all.

"I just don't trust her, Dr. Baldwin. She's got this way about her...I can tell she's lying to me every time she meets with me. She doesn't even want to help me get better. She just wants me to tell her the truth about the bad stuff I did so I can get locked away forever."

Autumn's body turned to ice. How dare he? She was one of the *only* people on the damn planet who genuinely cared about helping Justin Black after the heinous crimes he'd committed. The hours she'd spent awake at night...

But should she have expected less? Justin was a serial killer. Lying was as natural as breathing for him. Of course he would display no loyalty to her simply because she was emotionally invested in his case.

And that was the problem. She had to stop allowing her emotions to affect her training. This was the very reason

Winter hadn't been allowed to take part in the Albert Rice case.

Feelings had no place in the FBI or in Autumn's profession of forensic and criminal psychology.

Justin Black wasn't her best friend's little brother. Not today. He was a demented psychopath, and his affinity for dishonest interactions was the standard operation of those afflicted with his diagnosis.

"Honestly? I bet Dr. Trent would suck my dick if she thought that a blow job would make me tell the truth." He let out a haughty, disgusted laugh. *"Hell. My sister would do the same thing. Winter's so guilt ridden that she'd probably do anything I asked."*

"What kinds of actions do you believe your sister would take for you, Justin?" Philip remained calm and unreadable.

"Winter's got it bad. She's got the guilts. *She abandoned me when I was just a helpless little kid, and she can't ever take that back. So now, I'd say there aren't any limits to what she'd be willing to do."* Justin's confidence was appalling.

"No limits at all?" Philip challenged. *"Your sister is a federal agent, Justin. It's safe to say she has many limits. You don't agree with that?"*

"Winter would do anything for me. Anything. She loves me. She'd bust me out of this place and probably even kill for me if she had to. That's the power of guilt, Dr. Baldwin. Guilt's the strongest motivator in the world."

Autumn stopped the recording so she could process her influx of thoughts. A terrible idea had entered her mind, and she was desperate to grasp the logic that would dismiss it.

How had Justin overpowered Dale Miller? Dale was on the larger side of average, with Justin the smaller of the two men by far. There was no question as to which man was the stronger in a physical sense.

And how had he also overpowered a highly trained FBI

agent such as Winter? How was that even possible? Armed or unarmed, Winter Black knew how to take down men much bigger than her baby brother.

On top of that, he'd made a magical escape from the hospital without anyone noticing or trying to stop him? The video cameras weren't up and running yet, and the staff was admittedly shorthanded, but there were still numerous sets of eyes that he'd have to get past to escape.

Guards on every floor. Nurses and orderlies scattered all over the place.

Yet he'd not only busted out of the building but escaped the hospital altogether.

And where was Winter?

Autumn couldn't begin to guess, but she did feel confident she could identify the one aspect of her friend's life that mattered more than all the rest.

Being there for Justin. Fixing things with Justin. Unearthing the good in Justin.

In Winter's mind, Justin outranked Noah, her friends, the FBI. Justin was her number one heartbreak. Her biggest regret. Her deepest hope...

Autumn's palms dampened as she sifted through the many conversations they'd had about Justin. Winter was a prisoner of guilt. She'd admit that herself, hands down. Her best friend couldn't escape the remorse...couldn't shake Justin off. She loved him too much.

She loved him too much.

Autumn hated to even consider the idea, but...what if Justin had been right?

A sudden chill iced Autumn's skin like a winter frost, and she rubbed her arms to ward off the chill.

What if Winter *had* helped her brother escape?

And worse...what if she'd killed for him?

7

Special Supervisory Agent Aiden Parrish stood on the cracked sidewalk and gazed up at the imposing edifice that was Virginia State Hospital. He was beginning to believe that the team would never be free of this cursed building.

Or Justin Black.

"You wanna take a picture or something?" Special Agent Chris Parker shuffled his feet with obvious annoyance.

Aiden's fists clenched at his sides.

You can't punch Parker. Punching Parker would cost you your job. Under no circumstance can you punch that son of a bitch.

The thought of disrupting Chris's unwavering, icy-blue stare and the preposterous blond poof that sprouted from the top of his head was almost enough to make any consequence worthwhile.

"Funny. You're very funny. Let's go, Parker." Aiden resumed his brisk stride, wishing he could leave Chris outdoors in the January cold. Forever.

The man's job skills made him worth putting up with, for the most part, but he rode every last nerve in Aiden's body.

He hadn't been aware that he'd stalled on the walkway at all. Aiden wondered if the momentary zone-out was indicative of the stress overload the last few weeks had provided.

Nearly losing Autumn to Albert Rice's revenge scheme had been a scare he still hadn't processed, and now Winter appeared to be in danger. If the agent was with her younger brother, then her situation could prove even more perilous than Autumn's.

Justin Black operated at a level of devilry few men ever reached.

Judging by the large volume of Richmond PD cars already filling up the parking lot, law enforcement was on the scene as well. Justin's room would be taped off by now, and crime techs were certain to be recording every last detail of the site while combing the space for any possible pieces of evidence.

Mia had already arrived, and Noah was on his way. The purr of a vehicle parking behind them caught his attention, and a glance over his shoulder confirmed that Bree and Sun had just pulled up. The whole team was now present and accounted for. Good. Aiden had a solid premonition that they were going to need every last skillset and brain cell the group could contribute.

Winter's face flashed through Aiden's mind, and his mouth went dry. Had Justin kidnapped her? Hurt her? Or worse...the question he wished to avoid altogether.

Was Winter Black still alive at all?

They needed to figure out where the hell his agent had disappeared to, and fast.

Aiden charged into the hospital, with Chris close behind. Lately, the sterile white walls had become far too familiar. He'd even memorized the layout of the wings and floors, mostly to avoid setting foot in the damn elevators yet again.

They hit the stairwell and made the short three-story

climb in silence. When they reached the residential wing that Justin should have been locked away in, the area was crawling with officials. Autumn and Mia wouldn't have strayed far, so Aiden headed for the conference rooms. As he rounded the corner to the appropriate hallway, he recognized Autumn's voice.

He followed the sound to an ajar office door and was relieved to find Dr. Trent, Agent Logan, and a woman he assumed to be the interim medical director gathered around a desk.

Autumn's stricken green eyes rose to meet his. He wished he could offer words of comfort, but his tongue failed him.

After the events of the last twenty-four hours and her own near brush with death, learning that her close friend was missing and likely in harm's way must have been a gut punch she was ill-equipped to receive. Even under normal conditions, Winter and Justin both vanishing was a terrifying pill to swallow.

"Agents, this is the interim medical director, Dr. Maeve Carpenter. Dr. Carpenter, this is Special Supervisory Agent Aiden Parrish and Special Agent Chris Parker." Autumn gestured between them.

"Good to meet you, Dr. Carpenter." Aiden extended a hand.

The doctor smiled in return and gave his hand a firm shake. "Agent Parrish. Agent Parker. I wish it were under different circumstances, but a pleasure to meet you both as well."

Chris offered his own polite nod, and Aiden refocused on Autumn.

"Are you all right, Dr. Trent?" He asked the question before considering his audience. Parker's eyes had probably rolled out of his damn head.

Autumn answered with an unconvincing grin. "I'm fine. Just want to get going and find her. Find *them*." She gulped after finishing the sentence, and her haunted expression gave her away.

Autumn Trent was far from "fine."

Aiden's chest tightened, and he stepped closer, driven by an overpowering need to reassure her. "And that's exactly what we're going to do." Once again, he ignored the three other humans in the room who were also invested in the present situation.

"We haven't learned much from the tapes." She gestured toward the pile of recordings. "Justin was manipulative and deceitful in his sessions with Philip Baldwin, but I think that was to be expected."

Aiden studied Autumn's mannerisms as she spoke, catching the way her jaw tensed and how her gaze wandered off to the side.

His eyes narrowed. *What are you leaving out, Dr. Trent?*

"Is there anything you'd like to add to that?" Every face in the room turned toward him, the other occupants seeming to catch the inference that SSA Parrish suspected their red-haired colleague was holding something back.

Autumn locked stares with him. "No. Not yet."

Bullshit. Aiden was certain there was more. Autumn either had a hunch she was too unsure of to communicate right now or an idea too delicate to share with the others present.

There was the slight possibility that she had no intention of relaying her thoughts to him either, but he doubted that. They read each other incredibly well and shared a simple, implicit trust.

"I'm sure officers are searching every inch of the facility, and we can assist with that. No video footage means we need to seek out witnesses on our own." Aiden nodded toward

Mia, then Chris. "I'd like you two to start with questioning the nurses, orderlies, and guards on the first two floors. Dr. Trent and I will cover the third-floor staff."

Mia and Chris bolted out of the office while Dr. Carpenter raised a hand. "I'd like to help as well, Agent Parrish."

"Much appreciated, Doctor. Can you start by contacting those who worked last night? We need to interview each of them as quickly as possible."

Dr. Carpenter was out the door and gone before Aiden noted that Autumn was still seated and staring at the tapes. She seemed a million miles away.

Although Mia and the interim medical director had been privy to the exact same recordings as Autumn, he was again hit with the strong suspicion Dr. Trent had gleaned something from the audio the others hadn't.

"Autumn?"

She nearly jumped from her chair, grabbing her bag and hoisting it onto her shoulder while avoiding his gaze. "Let's go."

He wanted a chance to question her further about whatever worry was stewing in her mind, but she was halfway to the nurses' station before he'd hit full stride down the hallway. By the time he caught up to her, she was already midinquiry with one of the staff.

"And not one thing you saw struck you as out of the ordinary?" Autumn tilted her head and used a curt tone that he'd never heard from her before.

The nurse, an older woman who reminded him of a worn-down Hilary Clinton, fingered her whistle-bearing lanyard and shrugged. "Well, *everything* last night was out of the ordinary. This place was a madhouse. Full moon. Always causes an uproar."

Aiden struggled to maintain his indifferent expression.

"You believe *the moon* was to blame for the hospital's internal chaos overnight?" He glanced at Autumn, who lifted a shoulder in an "anything is possible" manner, which drove him insane.

"You think that's laughable, don't you, Agent?" The nurse's hands shot to her hips. He'd clearly offended her.

"I didn't mean th—"

"You come back for the next full moon and tell me something strange doesn't happen to the patients. You'll understand then. I don't care how smart you are or who you work for."

The nurse charged past them in a huff while Autumn shot him an aggravated glare for driving away her first interviewee.

Not his intention, but he was spared from trying to explain when Bree and Sun stepped off the elevator and headed toward them. They'd only made it a few feet when an officer burst from a different elevator car and rushed over.

"Agent Parrish. We've discovered something in the back lot that you'll want to see." The officer's weathered face was grim, and Aiden's muscles constricted as he followed the man back down the hall.

Before stepping onto the elevator, he pointed at Autumn, then Sun, and Bree. "Meet me on the ground floor."

There was a part of him that needed the five to ten seconds away from anyone who knew him. He would ride down with the stranger who'd given the alert and steel himself for whatever lay next.

The metallic doors closed, and Aiden met the eyes of the officer. "What did they find?"

The man flinched. "A gurney. An *empty* gurney."

Aiden forced himself to stay stone-cold as his insides turned and twisted.

An empty gurney. What could that mean?

He didn't speak to the officer as the elevator descended or when they exited the car. The policeman led him to a side door that opened to a cement walk connecting the front parking lot to the back.

In the distance, Noah was just hopping down from his truck.

Shit.

Noah was probably the last person who should accompany him to the initial viewing of this "discovery," but the ever-alert Agent Dalton had already spotted him and was jogging across the lot.

As the agent drew closer, Aiden suppressed a wince. Noah Dalton had morphed into the dictionary definition of a "train wreck." The man looked like absolute shit. His face was drawn and pale, and he seemed to have aged ten years since just that morning.

Just wait until he hears about the gurney.

Schooling his features into a neutral mask took Aiden more effort than usual, but he was fairly confident he'd succeeded by the time Noah stopped a few feet away. The agent raised his eyebrows, obviously wanting the scoop. Aiden waved a hand to indicate that he should follow them.

"They found a gurney out back." Aiden directed the words over his shoulder but didn't turn to witness the horror he suspected had flooded Noah's face.

The same horror that was corkscrewing his own gut tighter and tighter.

Rounding the back corner of the building, Aiden spotted the gurney resting behind one of the hospital's green dumpsters. He picked up speed, passing the officer and disregarding the other two policemen stationed near the find.

Noah did the same, and they arrived at the stretcher together.

Aiden scanned the contraption for any sign that Winter Black had been positioned there.

Nothing, nothing, nothing...*shit.*

For several long seconds, his lungs stopped working, and all he could do was stare at the single hair on the stark white pillow.

A long, black hair.

Just like Winter's.

A strangled noise from behind him yanked Aiden out of the trance. He turned to find Agent Dalton standing frozen in place, gaping at the strand of hair with the haunted expression of a man who'd just lost everything.

"Get some crime scene techs down here immediately!" Aiden barked at the officers standing by, his usual demanding tone edged with something he rarely experienced or expressed at all.

Fear.

The officers took off, and he returned his attention to Noah, whose eyes had taken on a wild blaze. Aiden read Dalton's intention a split-second too late, darting toward Noah just as the agent lunged forward and grabbed the dumpster lid.

Dammit.

Aiden managed to get a grip on the agent's upper arm. "Agent Dalton, if you contaminate a possible crime scene—"

Between the agent's larger size and adrenaline rush, Aiden might as well have been attempting to restrain a charging elephant. Noah flung the lid back with a creak of metal before Aiden could even finish the warning.

Dread crawled up his spine when the empty space yawned open before them. Preserving the crime scene had only been one of the reasons he'd wanted to stop Dalton.

The second reason being that he wasn't sure either one of

them was mentally prepared to view what lay inside that dumpster.

The damage was done, though. The lid was open, and there was no turning back now. No matter what the outcome, Aiden needed to know the truth just as badly as Dalton.

This is the moment. This is when you find Winter Black's cold, dead body and have to face the fact that after all of your attempts to protect her...none of that mattered in the end. You failed.

Aiden mirrored Noah and leaned forward. His heart slammed against his rib cage as he forced his eyes to sweep the contents. Dreading what they might find.

Noah reacted first, releasing his grip and dropping to the pavement as a few choked sobs escaped him.

Aiden caught the lid and stared for several heartbeats longer, needing to reassure himself that what he had witnessed was accurate.

Garbage bags. A haphazard layer of garbage bags. Piled high enough to show that the trash hadn't been collected in the last twenty-four hours and low enough to ensure that a human body wasn't hidden underneath.

No Winter.

The lid clattered shut while Aiden tried to breathe through the volcano of emotion erupting in his chest. He crouched to the ground beside Noah, and for a few moments, neither of them said a word.

Blue. All Aiden could think of were the giant blue eyes of a very young Winter Black. Eyes filled with sadness and loss. Despair. He'd sworn to himself then that he would help that little girl. Keep her safe.

Even now, when she was a full-grown adult and tough as nails, he stayed beholden to the promise. And that split second before they'd seen proof that Winter was not lying dead amongst the reek and rot of a standard commercial dumpster—

"*I thought she was in there.*" Noah's head hung between his knees. "I thought she was in there, Aiden. Dead. I thought Winter was *dead.*"

Aiden slowed his ragged breathing and attempted to pull himself together.

He was supposed to be in charge. Part of his job was keeping everyone else calm. In line. There was untold relief in not finding Winter dead, but she *was* still gone, and they had to find her.

There was no time to waste.

"She *wasn't* in there, and she *isn't* dead." Aiden clapped the other man on the back and stood. His legs were weak and shaky, but he offered Noah a hand, assisting him back to a standing position. "We need to get to work, Dalton."

"We have to find her." Noah's dark green eyes met his. The man appeared slightly possessed...feral, even.

Aiden understood.

He was feeling more than a little feral himself.

"We will, Dalton." Aiden turned on his heel, dodging the crime techs rushing to the scene and striding back toward the hospital. Acid burned his esophagus, and he was on the verge of vomiting. He bit his inner cheek, letting salt and pain override the nausea. Any display of weakness would send a message to Noah that was the exact opposite of the hope the man needed right now.

Agent Dalton was already drowning in his own despair, and Aiden intended to snap him out of it. Winter Black was a fighter, and they would find her *alive.* Aiden refused to entertain any alternative ending.

The team had gathered in the lobby, except for Autumn. He assumed she was still questioning the staff upstairs and would join them soon.

All eyes homed in on him and Noah as they joined the group, though Noah trailed several feet behind.

"Let's step into that conference room." Aiden pointed at a large, vacant space nearby. The last thing they needed was a host of curious ears taking in their conversation and leaking the words straight to the media.

Once inside, Chris wasted no time sharing his gathered info. "I searched the lots and the parking garage. Winter's Civic isn't here." His exaggerated hand gestures relayed the frustration that Aiden knew they were all experiencing.

Agent Parrish turned to his tech-savvy ex. "Sun, if you could get an APB out on Winter's—"

"Already on it." Sun held her iPad and swiped with maniacal speed at the screen.

"Law enforcement discovered an abandoned gurney in the back lot." Aiden prepared for the influx of questions about to shoot his way. "There appeared to be a strand of Winter's hair on the pillow, but we'll have to wait for forensics to confirm that it belongs to Agent Black."

"You think she was pushed out on the gurney?" Mia's brow furrowed deeply at the assumption.

"It's possible." Aiden had a lot of theories, and none of them were especially uplifting.

"But we have no way of knowing if she was conscious or not. She could have been severely wounded." Chris's callous musing earned him a sharp glare from Noah. "Although you didn't mention any blood. Was the gurney bloody?"

Aiden wasn't sure Agent Parker would make it through this investigation without taking a punch to the face at some point. Dalton was on edge, and his own self-restraint hovered at an all-time low.

"We spotted no blood. Again, the crime techs are combing the scene. If there is blood or any other trace of DNA, they'll find it." Aiden hadn't mentioned the dumpster, though he knew its contents would be closely scanned as well.

The sooner he could forget that horrible moment in time had ever occurred, the better.

"There are a multitude of possibilities as to how this played out. No reason to assume the worst already." Bree placed a comforting hand on Noah's arm.

Noah remained mute.

"I'm apt to wonder if this all could have been prevented." Parker looked around the room, his lip curled in a smugness Aiden wanted to punch off his face. "Surely Justin displayed some behavior that should have set off major alarms. He had to have said a lot of things that would lead a *trained* agent to predict this type of scheme."

Aiden's eye twitched at the obvious attack on Autumn, who was the only team member to have worked with Justin in close capacity.

Mia poked Chris's arm and whispered something when he bent his head toward her. Aiden hoped she was tearing him a new asshole.

Poor Mia. She was always getting teamed up with Parker. He never meant the pairing as a punishment. Agent Logan simply possessed an ability to handle Agent Parker's bullshit that exceeded the rest of them by far.

Chris shook his head in apparent disagreement with Mia's message. "All I'm saying is, going forward, I would think someone like myself would be a much better fit to work with Justin and create his in-depth profile. Autumn is obviously too close to Winter to be impartial. We can all agree on that."

"That's not fair, Chris, and you know it." Mia took it upon herself to do the defense work. "Autumn's amazing at what she does."

"I'm not taking away from all her fancy doctor crap."

Chris held out his hands with exasperation, as though he weren't the one slinging the attacks. "I'm just saying, given the current situation—the fact that both Justin and Winter Black have disappeared—I would have been a better choice for Justin's case."

"Hold up, Parker." Bree stepped toward him, taller than Mia and exuding a much more intimidating energy. "There is never a way to predict the exact actions any human will take, let alone a *serial killer*. You can't put that on Autumn."

"I never would have sanctioned visits between a patient still under evaluation and his sister. Never. Not when the stakes are this high." Chris was close to shouting now. "Black is not the normal criminal. He's a diabolical little turd. Winter would have been safe on my watch because she wouldn't have stepped foot in this building."

Aiden had heard enough. "Parker, why don't you shut your mouth and focus on the task at hand. Your opinions about the handling of Justin Black's case up until this point will in no way help us find Justin *or* Winter—"

He broke off when he noticed everyone staring at the door behind him.

Shit.

A pivot revealed what he'd already guessed. Autumn was standing in the doorway. How much of Chris's rant she'd taken in was uncertain, but the fact that she'd caught at least some of the little ass clown's ranting was obvious.

As stricken as she'd appeared when he'd first arrived, now she looked even worse. Her pale skin had grown even more pallid, her pretty features afflicted with a mixture of shock, despair, and grief.

Autumn didn't need her doctorate to ascertain the subject of their discussion. Though Chris had been the only voice against her, they'd clearly been going back and forth on two points.

The first one being, was she to blame for Justin's escape?

Aiden guessed the second accusation hurt far worse, though, and was the one wreaking havoc on those delicate features right now.

The allegation that Autumn Trent might be responsible for the sudden disappearance of her own best friend.

8

Noah Dalton stood with his arms crossed in a corner of the conference room, clinging to the tether that leashed his fury while he considered his options. The safest route would be to swallow his rage, for now, releasing it later in the gym or a sprint down the track.

Except he didn't trust his self-control enough at the moment to wait until such an opportunity presented itself.

Plan B was something along the lines of punching a hole in the damn wall. As appealing as this option was, Noah was well aware that the cement blocks of Virginia State Hospital would win that fight. A broken hand seemed like a very unattractive addition to the hell he'd already entered.

Winter was gone. And while he refused to accept that she might be *dead* and gone, the fear still ate away at his bones.

Especially when his dipshit colleague, Agent Parker, presented queries such as, *"Was the gurney bloody?"*

Chris kept churning out word after word in his damn nasally drone while his asinine poof of blond hair flopped around on his giant, idiotic head. Noah was dangerously close to putting a hole in Parker's face in lieu of the wall.

That was Plan C and Noah's favorite thus far.

He wasn't sure if Chris was capable of loving someone the way he loved Winter. Maybe if the asshole had just been faced with the possibility that his better half was cold and stiff inside a rusty, filth-covered waste receptacle...*just lying there like yesterday's trash*...he'd be more careful with his words.

The first thing Noah had spotted when peering into that dumpster was a black trash bag. In the initial split seconds of viewing, he'd been sure he was staring at Winter's long, dark hair.

The horror of that mistaken moment in time would haunt him forever.

Noah wiped a damp palm over his face. The hunt for the Black siblings had barely begun, but Noah could swear he'd aged by ten years already. The toll each terrifying second took was undeniable.

And also, irrelevant.

He'd keep searching for Winter until his heart stopped beating.

"...never would have sanctioned visits between a patient still under evaluation and his sister. Never. Not when the stakes are this high. Black isn't the normal criminal. He's a diabolical little turd. Winter would have been safe on my watch because she wouldn't have stepped foot in this building."

Parker's voice was still a nasal assault on Noah's ears, but the man had a point. Hell, Noah had thought the same exact thing on numerous occasions, but everyone had seemed so sure that Autumn was perfect for the job. He'd felt as though the whole damn FBI was in favor of Autumn Trent assessing Justin Black.

He hadn't protested, though, because his personal investment in Winter's welfare had seemed like a conflict of interest. He *was* biased, and if he'd tried to interject, his superiors would have played that card immediately.

However, pretending like Autumn *wasn't* biased when Winter was involved was just as laughable. All the education and degrees in the world wouldn't stop Autumn Trent's feelings from seeping into her professional decisions. Not when her best friend was part of the equation.

Even *Justin* had wanted Autumn to be his shrink. That bloodthirsty bastard had pushed hard for Dr. Trent's services.

Noah didn't have to wonder why. Justin obviously believed he could manipulate Autumn. The kid knew how close she and Winter were.

And apparently, whatever he'd planned had worked out splendidly.

For Justin.

Winter's situation was less than ideal.

Noah's hands curled into fists. All this mess could have been avoided by simply keeping the siblings apart.

Now, Autumn's refusal to make that call could cost Winter her life.

"Parker, why don't you shut your mouth and focus on the task at hand. Your opinions about the handling of Justin Black's case up until this point will in no way help us find Justin or Winter—"

Noah spied Autumn in the doorway behind Aiden at the same time as the rest of the team.

Her green eyes appeared wounded and too large in her ghost-white face.

Good.

The vicious thought caught Noah by surprise. He tried to push it away, but the sentiment lingered and burned in his throat.

"Winter would have been safe on my watch because she wouldn't have stepped foot in this building."

Even Chris Parker had known, and Chris was a bona fide idiot.

How had a psychologist let this slide through the cracks? Weren't those degrees, that auspicious title, supposed to fucking mean something?

Too much. It's too much.

He stalked toward Autumn, her *"But I'm innocent!"* expression yanking at the reins of his control.

Maybe she believed her own innocence bullshit. Maybe most of them did.

He didn't.

"Would you like to explain to me how you, *a trained professional*, failed to understand how dangerous Justin Black still is?" He wasn't yelling. He refused to yell at Autumn or any other woman. The low growl emitting from him seemed more offensive than shouting, though.

Shock widened her eyes before a series of other emotions flashed across her face. Noah read guilt and remorse before her nostrils flared and her chin jutted out. "Of course I knew how dangerous Justin is. I was always aware of that and shared my viewpoint with anyone who asked. *Including Winter.*"

"You knew there was no way in hell she'd listen to you!" Autumn's bullshit defense caused Noah's own fury to pound through his veins like a drum.

She'd messed up. She needed to admit that much.

"You're right, but I still tried repeatedly. Winter knew my exact opinion of her brother's condition. And keep in mind, I barely spent more than a few interview sessions with Justin, during which my focus was to establish competency and then insanity. I was never meant to 'treat' Justin!"

Autumn was the first to shout, and Noah reared back a little. He couldn't recall her ever yelling before.

At least, not at him.

Something inside him snapped. "That's my point! You knew the little psycho's 'road to recovery' was just starting. You should have done more!" He was yelling now and couldn't bring himself to care. Autumn could have stopped all of this from ever happening.

"What more could I have done, Noah?" Autumn had regained a bit of her calm. The volume of his voice had probably shocked her self-control into returning.

His own fury was still too intense to dial it back so easily.

"Hm. How about, oh, *I don't know*, barring Winter from visiting Justin altogether?" Noah threw his hands up, his sarcasm unmistakable.

"I wish I had." Autumn blinked several times in rapid succession, appearing to be on the verge of tears.

"All the damn wishes in the world might not help Winter now." Noah pictured the single long, black hair on the gurney pillow, and his stomach wrenched. The burning behind his eyes suggested his own tears weren't far behind.

"I know that, Noah."

Her trembling lip only pissed him off more. "You ever consider that maybe you were transferring your need to find Sarah, *your* long-lost sibling, into Justin's case? You let it blur your vision and your judgment. Your personal bullshit is the reason Winter's gone."

Noah regretted the words as soon as they left his mouth, flinching when Autumn's face crumpled. Bringing Autumn's sister into this was the lowest of blows, but his emotions boiled too hot and close to the surface for him to control.

"That's not fair." Autumn seethed through tear-brimmed eyes.

Winter would have hated this. Her boyfriend and best friend at each other's throats. She would have despised him for speaking this way to Autumn.

His jaw tightened. Except Winter wasn't here, and that remained Autumn's fault no matter how he spun the picture.

"Just because you don't want to hear it doesn't make what I said unfair or untrue. You. Could. Have. Stopped. This."

Aiden pushed his body between them, forcing Noah and Autumn to take several steps back.

"Enough. Finger-pointing and fighting amongst ourselves won't save Winter. If we're going to find her *before* something horrible happens, we have to band together." SSA Parrish gazed from Noah to Autumn and back again. "Dalton, step away. Catch your breath and compose yourself."

There was a clear warning in Aiden's cool blue stare that this was not a wise time to argue. Noah shook his head and started for the door. He'd obey, but he refused to apologize.

Before he could reach the exit, Bree was beside him. She grabbed his arm and nearly dragged him out of the waiting room, through the lobby, and back into the crisp January afternoon.

"You need some fresh air almost as much as you need a good ass whooping. Pull your shit together, Noah Dalton!" Bree wasn't impressed by his significantly larger stature, and he bet the fearless woman wanted to deliver the aforementioned butt kicking herself.

Noah rubbed a shaky hand across his forehead and slumped. "I didn't mean to...go off like that. I didn't." He wasn't himself. Special Agent Noah Dalton didn't often lose his cool, and certainly not on his friends.

"I don't give a damn if you meant to. Aiden is right." Bree crossed her arms, daring him to argue. "We have to remain a team if we want to find Winter. If you really love that woman, and *I know you do*, you'll drop the blame game and get to work *finding* her."

"This didn't have to happen, Bree." His throat was dry,

and now that his anger was spent, the fear fueling it reemerged and threatened to drown him.

Agent Stafford didn't miss a beat. "That doesn't matter. It happened. You have to deal with this just like the rest of us, and making Autumn feel like a piece of shit isn't going to help you feel better about Winter being gone. Autumn is a good person, Noah. She's a good friend, and she didn't deserve that." Bree's hands went to her hips, and he figured she was more than prepared for his rebuttal.

He didn't have one. Autumn *was* a good friend. For god's sake, she was *his* good friend. Never in a billion centuries would she put Winter in harm's way.

Not on purpose.

But the bitterness still lingered, and he wasn't sure he'd ever be free of its grip.

Doesn't matter. Finding Winter matters. Assuming she wants to be found.

When the last thought registered, Noah's entire body went still. Where had that come from? Because the notion that Winter didn't want to be found was ridiculous. Out of the question.

Only now that the possibility had invaded his mind like an aneurism, he couldn't seem to force it away.

Winter had been desperate to help her brother. Her love for Justin had tortured her every waking second of each day. Noah had front-row seats to that anguish.

Would that anguish push her far enough to help Justin escape, though? Would Winter Black break her brother out of the hospital?

He jerked his head. No. No way in hell. Winter was the best person he'd ever met. Her moral compass never wavered. Not even for her little brother.

She would never cross that line.

Noah shoved the painful thought aside and met Bree's intent gaze. "I'm not going to lose my cool."

"Good, then let's get back to work." She spun and walked back toward the front entrance. Noah followed, resembling a penitent, misbehaved puppy.

When they reentered the doorway into the waiting room, a new conversation was taking place.

"I'll just go to the Wellington and ask for him. If Sun says he's there, he's there." Autumn's statement earned her a rare nod of approval from Agent Ming.

"You can go, but you're taking Chris with you," Aiden said. "None of my agents are going out in the field solo while Justin Black is at large."

Protest flooded both Autumn and Chris's faces. Noah had an inkling that, pre-argument, Aiden might have sent him with Autumn instead.

Now she was stuck with Parker, and the part of Noah that still flamed with anger toward Dr. Trent was happy to witness her trapped with the whiny agent.

Autumn gave Aiden a reluctant nod.

Chris cracked his knuckles and shot Aiden a peeved stare. "Just what I wanted. To spend more time with that Baldwin jackass."

Noah wondered if Chris was afraid of sharing the douchebag limelight with another man but kept his mouth shut.

He'd said more than enough already.

"Dr. Baldwin isn't really that bad."

Chris chuckled in mock amusement at Autumn's quick defense. "Sure. And Winter isn't really that missing."

Though Noah applauded the comment in silence, Aiden took an aggressive step toward the agent. "I trust that you'll keep your opinions to yourself and do your best to assist Dr. Trent as needed?"

Chris sneered back at Parrish. Parker had been very vocal about his problem with Autumn's "special treatment," and Noah found himself agreeing wholeheartedly with the dick yet again. The baby glove approach that Aiden always used regarding Autumn Trent was getting old.

"I'll be a good little boy. Don't worry." Chris began walking away, not seeming to know or care if Autumn would follow him.

"Or maybe try acting like an adult who displays the exemplary behavior expected of a representative of the Federal Bureau of Investigation," Aiden called after him. "Can you handle that, Agent Parker?"

Chris gave no response, but it was impossible that he'd missed the SSA's booming voice. Autumn shot Aiden a last glance that clearly relayed her dissatisfaction with the pairing before she took off after Parker, squaring her shoulders as she went.

Aiden was clearing his throat to continue the meeting when his phone buzzed in his pocket, loud enough to alert the remaining team members.

Noah's pulse accelerated as Parrish pulled his device out and swiped twice before pausing to read.

Please don't be bad news.

After what seemed like hours, the SSA lifted his head. "They've found Winter's car at the edge of Dragon Run State Forest. It's a small patch of woods only an hour away."

A small patch of woods.

A perfect place to dump a body.

Fear paralyzed Noah as he waited for the rest, but Aiden only scowled. "What are you all standing around for? Let's go."

Relief hissed from his lips before he and the rest of the team darted for the door. They ran through the lobby, picking up more speed once they burst outside. Sun and

Bree arrived together and automatically headed for their vehicle, with Mia following closely behind to jump in their back seat.

Noah turned toward his truck, but Aiden's hand clamped down on his forearm, stopping him.

"No solo agents, Dalton."

Any other day, Noah might have argued with the SSA's barked order, but this day was unique. There wasn't time to express how badly he wanted to be alone and speed down the highway like a bat outta hell.

He jogged to the passenger's side of Aiden's car and opened the door.

The fact that he didn't care for Agent Parrish made no difference. Their personal opinions of each other had been momentarily pushed aside in favor of one clear, mutual goal.

They had to save Winter Black.

DRAGON RUN STATE Forest should have been an hour away, but Noah and Aiden arrived in forty-five minutes. Agent Parrish possessed a lead foot he apparently wasn't scared to use when the situation called for it.

Noah approved. His own truck, Beulah, wouldn't have gotten him there any faster, no matter how much he'd punched the gas.

When they pulled up to the scene, Winter's Civic was exactly where they'd been told to search.

Noah and Aiden jumped out of the car and approached the Civic with extreme caution just as Bree, Mia, and Sun accelerated into the lot.

Noah took the driver's side while Aiden circled around to the passenger side. They peered through the windows in unison, and the cramp in Noah's chest eased.

Nothing alarming was visible through the glass. No signs of a struggle. No bullet holes. No blood.

And no bodies.

"It's locked."

Noah had ascertained as much before the SSA's announcement but understood Parrish was keeping the other agents who were hurrying over informed.

He fished through his pants' pocket. When his fingers closed around the cold metal of Winter's spare key, he waved it overhead. "Not for long." Noah pulled a pair of plastic gloves from his jacket pocket and swiftly tugged them on.

A simple turn of the key unlocked the driver's side door. Crouching down, Noah poked his head into the car, careful not to touch anything. The last thing he wanted to do was screw up any evidence that might shed light on Winter's situation.

Nothing appeared out of place. Still no signs of a disturbance. Frustration growing, he backed away and headed straight for the trunk. Aiden followed suit, and once again, tension crackled between them as they braced themselves for the worst.

Not that there was any real way for Noah to prepare himself for the sight of Winter's dead body.

Noah sucked in a steadying breath before jamming the key in the trunk lock, refusing to let the thought fester. She wouldn't be in there. His girl wasn't going out like that. She was a fighter. She was—

His heart launched into his throat when he spotted the white hand. An arm. The pale skin of a bare human back.

Oh, god. *Winter.*

Swaying on his feet, Noah opened the trunk all the way while pain detonated in his chest. This was how his love story ended. After everything she'd fought through, Winter was naked and stiff in the back of her own car.

A simple, clean-cut conclusion to a complex life full of tragedy.

His legs were starting to give out when the details finally penetrated his traumatized brain.

Short hair. Wide shoulders. Burly legs and copious arm hair.

The body wasn't Winter's. Whoever was dead inside of that trunk was a man.

As relief swept Noah's body, a wheeze to his right suggested that Aiden had fallen prey to the same illusion upon first glance.

How many times are we gonna go through this, Parrish?

Maybe he and Aiden would find their breaking points today. Together.

After taking a few moments to regain his composure, Noah leaned over and placed two fingers against the man's neck, pressing gently on the carotid artery.

Twenty seconds passed. "No pulse, and nothing else in this trunk." Noah stepped back, fighting the urge to scream.

"No identification." Until she spoke, he hadn't even noticed Bree standing to his left. Her trained eyes scanned the corpse in calm, focused sweeps.

"Clothes. Justin killed him and stole his clothes." Aiden's speculation made perfect sense.

"Then took off in his car." Mia's dark eyes remained transfixed on the body.

"Justin would know we'd immediately be searching for Winter's car." Aiden met Noah's gaze as he spoke. "He never meant to use her vehicle for long. That would have been a reckless choice, and this kid thinks everything through. He doesn't make mistakes."

"We need forensics." Bree turned to locate Sun, who was standing behind the rest of them.

"Already done." As Sun gave them a curt nod, her iPad in

one hand and phone in the other, Noah was hit by how indispensable Agent Ming was to the team. She wasn't going to win any Miss Congeniality awards, but who the hell cared?

Anyone could smile and fill you full of shit.

Justin Black, for example.

"We have to ID this body." Noah barked the statement, frustration making his voice more aggressive than usual. "Winter and Justin might still be in this guy's car. ID the man, figure out what make and model he drove, and we could have the lead that takes us straight to Winter."

Murmurs of agreement were shared as he began to examine the surrounding area. Waiting for the crime scene techs was going to drive him insane, but he knew how important every last detail they discovered could be.

He was aware that tearing through the car or anything near it, which his instincts were screaming to do, could destroy valuable evidence.

"Just one breadcrumb, baby," he whispered as his gaze darted back and forth across the landscape. "Just give me one breadcrumb."

Logic said she couldn't hear him, but logic would also declare Winter's very real "special talent" to be impossible. Noah had witnessed many things in his time with Winter Black that defied the accepted laws of mankind.

A stand of bushes caught his eye. Dwarfed spruce, maybe Albertas or Norways. They retained their evergreen foliage throughout the Virginia seasonal changes. A few winterberry shrubs also dotted the deep green with their bright crimson clusters of fruit.

He headed toward the bushes, instincts flaring.

Winter had been here. Alive. He was sure of it.

He wanted to charge through the greenery and assure himself that Winter had also *left* alive. The absence of her body in the surrounding area would fuel his hope that they weren't far behind Justin Black and his trail of destruction.

When they found Justin, they'd find Winter.

Unless she's in those bushes.

Noah moved toward the stand, but Aiden's firm hand landed on his shoulder after only one step. On his other side, Bree scrambled over and hooked her arm in his.

His muscles coiled, quivering with the urge to shake them off, but he curbed the impulse with a series of deep breaths. As much as he hated waiting, his colleagues were right in using their restraint to manage his plummeting self-control.

They were a team.

And now he had to stand by and wait for someone else to search for Winter's body.

The seconds ticked by in his brain like the countdown to a bomb. Sooner or later, an explosion would rock this case. He could feel it in his bones.

Noah stared off into the shadowy woods and prayed that they'd find Winter before the clock struck zero.

9

W inter Black sprinted down a narrow, dark hallway, her lungs burning and legs aching from the infinite effort.

How long had she been chasing Justin? How many hours... months...years...had she been running after him?

Had they always been in this blackened corridor? Why was her baby brother so determined to get away from her? What had she done?

She couldn't remember. She only knew that she had to catch him. She had to stop Justin before something terrible happened.

Winter pumped her legs harder, but her brother was too fast. Tireless. She'd become convinced that he could run forever.

And maybe he would. Maybe she would as well.

Without warning, Justin stopped up ahead. Excitement bubbled beneath Winter's skin as she shortened the distance between them. She'd almost caught him when her feet froze to the floor, locking her into place just far enough away to prevent her from touching him.

No. From stopping him.

He closed his eyes and began to shrink...morphing like potter's clay into a much younger version of himself.

His hair grew long. Silky. His t-shirt and jeans faded into snug SpongeBob pajamas.

Justin was six years old again.

Winter's heart soared. The chase was over. She'd found—

Her joy faltered when he whipped a knife from behind his back. The metal glimmered like silver as he toyed with the weapon, his soft-cheeked little face transfixed by the blade. The weapon appeared gargantuan in his tiny hand.

Worse though was the awe...no, the absolute glee that widened his grin into an obscenity.

The lewd mask was so unbearable that Winter shuddered and dropped her gaze. When she did, her attention caught on the red stains on his pajamas.

Blood.

A blurred figure sprawled on the ground beneath him. Justin considered the form for a moment and then raised the knife high above his head.

He was going to kill. He was going to murder. Again.

Horror froze Winter's veins to ice. She had to stop him. Convince him not to commit the horrendous deed... He was just a baby now. He'd listen to his big sister.

"Stop!" she screamed. "Justin, please! You don't have to do this. You can walk away. Come to me! Please!"

His small head swiveled toward her. His grin was gone. Brilliant blue eyes, her baby brother's eyes, stared up at her blankly.

He didn't trust her. Winter could sense it in her bones.

"Please." A sob escaped her as she held out a hand, beckoning him to come. "Please stop, Justin. Please listen to me."

His head tilted, and his eyes returned to the long, shiny blade. "I want to stop, but I just don't know how, Sissy."

Before Winter could utter another word, Justin plunged the knife deep into the figure. A spray of crimson exploded through the air, showering her body in blood.

The liquid infiltrated her eyes...her mouth. She drowned in the ceaseless fountain of blood as it ate away at her flesh like acid.

Unable to move or act, she was crushed by the brutal truth that she couldn't stop him...

Couldn't stop him...

Couldn't...

Winter jerked awake with her pulse pummeling her ears. She tried to sit up, but just like in the dream, her body was frozen. This time in a different way.

Her vision blurred, but not from the explosion of blood in her subconscious. Justin had injected her with something. She remembered the sharp prick that had sent her tumbling into the abyss.

She remembered where she was.

"...approximately...six hours and forty-five minutes away from your beloved River City and all your dumbass Fed buddies..."

Almost seven hours away from home, trapped in a decrepit RV that harbored the overwhelming scent of dog piss. Camping with her little brother.

Quality sibling time.

You wanted this. You wanted to be with your brother. You wanted to bond with Justin so badly that you ignored every last warning your friends, boyfriend, colleagues, and the entire world gave you.

Here you go, Agent Black. He's all yours.

Winter turned her head and found her brother's familiar face staring right back at her. But his face was where the familiarity stopped.

Justin's jet-black hair was lighter now. She tried to focus, willing her hazy vision to clear. Not just lighter. Justin's hair was platinum blond.

She sniffed and detected the bleach still lingering within the RV. Though pungent, the fumes were a step up from urine.

Justin's eyebrows were lighter as well, and his eyes shone a rich chocolate brown instead of her identical piercing blue. A stylish pair of square-rimmed glasses sat on his nose, giving him a nerdy, hipster vibe that only accentuated his handsome features.

He shot her a wide toothy grin and tousled his new hairdo. "How you like it, Sis?"

Groggy and dazed from the injection, Winter struggled to form an answer. "I need to pee." And she did. Badly.

Justin's smile didn't fade at all. "Go ahead. I put one of those adult diapers on you."

Horror swelled in her stomach at the thought of Justin removing any of her clothing while she was passed out. What else had he done? There was no tell—

"I'm kidding." He laughed, throwing his head back as amusement racked his body. Seconds later, his smile faded, and the evil Justin she'd come to hate reappeared in a flash. "Okay, dear sister, this is how your potty break will go. First, your jewelry. Only the finest for you." Justin proceeded to tie a belt around her neck and then slid another needle into her arm. She hadn't been cognizant of the fact that he'd even been holding one.

"Stop. I don't want...I don't want whatever that is." The instant relaxation flowing through her muscles interrupted her thoughts, removing her from the world while allowing her to still partake, somehow, in the land of the living.

"This blend won't knock you out. At least, I don't think it will. I'm going for nice and calm, but I'm still mastering my craft. How bad would this adventure suck if you were all tense and brave and did something *stupid*?" He tapped a finger to his chin as though considering the scenario.

The finger and his face grew fuzzy as Winter's surroundings resumed their former blur.

"I'd have to *kill you*. That's not epic movie-worthy at all.

We're supposed to be Bonnie and Clyde. Not Dumb and Dumber. *So behave."* His nonchalant delivery made the threat to murder her all the more menacing.

Or at least, it should be menacing. At the moment, Winter didn't seem to care.

She squinted at the discarded needle on the nearby countertop. "What…did…that…" Her mouth refused to form coherent sentences.

Justin glanced at the empty hypodermic needle and laughed in a way that reminded her of an evil professor in his sadistic lab. "Oh, I just gave you a little dose of rama-lama-ding-dong. Produces a nice shoo-bop-sha-wadda-wadda effect. Don't worry about all that. Let's get your bladder emptied in the *proper* disposal area. Cuz, Sis, I am *not* cleaning up any of your shooby-doo-wops."

He cheerfully unbound her body and helped her to a sitting position. Justin had shifted moods yet again without any apparent reason. Her head spun, and she wondered if she was still dreaming. The floating sensation her "special medicine" induced was so soothing, she wasn't sure she could tell the difference.

Strings of some sort swung into her eyes and grazed her cheeks. She tried to push them away, missing her face entirely with the first two swats. On the third attempt, she made contact.

When she tugged at the bothersome threads, she noticed a corresponding pressure in her scalp. Weird. The strings were attached to her hair somehow.

Her sluggish brain put two and two together. Those strands *were* her hair.

Euphoria welled inside her, and she giggled while tugging the strand in front of her eyes. Her long, dark tresses were now shoulder-length and a reddish-black color.

Something told Winter she should be upset by this, but

the concoction Justin had injected into her body only allowed for mild curiosity. She tilted her head and yanked on the strand again before turning back to her newly blond brother.

Justin bounced up and down, obviously elated with her discovery. "You like it? I think the style suits you *much* better. And don't worry." He rolled his eyes. "Mine was bleach, but yours was just some coloring wax gunk. Washes out. Eventually. I think."

"You cut it." Her tongue couldn't manage more than those three words.

"Sure did." His gaze hardened. "No more whore hair for you."

Justin tightened the belt around her neck and pulled until she had no choice but to stand up. He guided her along the pitiful three-foot path to the bathroom door and gave her enough slack to reach the toilet.

She wondered if he might insist on watching, but he turned his back like a gentleman.

A gentleman serial killer leading his sister around like a pet zombie on a leash and allowing her to piss without an audience, how nice.

The thought zipped into her head, but she wasn't angry. She wasn't sure she was capable of experiencing much of anything right now, beyond this sense of peaceful bliss.

Peeing took a little long to get started, but that wasn't the hard part. Wiping, flushing, standing, pulling her pants back up, and staying on her feet while she washed her hands were all seemingly impossible tasks.

But she managed.

Once she finished, she peered into the mirror above the sink. She could now take in that her hair was a red-and-black-streaked catastrophe.

"So ugly." She whispered the comment without inflection

or remorse before her gaze drifted to the rest of Justin's alternations.

Her pupils were tiny within eyes that were heavily outlined in black, and the lipstick he'd applied was just as dark. He'd also changed her clothes.

The new outfit reminded her of a leftover goth kid from high school. All black. Black shirt, black pants, black boots.

As she studied her new persona, words she would never escape whispered through her mind.

"Grandpa had a hard-on for you, big sister. I do too."

Winter gripped the edge of the tiny sink, bracing herself for the violent reaction that always followed the memory, except nothing happened. The blue eyes gazing back at her remained hazy and dispassionate, even when she wondered if he'd touched her while she was unconscious.

Would Justin do something so vile to his own sister? Probably, but she couldn't summon enough emotion to fret about it, one way or the other.

What in the hell did he give me?

That question was too hard to focus on for long, though. Besides, if Justin had really raided the med cart before escaping the hospital, then the answer was, *pretty much anything.*

She stared at her unblinking reflection. *Come on, Winter. Fight this. Whatever this was.*

The drugs flowing through her veins were simply too strong, though, dampening her emotions and anxiety the way noise-canceling headphones dampened sound.

Justin tugged on the belt. "You done starin' at my fantastic artwork? You flushed like eighty years ago. The makeover *is* genius, but nobody likes a vain woman, Agent Black."

He yanked again, and she emerged from the bathroom, knowing another jerk of the belt might send her to the floor. With her reflexes medicated into such a sluggish state, her face would more than likely take the brunt of any fall.

Even medicated, she understood that the last thing she needed right now was another head injury like the one inflicted by Douglas Kilroy years ago, granting her that inexplicable ability.

She closed her eyes as the vision from a week ago resurfaced. A faceless nurse pushing Justin on a gurney. She'd told Noah that the vision felt "off" somehow.

Too late, her wandering mind made the connection. The premonition had seemed off because *she* was the Black sibling on that gurney. Justin was the nurse, who hadn't been so faceless after all.

As Winter float-walked out of the bathroom, a tiny voice in the far reaches of her mind screamed to run...to *fight*.

That seemed like so much work, though. Especially when putting one foot in front of the other was such a struggle. As incapacitated as she was, she wouldn't even make it out of the RV.

Justin led her to a tiny, cracked Formica table and sat her down on one of two chairs bolted to the floor. A paper plate was already waiting for her.

Her brother had prepared a thick peanut butter and jelly sandwich, sliced into four triangles. Half a banana and a pile of what resembled Cheez-It crackers rounded out her gourmet meal.

This was the exact dinner she'd made for Justin many a night when babysitting duties had fallen in her lap. He'd always requested the combination and insisted on eating right beside her on the couch.

Sometimes, she'd found the closeness adorable. Other times, she'd been annoyed and bored out of her mind with whatever cartoon her little brother had convinced her to put on the screen.

Not that any of that mattered now.

Winter swallowed with effort as she gazed at the familiar food, wondering idly if he'd made the meal on purpose or due to an attachment to the past…even one he wasn't aware of. Maybe that little boy she remembered was in there somewhere, trapped and buried under mountains of Kilroy's brainwashing.

The notion lit her heart with a tiny spark of hope before drifting away.

Justin motioned toward the food. "Eat, Winter." His voice wasn't unkind, but she sensed the warning in it.

How long had she been out for him to prepare all of this? And what if he'd laced her food with something even stronger than the drug already coursing through her veins?

Winter tilted her head, considering. She *was* hungry. Or she thought she might be. Her stomach had grumbled several times since waking, but the actual *desire* to eat hadn't registered at all.

Justin let out a frustrated grunt and picked up a sandwich triangle, pushing the food past her lax lips and into her mouth. She chewed, all the while certain that she shouldn't.

Making her brother angry seemed like an even worse move, though, considering she could do nothing to protect herself from his unpredictable reactions. And there was the lingering idea in the back of her mind that maybe if Justin could relax a little—trust her even a *tiny* bit—he might let his guard down long enough for her to escape.

Even if he did, Winter had no idea how to go about acquiring the motivation.

The happy yell of a young boy reached them through the thin RV walls, and Winter's head jerked up, triggering the instant pinch of the belt as it tightened around her throat.

Justin held a finger to his lips. "Ssshhh, Sissy. You can peek, but don't say a damn word or I'll cut your mouth off."

Winter wanted to argue that she couldn't put together a cry for help if she tried, but forming words was still too hard.

Justin drew back the curtains from the small, rounded window enough to grant them both a peekaboo view. As he peered through the glass, a malicious grin crawled across his face.

A boy, maybe eight or nine, tossed a baseball back and forth with a man who appeared to be his father. They both shared the same shaggy, light brown hair and wore matching orange hooded sweatshirts with a black Hillside Tigers Elementary School emblem across the chest.

Fog escaped from their mouths every time they spoke or laughed, and they laughed a lot. The cold didn't impede their enthusiasm at all.

Happy. They were happy.

Winter slid her gaze to Justin, whose smile had disappeared. His jaw flexed as he observed the father and son joke and play. She wondered if he was thinking of the childhood The Preacher had taken from him.

Or maybe he was reliving the childhood Douglas had *given* him instead and comparing his experiences to the loving scene of normalcy on display.

Either way, Justin's face was hard-set when he finally turned to her. "Effing tigers. Apparently, the *Brady Bunch* out there likes ferocious, carnivorous beasts. Lucky for them, they're about to meet one."

The drug pumping through her system told Winter to disregard whatever her brother was saying and drift along in a calm, easy dream. To take the simple path for once by letting go of her worries and embracing the peace.

Beneath that peace, though, a discordant note rang. An alarm bell, urging Winter to fight harder and snap out of her robotic state.

Come on, Winter. Wake up.

She dug her nails into her palms, but blood welled in the crescent shapes without Winter ever feeling a sting.

It was like her pain and emotions were neatly locked away in a steel safe.

She blinked at the red marks. Maybe she was better off that way.

The internal distress signal grew more insistent.

Wake. Up.

Even high as a kite, some part of Winter understood she had to warn that family. Justin wouldn't just drive away from them. Not now. Not after their genuine love for each other and enthusiasm for life had been dangled in front of his eyes like a coveted jewel he could see but never grasp.

They'd insulted him. It was written all over his face.

But how? How could she warn them when she could barely talk, and there was no way in hell Justin was going to let her meds wear off anytime soon? Earning his trust would take time, assuming she could ever pull the feat off at all.

That family doesn't have time.

Justin picked up another triangle and pressed the sandwich against her lips until she opened her mouth. "You're smearing your lipstick. I worked damn hard putting that shit on you." He huffed with mock frustration. "Ha. Just kidding. This works better the messier you are."

He glanced out the window again, and Winter frowned as she chewed. What worked better when she looked messy?

Nothing good. Of that she was certain.

She finished chewing and swallowed, hoping the act of eating might help her work up the strength and focus to ask her brother about his plans. He was always proud of his work. His creativity. Maybe he'd gloat and share some information that could help her prevent the impending horror movie about to take place in this frigid RV park.

"...six hours and forty-five minutes away..."

Everyone she loved, aside from the monster in front of her, might as well have been on different planets. None of her friends were close enough to save her or the nearby family.

If she wanted to escape, the challenge rested solely on her shoulders.

She just needed her brain to cooperate.

Justin shoved another bite into her mouth. "You have to eat up, Sis. You're going to need your strength." He turned back toward the window, leering as the man and his son continued to toss the ball. "We're going to have some fun very, *very* soon."

Winter forced her jaw to continue working, even as goose bumps pebbled across her skin.

Justin's warped idea of fun was the thing that terrified her the most.

Or it was, right up until another prick in her arm created another calming wave and soothed her fear away.

10

Nicole Stewart sulked in the corner of the RV's kitchen, wishing she could scream at the top of her lungs. If not to release her frustration, then to scare the hell out of her mother. Technically, both of her parents had forced her to come on this damn camping trip, but her mom was the one always pushing for more "family time."

Her dad just went along with whatever her mom wanted because that was easier and seemed to be what married people were supposed to do.

Nicole kicked the fake wood cabinet. She planned on never getting married. She'd witnessed her parents' boring as crap relationship—which only grew more boring with each passing day—long enough to know better.

She wasn't tying herself down to one stupid guy and popping out his kids for the grand prize of living like a prisoner chained to the suburbs for the rest of her life. Hell no.

There was a great big world out there, and she was going to roam every last inch of it. Of course, there would be men along the way. Lots of them. She'd make them all fall madly in love with her, but she'd never commit to a single one.

Her mom bumped her hip on the edge of the tiny kitchen counter. "Oh, darn it all to heck! Good gracious, that hurt!"

Nicole didn't bother to ask if her mom was okay. She was too busy trying not to puke at how disgusting and lame parents were. Especially her mother.

"Darn it all to heck! Good gracious!"

Like her mom was a freaking nun or something. She obviously wasn't, because she'd had to have sex at least twice to bring Nicole and her little brother into the world. Nicole doubted her mom and dad had done it much more than those two times.

She shuddered at the visual. Parent sex was gross. If Nicole were either one of them, she'd rather die than be forced to see the other one naked. Barf-a-rola.

Plus, her mom drank wine coolers on occasion back at home, and nuns didn't drink wine coolers. Why couldn't her parents just act like normal human beings instead of trying so hard to be these cheeseball *Full House* wannabes? Why couldn't they say "damn" and "hell" like normal parents?

She'd get grounded for a week if she said either of those words even once.

So, so lame.

"Are you okay, honey?" Her dad appeared from the back of the RV, where he'd been trying and failing to get the heat to turn on. This wasn't even their stupid RV. Just some junkwad her dad's friend had let them borrow.

Her mom smiled. "I'm fine, Greg. But I think little Nicki-Poo-Grumpkins could use a pep talk."

Her parents gave each other a disgusting, senior citizen smooch before her dad came to sit beside her on the padded bench that served as half their dining room.

"Remember, sweetie, we talked about how good it would be to put the screens away and breathe some fresh air for a couple of days? This is a healthy break for all of us, Nicki-Poo."

She shot him the meanest glare she could manage. "I've told you both to stop calling me that. You guys *never* care what I say. Never."

Her dad sighed, and a pang of guilt assailed her stomach before her shoulders stiffened. Screw him. Even if this camping trip wasn't his idea, he'd still helped make it happen. He was basically just her mom's bitch.

Nicole wanted to be home, gaming and texting with her friends. Everyone else would be online right now while she was stuck out here in the effing forest with no service and no entertainment to speak of. In the middle of winter, no less.

Were her parents insane? The air sneaking through the door felt like it was negative one-zillion degrees.

Idiots.

"I'm sorry, sweetie. We've called you that since you were born. It's a little hard to stop now, but I'll try." Her dad added a firm nod to his promise and grinned at her. Apparently, he thought she was still young enough to believe parents ever meant anything they said.

She'd be Nicki-Poo until the day she died. Or at least until the day *they* died. And she was sure they'd live forever just to be able to try to run—*and ruin*—her adult life as well as her childhood.

"Nicki-Poo" would probably be on her gravestone if she died first. Her parents were *that cheesy*.

Nicole kicked the cabinet again and sneered at the fold-away table.

There was only one room in this ugly-ass RV, and when she'd asked her parents where she was supposed to sleep, her mom had pointed at the wall. The stupid grin on her face when she'd unfolded the built-in table to reveal a shitty and uncomfortable looking mattress had enraged Nicole.

Her mother acted like the contraption was genius.

So. Lame.

Nicole was certain she'd accidentally fallen through a black hole into some lower level of hell. She'd never share those beliefs with her friends because they'd laugh their asses off at her. But that stuff happened on TV shows all the time. Like *Star Trek: Voyager*.

She binged a lot of that show late at night. Netflix streamed the whole series.

Just one more thing my friends can never know.

Her mom plopped some chicken breasts down on the counter, preparing their family dinner. No matter how Martha Stewart-ish her mom *tried* to be, both her parents knew she wouldn't eat a bite of that crap.

Nicole had told them *an entire month ago* that she was a vegetarian now. She hadn't so much as touched a piece of meat in exactly twenty-nine days.

Well. Two weeks ago, she'd sneaked a chicken nugget off her brother's plate when he wasn't paying attention, but that had just been a stress-induced mistake. Junior high was *hard*. She couldn't be a perfect person *all* the time.

At least she was trying to do something good for the world. Her mom acted like *golly-gee-gracious* was an effing mantra for the morally upright, yet not wanting to eat a dead bird was "just plain silly." That's what her mother had said.

Silly.

"Oh yay. *Raw chicken.* Thanks, Andrea. Like this piece of junk camper didn't already smell rank enough." Nicole grabbed her coat and headed for the doorway, knowing her mother couldn't stand when Nicole called her by her first name. "Like I said before, you guys *never care what I say.* I'm not eating your gross murder meal."

Nicole stomped down the two steps to the crappy metal

door and swung it open as hard as she could, enjoying the loud slam that echoed through the campground.

Take that, assholes.

The satisfaction faded when she glanced around and realized there wasn't anywhere to go. They were the only idiot family in this stupid RV park right now.

She shoved her hands deep into her coat pockets. The air was cold as shit out here with the wind biting at her bare cheeks, but she refused to go back inside. Not yet. Let her parents worry and be upset for a little while.

They deserved it.

As she took a few steps across the hard dirt, a brilliant idea occurred to her. If her parents refused to accept her decision to become a vegetarian, she'd take everything one step further and become a vegan. That one would rock their world.

Nicole would wait until the next time her mom was pouring milk into a bowl of cereal for her moron little brother. She'd smack the jug right out of her mother's hands and scream, "Dairy is scary!"

Epic plan.

She snickered to herself, her breath forming little white clouds in the icy air. Her friend Raina had gone vegan for three months last year. She'd passed out cold in the middle of gym class trying to spike a volleyball, but that was because Raina hadn't done the research. Raina wasn't a *real* vegan. She didn't even like *dogs*. She'd just wanted attention.

Nicole was way too smart to not at least google some *Teen Vogue* articles and make sure she was doing it right.

In fact, she could probably walk into the wilderness, live off the land, and take just as good care of herself as any adult could. After all, her parents had purposely brought her and her brother to a questionable place with no heat in the dead of winter.

That should count as child abuse or something.

Every other RV in this whole godforsaken place was empty. Those were probably all owned by parents who loved their children and didn't want them to catch pneumonia or Ebola or whatever the hell else she'd probably come down with on this trip.

She walked a few more feet from their camper, not sure what to do with herself while her parents suffered their punishment. A baseball—her annoying little brother's baseball—rolled to a stop at her feet.

Their dad had been tossing the ball with Tim before he came inside to pretend he knew how to fix the heater. Tim was out here by himself now, and she almost felt bad for him. He'd been forced into this family trip too.

"Just toss it back? For a little bit? Puh-leeease, Nicki?" Tim's shaggy hair was so messed up that he could almost pass for a homeless kid. Her parents could probably get prison time for this.

Nicole stared down at the ball. Softball had always been her favorite sport. Coach had told her at the end of last season that she was the best pitcher on the team.

Raina had been *super* pissed.

She considered humoring the little butthead before remembering that he'd actually been *happy* about coming here.

Traitor.

Plus, the last thing she wanted was her stupid parents peeking out the RV windows and spotting her playing with her brother or maybe even accidentally *smiling*.

No. Absolutely not.

They'd never learn their lesson that way.

She pulled her foot back and kicked the ball back toward Tim before turning away and walking in the opposite direction. The view was way better in front of the RV, anyway.

The mountains stood stark and jagged in the distance, contrasting against the gray-blue January sky as the sun began its descent. Thin flares of bright pink and orange shot across the clouds.

Even with everything being dead and bare, the tree limbs that jutted out made dreamy, fairy-tale-ish silhouettes. Like a scene from *Snow White* or something.

Nicole grudgingly admitted that the view was pretty, but only to herself. Besides, skies were always pretty in their own way. This one wasn't that special or spectacular when she thought it through. She wasn't sure she even liked the view at all after considering how common the whole sunset and mountain thing was.

Getting excited about the sunset was added proof that her parents had dragged them to a destination *so boring* she had to walk around in the dirt just to find something interesting.

Movement in her peripheral vision caused her to turn. If Tim was wandering off alone, she'd totally get blamed for his stupidity. Better to go chase his dumb ass down now than wait for her parents to freak out. They always acted like there was a serial killer waiting around every corner.

Lame.

Instead of Tim, though, she spotted a couple—other actual humans—stepping out of another RV toward the back of the park. With no greenery or other visitor activity to obstruct her view, Nicole studied the pair.

The woman was dressed in black from head to toe and sported a pair of super cool army-style boots. Nicole had always wanted a pair like that…they were *so stylish* and punk…but her mom would say no because her mom vetoed anything that remotely seemed cool.

On top of the kick-ass outfit, the girl had funky red-and-black-streaked hair. Kind of like highlights, but *cooler.* Tougher.

Nicole fingered a strand of her own lank, dishwater-blonde hair. Her mom would never let her do anything that awesome. She wasn't even allowed to dye her hair one stupid, solid color.

So. Lame.

She focused on the guy next, and *holy crap*. He was hot. Way too old for her and clearly in love with the punk rock chick. But so, so cute.

The way he held his arms around the girl was adorable. Nicole hoped someone would hold *her* like that someday. Or even *look* at her like that.

What made the scene cuter and increased her jealousy all the more was the fact that the woman was trying to act like she didn't even like the attention. Pretending to push him away when she obviously could have broken free if she wasn't enjoying herself.

According to an article Nicole read once, girls were supposed to do stuff like that. Guys liked a chase, so you had to leave them panting for more. That's what this lady was doing. Pretending, teasing, building up the suspense…

Nicole planned to do the same herself. Lead the boys on and make them crazy.

She couldn't wait to grow up and get started. Her boobs had to fill in first, but after that, she'd have as many boyfriends as she wanted. They'd all think she loved them the most, and they'd all be wrong.

As she watched them closely, the guy spotted Nicole and flashed her a warm smile. He even tried to wave, but he had to wrap his arms around the girl again to keep her from stumbling. Was that lady drunk?

Nicole had tasted beer once. She'd gone to a party with her crush at the time while her parents thought she was staying the night at Raina's.

She'd desperately wanted to impress Wyatt with her

maturity. He was fourteen, *a year older*, and a full grade ahead, so hanging out with her at all was a huge compliment. She had to play things cool if she wanted to keep something going with an older guy.

She'd downed the first beer. He'd thought she was being a sexy show-off, but she'd actually just been worried that if she didn't drink the bitter stuff fast, she'd gag on it. The second one had tasted much better, probably due to some newbie taste bud adjustment period.

Nicole remembered walking the same way that girl across the park was walking now. Wobbly. Wyatt had been super stoked to watch her get two whole beers down. He'd kissed her and then asked her to go to the basement with him.

That was the point where she'd first become a little sick... and a little scared. She'd only kissed two boys before, and one of those times happened back in kindergarten. That didn't exactly count. Wyatt probably had all kinds of experience.

Older men always did.

When she'd worked up enough nerve to agree to "hang out" in the basement, he'd been all smiles. Whatever he'd planned for them to do down there must have been a lot of fun.

Except only a few seconds later, she'd thrown up...right on Wyatt's shoes. He'd never spoken to her again, and she was pretty sure she deserved that. Sexy girls didn't puke. They did sexy stuff, and lots of it.

Her first attempt at hooking up with a guy, and she'd totally failed. An epic living nightmare that left her in a perpetual state of embarrassment.

Her parents hadn't taken her seriously when she told them kids at school were bullying her, and that they had to move the family away to end her suffering. Granted, that hadn't been the truth. Not exactly. But the story was *close enough* to the real dilemma, and her parents had just smiled and shaken their heads.

Andrea had told her, "This too shall pass," and Greg had asked if she wanted him to call the principal.

The worst. Her parents were the absolute worst.   .

Nicole blinked back to the present and realized that the couple was walking her way. The closer they came, the more her heart raced. Forget cute. This guy was gorgeous. Short blond hair and a face that made her favorite pop star seem like a troll in comparison.

She smoothed her own hair as they approached, wishing she'd taken the time to put on some of her mom's lipstick before she'd stomped out the door.

"Hey there. What are you doing out in the cold all alone?" His voice was swoon worthy. Low and sexy and irresistible in a way she'd never experienced before.

Forget Wyatt. This is a real man.

"Just avoiding my stupid parents." She realized after she spoke that the answer sounded immature and lame.

The way he smiled made her forget what she'd said at all. His eyes were dreamy brown like Hersey's Kisses, and his gaze sent electric butterflies zooming around in her stomach. Similar to the sensation she'd had when Wyatt kissed her, but different.

Better.

"Ha. Parents are always a bummer, huh?" He laughed, and she giggled along with him. "Does your family live around here? Or just visiting?"

Nicole was old enough to know she shouldn't just hand out information to a complete stranger. This wasn't some weird old creep, though, just a cute guy and his girlfriend. He didn't have, like, an eye patch or a hook hand, and he wasn't driving a white kidnapper van.

He wasn't offering her drugs, or candy, or even smoking a cigarette.

"We're just on a lame little 'getaway.' We don't live anywhere close. Thank *god*." Nicole attempted her most dramatic eye roll yet, though she usually saved those for her parents. Although this was *about* her parents, so technically, same difference.

"I totally understand." He nodded in what she guessed was sympathy. He was grinning even wider now.

Nicole glanced at the girl. "Is she, um, okay?"

"She's fine." He gave a soft chuckle. "I'm Bill, and this here is Jeannette. Jeannette's just a little bit wasted right now."

Bill winked at Nicole, as though they were sharing some sort of secret while she wrinkled her nose.

Bill? Seriously?

Nicole had imagined his name was Xavier or Zander… something sexy like that. Though she supposed he couldn't help what his own stupid parents had named him. Jeannette wasn't much better anyway, so these two had both probably endured some incredibly lame parents growing up.

Did cool old people exist anywhere on the planet?

"I'm Nicole." She dipped her chin against her puffer coat collar, too tongue-tied at talking with such a hottie to manage more at that exact second. Raina was going to be *so jealous*.

"Nice to meet you, Nicole. Hey, we're having some trouble with the heat in our RV. Do you think your dad would be able to help with that at all?" Bill tilted his head, and between that adorable little gesture and the way her skin heated up when he said her name, Nicole was this close to telling him that *she'd* help him fix any damn thing, any damn time, and any damn where.

She might have, if she knew anything at all about RV heaters.

"We're having trouble with our heat too." She pictured her lame mother introducing herself to Hot Bill.

"Oh golly-gee-gracious, it's so nice to meet you!"

Blech. Andrea's greeting wouldn't be sincere anyway. Her mom was freaked out by girls like Jeannette, and she did *not* like older guys hanging around her daughter.

Why did her parents have to be involved in this? Nicole would love nothing more than to just keep flirting with Bill and observe Jeannette the Train Wreck try to keep her head up.

Oh my god. Did I act that dumb when I was drunk with Wyatt?

She hoped not, but that was done and over with. The next time she partied with a boy, she'd limit herself to one beer. Maybe she'd actually make it to the basement that way.

Nicole wiggled her freezing fingers inside of her coat pockets. She couldn't let these two go all night without a heater. Her dad had said a million times that tonight was supposed to get even colder. He'd told them if he couldn't get the heater fixed, they might even have to drive back home and forego the getaway.

She'd desperately hoped he'd fail, but she hadn't counted on it. Her dad always stuck with stuff until he figured it out. She was proud of him for that, although she'd tell him over her dead body. Some of her friends' dads were total assholes, and she was aware that she'd lucked out.

The bottom line, which she'd already accepted, was that they almost certainly wouldn't be leaving tonight. Helping Bill and Jeannette was the decent thing to do.

Plus, Bill was way too handsome to die young by freezing to death.

"My dad is kinda good at that stuff. I'm sure he'd help you guys out. I can go ask him." Nicole beamed at Bill, showing him that she was a *good person*, after all. All vegetarians were.

Duh.

"That would be fantastic." Bill's gratefulness was apparent. He might have even hugged Nicole if he wasn't holding up wasted Jeannette.

Nicole sneaked another peek at the woman, who was staring off into space at nothing. Couldn't he just leave her in the RV? Even without heat, it had to be warmer inside than out here. Plus, if Jeanette stayed in their RV, Nicole could flirt with Bill much more openly.

Not that Jeannette seemed capable of noticing anyway.

"Heads up!" Tim shouted from the other side of the RV just as his baseball came flying over, landing several yards away from them. Nicole wasn't sure if he'd meant to hit them or just wanted some attention. Either way, Tim was so, *so* lame.

Nicole scowled at the ball and met Bill's chocolate eyes. "Think you could kill my little brother in exchange for my dad's help?" She giggled and batted her eyelashes at him.

Bill stared at her, his gaze so intense now that the electric butterflies in her belly flapped their wings again. "I could probably help you out with that." His features altered for a second, sending a cold chill down Nicole's spine.

Run. Get your family and leave. Now.

Nicole tried to sort through the absurd thought that had almost seemed like a whisper in her ear. Bill was smiling again before she could focus, and she was mesmerized in an instant. He was just *sooo cute*, like, Hollywood cute. Nicole was pretty sure she'd fallen a little in love with him already.

The alarmed voice from seconds ago faded away until she forgot the warning completely.

Flashing him a flirtatious smile, Nicole walked to the ball, careful to sway her hips like the models always did on the runway. When she reached it, she made sure to bend just right, pushing her tight ass out the way she'd learned from the reality shows she binge-watched. She knew the move drove boys crazy.

She hoped to god that she could drive Bill insane, even just a little bit.

Straightening back up as slowly as possible, she turned and gestured. "Follow me." She led the couple to her family's RV, her earlier sour mood gone.

Now that Bill was here to spice things up, this might turn out to be the most unforgettable camping trip of her life.

11

W inter willed the world to stop spinning. This poor teenage girl had no idea who she was talking to. Flirting with.

Nicole stood in front of them wearing a dark purple puffer jacket over gray leggings that were way too thin for the cold. She had beige Ugg-like boots on and a purple beanie on her darkish blonde hair to round out the ensemble.

Winter's head started to droop as she nodded off. She caught herself just in time and jerked her eyes back open.

No, no drifting. Focus.

A figure swam in Winter's vision before her acuity sharpened. Right. The girl. How old could the child possibly be? Thirteen? Fourteen? Whatever the answer, she was too young to have her entire life ruined. Winter didn't know exactly what Justin planned to do to this family, but she was certain little Nicole would never be the same again.

If she survived at all.

She's just a kid. A cute, innocent, clueless kid.

Winter wanted to scream…or even just *whisper* for the

girl to run. Gather her family and leave *now*. She couldn't communicate the warning in her current drugged state, though. She could only think it.

Even if she'd been able to make her thick tongue say the correct words or any words at all, Justin had her gun. She hadn't been surprised that he'd found the weapon before switching out cars. He knew what she did for a living and the "accessories" she toted around as a result.

He now had the weapon hidden in his pocket, the barrel pressed tightly to Winter's side. What Nicole was certain to perceive as an adorable cuddle between two people in love was actually Justin making sure that Winter didn't forget the consequences of saying the wrong words.

In addition, Winter's muscles were so loosey-goosey that she would have fallen over if her brother wasn't propping her up against him.

Justin had warned her before they exited the RV that doing something foolish would not only result in him shooting her…he'd also be forced to kill the family, and that would be *her* fault. If that happened, he'd promised to care for her gunshot wound and keep her alive so that she could fully experience remorse over what she'd done.

"You already ruined *my* life, Winter." He'd swiped at a fake tear and sniffled. "And 'in the name of the beautiful, wonderful law' or not, you've ended quite a few other lives with your hotshot career. You really wanna add a sweet little family to that? Is that who you are now? Are you a *killer*, Winter?" He'd let out a few hysterical laughs after asking her that.

All she'd been able to ask in response was, "What…you… do them?"

Justin's evil grin had transformed his handsome face into the ghoul-like façade of Kilroy. "Oh, Sissy. Always wanting to know everything. Just be *patient*. You'll find out soon enough."

"Soon enough" was nearing, and she still hadn't figured out a way to prevent Nicole's family from being harmed. She could barely work out a way to get from point A to point B without collapsing. Every step Winter took seemed impossible. Her legs were dead weight, and lifting them at all required every last ounce of energy and focus she could muster.

Her pulse pounded in her ears just as loudly as when she had her headaches but without the pain. Winter wasn't sure she could register pain right now, even if someone shoved a knife through her hand.

Justin must have combined sedatives with painkillers.

As they approached the family's RV, she attempted to lift her head, hoping to make eye contact of some sort that would at the very least prevent Justin from entering their temporary home. These people didn't have to know he was a serial killer. They simply needed to be uncomfortable enough to flee the park.

Alive.

The effort of lifting her head was too much, though. She had nothing left for anything else. Maybe they would witness how ill she was and insist on calling for an ambulance if they were able to catch a signal at all out here in the boonies. Winter didn't know their exact location, only that Justin had done his best to remove them from civilization.

Before she could even finish the thought or hope that a call would go through, her heart sank. The second a single one of them picked up a phone, they'd receive a swift bullet to the head. Justin wouldn't hesitate to take one or *all* of them out.

They rounded the corner of the RV, and Winter spotted the father and son. Nicole's dad frowned when he noticed the two strange adults following his daughter. His frown deepened with considerable disgust as he absorbed the state she was in.

Incapacitated, which was true. On drugs, which was also true. No doubt, when Nicole's dad looked at Winter, all he saw was a wasted, loser, drunk woman who could only ever be a bad influence on his little girl.

Justin wasted no time spinning his tale. "Hello, sir. I'm Bill, and this is Jeannette. We're having a bit of heater trouble in our RV, and your kind daughter mentioned that you're rather handy with those types of things."

Bill and Jeannette.

Bile rose in Winter's throat as Justin dared to use their parents' names. If they were still alive, the knowledge of what their son had become would kill them all over again.

"Okay. I might be able to help. Name's Greg. This is my son, Tim. And I guess you already met Nicole. But…" Greg's blatant stare at Winter spoke volumes. "What's wrong with your girlfriend?"

Justin's winning smile faded into a somber expression. He ducked his head a little as if embarrassed. "I know, she looks rough, but she's just lost her parents in a terrible car accident. A ten-car pileup and…there were *semis* involved." He released a heavy sigh. "I wanted to get her away from all the relatives and family friends who just kept coming at her. They meant well, but she needed to grieve in peace, ya know?"

Greg's countenance softened by considerable degrees.

"She drank and sobbed most of last night. I think she's only slept three or four hours since…since she lost them…"

Winter wasn't sure how long she nodded off for, only that Justin was still talking when she woke to him squeezing her ribs. "I've been keeping a real close eye on her, though, making sure she's safe and all. Haven't let her out of my sight."

"Grief is a rough one." All the judgment left Greg's tone, and Winter had the fleeting idea of what a good man he must be. A loyal husband. A caring father.

"Sure is, sir. Sure is." Justin let out another sigh. "So, I guess things are going just about as well as they can right now except for that darn heater situation. Conked right out on us. Super bad timing. I'd just drive her home right now, but Jeannette's still so hung over. I'd hate to let her get attacked by relatives for falling apart a little. You have *no idea* how rough her family tree is."

Greg shook his head. "Everyone has an opinion when the tragedy isn't theirs. It's a shame."

Justin gave a vigorous nod. "You are exactly correct. People always judge what they don't understand." He waited what Winter guessed was a very calculated number of seconds before returning to the situation at hand. "So, are you as good at electrical systems and stuff as your daughter bragged you were?"

"You betcha. Let me just grab some tools and fill in my wife on your predicament." Greg stepped toward their RV just as the door swung open.

"Greg, honey? What's going on?" The female voice had to belong to Greg's wife. Winter thought she sounded sweet but wary. Motherly.

Greg introduced his wife as Andrea before pulling her off to the side to share the tragic story of Jeannette's recent loss, along with Bill's attempt to guide her through this hard time. Despite his low voice, Winter caught every single word and was positive that Justin, Nicole, and little Tim had as well.

Leave it to her mastermind demon brother to figure out a way to keep his highly trained, federal agent sister from using her strength and skills in any capacity while *also* coming up with a backstory that made people pity the mess he'd transformed her into.

You should have stayed away from him.

Winter must have drifted off again because, one moment, Andrea was a good fifteen feet away, and the next, her gentle hand was on Winter's arm.

The woman spoke in a soft voice. "Oh, sweetie, I get it. My own parents passed in a car accident just four years back. It's a terrible thing to have the ones you love ripped away from you with no warning. If I could've escaped and drank away my sorrow for a few days, I would have."

The affectionate pat following the kind words caused a dull ache in Winter's chest. These were good people. Not perfect. No one was perfect. But kind, well-meaning humans who probably wanted nothing more than to live out their lives with their children...and their children's children...

Beneath her clothes, her skin broke out in a cold sweat.

Justin can't. He can't hurt them. They're too innocent. He can't possibly plan to kill these people. Not if he still has a soul.

"I've got plenty of Tylenol, and we're stocked on Gatorade. It might help her feel bet—"

"That's so kind of you, ma'am." Justin cut her off in his polite, charming, deceitful-as-hell way.

"Andrea. Call me Andrea. None of this ma'am stuff." She gave Winter's arm another pat.

"Well, okay. Thank you so much, Andrea, but I think I'm just going to take her back to our RV and let her get some sleep. I thought the fresh air might help, but I think she just needs rest." Justin's tone was so convincing. So pure.

"A little shut-eye is the best cure for anything. That's what I always say. Why don't I go on over with you, and we'll get that RV nice and warm for you two?" Greg bounded off into the RV for the promised tools.

Andrea held up a finger. "Wait, Bill. Just one second. I'm

sending some ginger ale with you at the very least. Jeannette will need something to soothe her stomach when she wakes up."

Justin held Winter tight as the two adults ran their separate tasks, but at least he kept his mouth shut. Probably because Nicole was standing nearby, though Winter couldn't see her. She figured it was safe to bet that the girl was still drooling over "Bill."

Tim was easier to spot. He stood directly in front of them and was much shorter, allowing Winter a clear view without requiring the daunting task of lifting her head.

She squinted at the fuzzy figure, guessing he was a few years older than Justin had been when Kilroy took him. Tim's hair was a lighter shade of brown, and his cheeks were still rounded with baby fat. Even with her vision all wonky, Winter could tell the boy's wide eyes took everything in with great interest.

His life was just starting.

Just let them go. Please, let them go.

Winter's legs wobbled. Her chest ached again, and she wanted to go home. She just wanted to go home and crawl into bed with Noah and sob away the horror of this day. He'd stroke her hair, or what was left of it, and tell her everything was going to be okay.

She never truly believed that anything in life would be "okay." Not after the hell she'd lived. When Noah said the words, though, she could almost believe him. Almost…

Her eyes snapped back open as Andrea and Greg returned together, crunching twigs underfoot and chattering. So unaware of the danger they were in that Winter wanted to cry. Only her face was too numb to form any tears. Or talk, or try to warn them…

"Here. For when she wakes up." Andrea hung a small grocery bag around Justin's wrist. "And after Greg gets your heater going and Jeannette's feeling a bit better, why don't you two come on over for some dinner?"

No! No! No!

Winter managed a tiny moan and was rewarded with an immediate jab of metal into her side.

"That would be amazing." Sincerity rang in Justin's voice even as he shoved the gun barrel against her. A warning. "I've been so worried about Jeannette, I hadn't even thought about dinner yet. I'm so grateful to have met you and your family." His acting skills were so good that no one would question his intentions for a second.

Especially a normal, kind family who believed the world was mostly full of decent people, and serial killers were something that existed only in the scripts of TV shows like *Criminal Minds* and *Law and Order: SVU*. They had no reason to assume Justin…or Bill…was as ruthless and depraved as Ted Bundy, Jeffrey Dahmer, or John Wayne Gacy.

To them, Bill and Jeannette were just a couple of kids who needed a helping hand.

"I'll come with you. I can help get Jeannette comfortable and hand Dad the tools and stuff." When Nicole offered her services in a giddy voice, Winter wanted to scream.

No! Someone, tell her no!

Didn't anyone else see what was happening here? The lovestruck teen was only volunteering to help because she was crushing hardcore on Justin.

Winter sagged against Justin, and her brother's arms clamped tighter around her as her mind floated away. Growing up, she'd always been amazed by how well serial killers blended into society. How people who were so deviant and sociopathic could mimic such a normal outward appearance.

She'd been fascinated by them, but she'd never expected— nor wanted—to experience their talent for impersonating regular, law-abiding citizens up close like this. The reality was far more terrifying than intriguing.

Charisma. Charm. Chameleon-like abilities to adapt to any situation thrown at them. Plus, mind-blowing intelligence to back up all those attributes.

This class of evil—Justin's class—should come with giant red horns or some other telltale sign. Warning lights flashing above their heads. Fangs.

Instead, her brother was handsome and friendly. Likable. Magnetic.

His fingers didn't feel friendly, though, as they dug into her waist during the short walk back to their own RV, with Greg and Nicole trailing behind them. Winter wondered if the father and daughter would ever see their own camper again.

Winter couldn't let this happen. She just couldn't.

Planting her feet in the sludgy ground, which was muddy from the recently melted snow, Winter tried to stop them from going forward. The metal of her gun buried deeper into her ribs, and she opened her mouth to scream, but only a muffled sob managed to escape her numb lips.

Justin half-dragged, half-pushed her into the RV. Winter stumbled across the threshold and inhaled, hoping the sprays and air fresheners her brother had used to disguise the vehicle's putrid odor had failed. The dog piss stench was faint, though, and the interior now had more of a musty scent than anything. A little stuffy but camouflaged with a barrage of lavender and citrus.

Winter's heart plummeted as Justin led her to the bed. Everything was working in her psychopath brother's favor. How did she even begin to fight when the entire universe seemed to be on Justin's side?

Did Grandpa Kilroy actually wield powers from the grave like Justin suspected?

Hair raised on her arms at the thought.

"There you go, baby," Justin crooned and smiled down at her after she'd settled. He gave her a light poke with the gun just to remind her that her behavior would affect everyone.

Not like she could escape anyway. He'd rendered her body useless with the medications. All she could do was lay in the cramped space and listen in growing horror as Justin charmed Greg and Nicole, the three of them chatting together as though they'd known each other for years.

"Well, your vent is clogged for one thing." Greg's voice filled the RV with fatherly wisdom. "That can cause a whole plethora of problems over time. And that electrical screw right there is rusted out. If the parts aren't connected and sealed firmly, the ignition won't respond. Triggers a shutdown instead. That's for your protection, actually."

"Wow, Greg. How do you know so much about this stuff?" Justin's feigned awe made Winter's stomach turn.

She loved her brother. But oh, how she hated him too.

"You just pick stuff up here and there. My grandpa was great with cars and engines and whatnot. He taught me everything he knew."

Winter cringed at the older man's carefree, joyful response, fearful of just how badly Justin was fuming on the inside.

"That's awesome." Justin didn't seem overcome with rage. Yet. "*My* grandpa taught me a lot of stuff too. I guess you could say he taught me everything he knew. But I think his skillset was a lot different than yours."

"Is that right? And what was your grandpa's field of expertise, Bill?"

Winter sucked in her breath, expecting Greg was within milliseconds of being shot or stabbed. Or both.

"He was a preacher. A real smart guy. Unique." Justin's banter seemed lighthearted.

"Ah. A preacher. I must say that's one profession I was probably never worthy of." Greg laughed, and Nicole giggled along with him. "Nicki-Poo, hand me that black bag over there. Not the big one, the small one. I've got all the extra parts we'll need to help Bill and Jeannette out. Lean in here, sweetie. You never know when you'll find yourself stuck in a troublesome RV situation."

Nicole guffawed at that. "I think it's safe to say I won't be camping again anytime soon."

Winter drifted, recalling how her own father had taught her to change a tire when she was just twelve years old.

"I can't drive for like, four years, Dad." She didn't understand *why she needed to learn something that was so...adult-ish. But she liked being out in the driveway with her father in the hot summer sun—warm, peaceful, and happy.*

"If you start practicing now, you'll be a full-blown expert by the time you get your license. You'll never need a man who could very well end up being some psycho jerk to pull over and help you out. My little girl is going to be able to take care of herself. Grab that lug wrench over there. No honey, that's a hammer..."

Tears rolled down Winter's cheeks. She didn't often allow herself to think of her parents. Life was smoother when she kept them deep and quiet in her heart. The memory had assailed her without warning, though, rekindling the agony of losing them both at such a young age.

She wanted to curl into a ball and cry but forced her heart to steel over. She couldn't just stay here and give up. She had to think. *Focus.*

If she'd regained the ability to cry, didn't that mean the medicine was wearing off?

She grabbed the edge of the bed with one hand and pushed her opposite elbow deep into the mattress. Propped up on one arm, she concentrated on sliding her legs off the bed. As they dropped, the resulting momentum allowed her to push the top half of her body upward.

Once her feet found the cold floor, triumph flooded her mind. If she could do *this*, in a few more minutes, maybe she could—

She swallowed a scream when Justin appeared in the doorway. The fading sunlight illuminated him from behind, creating a ghostlike silhouette. Her brother was a nightmare apparition come to life, and he would never, ever, *ever* let her go.

He stepped closer.

"You'll want to stay put for a bit, Jeannette." In contrast to the warning in his brown eyes, his voice was cheerful. Excited. "Just take a little nap and let yourself recover. When you wake up, we'll get started on that fun I promised you. Here, let me help you lie down."

Before she could gather her strength to fight, he'd grabbed her left arm. The needle pricked her skin. Cold at first, then warm as the medicine entered her muscle. A small squeak of protest was all she managed as Justin pushed her back onto the bed.

Her brother's face grew blurry and fragmented before her head hit the pillow. A harsh voice echoed in her skull.

All of this is your own fault. You could have prevented this, but you wouldn't listen to anyone. This is happening because you're stubborn and stupid.

Her body drifted, and the yelling turned into a whisper.

He's going to kill you. You know that. Eventually, your baby brother is going to kill you...

Justin's deep brown eyes and sneering smile faded away as Winter sank into the silent shadows of her prison cell.

A utumn sat in the passenger seat of Chris Parker's SUV, trying to decide which horrible emotion was winning the misery competition blazing in her gut.

She wanted to focus on the upcoming conversation with Philip Baldwin. Get her questions organized, make sure she wasn't forgetting anything.

Pull her shit together.

Philip had been through enough in the past week. He didn't deserve a surprise visit from a frantic colleague who was fighting the urge to both scream and sob.

She guessed the doctor had checked into the Wellington Hotel to avoid the stress of returning to the home where Albert Rice had nearly murdered him. Autumn didn't blame him for that one bit. In fact, the house might still be a crime scene for all she knew.

Coming so close to suffocation only a day ago was something she'd rather not be reminded of just yet herself.

January had been one hell of a rough ride.

With Winter missing, time was of the essence. Autumn had to approach Philip with her ducks in a row...or at least her thoughts in some semblance of order. She needed the psychiatrist to share every last detail he'd learned about Justin so she could use the information like a machete to whack a path through the proverbial jungle.

That path had to end in finding Winter. And soon. Autumn had no doubt that the disturbed young man could snap and kill his own sister at any given moment.

He may have already planned out the exact way he intended for his sibling to die. He'd had plenty of time to contemplate murder fantasies and decide on a favorite.

Maybe there was a part of Justin, buried deep somewhere under all those twisted layers of Kilroy rot, that still loved Winter.

But he hated her too.

Justin had flat out told Autumn as much on more than one occasion. She'd also recognized the malice in his eyes and body language whenever he mentioned his sister.

Was that hatred enough to drive him to murder the only person left on the planet who loved him with her heart and soul?

If Justin were a normal human being whose brain functioned like the majority of his fellow species, the odds were good that no matter how much malice he held toward his sister, he would never take her life.

Unfortunately, Justin wasn't normal, average, or even sane. If he wanted to kill Winter, he *would* kill her.

End of story.

This was one of the reasons Autumn had cautioned her friend to consider avoiding visits to Justin and to temper her high hopes for a warm sibling reunion. Justin Black wouldn't simply snap out of his current state of mind one day and return to the sweet little boy Winter remembered. That was a pipe dream.

Deep down, Winter understood, but her love—and

extreme guilt, if she were honest—for her brother kept sending her back to the hospital and back to that room in search of the ghost of the sibling from her childhood.

Of course, Autumn now wished she had put her psychologist foot down and barred Winter's visitations. The thought had crossed her mind many times before, but she'd refrained from making that call.

Too soon. It'd seemed too soon.

Autumn had barely finished Justin's competency evaluation and only just begun to study him. She hadn't had the full opportunity to make a solid call on the benefits versus risks of his time with Winter.

He *was* dangerous. He *was* a serial killer. He *should* have been shackled. A guard *should* have always been present. Autumn had mentioned and re-mentioned these things to Winter.

At the same time, her educated, scientific brain realized that if there was any spark of humanity left in someone like Justin Black, the reassurance that someone—*anyone*—still cared was one of the few tools that might help grow the flicker of decency into a flame.

A family member sticking around through so much tragedy and horror meant more than a friend, or doctor, or shrink could ever hope to bring to the table in terms of healing.

Autumn had wondered if Justin might *need* Winter's love to ensure even a slight chance of improvement.

None of that changed the fact that the siblings never should have been left alone together or that Justin never should have been uncuffed in Winter's presence.

Now, Autumn struggled to appreciate the possible positives of allowing the siblings interaction at all.

Her closest friend was in great danger, a situation

Autumn could have prevented by simply requesting a court order to ban all visits.

She understood why Noah was angry with her. He was outraged for the same reasons she now berated herself. Someone they both loved dearly was gone, and there was no guarantee that they would ever get her back.

And Autumn was one of the people with the authority to prevent this scenario from ever happening in the first place.

She *despised* herself for not using that power to protect her friend, but she was also a forensic psychologist. The tragic irony of the situation was that her commitment to remaining unbiased was what led to her hesitation to bar the visits.

From a medical standpoint, Autumn stood by the decision.

If Justin were a random serial killer and Winter were a stranger, Autumn would have barely even questioned the visits. Granted, that may have changed as she dove deeper into her observatory sessions, but the short time she'd worked with Justin Black hadn't cemented the need for that action yet.

She'd allowed the visits *as a professional.*

As a friend, she'd failed to protect Winter and could never take that back.

Autumn accepted Noah's anger over that failure. The cheap shot about her sister, though…she hadn't deserved that blow.

If anything, Autumn being ripped away from Sarah had made her a more empathetic person. She was wiser and kinder for the loss, both personally *and* professionally.

Noah had crossed a line pulling Sarah's name into their fight. No matter how upset Autumn was, she would never, not in a million years, throw something so personal—*so off-limits*—in Noah's face.

Not for any reason ever.

What angered her further was that despite his disappointment in her—despite her disappointment in *herself*—she knew she was damn good at her job.

And she knew she was a damn good friend.

Her finger tapped nonstop against the armrest. She'd noticed a while ago but hadn't bothered suppressing the agitated motion. What was she going to do? Offend Chris Parker?

Heaven forbid!

If she could handle his attitude, he could handle her tapping. Furthermore, if they all had to put up with his fatuous blond Mount Vesuvius every single damn day…

Chris broke the silence in the same manner he generally did everything else. Like a complete asshole. "Why'd you even agree to work with the Black kid in the first place? You're an intelligent person. How could you have not seen the big orange cones surrounding that one from eighteen thousand miles away?"

Autumn whipped her head toward him, not caring if he was Goliath and she was an effing Sour Patch Kid. He was picking the wrong time to poke the bear. *The wrong time.* "I do not need to, nor will I *ever* explain myself to you."

Chris guffawed. "Cool down there, Trent. All I'm saying is what *everybody* else, *including* your good buddy Dalton, is thinking. You made the wrong call. Given your ties to Winter and all that bestie, girly bullshit the two of you have going on, you never should have agreed to handle Justin's case. Never."

"You sound like a broken record, Parker." Autumn gritted her teeth. She had no qualms being in the same room with nefarious, violent criminals, but a car ride with Chris was almost more than she could handle.

Almost.

"The squeaky wheel gets the oil, Autumn." Chris smirked after dropping the line, as though he'd just outdone Shakespeare.

"You know what? If you have that big of a problem with me or anything I've done, why don't you take the matter up with your boss? I'm sure SSA Parrish would be more than willing to address your concerns." She knew that wasn't exactly true. Aiden couldn't stand Chris any more than the rest of them.

That was between the SSA and Parker, though.

"Ha. Ha ha. You're hilarious." Chris shook his head in disgust. "You think I haven't shared my thoughts with Parrish? I have. *Loud and clear.* The man seems to be a bit too enamored with his handpicked redhead sidekick to do the right thing. Or even see straight, for Christ's sake."

Autumn's entire body tensed. She had, thus far, tried to avoid even thinking about Aiden and the perplexing dynamic between them. There was so much in her life that demanded her focus, especially after joining forces with the FBI.

Chris Parker had no right to put his giant foot on such personal ground. Especially not when Autumn had yet to step so much as a toe into that complicated arena.

"Is there something you'd like to say to me?" Autumn's nails dug into the armrest. "We're both adults. Why don't you drop the passive-aggressive commentary and use your big boy words?"

"Don't be a bitch. You know exactly what I'm saying. You were fast-tracked into this BAU because you're Aiden's little pet. Everyone knows that." Chris side-eyed her, sneering his resentment. "I'm guessing you two have a nice and tidy arrangement in place that pretty much lets you get away with whatever the hell you want."

Autumn's hands clenched into fists. Did Parker have the

nerve to suggest that she was sleeping with the SSA in return for special privileges?

Of course he did. Chris was a complete dick. He didn't care what lines he crossed, and he more than likely never would. Parker didn't have the capacity to even *recognize* the lines.

She glared at him, icy rage pumping through her veins. "I'll thank you, Agent Parker, to keep your suspicions about my private life to yourself. Unless you'd like to be hit with a workplace harassment claim."

Chris let out a bellow that was more scoff than laughter. "Yes, Dr. Trent. I've gathered that launching such complaints is quickly becoming one of your personal specialties."

Had Parker ever been kicked in the balls? Was that the experience missing from his life that caused him to say such things so freely?

Autumn would never openly condone violence. However, if someone happened to give a solid punt to Chris's nether regions, she wouldn't shed any tears for the man.

Chris brought the vehicle to a hard stop in the Wellington Hotel parking lot. He exited the driver's side and slammed the door with enough force to shake the entire SUV.

Autumn forced herself to inhale and exhale at a deliberate, measured pace. When she'd counted to ten, she opened the door and closed it calmly. This might be the day from hell or even the month from hell, but she'd be damned if Chris Parker would be the straw that broke the camel's back.

If a meltdown were in her future, that asshole wasn't getting the credit.

She entered the lobby of the Wellington, still seething but in full control of her demeanor. Chris was already at the front desk.

She hoped he hadn't already offended the desk clerk and needlessly screwed up yet another situation that could have run smooth as butter if anyone aside from Agent Parker had been the handler.

"I'm absolutely not supposed to give you that information, sir." The desk clerk was an older man with dark hair and an air of bravado who had clearly been schooled in the hotel's privacy policies long ago.

"I know you're not supposed to, dumbass. But the problem is that you think I'm *asking*. I'm not. You're going to tell—"

"We're with the FBI." Autumn interrupted in as pleasant a voice as she could manage. "The matter is urgent, and it would be extremely helpful if—"

"There." Chris cut her off with a flash of his badge to the clerk. "Still want to be difficult? Because I'm telling you right now, it's in your best interest to cooperate."

Autumn's toes flexed inside her shoes.

Just one kick. He just needs one good kick.

She shook off the thought and locked eyes with the now distressed man behind the desk. "Forgive my colleague, but time truly is of the essence. My name is Dr. Autumn Trent, and Dr. Baldwin is a friend of mine. I assure you he won't mind the bend in hotel policy. If he has checked in, all we need is his room number. Then I promise you we'll be out of your hair."

The clerk nodded, beginning to calm and putting his fingers to his computer keyboard.

"Type faster, guy. There are *lives* at stake here. You wanna be responsible for people dying? Do you?" Chris's pressure was uncalled for, and Autumn knew the agent was thoroughly enjoying his power trip.

The man's hands shook as he clicked across the keys. Autumn pitied him. Parker had no right to put the weight and responsibility of their dilemma on a hotel clerk's shoulders. Chris was being an ass simply because he could.

Autumn exhaled again, using a quick thought of Winter to help clear her mind and refocus on the important issue.

Saving her friend.

The clerk raised his eyes, pointedly addressing Autumn and avoiding Agent Parker altogether. "Second floor. Room two-zero-nine. The elevators are right around that corner." He pointed toward a hallway on the left.

Autumn offered the man a grateful smile. "Thank you so much." She immediately strode toward the hallway, not giving two whips if Chris followed or dropped dead on the hotel lobby's cold marble floor.

Parker's behavior and commentary were inexcusable, and his reference to her impending lawsuit against Adam Latham had made her blood boil.

She wasn't about to start her journey in the FBI by kowtowing to the likes of Parker's pompous ass. She *would* deal with Chris.

Later.

For the time being, she needed to devote all her mental energy toward finding Winter. Her friend had saved Autumn's life just this same week. Today, it was Autumn's turn to prevent Winter from succumbing to mortal harm.

Autumn's body was as tight as a bow as she marched down the hallway, picturing Winter's warm smile and sparkling blue eyes.

Winter, I promise, wherever you are, I am coming.

Nothing. Will. Stop. Me.

Nothing.

13

P hilip Baldwin eased himself into the sole leather chair of his Wellington Hotel room. The compression wrap around his rib cage did little to lessen the pain of his injuries. He had at least six weeks of healing to anticipate, and he was only on day two.

Damn...had the attack from Albert Rice happened just yesterday?

The Vicodin he'd been prescribed helped, but not enough, and the side effects were fast becoming more bothersome than the initial agony. Perhaps the edge had been taken off his physical suffering, but his mind was hazy from the painkillers. The spacey sensation sent him wandering in and out of chambers in his psyche that were better left locked and forgotten.

What did you do to earn yourself this punishment, Philip?

Memories, which usually slipped in like the whispers of wraiths, now charged through the proverbial front door of his mind like bold intruders, unfazed by the decades of effort he'd invested into silencing them.

Even without the pills, his mental fortitude was weakened

by the severe trauma of the past week, the last thirty-six hours or so in particular. All lines of emotional defense were down. Out of order.

Thus, the floodgates to his personal hell were open wide, and he had no strength to fight the incoming tide.

At the first realization of this fact, Philip had fixed himself a drink from the room's complimentary minibar. Rum and Coke, or more accurately, rum with a dash of Coke. The burn going down had produced a familiar warmth in his belly, the instant relief prompting him to fix a second drink.

Not ten minutes later, he'd faced the obvious consequence of mixing painkillers and alcohol. He wasn't surprised. Doctors knew better than anyone the side effects of such a combination, but he'd underestimated the swiftness and strength of the repercussions. Now, his mind was not only foggy but also willing to visit the worst realms of his subconscious.

"Why the closet, Dad?" Philip spoke aloud to his father, who had long been deceased. "You could have sent me to my room. Taken away the TV. Given me a list of chores. But you chose *the closet*. What *did* I do to earn myself that punishment, Dad? What? I was a *child*. I was *just a child*."

Philip was aware of being alone in his suite. Solitude had long been his norm, and he preferred to keep life that way. But there were times, such as this moment, where he wondered if he wasn't in need of a little companionship.

And therapy.

Autumn Trent's pretty face flashed through his mind.

How he had hated that woman at first. Persistent, fearless, and at times, she possessed an obnoxious clairvoyance...like she could see into not only his mind but his heart.

He'd *despised* her. Would have paid actual money to make her go away. Go *anywhere*.

When Albert Rice had taken them captive, though, the

dynamic between himself and Dr. Trent had changed. They'd bonded somehow. Traumatic situations often connected the humans who'd endured the crisis together.

He shuddered, thinking of the plastic bag wrapped around her head, sealing her long auburn hair tight to her neck before it splayed over her back and shoulders. How, beneath the clear layer, her green eyes bulged like they might pop out of her face as she tried and failed to breathe.

If the Feds hadn't shown up when they did, would Autumn even be alive? The human brain wasn't made to survive long periods of oxygen deprivation. There couldn't have been much time left before permanent damage or even death silenced that bright mind and its incessant inquisitiveness.

What a shame if the world had been deprived of Autumn so early in her burgeoning career and promising life. She had unique intelligence, empathy, and insight that made her special in a world full of shrinks and doctors.

And...she had those beautiful green eyes.

Not two full days ago, he'd loathed her. But now...

Philip grabbed his glass and sipped the remainder of his second drink. He hadn't intended to speak of his tormented past to her or anyone else. Not ever.

Yet he had. They'd spoken briefly of his childhood trauma, and Autumn had offered her help as a psychologist, maybe even a friend. They'd parted on decent terms.

Since then, Philip had wondered if he should seek her out again. Take her up on her offer. Let someone walk the halls of his inner hell beside him and assist with slamming the door to that haunted house forever.

Another sip, which he followed by shaking the cheap tumbler and studying the amber liquid as it swirled like a mini cyclone within the glass.

Did he really want to dig deeper into that mess of his past

injuries? He'd spent his entire life avoiding those memories. He'd entered the psychiatric field to help others in freeing themselves from *their* prisons.

In his case, the past was best left in the past.

Colleen Rice's young face swam through his mind. Albert's sister. The woman Albert believed Philip had pushed to suicide by some act of indecency or maltreatment.

Philip's grip on the glass tightened. He'd never been inappropriate with Colleen during the time that she was his patient. Not once.

He'd *pitied* her. He'd wondered how long her path to recovery would be, considering the depth of the girl's emotional wounds and her lack of desire to contemplate the future.

But he hadn't believed for a moment that Colleen was beyond recovery. And he hadn't been aware of her misguided attachment to him until that very last appointment.

That hug.

Her words.

"I think I've fallen in love with you, Dr. Baldwin."

He shuddered at the memory, recalling the terror and alarm that had flooded him as he'd broken away from her embrace. With his career, reputation, and *entire future* suddenly teetering on the edge of total ruination, Philip had been blunt about terminating his role as her clinician.

He hadn't meant to crush the poor girl, but he couldn't continue to treat her after that revelation.

Colleen hadn't actually been in love with him. Hers was a textbook case of transference where her feelings for the deceased professor had shifted onto her new therapist.

Philip's only desire for Colleen had involved helping her view the past relationship for what it was and convincing the young woman that she deserved much more and would find happiness. The first step she'd needed to take was to release the man she had loved, because remaining in a relationship with a dead partner trapped the surviving partner in a ghost world. Colleen had only required a little guidance to show her that she was capable of letting go.

Weren't you just speaking out loud to your dead father? You're the very definition of a hypocrite. You've been living in a glass house and throwing supercilious stones for years. Did you really believe you would ever be able to fix anyone else when you can't even fix yourself?

Philip stood, the pain in his middle protesting but dulled now. He walked to the full-length mirror attached to the same wall that held a large flat-screen TV and studied his reflection.

He'd managed a shower, so his dark, wavy hair was combed and clean, but his natural olive-toned skin was pale. Green eyes surrounded by bloodshot whites and circled with darkened skin spoke volumes of his current state.

Colleen killed herself. You couldn't fix her. You failed. That's what you do. You fail. That's why you deserve to be punished.

Philip frowned and received the same from his mirrored likeness. "No."

What did you do to earn yourself this punishment?

"Nothing. I didn't do *anything*. I *never* deserved that. I. Was. A. *Child*."

He glanced at the nearly empty tumbler on the tabletop across his room. Maybe it was time for a pot of coffee. He moved to the tiny kitchenette and began the brew.

A little time away from work might not be the worst idea. As for diving deeper into any emotional places—therapeutic or otherwise—regarding Autumn Trent, he believed it best to defer. At least for now.

Should they pass each other in the halls of Virginia State Hospital, a polite wave would suffice. Autumn didn't need any additional insight into the messiness of his mind.

She more than likely had far too accurate of an idea already.

He filled the oversized mug provided by the Wellington to the brim with black coffee, skipped the cream and sugar, and lowered himself gingerly back into the leather chair. The very least he could do while he waited for the caffeine to break through his self-induced grogginess was distract himself with the television.

Tapping the remote, Philip was greeted by the immediate blare of the local news. He registered that the skinny blonde newscaster was blabbing away about Albert Rice while standing in front of *his* hospital.

Or at least, it would be his hospital again once the doctors released him back to work in a week or so.

He grimaced and fumbled with the remote to switch the channel. He was far too intimately acquainted with the Albert Rice situation already.

Before he pressed the button, a picture of Justin Black flashed across the screen. Philip frowned, sitting up straight and wincing from the sudden movement.

He gave a few fervent taps to the volume button. *"...Black is believed to have escaped in the early morning hours. Officials have confirmed that at least one employee, a male nurse, was found dead inside the hospital. They currently suspect this to be the work of Black and have advised that the fugitive should be considered armed and dangerous..."*

Philip slammed his mug down, causing the steaming liquid to slosh across the table.

Justin Black had escaped? *Justin Black?* And *no one* had deduced that perhaps this was information he should be made aware of?

He was Virginia State Hospital's *medical director*! Someone should have filled him in on this development long before the story hit the local news.

His rage soared, undaunted by the knowledge that he was on official medical leave, and per hospital policy, would purposely not have been called. How was he supposed to relax on this little bedrest getaway when one of his most vicious criminal patients had made his *own* getaway?

Justin Black had no place in the free world. Not in his current condition. Anyone who crossed his path would be used as a pawn and eliminated in quick time.

He tapped the volume louder, his jaw dropping as an image of Justin's sister appeared on the screen. The camera returned to the newsroom, where a much more seasoned news anchor continued the report. *"...confirmed that Winter Black, an FBI agent based out of the Richmond Field Office, is also missing."*

Oh shit.

"Sources close to the investigation say that Agent Black's phone was found in a trailer truck north of Richmond, while her car was found in a separate, undisclosed location. A search of the vehicle revealed yet another dead body, this one found without clothing in the trunk. Police are working to identify the victim in this developing case."

Philip grabbed what was left of his rum and Coke and downed it.

No one knew better than he did the depths of madness lurking in that boy's mind. If Justin had somehow taken his sister...

The aging broadcaster leaned forward, his expression growing more severe. *"Agent Black's fingerprints were found on the steering wheel, transmission, keys, door, and car handles. Hers were the only prints found on the abandoned vehicle. The question now being asked is, was Special Agent Winter Black forced to drive her brother away from Virginia State Hospital, or did she aid in his escape?"*

Frantic flipping through the channels showed Philip that

nearly all the major broadcasting networks were covering Justin's developing story. The Black siblings' pictures graced station after station, sometimes separately, sometimes side by side.

As though the two were already being considered a team.

Was that possible?

Philip's mind flew through the scattered conversations of his sessions with Justin Black. There were many, and Winter's name had been mentioned in nearly every single one.

He'd only had a few talks with Winter herself, and those were brief, but he'd gathered that she was desperate to help her brother. She'd held on to the hope that his recovery was possible when the entire world had written Justin off.

As a professional, Philip had never believed that Justin Black would ever be "normal" in the way his sister wished. Improvements were possible in cases such as Justin's, but they weren't common. A full recovery after the life that boy had lived and the barbaric acts he'd committed...

He shook his head. In all likelihood, Winter's little brother would never recover.

Pointing a moral compass in the right direction was almost impossible when the device had been removed altogether. Justin not only lacked a sense of right and wrong but had no desire to develop one.

Philip had urged Winter to keep her expectations low. The guilt-ridden expression she'd displayed the first time he relayed as much had caused his weathered psychiatric heart to experience a rare pang of sympathy.

Winter Black blamed herself for not preventing Justin's kidnapping when they were both just children. She carried the burden of having not found him "soon enough," as well as the weight of being the agent who had hunted him down for his crimes.

In her mind, she'd abandoned him, lived a somewhat normal life while he dwelled in hell, and then stuck him in a cage like an animal years after he'd turned feral. Winter's guilt wasn't uncommon in these types of situations.

What was uncommon was the depth of the love and dedication she still held for her brother. Most of his patients who reached such a severe level of savagery had no one left in their corner, neither family nor friends.

Justin had the usual following associated with notorious criminals, but those types of groupies often came with their own slew of mental disorders.

Philip didn't consider them genuine supporters. He didn't consider them at all. And he knew that Justin would only view them as a means to an end, as tools to help him make his big break.

He wouldn't need many "tools." If his highly trained, federal agent sister ever decided to use her lethal skillset to assist his path to freedom, Winter Black checked off every box Justin could possibly have had on his list of requirements for a sidekick.

One of the most vital qualities she possessed, which worked heavily in Justin's favor, was her undying love for her younger sibling. No...not love. It was her relentless guilt over who he'd become that pushed her to save him.

Justin himself had given an incredibly accurate description of Winter's state of mind. *"Winter's got it bad. She's got the guilts."*

Guilt was a mighty motivator. Philip knew this, and so did Justin Black.

Philip decided to forego the half-spilled coffee and make himself another drink—the occasion seemed appropriate—when a firm trio of knocks interrupted him.

He stiffened. No one knew he was here. He hadn't *wanted* anyone to know he was here.

And what he really didn't want was for the newly "released" patient to show up outside his hotel door. A patient who may or may not have personal reasons to pay a visit to the medical director of the hospital that had attempted to "fix" him.

The knock sounded again, and Philip squared his shoulders.

There was only one way to find out if a sociopath had come calling.

He grabbed the empty glass off the table, clutched it close to his chest like a shield, and walked over to the door.

14

The Wellington Hotel wasn't large, but the establishment was elegant. The second-floor hallway presented the same marble floor as the lobby but with a strip of plush burgundy carpet running from end to end. Autumn barely registered the grandeur, hurrying past the elaborate, gold-framed paintings that hung from the tasteful beige walls between each doorway.

All she could think of was Winter and how much time they may or may not have to find her before something horrible happened.

If it hadn't already.

Chris gave a low whistle through his teeth. "Damn. Guess the doc is a little too important for the likes of Super Eight, huh?"

Autumn picked up her pace, wishing once again that SSA Parrish would have assigned any other agent as her partner for this task. Chris was the type of man who'd harbor resentment toward another man's good fortune while never hesitating to flaunt his own.

The double standard was obnoxious, but she expected nothing less from Agent Parker.

"Here." Autumn spotted the fancy calligraphic two-zero-nine gracing Philip's door and halted.

"Oh, goody. We found Waldo." Chris crossed his arms in disgust while Autumn gave the door three firm knocks. "Will you please tell me what you hope to gain from speaking to this asshole? We could be out there hunting Justin Black down *right now*."

She forced herself to focus on the delicate curl of the numbers. "First of all, we don't know where to even start searching yet. Second, Philip Baldwin has spent more time with Justin Black since his incarceration than anyone. If there's any information we could use to track Justin down, Dr. Baldwin is the person most likely to know of its existence."

Autumn knocked on the door again while Chris rolled his eyes. "Oh, please, like that stuck-up douche—"

The door swung open, revealing a very startled psychiatrist. He locked eyes with Autumn's, and neither of them spoke for a moment as memories of their abduction and torture by Albert Rice came rushing back.

Or at least they did for Autumn. She curled her fingers around the doorframe, digging into the wood while her brain filled with the very images she'd worked so hard to block out.

"Dr. Trent. I didn't, um, I wasn't expecting…"

The usually well-spoken psychiatrist stumbled over his words, telling Autumn he was just as thrown as she was. She cleared her throat. "I'm so sorry for intruding, Dr. Baldwin. There's been a development, or we wouldn't have bothered you."

He nodded toward the large flat-screen TV on the wall.

"Justin Black has escaped. I've been informed by our local broadcasters."

Autumn peered over Philip's shoulder and stared at the screen in dismay. There was Justin's image, split-screened with Winter's. The anchorman was spitting out details that should never have made it to the public so fast and certainly hadn't been released by any officials as of yet.

Anger and disbelief swirled in her stomach. Law enforcement agencies had more holes in them than a strainer, full of people who should know better than running their damn mouths to the news outlets.

The absolute last thing they wanted right now was a media circus. There were still too many question marks. The facts weren't clear enough yet to be shared with the general public.

As if to prove her worries true, a banner ran across the bottom of the screen. *Serial killer, Justin Black, escapes from mental hospital with possible aid from federal agent sister, Winter Black.*

Autumn glared at the reporter. That wasn't even *close* to being a confirmed theory, and the idea itself was preposterous.

For the most part.

"Please, come in." Philip stepped aside, holding the door wide open for them. His disheveled clothing and shadowed eyes made him appear battered on both physical and emotional levels. Her conscience twinged for adding to his worries when he needed to rest and heal, but there didn't seem to be a way around approaching him with the current debacle.

She needed the doctor's insight. Winter's life could depend upon it.

"You're familiar with Agent Parker." Autumn waved a hand toward her companion.

The men gave each other equally chilly nods. They'd interacted a handful of times throughout the Albert Rice case but never on friendly terms.

"I'm hoping you can help us, Philip. You've spent a significant portion of time with Justin Black. We're trying to figure out where he may have fled to. So far," Autumn shook her head in frustration, "we have no leads."

"Of course, I will assist you in any way that I am able to, Dr. Trent." Philip seemed off. Cautious and nervous and maybe a little bit...

Autumn eyed the empty tumbler on his table. The strong scent of freshly brewed coffee was the only smell she'd picked up on when they'd entered the room, but she had an inkling that Philip may have drunk a different sort of beverage pre-java.

Granted, he had every reason in the world to down a drink or two. She only hoped that he'd stopped there. She needed him clear. Present. *Focused.*

He wasn't slurring his words or wobbling as he moved about the room, and she took that as a good sign. Hopefully, that meant the doctor was only a bit buzzed, not three sheets to the wind drunk.

"Tracking you down took a minute."

He blushed at Autumn's comment, the reddish hue in his cheeks a drastic contrast to his abnormally pale skin. "I didn't share any information on where I was going. I thought getting away might make it easier to...I thought it might help me relax."

"Did these help you relax too?" Chris held up two empty minibar rum bottles. Autumn could have kicked him. Embarrassing someone whose help might be of vital importance to a case was such a damn typical *Parker* thing to do.

Philip's shoulders stiffened. "Yes, Agent Parker. Indeed, they did. I'm not sure if you're aware, but the legal drinking age is twenty-one in our beautiful state of Virginia. I realize federal law is your area of expertise, but I'd be happy to run over some basic state legalities with you when there are fewer pressing issues at hand."

Chris's nostrils flared, and his lips parted as though preparing to issue his usual snarky response. Apparently, he couldn't think of one, though, so he just stood there gaping like a hooked fish while Autumn bit back a laugh.

She'd been on the receiving end of Philip's sharp tongue quite a few times herself, but this was the first opportunity she'd had to *enjoy* the man's acerbic wit.

Dr. Baldwin turned his attention back to her. "The boxes. The boxes that I dropped in the hospital's parking garage when Albert…took us off guard." Philip coughed, his discomfort with the recent memory obvious. "They contained Justin's file and my notes on his case."

"You mean the boxes that the FBI already has possession of? The boxes we confiscated as evidence?" Chris whipped his gaze to Autumn. "I *told* you this was a waste of time. We already know everything he knows. This trip was unnecessary. We need to get our asses back to the crime scene."

"Actually, Agent Parker, you're wrong," Dr. Baldwin interjected. "I'm positive that the FBI does not have in their possession the notes inside my head or the additional pages of observation I kept at home. Or did you search my house and also scan my brain with some superagent power that I'm unaware of?"

Philip wasn't trying to be funny. He was seething, reminding Autumn of just how easy the man was to enrage.

She found herself amused, regardless.

"Your smart-ass remarks aren't going to help anyone, Dr. Baldwin. I don't have the time to waste on this bullshit." Chris glowered down at Philip, who wasn't short by any means. Autumn wondered if there wasn't a bit of optical illusion involved, considering the impressive volume of Agent Parker's hair.

"Agreed. Perhaps you should go wait in the car while I talk to Dr. Trent, since she's much more familiar with Justin Black anyway. I'm guessing she'd be a better spokesperson for the Bureau right now." Philip's voice had dropped to a growl. "And based on her performance dealing with Albert Rice while under extreme duress, I'd be willing to gamble that she can handle quite a few situations better than you."

Despite her name being thrown around quite a bit, both physician and agent seemed to have forgotten that Autumn was present at all.

Another needless pissing match amongst men. Shocking.

"You're right, Doctor. I've never been kidnapped by a strangle-happy psychopath. You know what else I've also never been? *A murder suspect.* Can't be the best at everything, I guess." Chris took an aggressive step toward Philip, who in turn advanced another step toward Chris.

"Any suspicions regarding myself and the hospital strang-lings have been proven false, Agent Parker. I'm sure you haven't forgotten that already, smart man that you are. However, the jury is still out on whether or not you're a giant asshole, but all evidence points in that direction." Philip offered Chris a menacing smile that was all teeth, and Park-er's hands clenched into fists before he whirled for the door.

"This doctors' conference is over, Agent Trent," Chris barked at her as he stomped away. "Parrish granted you your ridiculous little field trip." He snorted. "Shocker of the century, I know. Aiden gave you your way, but we're *done* here. We need to leave and meet up with the other agents."

Autumn bristled. She didn't appreciate being spoken to in such a tone, and she certainly wasn't taking orders from Chris Parker. Not today, not tomorrow, not *ever*. "I'll come as soon as I'm done conferring with Dr. Baldwin. Shouldn't take too long." She didn't wait for Chris's reply, and he didn't give one, other than to slam the door shut behind him much harder than necessary.

"Wow. Such a pleasant man." Philip's gait was stiff and slow as he headed back to his chair. Autumn guessed that squaring off with Agent Parker hadn't been the best move for his ribs.

She leaned against the kitchen counter and crossed her arms, the corners of her mouth turning up ever so slightly. "The world does seem to be full of difficult male specimens."

Philip met her gaze, his own lips twitching. "Fair enough, Dr. Trent. Fair enough." He grabbed the empty glass on the table and lowered his eyes. "What was all that nonsense about Agent Parrish giving you your way?"

Autumn tensed. She'd hoped Chris's comment would go unnoticed, but now Philip was avoiding eye contact. "Parker's just being an ass. He thinks I get special treatment or something ludicrous like that."

Change the subject. Change the subject. Please, change the subject.

"Oh." Philip's green eyes found hers again. "I wasn't sure if he meant that maybe you and Aiden Parrish were seeing each other…outside of work."

Philip may have been attempting to appear nonchalant, but Autumn read his mood shift like an open book. Her brain spun a few circles before she was able to recall why she was there in the first place.

Winter.

"No, of course not. Chris has a huge chip on his shoulder, that's all. Takes it out on anyone and everyone. I'm no exception. I do apologize for his behavior, though." She glanced at the still blaring big screen. "But I really should hurry. I'd love to peruse the other notes you spoke of, and I hoped to ask you a few questions as well."

Some of the tension lifted from her spine when Philip returned to the serious demeanor she'd come to expect from him. "Fire away, Dr. Trent."

"I know from personal experience that Justin talked a big game about wanting to make up for his crimes, be a better person, et cetera, but I always sensed he wasn't telling me the truth. His intelligence is astounding, to say the least. But his ability to manipulate is disturbing." Goose bumps covered her arms, and she was thankful for the long-sleeved blazer she'd grabbed that morning.

"Justin certainly displayed a rampant tendency for falsehoods during our private sessions. You've already listened to some of those recordings, I'm sure." Philip's fingers still played with the tumbler. "He seemed to enjoy pushing the envelope, so to speak. Bending the truth as far as possible just to discern whether or not I would react or argue. He possesses a brilliant mind, albeit one that has passed the limits of repair."

Autumn sighed as defeat stabbed her stomach. Of course, she'd guessed that Philip would confirm her own assessments of Justin's deviousness, but having him say the words out loud was crushing.

A part of her had hoped, if only for Winter's sake, that Philip would have uncovered some quality within Justin that provided even a glimmer of optimism. A light at the end of the younger Black's treacherous tunnel.

She should have trusted her instincts rather than clinging to false optimism.

There is no light where Justin Black treads. Only darkness. Always darkness.

"I wasn't supposed to be Justin's therapist." Autumn clenched the countertop. "My role was to provide the competency hearing and insanity exams. After that, my sessions with him were meant to be for study purposes toward my long-term work on better understanding serial killers. I was never meant to make calls about his treatment or the terms of his stay at Virginia State Hospital."

"Yes, that was my understanding of the situation as well." Philip's gaze flitted to the screen and back. His distress over the situation was, in some strange way, comforting. The doctor had been so horrible to her before their abduction that she'd questioned whether or not he had the appropriate empathy in his DNA to even attempt to help the disturbed minds filling his hospital.

She no longer believed him to be incapable of feeling or questioned his concern about his patients' well-being. That didn't mean she'd forgotten how callous Philip Baldwin could be. He had a long road of therapy awaiting him, should he ever choose to start the journey.

Autumn checked the judgment by reminding herself that she was by no means one hundred percent through her own healing process. Not even close.

"If I'd been treating Justin…if he was a complete stranger and I was in sole charge of his therapy, I may have observed him more closely through my therapist lens, you know? I tried to be professional and impartial and do what I was there to do while also not upsetting Winter. I didn't believe it was my place to make such heavy calls as barring her visits or restricting his visitations in general." Autumn rubbed her forehead, but the regret permeating her mind wasn't so easily banished.

"You were in a difficult situation." Philip summarized the chaos with one quick observation. "Too bad all of us in the psychiatric field can't just turn off our humanity with the click of a button like robots. Even when we try to do our absolute best, we can falter. And in this case, I wouldn't even say that you faltered, Autumn. You were shoved into a particularly gray area."

Autumn's throat burned as those very human emotions Philip had spoken of welled within her. "The circumstances got so muddied up. Agent Dalton blames me for Winter's disappearance. I should have done better. *More.*"

"No." Philip's voice was firm. "I've witnessed what you're capable of. You stayed calm and coolheaded with Albert Rice, even with the knowledge that he intended to kill us both. Justin's actions were impossible to predict even if you *had* been his therapist. I believe that you're incredibly skilled and that you will find him."

"I..." Autumn swallowed hard. She hadn't expected the depth of sentiment out of Philip Baldwin's mouth and was ill-equipped to process the compliment from a man who'd appeared so steel hearted.

He isn't the asshole you believed he was. He isn't even the asshole he wants the world to believe he is. He's a human being... some mixture of hard and soft, just like everyone else.

"I will help you in any way that I can, Autumn."

Judging by Philip's earnest expression, Autumn knew the offer was sincere. "Did Justin ever speak about how he would attempt an escape? He's pretty proud of his own intelligence. Maybe he boasted about how easy this or that method would be?"

Philip shook his head. "I'm sure he showed quite a bit of bravado toward his fellow inmates and may have even mentioned escape plans or ideas to them, but that was one subject that never came up in our sessions."

"What about places he'd like to visit if he were ever free? Or did he ever talk about Kilroy's family? Did he mention the possibility that any of them might take him in and protect him like they protected Kilroy?" Autumn spit out the questions one after another, hoping she wasn't forgetting any on her mental "ask Philip" list.

"I can't remember him opening up about anything like

that. Considering that he was likely always planning on escaping, he may have figured that family information was best kept to himself. Justin wouldn't have shown me any cards he meant to play in the near future. He's too smart for that." Philip stared into his glass, and Autumn wondered if he was considering fixing another drink.

She still didn't blame him, but…"Maybe hold off on the rum until we find him? I know you've been through a terrible ordeal, but I need you right now." Words she never predicted she'd be saying, yet there they were.

Philip gave the tumbler a light shove, sending it on a short slide across the table. "Of course. I promise to reexamine my conversations with him. It's possible he alluded to his plans in a less obvious manner without meaning to." He stood, wincing as his midsection stretched before grabbing the complimentary notepad and pen on his bedside table.

"I appreciate this, Philip." A ridiculous lump had formed in Autumn's throat, and she suddenly couldn't wait to be out of the room.

He ripped off a sheet and walked to her, holding out the tiny page full of scribbled digits. "This is my temporary cell phone number. My phone is still being held by the police, and there's no telling when I'll be getting it back."

Autumn accepted the paper, her finger brushing against his for a millisecond, if that.

Still, the short burst of emotion she received was undeniable. Philip Baldwin wasn't doing this just to help out law enforcement or because one of his many inmate patients was involved. He was offering his services because of *her*.

The realization, along with a rush of warmth and desire that Philip conveyed via his touch, alarmed her into taking a step backward.

"Thank you." Forcing composure to her face, Autumn smiled and took calm steps toward the door, though her brain wanted her to sprint. Everything was okay, she told herself. In another few steps, there would be a solid slab of pine between them.

"Anything. Anytime." Philip's eyes bored into her.

Uncomfortable to her marrow, she nodded and made a beeline straight to the elevators.

Whoever Philip truly is, and regardless of what he's thinking, you and he disagree on too much to even begin to entertain...whatever that was. And even if you didn't disapprove of the way he ran the hospital and treated his staff, guess what? You. Don't. Have. Time.

Considering Philip in the same manner in which he'd clearly begun to regard her was currently out of the question. She hadn't even started to sort through the tension between herself and her damn boss.

Stop. Focus on Winter. Winter is all that matters right now.

The elevator chimed, and Autumn darted inside like the hounds of hell were nipping at her heels. Relief swept through her when the doors slid shut, blocking the second floor and Philip Baldwin's room from view.

Justin Black *was* ridiculously intelligent, but he wasn't invincible. He'd been caught once. Autumn could catch him again.

And she would, as long as she kept her eye on the prize and her mind sharp and focused.

15

Agent Chris Parker waited in the Wellington Hotel's parking lot, fuming and tapping his fingers against the steering wheel. The fact that Autumn had insisted on staying and talking to Philip Baldwin when her supposed best friend was missing seemed more than a little stupid. And suspicious.

The nut-ward doctor was, hands down, the biggest douche of all the douchebags Chris had ever met, and that was a tough mark to beat.

Maybe there'd been alternative reasons for this stop. What if Aiden Parrish wasn't the only asshole Dr. Trent had set her sights on?

Chris sneered through the windshield. Autumn's fondness for shitty but powerful men was enough to warn him that partaking in any extracurricular activities with her was a dumb move. Yeah, she was hot, and getting in her pants didn't seem to come with too many obstacles, but she had obvious daddy issues to go for the men that she did.

Girls with daddy issues were insane. In his younger days,

he'd dated a few who'd put that crazy energy to impressive use in the bedroom, but he was too old for that shit now.

He didn't have time to waste on nutso girlfriends. The payoff of amazing sex wasn't enough anymore. He was a *federal agent*, so there wasn't exactly a shortage of women willing to go home with him for a one-nighter when the mood struck. Didn't matter if they were whack jobs if he never planned to spend time with them again.

Special Agent Chris Parker had a career and a duty to his country. That was his number one priority now.

Forget pretty women.

Like Winter, for instance. She was attractive too, yet she'd also picked a jerk. Noah Dalton attempted to act like he was the South's finest gentleman, but he didn't fool Chris. Not for a minute. The dude was a pussy-chasing ass just like every other guy on the whole damn planet. Winter was *way* too smart and gorgeous for him.

Every time Dalton called her "Darlin'" in that maddening hick drawl he often slipped into, Chris wanted to kick him in the damn teeth. But whatever. Winter had made her bed, and she could lie in it. Assuming she ever set foot in her own apartment again.

Chris scanned the Wellington's entryway. Still no sign of Autumn.

Unbelievable.

Baldwin had flat out admitted that aside from some mental notes and a few jotted-down rambles, the FBI already had his case files on Justin Black. If he remembered any detail of importance in that ancient, withering doctor brain, he could text or call.

This was *such* an obvious wham-bam-thank-you-ma'am session. And it was taking too damn long.

Chris couldn't fathom that Baldwin was much of a long

hauler in the performance department. The dude was old... thirty-five, maybe even older. If anyone was still going, Autumn was the perpetrator. Daddy-issue girls could never seem to get enough, and she, at least, was still in her prime. Though she was kinda at the tail end of that run.

Once a woman hit thirty, everything started heading south. Literally. Autumn only had a couple years left before she'd have to devote a substantial lump of her paycheck into the beauty upkeep department. Not that he cared.

Frankly, he didn't give a flying rat's ass about Autumn and her multiple partners.

So what if they were in there getting their rocks off? Big whoop. That was just stuff adults did. The timing, however, of this particular screw and shoo date was unacceptable.

Autumn knew better than anyone how evil that little Black shit was. Every minute she was in there killin' it with Philip was another minute that Justin was on the run *actually killing* more innocent human beings.

Then again, maybe Autumn didn't grasp the danger that Justin Black was. She'd obviously underestimated the maniac to the degree that one of their own agents might die. If she wasn't already dead. Chris's intuition leaned toward the latter. He didn't foresee "sibling love" keeping that psychopath from taking Winter out as soon as she'd stopped being useful.

If Winter was dead, the team was down an agent just like that. And given the thin strand of sanity that Dalton seemed to be clinging to, he'd be absolutely worthless to the Bureau for a very long time as a result of his loss.

Two agents gone meant a heavier, crazier workload than they already had. Days off would become a pleasure of the past while they tried to fill Winter and Noah's shoes. Longer hours...worse moods...

Chris grimaced and shifted his weight in the seat. He couldn't imagine Aiden Parrish being in a worse mood than he already was every day of his damn life. Unless Aiden figured out his girl was knockin' uglies with the cuckoo-house doc.

That might be a fun little piece of information to bring up on accident.

Maybe then the special effing treatment parade would come to a halt. Chris wasn't sure he could stand by and allow that crap to continue much longer. There was always someone with connections being awarded privileges they didn't deserve.

Always.

A sour taste filled his mouth. Even at Quantico. No matter how hard he worked, he'd never earned the favored student treatment from any of his instructors. He wasn't from the right stock, didn't have any flashy charisma, and hadn't ever known the correct way to kiss ass.

Chris drifted further back, all the way to high school. He'd sensed, even then, that he was part of a lower social class, and therefore, somehow "less" in every way that mattered. His parents weren't white collar. They were straight blue.

His father had worked his damn ass off sixty hours a week as a floor manager at a local power plant, and his mother had climbed her way up from waitressing to assistant managing a high-end steakhouse.

Their house wasn't a shack, but it was on the wrong side of town. Food on the table every night, but often it came straight out of the freezer and had to be flung into the microwave first. His jeans didn't have holes, and his shoes weren't falling apart, but they also didn't have the proper swoosh, stripes, or other name-brand emblems to prove he was worth taking two glances at when he walked down the high school halls.

He stayed out of trouble. He kept decent grades. No drugs, no alcohol, no bullying.

Chris knew he'd been a good kid. A *damn good* kid.

College had seemed far-fetched, but his parents encouraged him to apply for as many scholarships as possible. They'd do what they could to help, and student loans would hopefully cover the rest.

All he'd ever wanted was a career in criminal justice. He took their advice, kept his nose clean, and applied the shit out of any and every scholarship possible. He wasn't an A+ student, or a star athlete, or a gifted artist or musician.

But he knew his shit about law enforcement. He studied the subject in and out of class. And when he applied for a scholarship through the local police department that would have paid a hefty amount of his tuition, he'd been sure he was a lock-in for the award.

The stars were aligning, or so it had seemed. Until the day came when he'd finally understood—been *forced* to understand—just how the world worked. He could still remember that stupid bitch's face…

"Christopher. Hey. They're announcing the winner of the police department scholarship tonight. You gonna be there?" Melanie Dristol accosted him after Trig class, hand to her hip.

She was the high school principal's daughter, and as far as he knew, his only competition for the honor. He'd hated her since junior high, when she'd morphed from a spoiled brat kid into a spoiled brat teenager.

Melanie had gotten mean. He'd done his best to avoid her and her friends for the last six years. Graduation would come, and he'd never have to walk through these damn halls full of bitches and bullies ever again.

His height made him an easy target, though, and he'd been

humiliated more than a few times by Melanie and the kids who were like her.

That was almost over, though. Life was changing...looking up. There was no way in hell that Melanie would win the scholarship over him. Let alone the fact that she outright didn't need it in a monetary sense, he knew she couldn't have possibly written an essay as in-depth and well-researched as his.

All the Coach purses and manicures in the world weren't going to sway an official decision by the actual police department. No. No way.

"Yeah, I'll be there. Good luck to ya." He meant the words, but somehow, he'd set Melanie off bad. Right there in the high school cafeteria, which was teeming with his peers, she let him have a nice, big piece of her mind.

"Good luck? Are you kidding me? I don't need luck, Chris. I'm the principal's daughter, and my grades are way better than yours. You think they're gonna help some kid from the trailer park get a badge on his chest? You can't even comb your damn hair. Shit's been hanging on your head like a dirty fucking mop since third grade. Get some freaking hair gel, dumbshit!" She laughed, turned on her heel, and walked away with her usual trail of followers doing the same.

Melanie's group wasn't the only set of people the scene had amused. Laughter was coming from every damn corner of the stupid room. Every way he turned, he met eyes with someone who was giggling, grinning, or even worse, shooting him looks of pity.

He didn't need their damn pity. He needed to win that scholarship and get the hell out of this town.

His parents both worked closing shifts that evening, so he went to the award ceremony alone. Melanie was a bitch, and he couldn't change that. But she'd been wrong.

He didn't live in a damn trailer park, for starters. Near one, but not in one. And her grades were better only because the teachers *were under pressure to keep their boss happy. Melanie was a lack-luster student at best.*

He was the exact kind of candidate that this scholarship was made for. Smart. Determined. Very invested in his future career. He was an "up and comer," as his mom used to say.

But Melanie had won the money. She flashed him a ginormous smile while accepting the award from the sheriff. Her parents jumped up and down, clapping and cheering for their little girl.

Chris slipped out a side door with an EXIT sign above it and began the two-mile walk to his house. He stopped at the dollar store along the way, bought a bottle of hair gel and a Three Musketeers, then continued home, where he cried himself to sleep.

Chris brought a fist down on the steering wheel, remembering how much he'd hated everything and everyone that night. Including himself. The experience had been rough, but he'd learned.

Oh, how he had learned.

He'd had no choice but to take out the maximum in student loans, even after his dad borrowed money from his retirement fund through the plant. Chris worked two jobs... before class, in between classes, after class, and every damn weekend. He clawed his way through college.

Through the grapevine, he later learned that Melanie had studied criminal justice for one semester and then decided to take "a break." She went backpacking through Europe with her friends and eventually married an investment broker.

But Chris had gone the distance. He'd followed every damn step of the journey leading right up to this moment. Twenty-nine years old and a special agent for the FBI working in the Behavioral Analysis Unit.

That was some real shit right there. That was some effort. And now, here he was.

He should have been happy. Or at least satisfied. He'd

accomplished what he'd set out to do and still had a long career of ladder climbing ahead of him.

There were just so many unfair, biased aspects to life that drove him nuts. Pissed him the hell off. Despite all his hard work, the world hadn't changed. Not even one iota.

There were still people coasting through life for one ludicrous reason or the other while he'd barely had a chance to breathe since he was eighteen.

Autumn was one of those people. The coasters. Maybe not on the same level as worthless Melanie Dristol since Autumn *had* spent time and effort earning her education and accolades, but the fact that she was being fast-tracked into a special position Aiden had created just for her when she hadn't set one damn foot in Quantico was outrageous.

Out-fucking-rageous.

And what the hell? Aiden Parrish hated everyone. Yet somehow, he not only favored Autumn but also conjured up brand new jobs for her. Like he was Walt fucking Disney writing a princess movie script.

Chris pounded the steering wheel again. He hated Aiden much more than he hated Autumn. Aiden only held the title of Special Supervisory Agent because he'd aged into the position. He'd be *forty* this year. Jesus.

Clocking years away for the FBI didn't necessarily make you a good leader. The BAU needed some fresh blood, youthful energy, and new thinking. Aiden Parrish was dead set in his ways and always would be.

Unless, of course, the SSA glimpsed some shiny red hair and perky tits strutting past his office.

Chris curled his lip. Wrong. Aiden and Autumn's arrangement was just plain wrong.

His phone rang, interrupting the dark cloud of rage but doing nothing to subdue his frenzied resentment. The screen read "Unknown Number."

He went to accept the call but hesitated. The journalist contact who paid him for dirt on developing cases was admittedly sleazy, but a dropped detail here and there earned him enough money to go to Atlantic City every couple of months and have some fun. *Relief.*

Anyone who worked this job deserved that much.

He wasn't telling the media info they wouldn't eventually uncover anyway. He was just giving his guy a head start. A little journalistic boost.

Chris waited another second before jabbing the screen.

Screw his colleagues. They all needed to be taken down a few thousand notches. They were assholes, and he was sick to death of assholes always coming out on top.

"Gus," he greeted.

"Agent Parker. Paying double this time if you're up for it. What's the latest? Seems to be a lot going on behind the scenes." Gus kept their conversations short and to the point. He'd never once failed to come through with payment.

Chris snorted. "Like you wouldn't believe. I don't know what you've got so far. Haven't had time to check the news myself. But this one is bad. Justin Black didn't just magically escape from a maximum-security facility and happen to take his sister with him. We've all but confirmed that there's a damn good reason why he got out so easy. Winter Black is a lethal weapon as far as federal agents go and is super devoted to her psycho sibling."

That wasn't true. Well, except for the part about Winter's ability to kick ass and take names. Her involvement in Justin's breakout remained a question mark that they had no evidence to support at all.

Yet.

Chris wouldn't put anything past that bitch. Maybe he was the only agent who knew she was capable, maybe not.

Connection through genetics was a very real, scientific fact, though, and the Blacks were freaks.

"Hm. That *is* interesting."

He pulled a face at Gus's audible excitement. Chris actually loathed the man, but their arrangement never required more than a five-minute call. He didn't have to hang out with the guy or take him to lunch and pretend they were buddies.

They conducted quick and efficient business through phone calls and direct deposits.

"What's more interesting is the fact that the FBI's own Dr. Autumn Trent was in charge of Justin's psych eval and met with him frequently, even though she's Winter Black's best friggin' friend. The conflict of interest is blatant and totally jacked up." Just saying the words out loud made Chris angrier.

"That's good. That's *great*." Gus's breathing accelerated, and Chris recognized the scribble of pen on paper in the background.

"There should be a full-scale investigation into whether or not Autumn Trent crossed a professional line by providing her *BFF's little brother* therapeutic services. From the talk going around at the office, there will be. The courts gave initial approval, but Trent made some giant mistakes." Chris pictured the expression on Autumn's face when the newscast dropped that semi-accurate bomb and smiled.

Having two lovers was going to be the least of her problems soon enough.

The passenger door opened, and Chris almost pissed himself. Autumn's self-entitled ass *would* come back at the most inopportune time.

"Okay, Sis, I gotta get going," Chris said to Gus, adding a light chuckle for good measure.

"What the hell, Parker?" Gus wasn't the brightest bulb in the box, but he'd catch on at some point. Probably.

"Yep. Love you too. Take care." Chris ended the call and tucked his phone inside an inner jacket pocket. He turned toward Autumn, who was buckling in like a good little girl. "Did you have a nice *chat* with the crazy house doctor?"

Autumn met his gaze unabashed, and he wasn't surprised. She was a shrink. She knew exactly how to play this situation.

"I think I have a stronger handle on the situation. A more solid foundation." She offered him a polite smile. "We should probably meet up with the rest of the team now."

Chris shot daggers with narrowed eyes. "Like I need *you* to tell me that? I know what our next move is, Autumn. It's the one we should have made twenty minutes ago when you refused to leave Philip's room."

"Why do you seem so angry with me? Is it solely based on the fact that I worked with Justin Black, or is there more I'm missing?" She tilted her head in a way that would lead any normal person to believe she cared.

Chris wasn't normal. He saw through bullshit. Autumn might as well have been Melanie Dristol in that moment. The same fake *I'm such a good person* act, the same undeserved privileges. Teacher's pet. Well-liked. Pretty. Smart.

Bullshit. Bullshit. Bullshit.

He rammed the car into drive and headed straight for the parking lot exit, pulling onto the road without so much as a one-word reply. They needed to be back at the BAU office, and he was tired of talking.

All the words and effort in the world would never gain him acceptance into whatever the hell luck club Autumn and Melanie and everyone like them had been born into. Attempting to scale the sheer wall of the Bureau's democracy was exhausting.

Not impossible. He refused to believe that. But taxing. *Grueling.* And he was sick of the scales being so heavily tipped against him every damn second of his entire damn life.

Screw them all. And to be more specific, screw the team. Bitches and bullies...that shit *never changed*. Aiden, Winter, Noah, Autumn...the flawless foursome would soon publicly burn in a social media fire, and he was going to stand back and enjoy the flames.

16

W inter's eyes popped open, and she sat straight up in bed, almost colliding foreheads with Justin in the process.

"Whoa. *Down*, girl, down. That stuff works *faaast*." He made the weird giggling sound that always made her think of the Joker before tossing yet another syringe away. Their RV was turning into a hazardous waste disposal container in rapid form.

Her heart pounded as though she'd been mid-chase with a suspect. She was alert. *Mega*-alert. But even as every sense was screaming at her, she was also disoriented as to what was taking place or where she even was.

The combination was like a punch to the gut and a slap in the face all at once.

"What's happening?" Her hands gripped the mattress. She was terrified, but of what? Ready to run, but from whom?

Justin busted out a full belly laugh this time. "What's happening, dear Sissy, is that I am getting a crash course on how mental hospitals keep control of their nutso patients."

Winter blinked, struggling to absorb his reply. "What do you mean?"

"Drugs, Winter. Drugs. Duh. I took just about everything I could carry off the meds cart, but I admit I wasn't one hundred percent sure which did what. You've been an *amazing* lab rat, though. I think I've got it all figured out now." Justin gave her arm a congratulatory pat.

She stared at him, her mind blank while her body hovered on the precipice of fight or flight. He'd been shooting her up with drugs that he wasn't even familiar with?

"So, here's what I've learned so far." Justin held out his fingers and pointed to each consecutive one as he spoke. "Some drugs just knock a person out completely. Boom. You're familiar with those by now, of course. *Other* drugs wake you the heckin' crap up. That's the one you just got."

Just what her little brother had needed. A pharmacy at his fingertips.

"How do you know all this?" Winter asked, just to keep him talking.

He laughed. "Albert, of course. He was very helpful before you all killed him."

Winter stared at her brother, a ball of dread curdling in her stomach. "Did you have anything to do with Albert Rice going on a murder spree?"

Justin threw his head back and laughed. "Maybe a little." He laughed louder. "Or a lot."

Who was this person?

"What did you do to him?"

Justin lifted a shoulder and pretended to investigate his fingernails. "The man liked to talk, and when I learned he had gotten the job at the nuthouse to keep an eye on the head nuthouse doc, I might have suggested a few ways he could get even with the man." Justin chewed off a hangnail. "But in the end, I shot myself in the foot. Albert was killed, meaning that my main source of contraband was killed too."

Keep him talking...

"Why did they move your room?"

Justin's nailbed began to bleed, and he stuck the injured digit into his mouth, sucking hard on the skin. For a long moment, Winter thought he no longer wanted to share, then he smiled. "Sissy, I have friends in very high and very low places. When I learned they were installing videos in the hospital, one of my friends pulled a few strings and got me moved closer to an exit. Then, you appeared like an angel at my door." The smile dissolved from his face, his eyes sweeping down her body. "It was like I'd placed an order with Grandpa, and he delivered you."

Winter shivered. She should have listened to her instincts and left that place.

Justin blew a raspberry. "Anyway, back to med cart 101. As I was about to tell you, some drugs paralyze, and others make you loopy as shit. It's like you're alive and dead at the same time, and you don't even *care*. But it's all good stuff, right, Sis?" Justin landed a soft play punch to her shoulder.

Winter assumed the last medication he had spoken of was the reason she'd been able to wander around conscious earlier while also being *un*able to form a complete sentence. That sensation had been horrifying, yet at the time, she hadn't been able to experience the horror at all.

"I think that, if I hadn't become such a damn *amazing* leader, I would have been a fabulous pharmacist. But you know, people always say you should 'do what you love,' and what I love most is to free the planet of wasteful humans who do nothing more than inhale the oxygen that belongs to more interesting individuals." Justin was only a few steps away, grinning at her as though he weren't expressing his never-ending need to murder and maim.

Winter's muscles coiled.

I'm alert. Not bound, not paralyzed.

Without giving her intent a chance to register on her face, Winter launched herself across the RV, her hands reaching for Justin's neck.

A searing jolt of electricity stopped her midair, and pain exploded in all of her nerve endings at once while her body convulsed and dropped like a stone. On the plummet to the camper floor, her skull cracked against the RV wall. Hard.

The world spun like a runaway carousel, and black spots filled her vision, but the electric pain of the taser unfortunately kept her conscious. Agony seared her limbs as they jerked and danced against her will.

Through the searing vibration, she spotted her brother. His finger pressed the button, and pure pleasure flooded his features. He was *enjoying* her pain. Reveling in it.

Just when Winter was sure she couldn't take another second, the current ceased. She only had time for one full gasping breath before Justin climbed on top of her. He straddled her stomach, his weight threatening to cut off her air intake while pain still coursed through her body.

Stiff and horrified, she couldn't fight him, couldn't even move as he ran his fingers over her lips, down her neck, and then lower to cup her breast. He leaned down until their noses were only an inch apart. Winter wanted to spit in his face but didn't have the capacity to work up enough saliva.

"Been a while since I've been with a woman. I've been trying to figure out if I should break my fast with you or pretty little Nicole. Right now, I'd say I'm leaning in one delicious direction." His gaze wandered to where his hand remained frozen around her breast, and he licked his lips and smiled.

Her teeth began to chatter as control returned to her

limbs. She managed to summon enough force to knock his hand away from her body.

But only because Justin had allowed her to. He could do whatever he wanted right now, and they both understood that fact.

Whatever. He. Wants.

Winter swallowed the stomach acid that surged up her throat. She knew what he wanted. But he couldn't...he wouldn't.

Grandpa had a hard-on for you, big sister. I do too.

"You're s-sick." The words tore through her throat like knives.

Justin threw his head back and chortled. Just as suddenly, his hand whipped out to grab her face, squeezing so hard that the skin inside her mouth scraped her teeth. The metallic taste of her own blood coated her tongue, adding to the horror of the moment.

"You're just figuring that out, dumbass? Have they made you Miss Federal Agent of the Year yet?" His thighs clenched around her sides, and she spit a combination of blood and saliva in his face.

Instead of being revulsed or pulling away, Justin smiled and stretched his tongue out. She nearly gagged as he licked away every last drop within reach.

Winter shuddered. "I'm your *sister.*" Her skin crawled, and tremors wracked her hands, though she tried to feign a calm front. He was really going to do this. This was how her sweet baby brother meant to reunite with her after all these years.

Justin stroked her cheek with his hand, his eyes glazed over with desires she didn't want to define. "Grandpa told me it was always best to keep it in the family. That's what he did with me, you know."

Her chest tightened, and tears pricked her eyes as she

recalled the allegations Justin had made about Douglas Kilroy. She'd never asked him straight out about the matter.

Now, she needed to know. "Did he rape you?"

In an instant, a cold shutter dropped over his expression. "No. Grandpa would never 'rape' me. He *loved* me. And it only hurt a few times."

His matter-of-fact proclamation ripped into Winter, shredding her battered heart until she feared it would never stop bleeding. Part of her ached with pity for the hell Justin had lived through by no fault of his own. Another part questioned whether he was lying and pulling her further into his web.

Except there was no need to lie to her now. He didn't have to manipulate her into the position he wanted. She was already there.

"What are you going to do to me?" She hated to ask but needed to know.

His intense gaze focused on her, and his lips curved into a sinister smirk. "You should stop thinking my whole life was some chop-shop horror movie. Don't assume stuff. An ass outta me, an ass outta you…" The giggle returned, even higher-pitched this time. "C'mon. You *know better*, Agent Black."

Winter wasn't sure where his mind had shifted to, but she latched onto the hope that, for the moment, he seemed less intent on going through with his original plan.

"Grandpa taught me how to *hunt*. And no, I'm not talking about humans this time." Justin winked at her. "He taught me how to shoot deer, rabbits, squirrels…I even know how to make a few net traps. *And* I learned how to grow my own food. Do you know how vital that skill is? I could live off the grid and survive just fine. No one would ever find me."

She believed him.

"Why don't you?" Winter could imagine no better

scenario for Justin than for him to disappear, farming and hunting and never coming into contact with another human being ever, ever again. "Why don't you just find a quiet place to live out the rest of your days in peace? Why do you have to kill?"

Justin raised his eyebrows, grinning at her with a face devoid of actual humor. "*Power*, dear Sissy. A powerful man is feared, and a feared man never has to worry about loyalty. He will be followed...*revered*...without question. Love can't create that kind of power, and hiding out in the boonies like a damn hillbilly for the rest of my life won't create a world in which I have control."

There was no doubt in Winter's mind that he meant every sick word slithering out of his mouth.

"This world...this foul planet filled to the brim with repulsive beings...the way has been lost. By *everyone*." He settled his weight on her middle as he spoke, relaxed and seeming to have forgotten what he'd meant to do only minutes ago. "God's holy order has been forgotten. But a powerful, righteous man can change that. One filthy sinner at a time."

"What would you do with that kind of power?" She didn't want to know. Not really. But if sharing his visions for the future helped distract him, she might get that one chance to catch him off guard. She'd recovered the use of her body but was careful to remain still. Limp.

One chance. She had to make it count.

Justin didn't answer. He smiled, his twisted mind traveling into whatever deranged utopia he'd imagined for himself.

Now.

Winter bucked with every ounce of strength she could muster, but though her will had been strong, her body had been weaker than she'd expected, and Justin managed to keep his legs locked tight around her. The energy seeped from her muscles far too quickly, her strength diminished by the numerous drug injections.

Grinning like a clown, Justin held out the taser, and she braced for the upcoming agony.

Instead, he popped out the used cartridge and shoved in a fresh one. "I may have gone a little overboard the first time, Sis, I'll admit. I mean, watching you get all seizure-y is about the funniest thing I've seen since we escaped, but I don't wanna use this magic zapper up too fast, right? What a dumbass move *that* would be."

He succumbed to another giggling fit while she struggled to remember how many cartridges had accompanied the taser he'd obviously stolen from her car.

Five. You had five. And now he's down to four.

Her mind was clearing, allowing her to gather facts. The drugs were leaving her system. All she had to do was keep him talking. Given time, her body would do the rest on its own.

"Sissy, I don't think I need to tell you that I will happily use this again. You'd be better off behaving like we discussed earlier." He leaned down so close she smelled his breath. "Don't you get it yet? Every time you try and fight me, I just get so *angry* inside."

Winter stayed obediently still, though her mind created and eliminated any possibility she might currently have for escape.

For now.

"I mean, let's be honest, Sis. We can *at least* agree that angering a serial killer is pretty *stupid*, right?" He waved his hands at her in an oogey-boogey manner, grinning with the type of charm normally reserved for Hollywood heart-breakers and politicians. "Just no telling what I'll do. It's so exciting."

Gone. He's just gone. Keep him talking. Get more information.

Winter jumped at the abrupt clanging of an alarm, and she locked eyes with Justin. What did it mean? Was her time up?

He smiled and gently grazed her cheek with the taser. "Time to get ready for our date. Our new friends have invited us over for dinner." She expected him to rise, but instead, he gave a hard jab of his knee to her stomach. "I'm not going to drug you this time. That shit's like babysitting an effing zombie."

Her hopes soared at the mention of freedom, despite every bone in her body knowing that the danger...and possible tragedy...were far from over.

Yes. Don't drug me. Let me regain my strength. Nice and easy.

"But..." he held a finger against the very tip of her nose, "I swear to god and to everything you've ever loved that I'll kill that entire family if you do *one thing* that even makes me *think* you plan to run away or warn them." Justin tilted his head. "You know how you swipe your credit card at a grocery store? What do you think about when you're doing that, Sis?"

Winter hesitated. Was this a real question? "I don't know. I don't really think about it at all."

Justin nodded and gave her forehead an enthusiastic tap with the taser. "Precisely! Try to remember that's the *exact same thing* I'm thinking when I'm killing people. Nothing. I'm not thinking about it at all. You get it?" His smile disappeared. "I couldn't give two shits."

She forced herself to remain very still, even as her mind recoiled in horror. "I understand." And she did.

Justin couldn't feel guilt. Not anymore. It was like a piece of his brain had been removed. Winter couldn't repair that. *No one* could. Her baby brother was gone, and she should have stayed away from him. She should have *let him go*.

"Okay." He loosened his legs, allowing her to slide away but not moving an inch himself. "This is a test. I have to figure out if I can trust you. *Can* I trust you, Sissy?"

Winter nodded and stared into his strange brown eyes as he considered her for a long moment. She backed up until she hit the RV's wall, but there would never be enough distance between the two of them.

Not after this.

He stood with slow, cautious movements, the taser still primed and ready in his grip.

"You have fifteen minutes to shower and change. Brush your damn teeth because you look like you just ate raw steak or someone's stolen liver. Doesn't bother *me*, but you know," he twirled the taser in a circle by his ear, "people get freaked out so damn easy these days. Everybody's so *sensitive*."

She nodded again, rising on shaky legs that would never make it out that camper door before Justin got to her. Her body couldn't move quickly enough to knock his beloved zapper out of his damn hand before he lit her up like an electric fence.

Just play along. For now.

"There's some bodywash and a loofah and other girly crap behind you on the table. Why don't you pick that stuff up like a good little girl and head on into the shower?" He gestured toward the narrow bathroom doorway. "But Winter, don't wash your hair, or I'll just go ahead and kill you. I am *not* putting that shit in all over again. Phase One of the Trust Test begins...now."

On legs that felt as if they would fail her with each step, she wobbled over to gather the sack of toiletries he'd bought at some unknown point along their journey. She held the sack in one hand and ran the other against the wall, using the surface to steady herself as she made her way to the tiny bathroom.

The mirror showed her Justin's striking alterations once again. She was much more aware now and able to process the shock. As she carefully braided back locks that stopped well above her shoulders, the tears she'd been holding at bay began to pour out.

It's just hair...get over it.

But it wasn't about the hair at all. It was about how powerless she'd been to stop him from doing whatever he wanted to do with her. She'd gone to the academy and taken so many self-defense classes that she could take down most any punk on the street...but she could barely lift her head right now.

Winter stepped into the shower, which was so small that turning around was a feat of gymnastics. The water was just above lukewarm, but she savored the sensation of being cleansed.

The tears continued while she washed. Maybe mourning hair was a silly thing to do, especially considering the full picture of her situation. Her mother had always worn her hair long, though, and Winter had chosen to follow suit in part to keep her mother's memory alive.

She surrendered to her sadness, allowing herself a much-needed breakdown, but kept her hand clamped tight over her mouth as she sobbed.

By the time she turned off the shower, she'd made herself stop. She dressed in haste, unsure just how many of her allotted minutes were left.

No more tears. There wasn't time for them.

Focus. Concentrate.

Winter had to come up with a way to save herself and the family who had been unlucky enough to choose this very same RV campground on a cold January day.

Justin's plans were unclear, but the fact that he harbored

no qualms about murdering four people who'd done absolutely nothing wrong was obvious.

Just like swiping a credit card.

If Winter didn't take control of the situation soon, this deserted campground might very well turn into that sweet family's graveyard.

17

Nicole scrubbed her teeth with her neon pink toothbrush until her gums were sore. She'd wanted to get a whitening treatment at the dentist like her friend Raina had, but her parents had deemed the cost unnecessary.

"Just brush twice a day, Nicki-Poo. You'll get the same results."

Her dad had assured her of this, but months had gone by, and her teeth didn't glow white like Raina's did. Until Nicole had a blinding smile that made her friends' eyes hurt when they peered her way, she wouldn't give up harassing her parents for the treatment.

They might cave. Eventually.

Then again, they were from the stone ages when having teeth at all was considered an accomplishment. Her parents couldn't possibly understand the giant steps technology had taken. Their brains were too old and used up.

Her mom called Twitter "Tweeter," no matter how many times Nicole had corrected her. And her dad always said stupid stuff like "The Facebook" or "Instant Grams."

They were hopeless.

As long as they didn't humiliate her in front of Bill, she'd tolerate their lameness. For tonight, at least. But gaaawd, she was so sick of them. How was it possible that she was just thirteen? That meant at least five more years of having to deal with Greg and Andrea and all their annoying parent bullcrap.

Those years could *not* be over with soon enough.

She grabbed the darkest shade of lip gloss her mother allowed her to have and applied several layers. The result was shiny pink lips that shimmered in the overhead lights.

Perfect.

She appeared at *least* sixteen now. Maybe even seventeen.

If the weather had been warmer, she would have worn shorts. Her legs were long and smooth, but being that her parents were morons and the weather was akin to an artic blast, she'd settled for some nice tight leggings.

Her top was more of a cropped sweatshirt, which meant her backside wasn't covered. Nicole knew she had a nice, curvy butt. The boys at school were always whispering about her "hot ass." Raina was massively jealous because *Raina's* butt was flat as a pancake.

She just hoped the leggings were snug enough to make Bill drool a little. There wasn't a lot else to work with out here in this third-world deathtrap.

In comparison to Jeannette, she knew there was really no competition at all. Jeannette was a woman. She already had boobs and a butt and everything else that drove guys nuts. And she was super pretty. Nicole didn't think her own features would ever be that pretty, no matter how grown-up she was.

But Jeannette was a hot mess. Aside from the same parts every other woman in the world had to offer, what did Bill even see in her?

The whole time Nicole and her dad had been over fixing the heat in Bill and Jeannette's RV, which was a complete *puke-fest*, Jeannette had slept. She didn't even get up to thank them when they were leaving.

Nicole figured that the RV belonged to Jeannette's family. Bill dressed way too well to be the owner of that crappy old thing. Jeannette had probably forced him to come here instead of hanging out in, like, his own awesome penthouse apartment in the city. Maybe the junker reminded her of her dead parents or something.

Jeannette might not even show up tonight anyway, which would be super rude considering that her mom had made extra food *just for them*.

Bill was probably taken for granted, always having to do stuff for her while his hotness was wasted day in, day out. Absolute tragedy.

Nicole's conscience prickled just a tiny bit for being so snarky about the other woman. Jeannette's parents had just died, after all. But then again, Jeannette was like twenty-five or something. Her parents had to have been crazy old.

Did she expect them to live to one hundred? Jeannette really needed to get a grip on reality. Even Nicole understood that death was just a thing you had to accept. No one could avoid it *forever*.

She hoped that when someone close to her died, she wouldn't make such an embarrassing mess of herself like Jeannette had.

"Nicole?" Her mother's voice went right through the paper-thin walls of the bathroom. "Can you come help me for a second, sweetie? They'll be here soon."

"In a sec!"

Nicole stared at herself in the mirror and perfected her scowl. Of course, once Bill arrived, she'd be as pleasant as she knew how. Until then, she'd be damned if she'd let her parents believe that she'd had a sudden change of heart about this awful trip.

She walked out of the bathroom and straight into the kitchen, huffing when her mother handed her a stack of paper plates. "Can you set the table for me?"

Nicole grabbed the plates and sauntered a full two steps to the "dining room." She placed six plates on the Formica surface and then noted there was only seating for four.

How dare they…

She whirled toward her mother. "Where are Tim and I supposed to sit?"

Her mom grinned. "Anywhere you want except for the grown-up table. Isn't that fun?"

Nicole fumed, slamming plastic forks, spoons, and knives down beside the plates.

Just because she wasn't eighteen sure as hell didn't mean she was a little kid. With Tim sitting beside her, she was going to come off like a freaking preschooler. Right in front of Bill. He wasn't even here yet, and her fate was sealed.

Why did her parents always have to treat her like a baby? Some of her friends had already had *sex*. She probably would have too, if she hadn't puked on Wyatt. She'd be sitting here getting treated like a child, and she wouldn't even be a *virgin*.

I'm gonna do it as soon as I can. Take that, Mom and Dad.

She was almost fourteen, and *her* body was *her* business.

Could tonight even be the night?

Bill would be an excellent first for her. Her friend Ashley had said letting an older guy pop her cherry would be a good idea because they knew what they were doing. Boys Nicole's age didn't know jack.

Maybe later, after her parents had gone to bed, she could sneak out and go to Bill's camper. Jeannette was almost sure to be sleeping since that seemed to be her special talent.

Nicole would just ask Bill if he wanted to go for a little walk or something. The trees and the moon would make a romantic setting, and romance was an important part of enjoying your first time. That's what Ashley had said.

So, she and Bill could take a walk, and if he wanted to kiss her, she'd let him. If he wanted to do more than that, she'd let him do that too. Happily.

She wouldn't even have to be bitchy to her parents anymore. They'd get exactly what they deserved for dragging her out in the middle of nowhere and making her live like a homeless person.

Their "Little Nicki-Poo" would lose her damn virginity on this stupid "family together time" trip.

Perfect. Payback.

Nicole went to the counter, picked up the metal tongs, and began tossing the salad. Her mom's eyes almost fell out of their damn sockets. "Nicki-Poo, thank you. You're being such a good little helper."

The comment alone made Nicole want to chuck the tongs at her mom's head and return to the bathroom where she would not do one helpful thing or even come out until Bill got here. Before she could do either one, a knock came at the door.

Time was up.

Nicole lunged to answer, but snot-nosed little Tim beat her. He swung the door open and gave Bill and Jeannette a toothy grin. "Welcome to our humble home."

Where in the hell did this kid learn to say such stupid crap? The stupider Tim acted, the stupider she was going to appear sitting next to him. This was going to be a nightmare. She just knew it.

Bill was even more handsome than earlier. Nicole's legs got so weak just catching sight of him that she was scared she might fall down.

Then again, if she fell, he'd probably try to catch her, and that was romantic as hell if—

She eyed the beverages Bill was holding. A six pack of beer and two cans of Coke. The soda was obviously for Tim and her. Bill viewed her as a kid too.

Well, he was wrong. They all were.

Even though her previous joy had plummeted once she noticed the kiddy drinks, she held herself together. Now, more than ever, she was determined to entice Bill. Make him crazy.

Later, he'd pop her cherry, and she'd be even with her stupid parents.

The only tool she really had to work with was her ass, and she was happier than ever that she'd chosen the skintight leggings. Reaching across the counter for a fork she didn't need, she pushed her butt up high, making sure that her best asset was on display.

Bill couldn't have missed that. No way.

"Jeannette, you made it. So glad you're feeling a bit better." Her dad was greeting Bill's train wreck girlfriend like they'd known each other for years.

Nicole peeked over her shoulder when the pretty blue-eyed woman with the cool black-and-red hair entered their RV. Jeannette's skin was super pale...like a porcelain doll or something...which made the blue of her eyes even more prominent. And gorgeous.

Her funky hair now had some waves that reminded Nicole of the way her hair appeared after being braided. She was beginning to reach the conclusion that her curvy butt wasn't nearly enough to compete with the likes of this woman.

And to make matters worse, Jeannette wasn't even drunk anymore. Bill had his arm wrapped around her just as tightly as before. He had to be in love with her.

Nicole's stomach curdled like she'd just chugged a glass of sour milk.

This sucks balls.

How in the hell was she going to pull off her plan for later when the damn thing hinged on Jeannette still being in mourning?

Mourning. Riiight. Bill's code word for Jeannette being wasted.

"Hi, Nicole." Bill patted her shoulder, reigniting the electric butterflies in her belly.

She swallowed hard and forced herself to reply. "Hi." The single word came out more like a squeak. An immediate wave of embarrassment sent her back to tossing the salad with extra vigor.

"*Toss* the salad. Don't mangle it, dear," her mother admonished, letting out a chuckle.

Right. In. Front. Of. Bill.

Nicole wanted to sink into the floor and disappear. She'd never understand what was wrong with her parents. Never.

Pissed beyond her norm, Nicole tossed the tongs on the counter, successfully hitting the unneeded fork and causing a loud metallic clang that made her mother jump. She stomped away from the kitchen-dining-living room and went straight to the bathroom.

Committed to her dramatic exit, she slammed the door behind her. If her mom didn't mind humiliating her *own daughter*, then Nicole would return the favor by embarrassing the living crap out of her parents with this angsty scene.

Screw them!

She pressed her ear to the fake wood wall. Her mother and Bill were laughing. What in the hell could they be laughing at aside from her?

How humiliating. She'd just *die* if they were in there cracking jokes at her expense. She mashed her face against the wall but couldn't make out the actual words.

Well, one thing she wasn't going to do was stay in here forever while they made fun of her. No way in hell. Nicole gave the toilet a flush and then pretended to wash her hands for thirty seconds, counting them out in her head. Bill at least needed to know she had excellent hygiene, even if he did think she was a stupid kid.

Returning to the kitchen, Nicole willed her parents not to embarrass her again. She could stay quiet and pleasant, as long as they didn't make this night even worse than it already was. Although, there didn't seem to be any way circumstances *could* be worse.

A quick peek at Bill caught him glancing at her. He winked, and a hot blush spread across her cheeks.

"Thanks for helping us out earlier, Nicole. You're a lifesaver." Bill purred the words, and her legs nearly turned to noodles. She gave a quick lift of her shoulder in response and tossed her hair the same way the Kardashian sisters always did on their show.

She was more convinced than ever that an older man was definitely the way to go. If Bill could make her that giddy with just his voice, imagine what he could do with his lips or hands?

Her mom scooped food onto all the plates. Nicole gave her a distinct glare when the chicken breast came her way. For once, her mother seemed to understand and just gave her a nod and a grin, moving on to Tim's plate.

Miracles really did happen.

With the table full, the bed was the only other place to sit, and while the doorway did face in that direction, Nicole was removed enough to be left out of the conversation altogether. And worse, just as she'd predicted, Tim was being the same dipwad he always was and making her look moronic by proxy.

She listened with intent, wanting to learn everything

about Bill that she could. Details were important, *especially* when you were trying to seduce an older man.

"…I guess I'm something of a cryptocurrency expert," Bill told her parents.

"Fascinating. Never dabbled in that market myself, but I've always been curious." Her dad didn't even try to save a little face and *fake* some knowledge. He just up and admitted he was a clueless dork like that was no big deal.

So. Lame.

Nicole didn't know what cryptocurrency was, and she couldn't have cared less aside from wanting to impress Bill.

"And Jeannette here waits tables at a cozy little diner." He gave his girlfriend a squeeze. "You know, one of those places you go for the grease and possible heart attacks." He chuckled, and her parents joined him.

Jeannette, however, shot him an annoyed glare. Nicole figured she wasn't that proud of her flashy career as a waitress, and she wondered if the older woman maybe worked in a strip club instead.

"I'm going to be a doctor." Nicole blurted the announcement, desperate to enter the conversation and maybe raise herself a few pegs in Bill's eyes.

Instead of acting supportive, her parents stared at her like she'd grown two heads. Her idiot brother busted into loud laughter. "Guess you better stop failing science then, huh?"

Nicole's face burned. She hated her family. All three of them. They were the most horrible people on the planet, and now she just wanted to die somewhere.

She jumped to her feet, chucked her plate at the trash can, and stormed out the RV door into the night.

As she stalked away, she glanced over her shoulder several times to see if the door opened. Her dad would come retrieve her. At least he always apologized, even if he *was* a moron, and the night air was freezing. He'd be worried.

But as one minute turned into five and no one came, Nicole's fury grew.

They were just going to let her freeze to death out here? They could go to prison for that. She was almost positive. Child neglect or whatever the courts called it.

Nicole stayed outside until her teeth chattered so violently, she began to worry that every tooth in her head would fall out. She stalked over to Bill and Jeannette's RV, but the door was locked.

Dammit!

She jumped up and down and stomped her feet, but that did nothing to help her handle the cold. Maybe her parents didn't care if she died, but she refused to go out like this. She still had her virginity to lose, and they were not going to ruin that plan for her just like they'd ruined everything else in her whole entire life.

With no choice left, she marched back toward their camper. When she reached the stairs, she took a moment to wipe her face on her sleeve. She wasn't going to make this entrance with tears and snot all over her cheeks.

Nicole lifted her chin, determined to return to the RV with pride.

When she first opened the door, the light that cascaded into her eyes was blinding. As her pupils adjusted, she froze. She blinked frantically, sure that her eyes must be playing tricks on her.

The scene didn't change, though. Her mom and dad were still tied to chairs with duct tape over their mouths. Tim was bound and gagged, curled into a ball on the table.

Her stomach bottomed out when she spotted Jeannette handcuffed to a steel grab bar in the wall. The wide-eyed terror in each gaze she met escalated her own, quickening her breathing until she was panting for air.

"Wh-what—"

She screamed when a hand grabbed her arm. Desperate energy flooded her body, and she thrashed, using all her strength to try to escape the firm grip.

No! She had to *escape*. Get help.

Even as the fingers dug harder into her arm, Nicole fought back, kicking and hitting while her pulse pounded in her ears, drowning out everything else.

She fought until the freezing cold metal poked into her temple.

"Don't make me shoot."

It took a second poke at her temple before the voice and words came together in Nicole's brain. She stopped struggling and began to shiver instead.

A gun. Someone was pointing a gun at her head.

No, not someone. *Bill.*

Fear like she didn't know was possible weakened every muscle in her body as the danger sank in.

Bill isn't cute at all. He's a bad man. A very bad man.

Nicole trembled in silence, wishing she could take back every mean thing she'd ever said or done to her parents. Even the things she'd only thought in her head. She hadn't meant any of that crap. She wanted to fly into their arms and tell them how much she loved them...that she loved them more than anything.

She didn't get the chance.

Bill yanked her close to him, leaning in from behind like he had when she was mixing the salad. But there were no butterflies now. No electricity. Just icy fear filling every part of her body, weighting her down until it was impossible to move.

"Welcome back, little Nicole." His breath was hot on her ear. "You're right on time."

18

The last place on Earth that Special Agent Noah Dalton wanted to be was cooped up inside the Richmond Field Office, but he was levelheaded enough to admit the technology available within the building was their best chance at getting a lead on Winter's whereabouts.

He'd walk barefoot over hot coals if he believed that might bring Winter back. Stuck in a chair in a stuffy office should be easy.

Except, Noah wasn't made to sit at a desk and click away on a computer screen for long periods of time. He was a former Marine. An athlete. A *doer*.

He glared at the monitor while his knee jiggled with nervous energy. The moment they uncovered the smallest bit of information pointing them in *any* direction, he'd be out those doors and flying down the highway in a heartbeat.

Instead, the search was still active, and he was considering sticking his head out a window and screaming into the cold air at the top of his lungs.

Aimless. He had no direction, and the frustration of that

mental "my hands are tied" sensation grated away at his nerves. Anxiety was threatening to tear him apart.

He straightened his spine, expanded his chest, and tried to fall back on his military and Bureau training. Focus. Calm. Mission-minded.

Sweat trickled down his neck. When the mission involved his missing girlfriend and her psychopathic sibling, "finding his center" became an impossible task.

Noah was terrified. Utterly terrified.

The media had been doing an amazing job of spreading unfounded rumors that Winter helped Justin escape. Reporters and anchors posed the question that his own team had barely begun to touch upon.

How did *anyone* escape from the maximum-security section of a mental hospital without assistance?

Only Winter's fingerprints had been found on the driver's side of the car. That info had been leaked to the media maybe two seconds after he'd found out himself. Some asshole, or possibly many assholes, with the inside scoop had loose lips.

Noah would love to find and punch that flapping mouth right off its owner's face. Instead, he vented his anger on the desk, pounding his fist against the wood until his skin turned red.

The newscasts were making Justin and Winter out to be a modern-day sibling version of Bonnie and Clyde. Every time someone mentioned the duo on the flat-screen television of the BAU office, he fought the intense urge to smash the glass.

Winter was *not* teamed up with Justin. She would *never*. Yes, she loved her brother and of course wanted his condition to improve.

But Winter Black wasn't a criminal. She couldn't commit murder, and she would never assist her brother in doing the same. Not. Ever.

The comparison made for a great breaking news story, but it was all bullshit.

Not my girl. Not in a million years.

Noah slapped the desktop one more time for good measure. Why were the techs taking so damn long to identify that body? The entire world seemed to be moving in slow motion.

He tried to assure himself that everyone was working as fast as ever. His personal interest in the case was messing with his perspective.

A second was a minute was an hour was a day.

On top of facing the reality that the woman he loved was still missing, his gut churned with guilt for the things he'd said to Autumn earlier. What kind of a jerk spoke that way to their friends?

Noah had yet to run into Autumn since their heated exchange. He knew she was somewhere in the building scouring through Philip's case notes and that she was just as terrified for Winter as he was.

Shame poured over him, thick and heavy like an oil spill. Blaming Autumn had been a dick move. He should have taken the fact that he was agreeing with Chris Parker about *anything* as a sign that he'd lost touch with reality.

This nightmare wasn't Autumn Trent's fault. He'd heard her with his own damn ears tell Aiden and Winter that she didn't think it was a good idea for her to be the one to do Justin's competency assessment.

Winter had begged her, though. Justin's attorney had pushed for Autumn's services as well. The courts had approved Autumn's assignment to Justin, and she'd taken on the responsibility with complete professionalism. She never would have given the task anything less than her best. Furthermore, he knew she'd remained as impartial and fair as any human could in that situation.

Autumn had even pissed Winter off with her trained, unbiased analysis of Justin.

No, this wasn't Autumn's fault.

Noah bowed his head and squeezed his eyes shut while the guilt pounded through his body.

Deep down, he knew why he'd attacked her with such viciousness. If he couldn't pin Winter's disappearance on Autumn, there was only one other person left to blame.

Himself.

He didn't share all of Autumn's doctorial merits, but he was still a man who'd been trained not only by the U.S. Marine Corps but also the Federal Bureau of Investigation.

Noah had no excuse for not having prevented this catastrophe.

He'd perceived the danger. He'd known the possible consequences. He spent more time with Winter outside of work than anyone else.

And how would you have stopped her from visiting her brother? Were you going to throw her over your shoulder and skip the country for the duration of Justin Black's life?

A sad smile crept across his lips. Winter would have kneed him in the damn balls for even trying to stand in her way. She would have kicked his ass.

Nobody told his Winter what to do.

His smile faded as he realized that there was another reason he hadn't put his foot down.

He hadn't wanted to lose her. If he'd pushed too hard about staying away from Justin, she would have ended their relationship. He was sure of that.

So instead, he'd tried to walk the "agree to disagree" line with her.

You didn't want to lose her. Funny how you lost her anyway.

If anything happened to her...Noah shuddered. He'd

never forgive himself for being so selfish. His effort to keep her close could wind up being the cause of her death.

Single and living in a world where Winter Black existed beat "former boyfriend of Winter Black, the federal agent who'd been murdered" any day of the week.

Good job. She didn't break up with you. Instead, she might die. Or be dead already.

Noah braced his hands on the desk and shook his head. *Stop it.* He had to stop thinking that way. A defeatist attitude wouldn't help find her any faster, and he wasn't a quitter. Not even close. He fought 'til the end, and so did Winter.

He had to keep believing she was out there and that the team would track her down.

That might be easier to do once they had an identification on the body and a make and model of the vehicle Justin had stolen.

"Give me a lead and let me get out there." The blank computer screen didn't reply to his mumble. "Give me a damn lead, and I'll find her. I'll find *them*. And I will make that little bastard pay for what—"

"Noah?"

He whipped his head up. Mia stood with two cups of coffee, one of which she extended to him. She appeared nervous…probably unsure if he was capable of human interaction at all.

"Thank you." He accepted the beverage, though his body was pumped full of caffeine already. His hands needed something to do, even if that was just holding a hot mug. "Are you here to save me from my self-flagellation?"

Mia pulled an empty chair from a neighboring desk toward him and sat. Her expression held a soft quality that he'd only ever seen displayed with such prominence on Autumn's face.

Empathy.

"You can't do that. You can't blame yourself." Mia sipped her coffee, peering at him with her big brown eyes over the rim of her cup. Her hair was as dark as her irises, though not black like Winter's long locks. Mia's hair grazed her shoulders and had a wave he guessed was natural. She didn't seem like the salon type.

"Can't I? I'm pretty sure I have. In fact, I've finally found the *right* place to lay the blame. You know, after ripping Autumn's head off." Noah cringed at the recollection.

"Autumn will forgive you. You know that." Mia twirled a spoon in her cup. "And what's happened is no one's fault. That's why it's so hard, Noah. There isn't anyone to blame. A shitty thing happened because shitty things happen in life sometimes."

Based on their few interactions, Noah had detected that Agent Logan wasn't a big talker. She was tiny, excellent at her job, and ridiculously patient…or so he assumed as she hadn't physically harmed Parker yet.

"I can guess what you're thinking. What the heck do I know, right?" Mia diverted her eyes to the carpeting. "But you'd be surprised at how well I understand what you're going through."

He cocked an eyebrow. He doubted she could even come close to understanding his worry, but the genuine concern in her voice was comforting. "Thanks, Mia, but you don't have to do this."

"Do what? Empathize? Try and stop me." She gave him a grin, but he sensed the pain behind it.

"Okay. Shoot." He crossed his arms, giving her the proverbial floor.

Her shoulders rose as she took a deep breath. "A few years back, I got a call from my brother. Ned had just gone through the breakup of his relationship…and I mean *just*. He was heartbroken and *so* upset, I could hardly get a word in to calm him down. I urged him to just keep talking to me and not do anything…rash." Mia was staring past Noah now, clearly reliving a nightmare on an invisible movie reel.

"This is where the shitty thing happens, right?" Noah needled her with a strained attempt at humor.

Mia refocused on him. "The breakup was sudden. His girlfriend, Sloan, had shared some upsetting news and…" She took another sip of her coffee. "Well, anyway. He wouldn't listen to me. He took off for a drive, and my family and I spent hours without any contact from him. Couldn't get him on the phone. No friends had seen him."

Noah was beginning to make the connection, and he was also very aware when Mia's chin trembled as she spoke.

"I just meant to tell you," she gave his arm an encouraging pat, "I know what it's like to wait for the news of a loved one's fate. The minutes drag on and on…but they *will* pass. This won't last forever, I promise you."

Mia stood as if to leave, and Noah stopped her with the inquiry burning in his throat. "Did you…did you receive some good news in the end? Was Ned okay?" His stomach clenched as her countenance fell.

"No. Ned's story didn't have a happy ending. He died in a car accident." Mia smacked a small hand over her eyes. "That was so stupid of me to share right now. I'm so sorry, Noah. We *are* going to find Winter. Ned's fate isn't hers."

Noah's own pessimism throbbed at his temples, but that was in no way Mia Logan's fault. "Don't apologize. I do appreciate that someone involved in this case gets it. I do."

"I just wanted you to know you weren't alone. Instead, I increased your worries." Mia's cheeks had taken on a subtle pink tinge.

Noah returned the consoling arm pat. "Hey. You didn't increase my worries. A shitty thing happened because shitty things happen in life, remember? I'll try my best to stay on

Team Positivity with you and believe that everything works out okay. And Mia, I'm sorry for your loss."

Mia couldn't help giving Noah a warm hug before retreating to her desk. She'd messed up in sharing the Ned story, and even though she was positive that Noah wouldn't hold it against her, she'd remember this cringe-worthy moment for the rest of her life.

She plopped down in her chair, her brother foremost in her mind. His photo hung on her bulletin board. Ned's grin had always been contagious, and she found herself smiling back at him. His dark brown eyes and even darker brown hair were a match to her own. They even shared the same hints of dimples when they smiled.

Somehow, he'd lucked out and gotten the skin that tanned while she just burned and burned some more. But when it wasn't summertime, they were often mistaken for twins.

With only two years between them, they had always been close. Inseparable as young children, teens, and into their twenties.

Her brother was the only person on Earth who knew she'd written Brad Pitt a lengthy letter as an eleven-year-old, proposing marriage.

That one definitely didn't work out.

Ned had broken it to her when they were in high school that their parents had tucked the letter away in a keepsake chest instead of dropping the envelope in the mailbox. Apparently, *Brad Pitt, My Favorite Actor, Brad Pitt's House, Probably California* wasn't his official address, and therefore, the letter would have been doomed to languish at the post office.

Mia didn't mind, though. She was happy Ned was the only one who had known and laughed just as hard as he did when one of them brought the letter up. She still laughed when she thought about it.

Most of the time.

She'd known her brother's secrets too. No one else would have guessed how much Ned hated dolls. He'd called them the creepiest things to exist and claimed they were only fit for horror films. At age ten, Mia had packed her Barbies in a box and pushed them to the back of the closet so that her big brother wouldn't have to worry about them. Ned was two years older, but if it was in her power to protect him from anything, she would.

She always had.

The only time she hadn't been able to protect him at all was when Sloan came into his life. Mia's eyes wandered from Ned's happy face to the hand on his shoulder. She had tried to crop Sloan Grant from the photo completely, but the feminine hand wearing an aquamarine birthstone ring still rested on her brother.

Appropriate, considering Sloan's the reason he's dead.

Mia shook the accusation off, just like she had hundreds if not thousands of times since losing her brother. She'd blamed Sloan in the beginning, but over the years, she had tried to work through her grief and accept how life had played out for Ned.

A shitty thing happened because shitty things happen in life.

The words had come out of her own mouth during a counseling session, and she'd held on to them as a mantra ever since. Therapy had enabled her to move past the loss and to forgive Sloan for the part she had played leading up to his car crash.

But nothing gave Mia the ability to forget.

What she'd left out of the conversation with Noah was

that Ned had called her so upset not because of a simple breakup but because Sloan, the woman he'd proposed to, had admitted to sleeping with another man shortly after the proposal.

To her credit, Sloan had shared the information of her own free will. She'd been honest. Or at least, she was honest after the fact that she'd been *dis*honest. But Sloan came clean, and in doing so, crushed Ned's heart to pieces.

Deep down, a part of Mia still held Sloan responsible for Ned's death. He wouldn't have been so upset, wouldn't have taken off driving so recklessly, wouldn't have crashed and died if Sloan hadn't existed in his life at all.

But Mia didn't want to be that person...the one who couldn't let go. When people didn't let go of hurts and wrongs, they only grew more and more bitter by the day. Their wound transformed them into someone else.

Mia wanted to stay Mia.

And while her colleagues were quick to congratulate her on her ability to deal with Chris Parker, her penchant for patience was only one reason she never unleashed on Chris and gave him a good piece of her mind.

Chris hadn't had an easy childhood. He'd mentioned a few things here and there, sometimes meaning to and sometimes not. The bits of info he did share was enough for Mia to gather that Chris's life had been a grueling, uphill battle.

His family had been loving but far from well-off. He'd nearly missed out on going to college altogether because of favoritism in his small town. Chris had a giant chip on his giant shoulder, and Mia hoped over time he might learn to let a few things go.

She wasn't an idiot, though. Chris had a long road ahead of him if he was ever to soften that hardened heart to any visible degree. He didn't seem remotely ashamed of his behavior or even aware of just how nasty he was most of the time.

Maybe he'd never change, but Mia wasn't one to give up on people.

She fiddled with the spoon in her now cold coffee, reminding herself yet again that Sloan was a person too. She surely had reasons for betraying Ned. And that was enough for Mia because it had to be.

She didn't want to know the reasons or ever talk to Sloan again for the rest of their lives. They'd been friendly, maybe even close, while Ned and Sloan were dating.

That closeness had ended the day her brother died.

Now, Mia just did her best to avoid Sloan and the painful memories that inevitably came with her.

If Sloan hadn't been employed by the FBI and working in this same building day in, day out, the task would have been easier. Thankfully, Agent Grant was a part of the counterterrorism unit. Sloan had spent time training with the Army overseas before becoming a federal agent, and she specialized in defusing bombs.

Their paths rarely crossed, regardless of the fact that they both were in the Richmond Field Office. Mia had only passed Sloan in the hallway maybe two or three times since the tragedy, and she'd simply put her head down and kept walking.

Not to be cruel, but the opposite. Mia didn't want to risk her face twisting into some horrible expression that could intensify Sloan's guilt. As much as Mia struggled to not blame Sloan for Ned's death, she was sure that Sloan struggled even harder to do the same.

The past was the past. She couldn't forget, but she could walk away.

And so she did.

Another glance at Ned's smiling face solidified her

resolve to let the past go. Ned would have wanted her to live out the rest of her life happy and free from the chains that a grudge locked around the human heart.

She sighed. Time to turn away from the picture and focus her attention on the investigation. Maybe the Logans' story had a sad ending, but the Blacks weren't beholden to the same fate. No one had to die in this mess.

Ned didn't have to die either.

Closing her eyes, Mia resolved to make that voice in her head shut up once and for all. As long as Sloan stayed out of her life, Mia could retain her center.

The calm and forgiveness that she'd worked so hard to find after Ned's death was too precious to throw away into a pile of hatred. Not that Mia hated Sloan...she just never wanted to see her face again.

She straightened in her chair, determined to banish the past for now. At this moment, all that mattered was saving Winter Black.

Mia couldn't take any more needless deaths.

When Autumn pulled up to Philip Baldwin's country home, the officers on-site warned her that she was venturing onto an official crime scene. They instructed her to go straight to Philip's office, gather what she needed, and come right back out, touching nothing else.

Get in, get out. That was what Autumn told herself as she headed up the walkway to the oversized front doors.

As soon as she stepped inside the foyer, the plan went out the window.

On an intellectual level, Autumn realized what preserving a crime scene meant. On a personal level, experiencing the untouched crime scene where she'd come close to exiting this world only a little more than twenty-four hours ago was a rude awakening.

Autumn didn't get far before she froze, her pulse ratcheting up as her surroundings sank in.

The chair she'd been bound to sat in the same exact spot. Almost like it was waiting for the next victim.

Broken glass from Philip's pictures was still scattered across the floor, glittering like diamonds beneath the fancy light fixture. The red stain was a macabre reminder of Albert's gunshot wound.

She touched her neck, recalling the way the plastic had dug into her flesh. So close. She'd come so close to dying. If Philip hadn't gained control of the weapon when he did, she wasn't sure either of them would have survived.

The plastic bag was gone at least, but that was only because the cursed thing had been carefully collected and taken as evidence.

She edged forward, skirting the yellow crime tape. Every step echoed off the high ceilings. Her skin flooded with goose bumps when she recalled Albert talking to his dead sister, his mood alternating between rage and sorrow. He'd acted like his sister had been standing right there in the room with them.

Maybe she was. Why are you so sure that she wasn't?

A violent chill ran down her spine, and she scurried in the direction of Philip's office. The sooner she located the additional notes Philip had kept on Justin and got herself the hell out of there, the happier she'd be. A part of her wondered whether Philip would sell his property, considering the events tied to the grounds.

Autumn couldn't imagine him wanting to live there now. Were it her decision, she might just burn the whole damn house down, leaving nothing but a pile of ashes as a reminder of the horrid ordeal.

She found the notes right where Philip had told her they'd be and hurried back out, clutching them to her chest. As she passed back by the crime scene on the way out, her gaze was drawn back to the chair where she'd gasped for oxygen.

On second thought, maybe she should do Philip a favor and go ahead and toss a match now. She'd just read an article the other day about how symbolic cleansings were often helpful when an individual was attempting to move past a painful event in their life.

She doubted law enforcement would consider setting someone else's house on fire a symbolic cleansing, though. More like a literal felony. Somehow, the idea of adding convicted felon to her list of achievements didn't quite seem worth the trouble.

Autumn's newfound pyromaniac tendencies faded as soon as she was back in the safety of her own car. She returned to the field office as quick as the speed limit allowed, recruiting Bree and Sun when she stepped inside to help her go through Philip's case notes.

Both agents seemed eager to assist, even Sun.

"You think this will give us the insight we need to find them?" Bree posed the question while they walked to an unused conference room and set up shop at the wide table.

"I'm not sure." Autumn divided the notes into three stacks. "I just keep thinking that if there is any pebble of information we're missing about Justin Black, Dr. Baldwin would be the most likely person to have it."

"They've gotta be getting the results back on that body soon." Sun frowned as she shuffled through the notes. "If we can't find anything here, at least it's something to do until then. I keep waiting for some lead to pop up, but..." Sun's show of uncertainty was shocking, but Autumn didn't let an ounce of her surprise show.

If she and Sun Ming were ever going to be friends, Sun would have to lower her defenses. Autumn hoped that maybe she was witnessing the first baby step in that process.

"I agree. Thank you for your help." Autumn made sure to meet eyes with both women as she spoke. Sun needed to know she mattered and was appreciated just as much as the other agents.

Stop shrinking your colleagues and read the damn pages.

They'd started with a sizable stack, but after tackling the task as a trio for a good twenty-five minutes, that pile was almost gone. Autumn was grateful because her mind was all over the damn place.

As though she hadn't been distracted enough over Winter's welfare, walking back into Philip's home had felt like a literal haunted house encounter, and the tension from that visit was still alive and well in her abdomen. She was miles away from Philip's country dwelling, but a part of her was convinced she'd never completely leave that house behind.

Good thing her desire to help the millions of inhabitants on this rock they all shared overrode her need for tranquility because her profession didn't provide a lot of peace and quiet.

"He really is the *master* of manipulation, huh?" Sun gaped at the pages before her. They were almost through everything—three people sped the process up considerably—and there hadn't been any type of breakthrough discovery.

Some interesting notes, Autumn had to admit. Philip apparently did a lot of his deepest patient analysis after he'd left the hospital. Though the pages were much more rambling than his in-office notations, they proved that when Dr. Baldwin went home at night, his troubled patients were still very much on his mind.

Philip wasn't a man who oozed charisma and charm, but he was devoted and nuanced. Complicated. And very possibly, more than a little misunderstood.

And you're thinking about this why right now?

There wasn't a good reason, or at least not one she cared to define.

"Sounds like Baldwin was heading toward barring Justin's visitations himself." Bree tossed a page aside as she commented.

"If the medical director had the thought and hadn't acted on it yet, blaming *you* for not doing the same when you don't even work there is just straight unfair bullshit."

Autumn blinked at Sun's declaration. That was easily the most heartfelt sentence the other woman had ever uttered to Autumn, even laced with profanity.

Not that Autumn minded the cursing. She'd take whatever she could get from Sun Ming, and someday...someday, they were going to be friends.

Autumn was determined.

"Honestly, I'll take the blame. I don't even care about that anymore. I just want to find Winter. Alive." Autumn closed her eyes and envisioned her friend, willing Winter to be unharmed.

"And find that little shit brother of hers and make sure he's put in a cell he couldn't bust out of with an atomic bomb." Sun's additional commentary was extreme but summed up what they'd all been thinking...more or less.

Catch him. Lock him up forever. Throw away the key.

"He plays on emotions very well. When you consider that humans are full of them, that gives him quite the artillery." Bree met Autumn's gaze as she spoke, her dark eyes broadcasting her concern.

"Unlimited power." Autumn remembered her first meeting with Justin Black and the morbid awe she'd experienced at his chameleonlike conversational skills. "All he has to do is tell people what they want to hear, and he's an expert at that. That was one of the reasons I signed him as being incompetent for trial. The courts didn't give me adequate time to fully assess Justin, but the fact that he could and *would* do everything in his power to say whatever was necessary..."

She blew out an audible breath. Nightmare. Justin was a living, breathing nightmare.

No one capable of the gory deeds he'd committed should be able to wield such intense powers of charisma, appeal, and relentless charm. The ease with which he controlled his "moods," despite being a bloodthirsty psychopath, was what elevated him beyond a typical killer and pushed him into monster territory.

When he wanted to be, Justin Black was extremely likable. He could even pull at a heartstring or two if the need arose.

"Sending him to trial would have been like giving an Oscar-winning actor a grand central stage, with the entire world as their audience. He would have given the performance of his life and *enjoyed* the trial." Sun's disgust twisted her features in a comical manner. Autumn imagined a "BLECH!" word bubble hanging above Agent Ming's head, but the humor fell flat even inside her mind.

This wasn't a cartoon, and nothing about Winter's perilous situation was funny.

"You're absolutely right. But he also knew that there was no guarantee he'd be saved from federal prison at the end of that performance. Justin was very aware that he needed to stay at Virginia State for the time being. And I figured between the psychiatrists working there and my observational meetings with him, maybe the Justin Black tornado could be unraveled." The window for unraveling that tornado was closing, though.

Frustrating, because Autumn had planned to put her work with him to good use. The insight she might have gained from one-on-one interaction with a serial killer could have proven invaluable. The fact that Justin had been raised by a serial killer himself made for a fascinating conglomerate of nature versus nurture discourse.

Often, these criminals were written off as hopeless since the moment they took their first breath. In utero, even. The world labeled them defective. Wrong. They never stood a chance. That was the popular opinion.

In truth, many different aspects affected a psychopath's fate, beginning at birth and extending throughout the developmental years. Many CEOs, politicians, military leaders, surgeons, and famous actors checked all the boxes that technically earned them the psychopath title, yet they somehow managed to avoid murdering people.

Becoming a serial killer was never engraved in stone for any child, and Autumn firmly believed that intervention at a young age was one of the keys to preventing the need to kill.

There were, for instance, studies that used brain scans to find children genetically predisposed toward psychopathy based on the size of the amygdala and other known scientific precursors.

In one of those experiments, the at-risk children were exposed to enrichment classes—art, culture, social interaction, enjoyable physical activity—and received nutritious diets instead of the common high levels of saturated fat, salt, and processed sugar prevalent in many kids' everyday menus.

This treatment changed the outcome for the children involved in the study, allowing them to grow into high-functioning members of society with no tendency toward mental instability. In some cases, the size of the amygdala was physically altered.

If Autumn could help the young, she could change their future. And even if she changed only one future at a time, the ripple effect would better the entire world.

Less hatred. Less violence. Less sadness.

Justin Black's life was a *tragedy*. She experienced real sorrow for his wasted potential and had hoped that interacting with and learning from him might prevent similar tragedies.

But Justin being a part of that process was unlikely now. If they...*when they* captured him again, Autumn didn't foresee the courts granting her access or visits. They wouldn't blame her for his escape, but the law would want to start fresh.

A new shrink. A new public defender, even. And possibly a new hospital altogether.

Or, considering he'd had the wherewithal to escape so easily, Justin might find himself in the courtroom sooner than he'd hoped. He'd be facing far more serious charges than escaping a mental ward, and his downtime would be spent in an actual federal prison.

She couldn't know any of that for sure, but she could make an educated guess. Her degree in criminal psychology and Juris Doctorate let her mind envision a rough outline of the path Justin's future would take.

That future was bleak.

Autumn's mind conjured an image of Winter, tied up and bleeding, and she squeezed her hands together.

Bleak, maybe, but no more than Justin deserved.

"What I keep thinking is that even if he'd told Dr. Baldwin every detail of his plans to escape, he never should have been able to pull the actual getaway off." Bree tapped a pen so rapidly that Autumn thought it might take flight.

"You're right. He shouldn't have. Every piece of mail Justin received was scanned. Even his visitors were searched and scanned. Medical staff and law enforcement were the only exceptions. Jane or John Doe couldn't have just walked in off the street and gone to his room." Autumn had been running into this same conundrum repeatedly.

He couldn't have gotten out alone, but no one could have helped him, either.

She continued going over the maximum-security hospital's visitation procedures, which were just as extreme as the crimes of the patients receiving the visits. "There's no way he received assistance from a fan or family member. Security protocol wouldn't have allowed the slightest chance of that happening."

"Virginia State is no joke. Any family member who comes across as the slightest bit troublesome makes a list, and that list involves a mandatory strip search *and* full body cavity search before they're allowed to meet with their convict." Sun scrunched her nose. "I'm just saying, if I got pushed into that job duty, I might have to switch careers."

"Why? There's no blood involved. Probably." Bree shot Sun a grin, and Autumn tried hard to keep a straight face but failed. Even Sun's lips upturned ever so slightly.

Agent Ming and bodily fluids didn't get along.

Despite the moment of humor, Autumn's mind circled back to the same question she'd been burdened with since first learning of Justin's escape and Winter's disappearance.

How? How would Justin have gotten a weapon or been able to overpower a federal agent *and* a male nurse?

A firm but gentle hand came down on her shoulder, causing her to jump. Fleeting currents of anxiety mixed with…affection, maybe…jolted Autumn to attention. She turned as Aiden pulled out the chair beside her and took a seat, his cool blue eyes fixed on her face.

"How are you holding up?" The genuine concern in his voice was both heartwarming and embarrassing.

There are two other people at this table, Aiden. Two. How are they holding up?

Autumn forced herself to respond with a smile but doing so felt akin to holding a million pounds of weight above her head. "I'm okay. Frustrated."

Her eyes slid to Sun and Bree, both of whom had ceased all activity to watch the interaction play out.

"I think I'm just gonna slip out and grab my eightieth cup of coffee for the day. Holler if you need me again, Autumn."

Bree tastefully made her exit, giving Sun an almost imperceptible tap on the shoulder as she walked away from the table.

Sun, who had been significantly more cordial toward Autumn than usual, narrowed her eyes at the pair. "I don't need any damn coffee. But I wouldn't want to interfere with your *work*, Agent Parrish." She shoved to her feet with a screech of the chair before stalking out the door.

Whatever bubble of hope Autumn had been holding for the improvement of relations between herself and Sun Ming popped and deflated. Someday, Autumn was going to find out exactly how Aiden and Sun's short dating stint had ended. Once she understood the circumstances, maybe she could talk to Sun and—

"Rude but expected." Aiden shrugged off Sun's statement like water off a duck's back.

Autumn exhaled a long sigh and reminded herself that there was no time to waste on dating drama. "I was actually enjoying her company, if you can believe it."

Aiden's eyebrows shot up his forehead, providing all the answers Autumn needed.

"Okay then. Well, let's focus on Winter and what we know so far." Aiden flipped through some of the pages in Autumn's pile of notes.

"Honestly, Aiden, I'm presuming that we don't know anything more than we knew before. Justin is calculating, devious, and manipulative to an infinite degree. He never spoke of escape plans to Philip. And even if he had..." Autumn shook her head, her thoughts returning to the main issue at hand.

"Even if he had, how does one young man make his way out of a maximum-security facility such as Virginia State Hospital?" Aiden finished for her.

Autumn decided there was no point in avoiding the other

worry that plagued the team. "I refuse to believe that Winter willingly helped Justin escape. She loved him, but she knew he was where he belonged for the time being. And she never, *ever* would have killed a nurse in the process. Winter isn't capable of murder."

"I agree." Aiden cleared his throat, just as uncomfortable with the idea of *their Winter* being an accomplice to Justin's evil doings as Autumn. "But the press is running with the theory that the Black siblings teamed up. And by 'running with,' I mean they're blasting the belief on every news channel."

"They have nothing to base that on. *We* don't even have evidence to substantiate that claim." Autumn whirled toward Aiden, cheeks hot with indignation. "Do you believe Winter could have done that? Helped Justin break out?"

Aiden shook his head but kept his gaze averted. Autumn considered touching his arm to ascertain just how honest he was being but refrained. He deserved to have a safe place for his own thoughts.

Plus, she didn't want the action to be misconstrued by Aiden or anyone else who might just happen to be walking by. Stirring that pot would in no way help them find Winter.

Step away from the pot.

None of that would help save her friend. They needed to find whatever detail they were missing. An option they hadn't considered yet.

"We keep asking how he did it with the unspoken understanding that we all believe getting out of that building is impossible. But he got out. We're going to have to accept that escape from Virginia State is possible because *it happened*." Autumn shifted gears to focus on her mental blueprint of the facility.

"As in quit concentrating on all the factors that made his disappearing act so challenging and concentrate on the ones that might have helped him." Aiden nodded, seamlessly following her train of thought. "Security at the hospital isn't as locked down as an actual prison, but it's still tight. Lots of security checkpoints, on top of guards who walk the halls the entirety of their shifts."

"And that didn't stop him." Autumn chewed the end of her pen. "Dale Miller was naked, so his clothes could have been utilized as a disguise."

"A disguise for Justin? Or Winter? He's a very well-known face at that hospital. Winter stood a much better chance of wheeling Justin out than the other way around. The gurney would have helped contribute to the disguise plus hide one of them from scrutiny, but we still have no clear indication as to who was pushing the damn thing. If we even so much as mention that possibility to the press, they'll be twice as inclined to declare this a sibling breakout."

Aiden was right. Someone was talking, and that individual could be anyone, from an over-attentive nurse's assistant to a cop to a federal agent. Autumn refused to add any more flame to the media fire. She trusted Aiden, and in this moment, that was enough.

"Video surveillance would be helpful right about now." Autumn couldn't help but grind her teeth and think of Philip's stubborn refusal to use cameras in "his hospital."

"Philip Baldwin is an arrogant man. Arrogance always comes at a cost...eventually." Aiden seemed to be speaking from personal experience, but there wasn't time to delve deeper into that black hole. Not now.

"Well, the cost might end up being that Winter is injured or even..." The growing lump in Autumn's throat prevented her from finishing.

Aiden leaned closer and held her gaze this time. "Hey, she's not dead, Dr. Trent. You can't allow yourself to think that. She's alive, and we're going to find her."

Autumn swallowed with difficulty, allowing the truth of his words to sink in. She had to stay positive. Nothing threw off an investigation worse than despair. The human brain lost focus and sharpness when desolation was allowed to enter. Details were forgotten, clues missed altogether.

But as Winter's best friend, Autumn's worry ran deep. Justin was sick. *So sick.* The things he might do to his sister—mentally *and* physically—before ending her life were limitless.

Autumn's stomach clenched before she focused on her breathing and pulled her mind back to the now, shutting down the parade of worries.

Winter's alive, and we're going to find her.

With that mantra buoying her spirit, Autumn could think more clearly. "The timing for Justin's escape was perfect. The entire hospital was up in arms over the Albert Rice murder fiasco. Some of the staff had taken leave or quit altogether because of safety concerns. On top of that, having the medical director absent made the situation a perfect storm."

"If there was ever a time when the employees would have been distracted, this was the winner. For lack of a better word." Aiden lifted a shoulder in mild exasperation. "The only real win here was for Justin."

"With Philip giving the green light for video surveillance equipment to be installed, Justin's perception may have gone beyond believing that this was a good time to attempt a breakout. He might have decided it was his only chance. The cameras could have triggered his urgency to escape that particular night." Autumn imagined what Justin must have experienced when he learned of the security upgrades in the form of twenty-four-hour video surveillance.

She guessed a large part of him had been enraged, but like any animal being backed into a cage, he would have focused on avoiding the trap rather than wallowing in self-pity. And when Justin Black focused, things happened.

Horrible things.

Aiden shook his head. "He couldn't have made the decision just like that. He would have needed a plan."

"You're forgetting all the time Justin's already had to ruminate. He'd probably formed dozens of ideas regarding escape, even if the methods of executing those plans were foggy. Winter's visit that evening wasn't expected. Maybe he just saw an opportunity, possibly his last, and took it."

"Okay. Let's say that's exactly what happened. An opportunity presented itself, and Justin pounced on it. That still doesn't explain how he overpowered two strong people, both of whom would never have been relaxed in his presence. How?" Aiden brought them back to the original maddening question.

Autumn kneaded the back of her neck as she searched her brain for an answer that made sense. "Could he have had a weapon of some sort? A tiny object he hid away until the right time came?"

She was positive that Justin had to have some type of device. Saying the words out loud only convinced her all the more.

"I checked with security. I asked them about their protocol for room searching. Every room was checked each week for contraband, and the checks were never scheduled. The patients never knew when they'd be getting searched, and there wasn't a place the guards or orderlies wouldn't have examined regardless. Justin had no true privacy, even without the cameras." Aiden was growing more and more irritated, but Autumn knew she wasn't the cause.

This. This talking in circles while no progress was made whatsoever in actually finding Winter was driving them all insane.

Aiden straightened in his chair with an abrupt jerk. "Who, aside from you, Winter, and Justin's attorney visited Justin? Do we know?"

Autumn scanned her memory for any mentions of other visitors. "To my knowledge, no one else ever visited him, but I haven't exactly dug into that."

They locked eyes, hope swelling in Autumn's chest as a new idea passed between them in silence.

Could this be the detail they'd been missing?

"We need to find out. ASAP." Aiden stood and pulled out his phone, heading for the doorway. "I have to return a few calls and try to get this media wildfire under control, but I think it would be wise if you checked out Virginia State's visitor log."

"On it." Autumn sprang to her feet with fresh determination blazing in her mind.

They finally had a direction to follow. A possible crack in the case.

And when the mystery was solved, Autumn was certain that Justin would be behind bars once again, and Winter's innocence would be proven.

First, though, they had to gather all of the pieces together, including one neglected piece that, when added to the puzzle, might help them answer a crucial question.

Could Justin Black have recruited other people to his corner, and if so, who?

20

I nside the cramped quarters of the RV, I caressed the sleek metal of my sister's gun and sighed in delight as everything fell into place.

Grandpa was here. His spirit was alive and well inside of me. He was staring down at me from the heavens and aligning the stars in my name. He was clearing the path for me just as Moses had parted the waters of the Red Sea. With his blessing, nothing and no one could stop me.

I was carrying out his plans and fulfilling his purposes, just as he'd said I would.

My gaze swept the trio of faces, excitement making my skin tingle. Pretty, young Nicole had done me a huge favor when she'd thrown her tantrum and skulked off. I couldn't have planned a better distraction.

Greg and Andrea were both seated in their cheap RV chairs and subdued for the moment, but that had taken a little persuading. Right after Nicole left, they'd launched into immediate "Oh, honey, go get her or she'll freeze to death" mode and all but forgotten my existence.

While they'd been distracted, I'd pulled the gun out. Tim,

the cute little booger, was the first to even notice. He'd frozen on the spot, which I applauded. Smart kid.

Andrea, on the other hand, had started shrieking and reaching for kitchen utensils. She managed to throw the salad tongs at me before I got things under control. Quite the arm on that suburban mom. Impressive. And her ridiculous attempt to defend their innocent, perfect family only made the footage funnier.

I was recording the whole thing on my phone.

Greg had started some misguided lunge toward me, but he stopped short when I pointed the gun directly at precious Tim. That was always the key. No matter how physically strong a man was, if you threatened what he held most dear to his heart, he turned into a giant pussy in about point two seconds.

Weak.

Had I kept the gun on Greg, he would have valiantly taken a bullet if that allowed him to take me down and save his family. He was hardwired to protect, which was hilarious and sad at the same time.

That poor middle-aged dumbass had no idea what delectable freedom was available to him were he to simply stop giving a crap about stupid matters like his wife, his kids, his mortgage payment, and all that other insignificant bullshit. But he was never going to figure that out. Greg liked to think of himself as a good man.

Too good.

Even now, in the midst of their terror, Greg's eyes managed to spit fire, and Andrea kept trying to send Tim reassuring glances, trembling chin and all.

Great parents, those two. They obviously loved their offspring. But man, what a huge mistake. I didn't even have to figure out a way to take them off guard.

These idiots had their guards so far down it was like they

wanted to die.

I shrugged and returned my attention to the new toy in my hand. I loved Winter's handy-dandy piece. So shiny.

The gun kept everyone in line, including Winter, which was the ironic cherry on top. Persuaded by her own persuader.

I ordered my ever-helpful sister to bind Greg and Andrea to the chairs with the duct tape she'd carried in with her. Purses were great. Women always had them, and no one ever suspected that anything beyond some lipstick and a pack of Mentos was hiding inside.

Winter could have been packing a damn machete for all they knew.

Morons.

When she finished, I inspected her handiwork. Greg and Andrea were bound to the chairs with thick gray strips like partially unraveled mummies. "Good work, Sis. Now do their mouths."

Andrea's whimper turned into a shriek, and I sighed, shaking my head. How quickly they forgot. I shoved the gun's muzzle against Tim's skull with one hand and used the other one to put my finger to my lips. "Shhh. It'd be a shame for little Timmy's head to explode just because his mother couldn't shut her trap."

That worked like a charm. The annoying screeching ended, and even Greg stopped swearing and making point-less threats.

I ran the barrel down Tim's skull. "Better hurry, Sissy, before she starts up again, and I get trigger happy."

Winter hurried to obey like a good little minion. She made quick work of tearing tape strips off the roll and pressing them over our prisoners' mouths.

Ahh, so much better. Now, the only irritating noise came from Tim, who was sniveling like a baby. I supposed I'd give him a pass, though, considering his age and otherwise exemplary behavior.

Still, I didn't trust him not to snap out of the sobbing fit and bite my ankle or something equally as annoying once the initial shock wore off. Kids were unpredictable little turds.

"Now him." I nodded at Tim, enjoying how Winter's jaw clenched at the command. Sissy wanted to resist so badly, but she wouldn't because she was a do-gooder. Because she cared what happened to these meaningless strangers.

One way or another, I'd break her of that human frailty. Baby steps. I could be patient when necessary.

She did as I ordered, binding Tim's arms and legs and covering his whiny mouth with duct tape before lowering him flat onto the table.

"Good, Sissy. Now here…catch!" I tossed the handcuffs I'd tucked into my pocket at Winter's face. She snatched them out of the air. "Handcuff yourself to that bar." It was the handicap kind, guaranteed to be extra sturdy.

She opened her mouth as if to argue, so I aimed the gun at Tiny Tim. That shut her up.

I giggled as she followed orders, snapping one cuff to her wrist and the other one to the metal rod. Adrenaline rushed through my body and turned me giddy. This was all so perfect. Tim was out of the way, but he still had an excellent view of the show.

And there was going to be an *epic* show.

I'd made the vast majority of my money from snuff films, and this would be the masterpiece to top them all. The amount of bitcoin I'd gain on the dark web from our little family video was going to be outrageous.

Since I was in a particularly good mood, I might even have to share the reel with the rest of the world on the regular internet. The views would be endless. Monumental.

That was the secret to mankind that I'd figured out all on

my own. The upstanding citizens of Earth who wouldn't dare take one click into the dark web were just as blood-thirsty as the sickos who flooded the evil side of cyberspace.

If it was on YouTube, you could bet your balls those upright souls would be glued to their damn screens. That's why videos of terrorists beheading journalists and the like were so fascinating to the good guys, because the truth was, they weren't good at all. No one was.

Some of us were just quicker to accept that fact.

My excitement grew as I surveyed my three helpless victims with a director's eye. This footage would go viral in a hot second. I was counting on that, actually.

Almost as though she'd been given a stage cue, the RV door creaked open, and Nicole reappeared.

I pressed the gun to her head while she was still blinking like an idiot. "Don't make me shoot."

That wasn't very fun, though, so I grabbed her by the arm next and pulled her soft adolescent body tight against my chest.

Now, *that* was fun. "Welcome back, little Nicole. You're right on time." As I whispered into her ear, I caught the scent of lavender and went hard as a rock.

Dang. All work and no play...

Then again, my work *was* play. Maybe I wouldn't be popping Nicole's sweet red cherry today, but I was going to have a blast anyway.

"Okay. We're going to play a game. The name of the game is 'Which Parent Should Die First?' and *you*, luscious little lady, are the one and only contestant. The rules are simple," I raised my voice to ensure I was successful in drowning out Nicole's annoying whimpering, "as I'm sure you already figured out. All you have to do is pick. Who dies first, Nicki-Poo?"

Her struggling turned frantic as she kicked and twisted

and tried to break away. So exciting. I tightened my grip around her body until I was sure her ribs were compressing.

Metal clinked, and I flinched. What the hell was that awful noise? Still clutching Nicole to my chest, I swiveled my head.

Winter was yanking at the handcuffs, desperately trying to escape.

"You might be strong, sister dear, but even you can't over-power metal. I suggest you relax while you can. You're gonna need your strength real soon."

Nicole bucked against me. "I don't want to play! *I don't want to play that game!* Let me go! Leave us alone!" She broke into a full-on sob, which was no surprise but super aggravating. I had to grit my teeth to curb the urge to punch her in the head.

A game wasn't a game if the sole player was unconscious.

"Oh, Nicole. Nicooole." I singsonged the word, drawing it out until goose bumps raised on her arms. "You have to accept things in life for what they are. Not what you want them to be." I began swaying, pulling her rigid body to and fro. Just like a middle school slow dance…aside from the gun and the terror and the duct tape and whatnot, of course. That would be a pretty messed up educational institution, even by my standards.

"No! *Nooo!*" She acted like screaming and shaking her head could change reality and wake her up from what probably seemed like a giant nightmare. Silly girl. Didn't she realize the most horrifying nightmares were the ones that happened while you were wide awake?

Those were the doozies.

She needed to understand that the scene before her was real. This was happening. And she *would* pick a parent. Her refusal to listen to a word I said was beginning to piss me off.

Thirteen was young but old enough to know that you

should never anger a psycho, especially one who was holding a firearm. Common freaking sense. What were the public schools teaching kids these days, anyway?

The metal clinked again and again, louder this time. Such a noxious, awful racket. Why did Winter have to be so annoying?

I ground my teeth and focused on Nicole. No way was I letting my do-gooder sister deter me from my fun. "Dad or Mom? Mom or Dad?" I swiveled the gun back and forth between the two faces as I spoke.

Everyone was sobbing now. Thank god their mouths were all taped shut. Otherwise, enduring four people losing their crap at the same time would be insanity-inducing.

God forbid I lose my mind.

I chuckled and glanced at Winter. I knew she wanted to try and rip the handcuffs straight off the wall. She probably could too, crazy-strong freak of nature that she was.

But Agent Black hadn't forgotten my promise to kill every single member of this cuddly cute family were she to try anything. *Anything.*

Even now, when it was becoming obvious that I was definitely going to kill someone, she'd try to save as many of them as possible with her compliance. My sister was a hero at heart, or so she thought.

Hearts could change, though.

Winter's eyes met mine, and I grinned. I fished my free hand into my pocket, pulled out a key, and tossed it to her. "Unlock yourself and go stand behind Greg and Andrea. *Now.*" Fear flooded her face, but she didn't hesitate to obey.

Siblings always knew each other better than anyone else ever could. Winter had taken heed of my warning before our dinner date because she fully believed I would act upon it should she screw up. Big sisters could tell when their little brothers were bluffing.

I hadn't been.

When Winter was in place behind the lovely couple, I was ready for the game to proceed. The action was moving at a snail's pace, and I didn't want my phone battery to die before catching all the real fun.

"Okay, Nicole. I'll make this easier for you. If you don't choose dear old Mom or Dad, I'll just kill both of them. Takes the pressure off. Then again, you're making yourself an instant orphan, and that seems a bit stupid. But you gotta do you." When I raised the gun again, the girl really started to lose her cool.

She was a screamer, just like her mother.

Greg was mumbling as loudly as he could beneath the tape, trying to catch Nicole's eye and—gag—be valiant again. I imagined he was yelling, "Choose me!" or some equally idiotic command.

I rolled my eyes. Was Andrea really worth dying for? The kids, sure. But couldn't he imagine his life without that woman beside him and realize that not a lot would change for the worse? He could chase tail again. Experience things he'd never even tried before getting saddled with all that responsibility and family baggage.

Just when I thought I'd lose my mind from all the screams and muffled screams and sobs and muffled sobs, Nicole broke. "My dad! I choose my dad!"

She went limp in my arms after saying those words. This kid was permanently jacked in the head now. She'd never forgive herself.

My heart warmed over the prospect. Such delicious, sweet defeat.

I was sure everyone expected a gunshot to rip through the air, but I had much better plans for my movie. "Winter. Take care of him." My voice was flat now. Dead.

Winter stood there like a statue, her blue eyes all big and round and her cheeks as pale as Grampa's ghost.

I huffed an impatient breath. My sister, the Fed, ladies and gentlemen. Was she seriously surprised by the fact that a serial killer wanted to actually murder people?

Spending time with those idiotic feebs had clearly rotted her brain. Good thing she had me as a brother to steer her right.

At least ten seconds ticked by before she found her tongue. "No. *No. I won't*, Justin. I won't."

As a reply, I shoved Nicole to the floor and yanked Tim off the table. I swung the gun back and forth between them, giggling when they flinched and cowered near my feet.

Yeah. Bob and weave. That'll save you. Idiots.

"Don't test me, Winter. You off Papa Smurf right now, or one of these two bites the dust." I admired my sister's attempt to still be a badass FBI bitch, but her refusal was pushing a button in my brain.

My head was starting to pound from all the screams. Stupid, cheap-ass duct tape. When this was over, I was going to file an official complaint with the company.

"Ten, nine, eight…" I kicked off the countdown and focused the gun carefully on Tim's little head.

This was so much fun.

21

"Ten, nine, eight..."

The RV closed in around Winter like a trap, pressing down on her from every direction and squeezing her lungs so tightly that she wheezed with each inhalation. Shock held her in place. She couldn't even move her lips to speak.

As an FBI agent, she'd made life-and-death decisions before, but not like this.

Never like this.

There has to be a way out. There has to be. Quit panicking and think.

Except, there wasn't. In the short span of time since she'd unlocked her cuffs, Winter had assessed and reassessed the situation, always coming to the same horrifying conclusion.

She was cornered. Trapped in a horror of her own making.

Everyone tried to tell you, but you refused to listen.

She should have predicted this. Justin blamed her for Kilroy kidnapping him. Of course he wanted to punish her.

Sounding like a mix between the Joker and Pennywise,

her brother swung the muzzle back and forth between the boy and his father in a demented version of eenie-meenie-miney-mo. "Come on, Sis, what's it gonna be? The kid or the geezer? Seven, six..."

Desperation merged with panic as Winter's every instinct revolted against obeying Justin's sick command. She was a trained FBI agent. She helped people. Executing innocents was anathema to the essence of who she was.

The adrenaline surging through her veins backed this up, injecting her muscles with a taut energy that left her quivering and poised on the verge of attack.

Her fingers flexed. Her breathing quickened. But logic prevented her from lunging at her brother.

She'd never make it in time. As fast as she was, bullets were faster.

"Five..."

Nicole and Tim sobbed while Andrea moaned. Greg raged against the duct tape, his curses muffled, but the fury in them clear.

Four innocents. A happy family who'd escaped to the campground for a quick getaway. Had they picked any other site, the Stewarts would be safe right now.

Instead, they'd picked the one campground where Justin Black was hiding.

Wrong place, wrong time. A twist of fate. A fluke. None of this should be happening, but it was, and Winter couldn't fight her way out. Couldn't outsmart her brother fast enough to make a difference.

With that gun pointed at the kids, he held all the cards. She was at his mercy. Failing to choose was the same as putting the gun to Tim's head and pulling the trigger herself.

Kill the father, or Justin would murder the kids.

"Ticktock, Winter. Four...three..."

A heartrending cry escaped little Tim. The noise ripped at Winter's defenses, shattering something inside her.

She battled the anguish that threatened to drag her under. She was an agent. Calm under pressure, cool under fire. Emotions couldn't help her now, so Winter locked them away, allowing clinical detachment to descend instead.

She had a choice to make.

The dad...or the kids.

"...two..."

Out of time.

When Winter glided forward, her legs didn't even feel like her own. Nor did her hands as they reached out to cradle Greg's head. She registered the warmth of his skin, and the stubble that prickled her palm.

"...one..."

There was no more thinking, only instinct and muscle memory carrying her through the motion. A sharp, forceful twist and—

Crack!

The snapping of his cervical vertebrae ricocheted through the RV. An awful, violent noise, but Winter knew that wasn't what would kill him. The lethal part was the silent severing of the spinal cord.

If Greg wasn't dead yet, he would be soon enough. Without medical attention, the respiratory paralysis would kill him within minutes.

When she released him and stepped back, Greg's head fell forward, dangling on his neck like a rag doll.

Nicole gasped, right before the screaming started.

Somehow, Justin was louder, cackling and smacking his free hand on his thigh. "Yes! *That's what I'm talking about!* Holy hell! Amaaazing! You're like a living lethal weapon!" As quickly as he started laughing, he stopped, sticking his lower lip out in an exaggerated pout. "Aw, what's the matter? Is

Sissy sad? Whatever you do, don't hurl in the RV. I don't wanna have to smell that."

As he crowed in victory, a new emotion pumped through Winter's body, scalding every cell and crevice. When she raised her eyes to his, she seethed with it.

Hatred. Right here, right now, she hated her brother more than she'd hated anyone or anything else in her life.

Justin's eyes widened as he studied her expression before his mouth stretched into an even bigger grin. "There you are, Sissy. I knew you had it in you." The smile flattened, and he jerked the gun at Andrea. "Now, take off her tape."

His tone warned her not to argue, so Winter reached for Andrea's face and removed the silver strip with one quick *riiiip.*

The woman emitted a high-pitched keening, her head swiveling between her dead husband and her children.

Not just dead. Murdered. By me. In cold blood.

Nicole and Tim sobbed like their hearts were breaking. Together, their voices combined into a razor-wire cacophony that scraped at Winter's raw nerves and hacked away at her very soul. She was frantic to help, but she couldn't. There was nothing she could do to end their suffering. No way to stop this.

"Okay." Justin's smile was gone. "Now, take care of Andrea."

A heartbeat of silence descended as shock rippled through the RV. The screaming returned almost immediately.

Winter knew there was no use arguing, but the agent in her had to try. "I won't. I won't do it."

Justin grabbed Nicole by the arm and yanked her to her feet and back against his chest like a human shield. "Do it now. *Now.*"

He wouldn't do it. Wouldn't kill a piece of his leverage.

Defiance made Winter growl. *"No."*

Justin clucked his tongue and the Joker-like smile returned. Before she could even take another breath, his gun hand moved, and without another warning, sound exploded from the weapon's barrel.

Bam.

Time seemed to slow as Nicole's head jerked back. A red circle bloomed on her temple, and droplets sprayed the air before Justin released her. She crashed to the floor, her eyes glazed over.

Limp.

Dead.

Winter stumbled backward a step, shaking her head in feverish denial while her mind screamed a single word over and over.

No. No no no.

"Sissy, look what you made me do. What a waste of a perky ass."

Winter stared down at Nicole's unmoving form, and the pain in her heart swamped her, threatening to drown her right there on the spot. Her head spun, and she teetered on the verge of consciousness.

Too much.

Self-preservation yanked her back from the darkness, sweeping her to that empty place beyond the chaos where their voices couldn't hurt her.

Where nothing could hurt her.

"Come on, Sis. How will we ever reach Rockstar Killer Sibs status if you don't take me seriously? You gotta stop with your Pollyanna belief that I have a limit because...guess what? I don't even understand the concept of limits, let alone have any. Why would anyone want to restrict their fun? Stupid concept, if you ask me." Justin turned to glare at

Andrea. "And you, could you shut up already? You're giving me a headache."

Winter drifted along like a leaf floating in a river, observing the events as if she were watching a play. None of this was real. Justin must have dosed her with a potent hallucinogen. This entire RV nightmare was all in her head. Conjured up from her worst fears.

An acid-like trip was a temporary hell she could accept.

Not this scene. Not this story.

She would never break a man's neck or end a man's life simply because she was ordered to.

Agent Winter Black wasn't a murderer. She was a hero. A fighter. She found a way out. A way around. *A way through.* She never gave in, and she never gave up.

And Nicole...

Winter's gaze slid to the lifeless body on the floor. The long blonde hair that flowed out like a cape. The girl had been in the same position, blank brown eyes open wide and staring at nothing, for far too long.

Get up, Winter urged as her hands balled into fists. *Get up get up get up.*

But of course, the girl didn't comply. She couldn't because she was dead. Likely before she'd ever hit the floor.

Winter's breathing quickened, increasing in tempo as she took in the blood splattered across the cupboards, the counters, the walls. The red splotches were speckled with tiny bits of flesh, the healthy pink color already starting to turn gray.

Brain matter. Sliding down the wood-slabbed walls.

Justin's maniacal laughter filled the RV, and Winter's skin iced over.

She wasn't hallucinating. This *had* happened. She'd killed a father. Justin had shot a daughter. Two innocent people dead, and every last bit of the tragedy was her fault.

Selfish. Stubborn. And now you're a murderer.

Every single person in her universe who truly knew her and cared about her well-being had told her. Asked her. Begged her.

Stay away from Justin.

But she'd refused to listen. Arrogance had taken hold of her heart like a parasite, and she'd fed that mania…kept it alive. She'd insisted, if only to herself, that she could save him. She could save her unsavable brother. Maybe everyone else had given up, but *she* was Winter Black. She would never give up on…

Her eyes slid to Justin, who was still lost in a happy fit of hysteria. He crowed as he crouched down and grabbed Tim, pulling the boy up to press the gun to his temple.

Poor little Tim appeared almost catatonic, like the latest horrors had forced him to retreat into his own mind.

Meanwhile, Justin cackled, delighted by the destruction he'd inflicted on this frigid January evening.

His bleached hair was still so foreign. But his laugh.

Winter shivered. With or without the mad edge that laced each howl, she would have known that laugh anywhere.

As a child, the slightest amusements had made her baby brother giggle. A simple funny face she flashed him over the dinner table. An icicle dropping from the gutters above their kitchen window. The neighbors' dog howling through the quiet evening air, setting off every canine within a five-block radius in a chorus of bellows.

Who might Justin have become if The Preacher had never killed their parents, never taken him away from her…? Maybe he'd be dancing around the room celebrating the birth of his first child right now or proposing to a woman. Graduating from college. Landing his dream job.

Now, none of those fantasies would ever come true. Under Kilroy's tutelage, Justin had undergone a complete metamorphosis, changing from ebullient child into a man who rejoiced over forcing his sister to kill. The kind of man who celebrated the splattered remains of a young girl's brain.

She shook her head. Not a man, but a monster.

A broken, demented creature lived within her little brother's body, and that creature only knew how to do one thing.

Kill.

Justin kept one arm latched around Tim's neck and used his gun hand to ruffle the boy's hair. "Who's ready for round three?"

The frost that coated Winter's skin seeped inside her, freezing her entire body until she was one big block of ice. "Please, Justin. Let's just leave. We can go anywhere. You don't even know what you're doing anymo—"

His laughter stopped in a split instant, and a madness she knew was incurable spread across his features. "I know *exactly* what I'm doing! When are you going to accept that? I'm *fucking nuts*, Winter! I'm a living nightmare! And I *love* it! Do you hear me? *I love what I am!* You will *never, ever* change me! There's no cure for this!"

As he raged, Justin's proximity to Tim birthed a new dread. Would her brother kill an eight-year-old boy?

Was that even a real question?

Of course he would murder Tim. He wouldn't hesitate or even blink.

Just like swiping a credit card.

As if he were reading her mind, Justin ground the muzzle into Tim's temple. Giant tears dripped down the boy's face. Spattered blood drops covered his orange hoodie like a gruesome game of Connect the Dots strewn across the Hillside Tigers emblem.

Justin had been right. The Stewart family was destined to meet a ferocious, carnivorous beast that day. They may have fared better against an actual wildcat than her maleficent brother.

Tigers could be distracted. Frightened. Tamed. Wounded.

Justin was a beast of a different sort. The kind that spawned straight out of the deepest level of hell.

"It's time, Winter. Take care of her. Five! Four! Three!" Justin screamed the countdown. His contact-darkened eyes were glazed with insanity.

There was no point in attempting to call his bluff.

He had no bluff to call.

Winter briefly wondered if she should let Justin kill Tim and save the boy from the lifetime of agony and remorse that awaited him.

Tim's giant brown eyes met hers, his shaggy hair pasted against his head with a mixture of sweat and tears. Pain stabbed between Winter's ribs.

She couldn't let that child die. She just couldn't.

There were no guarantees that Tim would wake to another morning even if she obeyed Justin's command to kill his mother, but she *was* certain her brother would kill Andrea either way.

Andrea was never going to make it out of this campground.

"Three! Two!"

Winter stepped forward and wrapped her arms around Andrea's neck. The woman had already accepted her fate and spoke to her child through her tears. "Timmy, Mommy loves—"

"One!"

Crack.

Husband and wife sat side by side, bound to chairs they no longer needed inside of a camper they no longer could see, and sheltered from the winter wind that would never chill them again. Their heads dangled at identical angles. Wrong angles.

Dead angles.

You did that. You murdered them.

A sudden calm came over her, a calm as still as the dead woman in front of her. She understood so clearly what she had to do.

What she *would* do.

Justin's high-pitched, feverish cheers were mere white noise now. He pushed Tim to the floor, and the boy, still bound, tried to scoot toward his mother's dead body.

Wait.

Winter absorbed the tragic scene, her resolve hardening at the way Tim's eyebrows arched up in misery and the rivers of tears cascaded down his ashen face. The child wasn't out of the line of fire, but the gun was no longer pressed to his skull.

Wait.

Justin stepped toward the counter, picked up his phone, and tapped a button. Winter didn't know or care why. She watched and waited.

She only needed one chance.

The split second Justin appeared fully engrossed in his phone, Winter charged. Leading with her shoulder, she put all her weight into one solid blow, colliding into her brother with a force that would make any linebacker proud.

Justin flew backward, crashing into the RV door. The flimsy lock gave instantly, and they both tumbled outside onto the snow-covered dirt.

Winter struck the ground hard, landing shoulder-first, but she ignored the pain and sprang to her feet. Without stopping, she reared back her arm and slammed her fist into her little brother's face, following the punch with another, and another, and another. Tears blinded her, but she kept on swinging.

She was going to kill him. She *had* to kill him.

Another fist raised high and—

Bam!

A bullet ripped through Winter's upper arm, sending her rocking backward.

Pain seared her flesh, stealing her breath away.

Can't. Stop. Now.

She let her left arm dangle while her right fist swung for another blow. Before the punch landed, the gun slammed down on her wrist. Fire shrieked up her arm before her entire hand and forearm went numb.

Panting, she lashed out with her legs, putting every bit of power into the kicks.

"I hate you! I haaate you!" Tears blurred her vision, but she somehow managed to connect with her feet. "I wish you'd died with Mom and Dad!"

The terrible words were still ringing in the frigid air when Justin's hand whipped out and latched onto her arm. Before she could pull away, his fingers pressed into the bullet wound.

She gasped, her vision flashing white with pain. Still, she kept kicking, refusing to give up even as her surroundings blurred.

Giving up wasn't an option. Not until Justin was dead.

Those cruel fingers dug deeper into the wound, ripping into her flesh and magnifying the agony to a point where she feared she would blackout.

Kick harder. You have to kill him. There's no other way.

The familiar prick of a needle sinking into her flesh sent a surge of panic through her body. The world fogged. Her legs went still.

She remembered his soft, pudgy-cheeked face for the millionth time.

"Sissy, I love you to the moon and around all the stars in the big, big universe."

But the little boy who'd said those words was dead. Justin didn't love her anymore. He didn't love anything because he no longer had the ability.

As the fog grew thicker and merciful blackness claimed her, Winter realized she didn't love him either. It was so strange...

All that time she'd spent fighting and raging against the truth only to discover that she loved a ghost.

22

A utumn drummed her fingers on the conference room table, passing the time while a never-ending tinny melody played in her ear. Being subjected to elevator music while placed on hold might be a feasible, death-free alternative to capital punishment.

Then again, she supposed enduring all four minutes of "Sailing" on her phone wasn't so bad when compared to her recent experience inside an actual elevator car.

Cheesy, soft-rock songs beat a dead nurse dropping through the ceiling any day of the week.

She groaned as the Muzak continued. Here she was, back at the Richmond Field Office, and yet she still couldn't escape interacting with Virginia State Hospital. Considering her career path, she'd known mental wards would be a permanent part of her daily life, but she was ready to be done with this chapter of her career.

She prayed they put Justin somewhere else when they found him. Somewhere far away. Of course, that was assuming they did find him.

Or Winter.

You will. You will you will you will.

Autumn's gut clenched. She desperately wanted to believe her own mantra, but every minute that ticked by intensified her internal battle with doubt and fear. Sitting on hold in an empty conference room while being bounced from department to department by Virginia State's receptionists wasn't helping either.

All she needed was Justin Black's visitor log faxed over to her immediately. So far, she hadn't even been able to get the full sentence out before being transferred or stuck back in the land of easy-listenin' tunes.

When a new song kicked off, Autumn decided she'd had enough. She ended the call and dug through her bag, searching for the interim medical director's business card. After Dr. Maeve Carpenter had scribbled her personal cell number across the back and handed over the card, she'd told Autumn to call if she needed anything.

Autumn didn't suppose the doctor meant at eight o'clock in the evening. Nevertheless, she needed Dr. Carpenter's help.

Before the first ring was through, the doctor answered her phone. "Dr. Carpenter." Her greeting was just as polite and professional as if the sun were still shining high in the sky.

"Hi, Dr. Carpenter, this is Dr. Autumn Trent. I'm sorry for calling you so late." Autumn hesitated, unsure if the pleasantries would continue.

"Oh, stop. I told you to call me whenever you needed, and I'm still at the hospital anyway. I'll probably be living here for a few weeks judging from today." The medical director's warmth didn't diminish in the slightest. "And please, call me Maeve."

"Only if you call me Autumn."

"Done. What can I help you with, Autumn?"

"Visitor logs. I need the records of Justin Black's visitor logs since he was first admitted to Virginia State. And if possible, his call logs as well." Autumn winced, hoping she wasn't asking too much. Maeve was already dealing with a giant storm of chaos by stepping in to fill Philip Baldwin's shoes.

"Well, I can have the visitor logs to you in a flash. And the call logs shouldn't be impossible to retrieve either. The phones here work much the same as the prison system, meaning collect calls only." The rapid clicking of a keyboard in the background told Autumn that either the doctor was jumping on the task already, or else Autumn's call had interrupted her mid-task.

"I really am sorry to intrude upon your time, Maeve. If this wasn't of such high importance, I would never—"

"No apologizing. I know what you're dealing with. *Who* you're dealing with. I want to assist in finding Justin Black however I possibly can."

"Do you have any idea how long pulling up those records will take?" Autumn was pushing, but the cause was worthy.

Winter.

"Not long. I'll get them out to you as fast as possible. Promise." The genuine kindness in Maeve's voice was like snuggling under a fleece blanket after a long, frigid day. Almost motherly.

"Thank you so much. Truly." Autumn would have hugged the woman had they been near each other.

"Not a problem. Hang in there, Dr. Trent. You're going to find her." Maeve ended the call, and Autumn sank into the plastic chair.

Now what?

Autumn was out of ideas regarding what to do next. There was an ongoing nationwide manhunt for Justin and Winter. All modes of transportation had received alerts and posted the necessary warnings. The staff and patients of the hospital had all been interviewed, and she'd pored over Dr. Baldwin's notes twice.

Exhaustion bleated from every muscle in her body. Her frayed nerves were on the edge of completely splitting apart. What else was there to do but scan through Philip's notes yet again?

Autumn pulled the files to her. She tried to tell herself there still could be worthwhile information in them. Human eyes were prone to missing even the most important details. Her third read over could be more effective than the first.

And your eighty-fifth could be more enlightening than your third. When are you going to admit that there might be nothing to find in those papers?

Rather than follow that thought down the rabbit hole, Autumn grabbed the top sheet with a steady, determined hand. She was interrupted, however, by the creak of the conference room door.

When Noah slouched his way inside without making eye contact, Autumn tensed, bracing herself for another attack. He kept his haggard face downturned, though, and walked straight to the table, dropping into the chair beside her in silence. His lips parted as though he intended to speak, but no words escaped before his shoulders started shaking, and he burst into tears.

Autumn's heart constricted, and she didn't hesitate to wrap her arms around him and squeeze.

"I'm so sorry. I didn't...I don't even know how I could have said those things to you. I didn't mean them, Autumn. I was just so...I'm so...I should have *stopped* her."

She stroked the back of his head while her own eyes flooded with tears. "I'm sorry too. I wish I had prevented this. I wish I had made the call."

They stayed locked in the embrace as seconds ticked by,

two heartbroken friends trying to help each other find a way through the madness and fear.

Neither of them would ever give up hope, but both of them desperately needed comfort as they faced the fact that the day was ending, and Winter was still missing. Every hour that passed was another hour that the unthinkable could have happened.

Heavy footsteps alerted Autumn to a new arrival, and she turned her head. Chris stared at them from just inside the door, a nasty smirk spreading across his face.

"Well, well. What have we here? You guys aren't even going to let Winter's dead body grow cold before you fire up the jets?" Chris followed the remark with a wink.

Noah was out of his chair in a flash. Autumn shot out a hand and latched on to his arm, pulling herself up and swinging her body in between the two men before Noah had the chance to crush Chris with the full force of his rage.

"You son of a bitch!" Spittle flew from Noah's lips.

"Apparently, you are too," Chris shot back.

Autumn put a hand on Noah's chest. "No. You can't do this. Not now." Her jaw clenched as she stretched her neck around toward Agent Parker, searching his face for any sign of intelligence. "Seriously. What is *wrong* with you?"

"*Me?*" Chris raised his arms in mock exasperation. "I'm sorry, but I wasn't the one mauling my best friend's boyfriend two seconds ago. What is wrong with *you?*"

Autumn was convinced the man before her did not possess a soul.

Aiden rushed into the room. Instead of acknowledging the obvious strife, the SSA picked up the remote to the wall-mounted flatscreen and began flipping through channels. His frenzied clicks and grim expression were more than enough to interrupt the two hotheads and command all their attention.

Sun and Bree raced into the room next. Both women's eyes shot straight to the screen. Mia skidded in after them, her attention also glued to the television.

The alarm bells in Autumn's head were ringing at full blast. There'd obviously been a new development, and she doubted it was anything good.

Aiden came to a sudden stop on a news channel. Autumn tensed.

Now what?

She didn't have to wait long to find out.

A video played under the sensational headline: FBI Agent Joins Serial Killer Sibling on Horrendous Murder Spree.

The reporter made a grim announcement. *"The violence in the following footage is very upsetting and difficult to watch. Viewer discretion is advised."*

The screen shifted, and Autumn's breath caught in her throat when she recognized the person featured in the footage.

The woman's hair was streaked with red and black like a punk rock concertgoer and cropped short, but there was no mistaking that face.

Winter.

Her friend stood behind a man and woman who were bound to chairs, their faces blurred to hide their identities.

Dread crawled across Autumn's skin, and the sensation intensified when her gaze shifted back to Winter's face. Her friend's expression was fixed in a mask of horror. Whatever was going on behind the scenes had put Agent Black in a state of acute distress.

Something terrible was going to happen. Autumn could feel it in her bones.

"Turn up the volume!" Noah yelled, charging toward the screen.

Aiden shook his head. "The video was uploaded with no

sound at all. Associated Press news received the video with a note that simply read, *'How an FBI agent gets the job done.'* Nothing else."

During the few seconds it took for that exchange, Winter's expression changed, morphing from horror to what Autumn perceived as resignation before her friend's eyes turned flat.

Oh, god...

Autumn lifted her hand, as if she could somehow stop the events from unfolding, while in the video, Winter stepped forward, her motions stiff and robotic.

In the next moment, Winter positioned her arms around the man's head and broke his neck with a single twist.

Autumn gasped as shock barreled through her. Had that really just happened?

The video glitched for a split second before the footage resumed. Winter was now stationed behind the woman, who was shaking and saying something Autumn couldn't quite understand, though lip readers would most likely be able to translate the words in a few seconds.

Winter's hands latched onto the woman and gave her head a violent jerk. She stopped moving after that. The camera showed her head dangling at a loose, unnatural angle before the video cut out.

A somber male newscaster appeared, replacing the horrific scene. He clasped his hands together on the counter before him and spoke with gravity. *"This disturbing footage was shared with AP news just within the previous hour. We had to cut the recording short due to the upsetting, violent nature, but it appears that there is a third victim as well, a teenage girl. While officials are hard at work to track the video's source, one thing has been confirmed. The assailant seen murdering two individuals and assumed responsible for the third is none other than Federal Agent Winter Black with the Federal Bureau of Investigation. Black went missing yesterday, the same day her criminally insane brother broke out of Virginia State Hospital. If anyone has information regarding the identities of the victims or Justin or Winter Black, here is the number to contact..."*

Autumn turned toward Noah, who had sunk into a chair, his face pale as death. She imagined his shock was even greater than her own. That was the woman he loved, shared a bed with, shared a *life* with.

She walked to him, kneeling to meet his blank stare. "She must not have had any choice. Winter would never murder anyone if she had even the slightest option to do otherwise."

Noah said nothing, and Autumn found she had no more words to share. The incomprehensible acts they'd just viewed Winter commit overwhelmed her mind, clouding up all channels of logic and reasoning.

There was nothing Noah or anyone else in the room could say. After what had just been broadcast across the nation, if not the entire world, Winter was ruined. Even if they found her alive and proved her innocence, her credibility as an agent would never recover.

And her mind...

Autumn bowed her head, her throat tight with unshed tears. She knew Winter's heart and couldn't imagine an existence where Winter Black was able to experience peace...*happiness*...after what she had done to those people.

Even though she'd been forced—Autumn refused to believe there was another explanation— Winter would forever view herself as a killer.

Even the strongest support from friends and lovers might not be enough to erase Winter's guilt over what she had done.

23

Aiden and his team arrived at the obscure campground near Cherokee, North Carolina, just after dawn.

Shortly after viewing the newscast, a family member of the victims had called the local authorities. They'd recognized their loved ones and knew where the family was camping. Though a nationwide, broadcasted home video was one hell of an awful way to find out that multiple people you cared about were dead—*murdered* at that—Aiden was grateful that they finally had a lead.

The short flight from Richmond to Asheville was followed by an even shorter drive in rented Tahoes to the outskirts of the tiny town. He, Autumn, and Noah led the way while Bree, Chris, Mia, and Miguel followed closely behind.

On the drive from the airport to Cherokee, a tech had tried to explain all the mumbo jumbo issues that were making the task of finding the email's origin so difficult. Cyber continued to attempt to trace the email, but the "gift" had been sent through a disposable email site.

As the tech who'd taken his call explained, "Whoever sent

the footage in wasn't playing. He used a live privacy distro and set the remailer to three hops with fifteen minutes latency. Cracking this code isn't quick work, Agent Parrish."

Aiden hadn't understood most of the terminology but had gathered that tracing the email was going to be more than a little difficult. The tech spoke as if the feat was damn near impossible, which caused Agent Parrish's frustration to compound upon itself yet again. "I don't care how hard this is. You're not paid to play with kittens. Do your damn job and keep trying," he'd barked into the phone before hanging up.

Neither Autumn in the passenger's seat nor Noah in the back had said a word.

What was there to say aside from a few choice expletives?

The proper RV was identified by local authorities before the federal agents had arrived, and the deceased Stewart family was found, as expected, inside. Aiden stood still in a designated spot near the camper door while the forensic team bustled about him, already hard at work. He scanned the bodies of Greg, Andrea, and Nicole Stewart, which thus far hadn't been moved.

Once every last detail and piece of evidence had been photographed and documented, the deceased would be removed with painstaking care and transferred for autopsy. The loss was significant. Father, mother, *and* child. But what bothered Aiden more was the fact that a fourth family member assumed to have been present for the camping getaway was missing.

Timothy Stewart was just eight years old. He had either survived the massacre somehow, or his dead body was waiting to be found. When Aiden considered that he could have been taken alive by the likes of Justin Black, the thought was immediately chased by another.

Maybe young Tim would be better off dead.

That wasn't a notion he'd be sharing with the family or even his agents, but Aiden was almost certain he couldn't be the only one to have considered the truth in that sentiment. The plans Justin might have in mind for that little boy were terrifying to contemplate.

Aiden caught the attention of the medical examiner, waved him over, and waited in silence while the older man made his way through a maze of tape.

"Special Supervisory Agent Aiden Parrish with the FBI's BAU out of Richmond. I'm hoping that you've been able to establish an approximate time of death." He studied the M.E., who bore the semblance of a man who belonged in a rocker by a fireplace and not out here in the frigid cold surrounded by corpses.

"I'm estimating the Stewarts passed between twelve to fifteen hours ago. Autopsies might narrow that window down a bit, and we should be able to establish the official order of the deaths. It's a shame." He glanced to his right, where the blonde-haired teenage daughter still rested amongst a macabre landscape of congealed blood and brain splatter. "It's a damn shame."

Aiden was already running the numbers through his head. That time frame would put the murders just prior to the video being emailed in.

Stepping back out into the fresh air, he inhaled deeply. Death had a distinctive scent, and he'd never gotten used to that particular stench. The biting January wind was a sweet and instant reprieve.

The entire surrounding area of the camper had also been taped off. A few feet away, a crime scene tech scraped up what appeared to be blood off the ground.

Fear wormed down Aiden's spine.

That could be Winter's blood. The worst may have already happened.

Aiden rejected the thought. Until they found her dead body, he refused to believe Agent Black wasn't still alive and breathing.

He spotted the local sheriff, Dennis Cagle, and approached the man without delay. "Sheriff Cagle, I'm Special Supervisory Agent Aiden Parrish. Here to assist, not to intrude." Aiden offered a leather-gloved hand, and Dennis shook it roughly.

"If this weren't my damn job, I'd hand the whole thing to ya gladly." The sheriff lifted his gaze to the sky, dark eyes surrounded by worry lines that Aiden guessed had been years in the making. The man wasn't old, exactly. Much younger than the medical examiner, who was going to need a replacement in the not-too-distant future.

But Aiden was certain Sheriff Cagle was older than himself, and that fact alone meant the man had witnessed a lot. Even a "quiet" career in law enforcement provided abundant views to the dark side of humanity.

"I understand. Not a pretty scene in there." Aiden tilted his head toward the RV.

Dennis shoved his bare hands deep into his coat pockets. "That's a downright nightmare in there."

Aiden couldn't disagree.

"I've seen a lot of shit in my day, and there's a lotta things stuck in this old brain that I wish to god I knew how to clear out. But this? This was the worst. This wasn't just murder. It was *torture*. We don't know if the kid witnessed her parents die or vice versa. They'll sort all that out, I expect. But there was no reason to…" Dennis's naturally low voice had turned into a growl. "The sick bastard *enjoyed* making those kids watch. That's what I think."

Sheriff Cagle obviously wasn't well acquainted with the sadist fiend that was Justin Black. Aiden was surprised that

Winter's little brother hadn't done worse. Raped the girl's dead body or another equally savage act.

Then again, they had no idea what had happened to Tim yet. Justin wouldn't be satiated by one or two or three killings. He would *always* need more.

It was part of his mission.

Dennis pulled a pack of Marlboro Reds from his pocket. "That girl was just thirteen damn years old. *Thirteen.* And the younger one, the boy, is only *eight.* Barely out of Underoos. God knows what happened to him." He scanned the distance, where an active search had been put into motion.

"We'll find out." Aiden wished there was some positive spin he could add to the statement, but based on the fate of the boy's family, the outlook of Tim's future wasn't bright.

"We've got multiple search teams out there. Missing person dogs. Cadaver dogs. And I can't lie, Agent Parrish. There's a part of me that doesn't want to know." He cleared his throat and stamped at the ground. "All we've found so far is an empty car parked back in the woods. It isn't the Stewarts' vehicle, which is missing too, by the way."

Aiden's interest peaked. "So, the car in the woods belongs to...?"

"Registered to a Roger Jones from Richmond, Virginia. We don't know the connection there yet, but I suppose everything will come out in due time. Always does." Dennis let out a ragged sigh. "A downright nightmare."

"Thank you for your time, Sheriff Cagle. Here's my card if any new and pertinent information should arise. I won't be far." Aiden handed Dennis his information and walked away to find a quieter spot.

Richmond's medical examiner answered on the third ring, sounding much more pulled together than Aiden could claim to be.

"We may have a name to go with the body from the trunk.

Roger Jones. Richmond resident." Aiden spit out the information in a rapid, emotionless voice.

"On it. I'll let you know." The M.E. was gone in a flash, and Aiden was grateful that he didn't have to give further instructions.

That would require energy and patience he lacked at the moment.

He rotated his neck from side to side, hoping to combat the ache starting to set in. All cases were taxing in one way or another. The light at the end of the tunnel was that answers would eventually be found, happy or otherwise.

The conclusion of *this* case, however, involved Winter Black's fate. Her life.

He would charge ahead as he always did, but the knowledge that the blanks would be filled in one by one carried with it a looming terror. This puzzle, when all the pieces were found, would show a picture of someone he cared for... someone he felt responsible for.

There was no way to predict what kind of image they were locking together.

He sucked in a few deep breaths through his mouth, allowing the sting of frigid winter air in his lungs to help him refocus. Letting his mind wander too far off would render him useless with anxiety. Aiden had to stay clearheaded for Winter, despite the fact that her involvement with this case had triggered his mental fog.

As he turned back toward the crime scene to gather his agents, he reminded himself that there were many brilliant minds working together to solve this case.

Oh, and Parker was on the job as well.

"Agents, we've got an estimated time of death for the Stewart family. The coroner gives a window of five to eight yesterday evening. The last person to have laid eyes on Black that we know of was his public defender," he looked at his watch, "about thirty-six hours ago. We need to take that time gap and fill it in." Aiden surveyed their faces, noting that Noah refused to make eye contact.

"You think that's gonna help us now? After all this?" Chris gestured toward the camper. His disapproval was expected, and yet Aiden still fought the urge to bury his fist in the man's annoying face.

"There's a possibility that whatever happened between Virginia State Hospital and this RV park could shed some light on where Justin and Winter might be headed next." Aiden answered Chris's question without even glancing at the man. "There's an APB out for the Stewarts' car, which appears to have been taken. Another vehicle registered to Roger Jones from Richmond has been found not far from here in the woods."

"That's our John Doe." Bree immediately ascertained what Aiden himself believed to be true.

He nodded at her. "My gut says yes. The Stewart's eight-year-old son is still missing. Justin may have kidnapped him, or the child could be..." Aiden didn't have to finish that sentence.

"If he's here, the dogs will find him fast. Sniffing out a dead kid is nothing for them." Chris's compassionless words earned him a sharp glare from Mia. Miguel stood beside her, blatant disgust blanketing his face at Parker's commentary.

"He may very well be *alive*," Autumn snapped. Her bright auburn hair whipped in haphazard waves across her face, and she shivered as she spoke.

Chris rolled his eyes. "And he may very well *be dead*."

"Enough," Aiden barked. "We have a timeline and a park full of RVs to consider. The park owner needs to be contacted immediately and a search warrant secured."

"I can work on that." Bree whipped her phone from her coat pocket as she volunteered.

"Every camper. Every single camper gets checked." Noah broke his silence with a suggestion that came across as a demand.

While Aiden would have found the tone obnoxious on a normal day, this was not a normal day, and he understood the gravity of Agent Dalton's words. He clapped a hand on Noah's shoulder and agreed. "Every single one, Dalton."

24

Noah stomped over the mud-covered ground with patches of snow still dotting the area, pausing to examine each and every RV parked in the enormous campground. He couldn't actually enter any of the vehicles yet, regardless of what he came across, and neither could his fellow agents who had split to survey the other rows.

Nothing prevented Noah from inspecting windows, though, and there were plenty of opportunities to do so. People apparently just paid to leave these beasts sitting out most of the year. If he had one, he'd be traveling around the damn world in that sucker.

With Winter at his side.

His lungs hitched as fear and longing clenched his ribs. No one had been able to make contact with the campground's owners. Noah considered that he'd picked the wrong career when he learned the couple was vacationing in *Europe*. Who knew owning an RV park was such a lucrative business?

Sun had taken over the hunt back at the Richmond Field Office, trying to find anyone from the park's maintenance team who would take care of common wintertime complaints. So far, Agent Ming had hit a veritable brick wall in that arena as well.

Though successful contact had been made with the owner's niece, she'd been the one to inform them that her uncle had switched maintenance companies the previous November. And as crap luck would have it, she did not know the current company's information.

She'd provided direct cell numbers for both owners and had promised to keep calling them herself as well. Noah wasn't an expert on leisurely world travels, as his time overseas had been spent dodging bullets and bombs in the excruciating desert heat, but he had a strong inclination to believe that random calls from the States weren't topping the couple's list of priorities at the moment.

Noah didn't give two damns about policies and permissions at this point. Searching the park *in full* was mandatory if they were to find any signs that Winter and Justin had been sheltered in one of the RVs. If he spotted something suspicious, his actions would be based on securing Winter's safety.

Not a godforsaken search warrant.

His entire life had been spent walking the straight and narrow path. Desperate times called for desperate measures, though, and the woman he intended to spend the rest of his life with superseded all else.

Why here? Why North Carolina?

The question came as a continuous swirl inside his mind. He knew the Black siblings' history well, yet he could think of no reason for the geographical direction Justin had taken. Noah also refused to believe that Winter had any control over the situation whatsoever. Wherever they were going, she wasn't making the calls.

There had to be a reason that little bastard was making

the moves he had so far. Justin was a calculating sonofabitch, if he was anything. He had a plan. Noah was sure of that.

Aiden hailed him from one aisle over as he reached a gravel cross-path that divided the park into "blocks" of sorts. Noah decided that he must have been searching the hardest because the rest of the team had already gathered around the SSA.

Heat seared his chest. Were they actually searching or just chitchatting their way around the damn things?

Aiden proceeded to speak before Noah had a chance to demand answers.

"I've just been informed that the fingerprints on the tape binding Greg and Andrea Stewart's wrists, as well as the strips placed over their mouths, are a direct match with Agent Black's. The bullet fired into Nicole's head was linked to Winter's service weapon." Aiden delivered the information in a calm manner, but the anger Noah sensed emanating from the SSA matched his own.

It was ludicrous for anyone to ever think that Winter was responsible for these murders or any of the mayhem that Justin left in his wake, and yet that was exactly how the media would spin the situation. With that kind of information circling through the masses, the general public opinion would all but convict Winter of multiple murders before she'd even been found.

Noah knew, as did Aiden, that Justin was conniving enough to orchestrate all of this. The shit-stain would love nothing more than to ruin Winter's good name, and the fact that he might be pulling the mission off made Noah's blood boil.

"Well, this implicates Winter's voluntary involvement. I mean, did he hold her hands and make her tape them up?" Chris opened his mouth, always the first to share and the last to understand. "She's *helping* him. She may be nursing some long-buried impulse to kill as a result of her ordeal at such a young age with The Preacher."

"That's ridiculous, Parker. Winter Black didn't just wake up two days ago and decide to become a murderer." Aiden seethed, staring at Chris with an unmasked anger Noah rarely witnessed from the man. "That's not how the brain works, and given your placement in the BAU, you should know that. If Justin has possession of her gun, there's quite a bit he can force her to do. Use your damn brain."

"She killed two people on video, and you're still defending her!" Chris roared back. "Wake up, Parrish. Winter Black isn't the golden child hero you want her to be!"

Parker's accusations snapped the thin thread of Noah's control. He lunged forward and seized the agent by his throat, barreling him backward against the nearest RV. Squeezing the air out of Chris's stupid throat seemed necessary. "Shut your mouth, asshole! Shut your damn mouth!"

Aiden and Miguel were pulling them apart in an instant, each of them taking one of Noah's arms and yanking him away from Parker. Chris coughed a few times, then a few more with added emphasis, before standing to face Noah.

"You just tried to *kill* me, Dalton! What the hell!" Chris straightened his coat and used both hands to pat around his hair, ensuring no damage had been done there.

"If I wanted you dead, you'd be dead, Parker!" Noah shouted back.

"Agent Parker, if you don't stop stirring the pot in the wrong direction every cursed chance you get, you will be off this case!" Aiden glared at Parker, clearly near the end of his rope with the agent's bullshit too. "Do you understand me?"

Chris shook his head, hands returning to his throat as his vanished cough made a reappearance. "My *job* is to create profiles on murderers! No one can deny that Winter murdered two, count them, *two people*. As the head of the

BAU, shouldn't you appreciate the unbiased effort I'm providing? Or are you too damn biased yourself to be able to do that, Parrish?"

Aiden didn't shout back. He emitted a low growl and took a step toward Chris. Noah was sure Parker was going to get attacked again and was more than happy to pop some corn and take a seat. Before Noah's bloodlust could be satisfied, the indignant agent threw his arms up and walked away, his blond pompadour unharmed.

Chris probably wasn't sure anyone would save him this time. And as far as Noah was concerned, retreating was the wise choice.

Noah glanced at Autumn, whose bright green eyes were wide with sad horror. This was not acceptable federal agent behavior, and they all knew that. The stress of losing one of their own was chipping away at their defenses, breaking them down hour by hour.

"We have to pull ourselves together." Aiden stared at the ground. His breathing was still audibly ragged, but Noah knew the man would steel himself over again in the following seconds.

Aiden Parrish didn't lose his cool. Ever. Noah had always found the fact annoying as hell. Somehow, knowing that he could and would go berserk for Winter was both comforting and bothersome.

Noah had never liked the bond between the two, platonic as it had proven to be.

"It might be possible to gather footage from business and residential cameras on all of the routes that exit the campground. The search for the Stewarts' car would go faster if there was even one or two glimpses of the direction they headed in." Bree appeared to have chosen to ignore the ill-behaved men altogether, which was probably the smart move.

"You're right. We've done it before. Excellent call, Agent Stafford. I'd appreciate it if you would head to the Cherokee Police Station and get that started right away." Aiden was himself again, just like that, and probably felt more than a little foolish for his behavior.

Still, Noah doubted any of them would be laughing over beers about what had just transpired anytime soon, if ever. Not at the annual Christmas party, not at the local bar...

Bree didn't wait to be asked twice. She jogged back down the lane to carry out her task while Noah and the remaining four dispersed to continue their search through the campground aisles.

If Noah stood still any longer, he foresaw spontaneous combustion in his immediate future. He needed to move. Seek. Find.

Looking through the windows no longer seemed good enough. Noah put his face to each one, blocking out the sunlight with his hands and searching every inch of RV interior that his eyes could reach. His process, though more thorough, was no doubt going to put him behind the others.

They'd be circling back before he'd made it to the end of his row, and then he'd be compelled to re-search their aisles.

And then you'll question your own searching and re-searching and be certain you missed something of consequence and lose your damn mind before you ever find your girlfriend.

He didn't expect a freaking burning bush, but a candle or even a spark of a clue wasn't too much to ask for, was it?

Noah was nearing the back of the park when he made out heavy foot traffic in front of an RV to his left. He stepped toward the run-down vehicle, smashing his face against the first uncovered window available on the old beast.

Messy. This camper was messier than the rest of the hibernating RVs he'd window inspected. From what he was detecting, this particular gem appeared used as well.

Recently used.

Hope sparked in Noah's chest as he walked to the door. He very nearly grabbed the handle then thought better of it, waiting until he'd pulled on a pair of gloves first. Instead of the blunt block of the lock, the door opened in one smooth motion.

Screw the warrant.

He stepped inside without hesitation and scanned the camper's interior as the faint scent of bleach and the overwhelming stench of dog piss assailed him. To his right, an ancient Formica table was bolted to a peeling laminate flooring. Pieces of the thin wood-paneled walls were broken off in multiple places throughout the vehicle, at times leaving only jagged slivers to insulate the inhabitants from the elements and wildlife alike.

There was only one main room and what appeared to be an attached bedroom in back. A very narrow door—the only interior door—stood next to the bedroom. He was almost certain it led to a bathroom. Whether or not the facilities were in working order was questionable.

Three kitchen cupboards above a rusted stainless steel sink were the full extent of the kitchen. Some half-empty water bottles sat scattered throughout the camper, and a paper plate on the cracked tabletop displayed a few cheese crackers beside a crust of white bread and a banana peel.

He wrinkled his nose. Craphole. The camper was an absolute craphole.

Noah took another step, almost knocking over a small trash can near his foot. Inside the container, an open box of hair dye and a used tube of red "Wax It Wild" gunk lay side by side atop a pile of...*used syringes.*

Noah's heart raced as he processed everything around him. Using only the tips of two gloved fingers, he picked up one of the hypodermic needles and read the label. The syringe had contained *haloperidol*, an incredibly powerful sedative.

Relief flooded his body, causing a rapid wave of dizziness. He'd been right. He *knew* he'd been right.

Justin had drugged Winter. *Heavily* drugged her.

Winter never would have done any of this on her own. Not in a million years. All he needed now was to make everyone believe him.

And he also desperately needed to find a way that allowed the team to search the RV without a warrant. Taking careful steps, he began to explore the tiny space. Yet another small trash can caught his eye near what he believed was the bathroom door. As he approached the basket, he spotted locks of long, black hair inside.

Every muscle of his body tensed, and his heart ached as he picked up a clump of strands, lifting them to his nose. One deep inhale was all he needed to know without a doubt that this was Winter's hair. He would recognize that sweet, perfect scent as long as he lived.

An idea came to him, and he moved in quick, careful motions to carry out the plan his mind had concocted in a split second of time.

Noah placed the hair on the floor right in front of the window he'd first peered into, exited the RV, and closed the door behind him. After yanking off his gloves, he pulled his phone out, calling Aiden immediately.

Maybe there should have been at least some guilt throbbing inside of him, but there wasn't. If anything, he only wished he could have told the lie sooner.

"Dalton?" Aiden's answer was gruff but expedient.

"I think I found something. I spotted some hair through a window on one of the RVs. It's long, Aiden. Long and black."

The sharp intake of air that Parrish took confirmed what Noah had already known. The falsehood was enough to sway the SSA. "That's cause for entry, especially under these circumstances. You wait right where you are. *Right where you are*, Dalton. I'll get the sheriff, and we'll check it out. We have to do this right. Dot every 'i' and cross every 't.' Sit tight."

Aiden ended the call, and Noah turned back toward the RV that Winter had been in not so long ago. Parrish could deal with the protocol because Noah didn't give a damn about any of that anymore.

He had only two clear goals to accomplish now.

Find Winter and kill her brother.

Justin Black had plagued the Earth for far too long, and it was past time Noah remedied that problem.

25

Autumn stared at the lengths of Winter's hair splayed on the floor of the RV. The sight wrenched at her abdomen, causing her physical pain and somehow making the reality of what was happening so much worse.

It's just hair. You're being ridiculous. Focus.

But the profound sense of loss that overtook her wouldn't be denied, whether she understood it or not.

"The syringes fill in the blanks." Noah's voice boomed through the tiny camper. "Justin's been injecting Winter with sedatives the entire time to keep her from fighting him."

Autumn opened her mouth to voice her agreement but stopped when Chris let out a dramatic snort. "Un-freaking-believable what the mind will do to deny, deny, deny."

Noah stalked toward the other agent, his hard stare latching onto Chris's insipid grin. Autumn jumped between the men just before another confrontation began, one arm stretched out toward each of them.

Maybe Parker *wanted* to be the fourth dead body in this campground. That would explain his atrocious behavior.

Aiden's phone rang, breaking through the ever-present

cloud of turmoil and sending all of them into stilted silence. He held up a finger, concentrating on the call. "Thank you."

Autumn held her breath as he repocketed his phone while Noah backed away from Chris, his full attention now on Agent Parrish. "Well?" he demanded.

"That was the lead crime scene tech. A quick cross-match with the blood outside of the Stewarts' RV confirms it was not Timothy's blood. His relatives shared that he was O positive, but the blood on the ground was AB negative."

Aiden directed the information at Noah, who'd gone deathly still.

When he spoke, his voice was uncharacteristically soft. "Winter is AB negative. We talked about it before. She said she had the rarest blood type of them all. I remember word for word."

Noah's face leeched of color, and even Chris's expression had turned grave.

"Do they know how much blood was spilled?" Autumn ventured the question, remembering the red puddle just outside the Stewarts' RV and how she'd worried over the severity of the wound.

Aiden held up a hand. "They estimate less than one unit. All is not lost, Agents." Again, he directed his words toward Noah.

Autumn relaxed slightly at the additional information. She'd once been in a serious relationship with a medical examiner, Dan Nguyen, and had learned all kinds of trivia from the man concerning this subject. If Winter had received an arterial wound, there would have been much more blood on the ground, and her chances of still being alive would have been far slimmer.

A flesh wound, however, would cause much less bleeding and explain the amount the tech had mentioned. Serious, but not fatal. Hopefully.

Her own phone rang. To her surprise, Dr. Philip Baldwin was the caller shown on screen. Autumn stepped toward the front of the RV and out the door. They all needed to leave this crime scene, and her movement also gained her a little privacy. "Dr. Baldwin?"

"Yes. I'm sorry to bother you in the midst of everything you're dealing with, but I viewed the news about the Stewart family murders, and I've formed a theory that I'd like to share with you." Philip's apologetic tone was matched by his evident urgency.

"Of course. Go ahead." Autumn would have taken a thousand interruptions if even one of them shed light on her friend's situation.

"I recalled Justin speaking to me one day while I was escorting him back to his room, which explains why the memory wasn't recorded in my notes. We were discussing what it would take for him to feel 'free' in the emotional sense of the word." The psychiatrist cleared his throat, and Autumn noted with relief that he seemed completely sober.

"And? What did he say?"

"He told me he could only be free if he was able to pass on all that Kilroy taught him. He needed someone else to join him in his murderous acts to ensure Kilroy's vision lived on. I wonder if this is what he's trying to do with his sister." Philip posed a possibility that Autumn had considered even before this new information was shared.

"I think there's a strong likelihood that he is attempting to do exactly that." She walked over to a window and looked into the dirty glass, staring at the mussed bed where her friend may have been drugged into sleep only hours ago.

"And do you believe Winter would be susceptible to such overtures?" Philip's voice was apologetic again, but Autumn understood that he had to ask.

"Absolutely not." Autumn stood firm in her stance.

"Winter isn't a killer. She doesn't have it within her to become one either."

"But—"

"I know what the video showed." Autumn was aware that an edge of desperation clung to her words. "I get that what I'm saying flies direct in the face of that footage, but I still believe with everything inside of me that Winter only killed the couple because she had no other choice. I'm asking you to trust me on this one. I know who Winter is."

If Winter were ever to live a semi-normal existence after this, there had to be a way to convince others, especially those in positions of high-credentialed authority such as Dr. Philip Baldwin. Agent Black would need a veritable army to stand behind her and defend her innocence to the masses.

"Okay. Then let's consider this. Is it possible that Winter would buckle and play along to ensure her survival, with the eventual intention of escape?"

Autumn considered the question. Philip had posed an interesting twist.

"If she's caught wind that Justin desires to bring her over to the 'dark side,' so to speak, Winter would likely play along enough to give him hope and give herself a chance to…" She couldn't go on, couldn't finish the thought.

"Live?" Philip finished for her.

"Yes." She closed her eyes.

No big deal. Just standing here discussing my best friend's chances of survival.

"If Agent Black has chosen to do this, perhaps the FBI should consider playing along as well."

Autumn tensed, following Philip's logic. "You're saying the FBI should publicly announce that they are *both* official suspects?"

"Indeed. Feeding into Justin's need to mentor someone the same way he himself was mentored could pacify him.

Even if that pacification was only minuscule, it would be enough to allow him to lower his guard a bit and would buy Winter more time. If the FBI declares Winter Black a criminal suspect, Justin will have the satisfaction of knocking her off her high horse, and his hopes for developing a sidekick of sorts in his sister will seem much more feasible."

"He'll be happy. A happy Justin lets Winter live. Or at least live longer." Autumn nodded, turning the idea over in her mind.

Most importantly, a living Winter stands a chance of escaping her psychotic brother.

"Precisely, Dr. Trent."

"Thank you. I'll be in touch." Autumn ended the call and turned toward the team, who had all left the RV and stood facing her with expectant stares, waiting for an update on whatever had sucked her into the phone call so thoroughly.

"What did Baldwin want?" Aiden studied her with his usual unreadable features, but she sensed a hint of annoyance in his tone.

"Two guesses. To be an asshole and…to be an asshole. What did I win?" Chris's douchebag-o-meter was limitless.

Autumn ignored him. "Justin had shared with Dr. Baldwin that he would only achieve true freedom when he found another soul to pass Kilroy's teachings to. He needed someone to join him. Philip seems to think that Justin might be trying to find a companion, a *sidekick*, in Winter."

"Pretty sure he's already pulled that off," Chris spouted.

Quick as a viper, Aiden pounced, slapping a hand to Parker's chest and shoving him back against a neighboring motor home's door. "This is your last warning, Parker! Shut your damn mouth, or I'm going to lock you in one of these RVs with Dalton and swear to any and all authorities that I never saw a thing!"

No one had expected that explosion, but the entire team

seemed to back up the sentiment. Noah's hands were clenched into white-knuckled fists, and Miguel had stepped back, apparently looking for anyone coming their way.

Autumn again wondered if she'd been sucked through a black hole without her knowledge or permission. The way they were all acting, the fact that Winter was missing, and Justin effing Black had escaped from the hospital…

The world had gone mad.

Chris shut his lips tight, appearing to understand for the first time that even the good guys had limits and that just *maybe* he didn't want to cross them. He folded his arms and lowered his eyes as Aiden stepped a few paces back. Autumn despised herself for the shot of sympathy in her chest.

Agent Parker deserved everything he got and then some, but he was still a human being. Her psychologist mind knew that his current attitude had its roots in years of events unknown to the rest of them.

Focus.

She ran a shaky hand through her hair. "Dr. Baldwin suggested that Winter would have figured this out by now and likely would play along to buy herself and any other innocent civilians they encountered more time. And furthermore, that if the FBI also played along, Justin would be even more pleased. Pleased and off guard. Relaxed."

"If he feels less pressure on top of satisfaction, he may make his next move at a much slower pace." Aiden nodded as he followed the proposed idea with ease.

"Slow is easier to catch." Miguel chimed in with the first hint of cheerfulness any of them had heard in days.

"I don't like it. We'd be asking the FBI to label one of its most exemplary agents as a murderer. Even if they retract the statement later with some type of explanation, that tag is gonna be on Winter forever. We all know that's true." Noah stared at Autumn, his expression severe.

"She could die a martyr, Noah. But then she'd be *dead*. Living and misunderstood is better than dead." Autumn wasn't sure that Noah could view the situation clearly at this point. She struggled to do the same herself.

Aiden pulled out his phone. "I'm calling Sun. We'll patch Bree in from the station. We need more opinions."

Autumn knew that what the SSA meant was they needed more unbiased opinions. The three of them—herself, Noah, and Aiden—were beyond invested in Winter's well-being. And with Chris not speaking at all, Mia acting as her partner's self-appointed babysitter, and Miguel ready to do whatever everyone decided was best, it was essential that the rest of the team weighed in.

After making the necessary connections, Aiden restated the dilemma and possible route of action to the entire team. Did they purposely allow the media to equate Winter Black with her serial killer brother if the move bought them time?

Bree voiced her immediate approval. Sun was quick to follow, adding her support with her "vote."

Noah took the nearly unanimous sentiment hard. He stared at Autumn as though the decision was theirs alone. "She might never forgive us for doing this, even if it keeps her alive. Winter will consider this as negotiating with terrorists, meaning you can't do it. She won't think saving her life was worth a lie of such…disgusting magnitude."

"Noah?" Mia's calm voice carried through the cold air. All eyes shot to the agent in surprise.

"Yeah?" Noah's attempt at an even tone missed the mark, leaving Autumn fretting that her friend was on the edge of a complete breakdown.

"Whether or not Winter forgives us is *her* call, not ours. She doesn't deserve to die, and if we can stop that from happening, we should. What happens after that isn't up to any of us…not even you." Mia spoke with kindness, but also with a firm conviction and confidence the team rarely witnessed from the quiet Agent Logan.

"Shitty things happen because shitty things happen..." Noah stared at Mia as he murmured the words, silent communication traveling between them.

Autumn didn't know what exactly he was referring to, but Mia seemed to. "Let's keep her alive."

He nodded, and Aiden picked up the phone, taking it off speaker. "Sun, I need you to work some magic. Fast."

As SSA Parrish put the plan into motion with the field office, Autumn went to Noah and curled a hand around his shoulder. The jolt of misery and doubt that poured out of him would have knocked her off her feet on a regular day. "I'll deal with the fallout when it's time," she vowed. "This is our best shot of catching up to them and bringing Winter home."

Noah put his hand on top of hers. "If it works."

"It will."

Autumn didn't voice the remainder of her thought, but the words echoed over and over in her head.

I hope.

26

W inter forced herself to crack open an eyelid. She'd been in and out of various states of consciousness the entire night and now well into the day. The one hazy fact she'd managed to gather was that they'd been driving nonstop. Justin had taken limited breaks, and she was almost positive that he hadn't slept at all.

She tried to straighten in her seat, wincing as the movement sent pain shooting through her arm.

You shot me, you sonofabitch. You shot me.

Granted, she'd intended to kill Justin…she still did. She would take ten more bullets if it meant her brother was actually dead.

She noted that her hands were bound together in a way that made moving her arms impossible, which explained the horrid pain when she'd attempted to do so. Justin had tied her bindings to the metal frame under her seat and done such a bang-up job of it that she couldn't move her hands any higher than her knees.

A soft flannel blanket that he must have stolen from the Stewarts was tossed over her lap, hiding the bindings from anyone else on the road who might have a view into the car. Between the ties and the sedatives, Winter was rendered useless once again.

Justin was on his phone...or *a* phone. Winter doubted he was dumb enough to use even a burner more than once. Her dear little brother thought of everything. But he didn't seem aware that she was awake.

She craned her neck to peer into the back seat. Tim was still sleeping, and she hadn't caught sight of him awake since their spontaneous journey began. What if Justin had given the boy the same amount of sedative he'd been giving her?

Her brother had flat-out admitted that he wasn't sure which was what as far as the medications went. Surely he had enough common sense to know a child that small couldn't handle the same dose as a grown adult.

Then again, he may have chosen to kill Tim via a needle. That was a much quieter and mess-free way to get rid of the only surviving Stewart family member. Later, her brother could just drop the body in a lake or river or ditch or dumpster.

Her awareness returning, Winter strained to eavesdrop on Justin's conversation.

"Yes, I ditched the effing Stewart vehicle. How stupid do you think I am? Seriously."

Winter glanced around, moving only her eyes and realized he was telling the truth. They were in a different car than the one she'd last fallen asleep in. This had to be what babies experienced when they fell asleep in one room only to wake up in another, moved by an invisible force whilst they slumbered. The switch was disorienting...upsetting.

The knowledge that she'd been so sedated that she hadn't even woken up when Justin transferred her from one vehicle to the next was just flat-out creepy. There was no telling what else he'd done to her while she slept.

"Grandpa had a hard-on for you, big sister, and I do too."

Winter suppressed a shudder. She was alive, and so was Tim.

At the moment, that was all that mattered.

"I *know* there's a lot of cameras in D.C. *Duh.*" Justin's anger was growing at what had to be a continual slew of questions. "It's a statement. You don't make a statement without cameras to capture it. Not in this world. And I'm planning to make a *big fucking statement.*"

Anxiety prickled her scalp. Big statement? What in the hell was he talking about? And who could he be talking to? Knowing that Justin had a "friend" on the outside who might be more than just a regular delusional fan was disturbing.

The last thing her brother needed was assistance from someone who was able to provide substantial aid.

"...and send the address. Thanks for the help. I gotta go." Justin ended the call and put the phone between his legs on the driver's seat. He glanced over at her, offering a wide smile. Winter noted the purple-hued swelling surrounding his right eye. His left cheekbone sported a crimson gash, either from his fall through the RV door or her multiple punches. His bottom lip was puffed up to twice its normal size. Handsome as her brother was, she'd managed to rough him up pretty well. "Good morning, dear sister."

"Who were you talking to?"

Justin ignored her and turned on the car radio, flipping stations until he hit a news channel.

"And the FBI has now confirmed that they are searching for a pair of killers in the wake of this gruesome series of deaths." A harried, breathless reporter spewed out the update.

Winter's eyes shot to Justin. *A pair?* He winked at her and turned up the volume.

"The first victim on this unthinkable murder spree was a male nurse at Virginia State Hospital in Richmond, Virginia. Dale

Miller was found dead in the facility's mental ward for criminally insane patients the same night that Black managed an escape."

Justin high-fived the steering wheel. "Right you are, reporter lady. Right you are."

"The trail continued with the discovery of murdered college student, Roger Jones, who was found in the trunk of Federal Agent Winter Black's abandoned car."

Winter whipped her head toward Justin, who just grinned and lifted a shoulder.

"But the worst finding by far has been the demise of the Stewart family, whose murders were taped and given to the Associated Press via an anonymous email. Though it is unclear who killed thirteen-year-old Nicole Stewart, the murders of Greg and Andrea Stewart were recorded. The couple appears to have been executed by Winter Black, who the authorities now believe is operating beside her brother willingly."

Justin busted into laughter at the end. Winter was so stunned by the report that she couldn't quite connect her mind to the horror burning deep in her chest at the accusation.

"So, be honest with me, Sissy. How bad does it suck to know that all of your coworkers and supposed friends turned on you just like that?" He snapped his fingers in front of her face. "That means your boytoy *and* your bestie think you have it in you to do aaalll of this. How's it *feel*?"

Winter didn't answer immediately. She tried to reason that the FBI must be putting into motion a much grander scheme. Civilians now had two faces to search for, which upped the odds of Justin being found simply by making her a target as well.

Surely no one who knew her held the actual belief that she'd broken her brother out of prison and helped him wreak this havoc.

"They would never believe that." She shook her head, fighting the tears stinging her eyes. "Never."

"Winter, why are you such a dumbass sometimes? You know the main thing I learned about your beloved Dr. Trent during her sessions with me? She's a flaky, over-hyped phony. She *knew* she was working with a psychopath harboring *major* abandonment issues, yet she kept disappearing. Hello! Trigger alert!" Justin sputtered out an incredulous laugh.

"Justin, that's not—"

"First, it was," he raised his voice a few octaves, "oh I'm sorry, Oregon, then welp, golly gee Pennsylvania, then oh darn it all to heck, Florida. And *then* she was too busy in *my own damn hospital* to even make it to my room? The heck?" Justin shook his head, displaying a dramatic exasperation that Winter knew was part acting and part true anger.

"Autumn was never your personal therapist, Justin. She had multiple jobs to do, and she was *kidnapped*, for god's sake." Winter tried to speak reason, if only to keep her own sanity. She knew what Justin was trying to do. Turn her against the people who had supposedly turned against her.

But she refused to believe that Noah or Autumn or even Aiden would ever accept that she was a killer. They knew her…

Didn't they?

She bit her cheek, uncertainty poking holes in her confidence.

Meanwhile, Justin's stern expression suggested that he didn't appreciate her defense of Autumn. Instead of jumping into a new rant, though, he burst into gleeful laughter. "I think you and I are finally making up for lost time, Sissy."

Winter's head throbbed, and she slumped into the seat. Her brother's mood swings were hard enough to handle when he was locked away. Now, in the free world, she couldn't keep up.

"You know, like I come home and tell you one of your stupid friends was mean to me on the playground. Like, knocked me off the monkey bars or gave me an atomic wedgie or any of that crap bitchy little kids do. You wouldn't believe me at first because you'd be all '*but Monica would never do that, Justin*,' and I'd bawl cuz your friends were jerks." He let out more high-pitched giggles, and his face flushed red with excitement.

Winter eyed him wearily. The crazy never stopped with Justin. He didn't even have a pause button.

"Then, you'd get *so* bothered thinking about someone picking on your baby brother that you'd confront the dumb ho, and she'd be *sooo* obviously guilty, and you'd tell her to get lost or get her ass kicked. You'd totally stick up for me in the end cuz that's what sibs do. Just like *I'm* sticking up for *you* right now and telling you that Autumn is a worthless piece of junk faker-friend, and dagnabit, you deserve better, Sis."

Justin had no idea how fast he was talking or how manic he'd become. Winter wasn't sure he remembered or even cared that she'd tried to kill him not long ago and had only been stopped by a bullet wound and heavy medication.

She instinctively opened her mouth to defend Autumn, but a sharp pain at her temples cut off the sentence. Just a flash of vision came this time, but the imagery was clear as day. The reel showed Justin tying her up inside a car and shooting the gas tank, causing the vehicle to explode.

Horror snaked through her veins. "No," she whispered.

"No, what? You know everything I'm saying is true. I'm a nutty guy, but I'm smart as hell. *Everybody* can agree on that." He laughed, pushing on the gas and flying down the road at breakneck speed.

Winter didn't know where they were or where they were going, but she knew her vision was a warning. A sign to shift gears and play along.

"You're right. I probably would have beat the crap out of 'Monica.' Then, I would have got detention and been grounded for defending your dumb butt." She smiled and shook her head as though the unreal memory was hysterical and sweet.

Justin bought it. He was on such a chemically imbalanced high that his ability to call bullshit had fogged. Her brother gave her leg a playful tap. "God, we woulda made a great team. But hey, we still can! Look at us. Look at us right now. Just cruising down the highway with ole Tiny Tim drooling away in the back seat. This is the stuff dreams are made of!"

Tim had been so silent that Winter wasn't one hundred percent sure he was even alive, but there was nothing she could do about that in the current moment. A stark thought sifted into her head, all the more terrible for its brutal truth.

You might be better off, little boy. Better off if you were dead with your family and not here, alive with mine.

"Tell me, Sis, and be honest. What'd it feel like to tie Greggy up before you killed him?" Justin glanced at her repeatedly, anticipating her answer.

His question yanked her back to that claustrophobic RV. Right to the sound the man's neck made just before he'd died.

Just before she'd murdered him.

Crack.

Winter's intestines cramped, and a wave of nausea slammed into her. "I don't want to talk about that, Justin. I should have...I wish I had been able to save him." She swallowed hard and stared out the window at the passing forest. Trees, trees, and more trees, with no end in sight.

As the green leaves flashed by, the nausea faded and was replaced by a welcome numbness. She felt detached from her own body, like she wasn't even real. Like none of this was real. Not Tim, or Justin, or the trees, or any of those bodies with the limp, dangling heads...

Or maybe she was already dead. Maybe she'd bled out on the ground back at the RV park, and this was her eternal punishment for murdering Greg and Andrea. A never-ending car ride with the insane brother she'd lost for good and the young boy she'd taken everything from. That made two little boys she'd failed to protect and save.

"Hey, the first time is hard, but you'll get past it. Trust me, you'll get waaay past it. And anyway, why *didn't* you save him? I mean, you followed orders like a trooper on that one." Justin put a hand to his chest as though he was shocked himself.

Fury flowed in and overpowered the numbness as she wrenched her head toward him. "I thought I could spare the rest of them. You told me you'd kill the entire Stewart family if I made one false move."

"Yeah, and you *listened to me*. How well did that work out for you, moron? You gotta stop believing what people say just because they say it. I kill people. That means if there are people involved, I'm going to kill them. Two plus two, Winter. Basic math." Justin's delight at lecturing her was maddening.

She swallowed the ball of rage that wanted to shoot out of her mouth like dragon fire and kept the charade going. "So, is my lesson learned now, Teach?"

Justin smirked and booped her nose with his pointer finger. "You're making progress. I can't deny that. But you've got a way to go yet, Sissy. I want you to grasp where I'm coming from and understand me in *every* way." He wiggled his eyebrows suggestively. "That takes time, but you just might get there."

Winter's stomach roiled. She wanted to vomit all over

Justin to give him a very clear picture of just what she thought about ever coming to "understand him in every way."

Except that wouldn't do anything beyond piss her brother off and send him straight into a rage. Justin's rage almost always ended with another dead body.

"I'm willing to try, Justin. To understand you, I mean." Winter spoke the words in the gentlest, most sincere tone she could manage.

"That's all I've ever wanted, Sissy. That's all I'm asking for." For once, his voice was thick with genuine emotion, and when his gaze slid to her, his blue eyes brimmed with unshed tears.

Joy flared in Winter's chest at the glimpse of the baby brother she remembered, but that emotion faded quickly, and she hardened her heart once again.

No matter what happened now, Justin's fate was set. The window for his redemption was closed.

It was Winter's responsibility to end this mess, and there was only one way to do that.

She had to kill her brother.

27

The utter elation coursing through my body filled me with an energy that was both electric and holy. I couldn't remember ever being so exhausted, and yet the lack of rest wasn't slowing me down in the least.

I pressed down on the gas pedal, turning the endless trees into a green blur as we raced down the deserted road. My skin hummed with power like I was invincible. Bulletproof. I was moving faster toward my destiny than I'd ever thought possible. Lightning fast. And I was covering every single base like a champ. No mistakes.

No mistakes.

With an irritated sigh at the reminder, I reined in my energy and eased my foot off the gas. Timewise, I could have already arrived at my destination, but using backroads was important. Yeah, they slowed me down, but that was a necessary evil. The amount of time I'd gain from leading the authorities in the wrong direction more than made up for the effort.

I'd driven west, toward good ole Chattanooga, Tennessee. I didn't need to actually reach the lights of the hillbilly metropolis. I just needed to make damn sure that's where I appeared to be headed.

A couple stops at convenience stores along the way were easy enough to make. At the first one, I made sure to stare straight into the camera while I paid for my gas. Maybe the footage would be checked, maybe not.

But even with my new look and the significant bruises gifted to me by Winter's awesomely uncontrolled rage, those Fed assholes would recognize me. They'd been obsessed with me forever. My face had to be emblazoned on their brains.

And they'd have more reason to check surveillance along my misleading path once they found the Stewarts' car abandoned behind a twenty-four-hour diner forty miles down the road. When they popped the trunk, surprise! They'd discover the dead, naked body of the driver stuffed inside.

I smirked at the memory. Who the hell tried, *in this day and age*, to help out a complete stranger in the black hours of the night with "car troubles" or anything else for that matter? An idiot who wanted to die, that's who. As far as I was concerned, I'd made that brainless doof's dreams come true.

Official cause of death...stupidity.

I'd also made sure to press Winter's pretty little fingers to the steering wheel and driver's side door just like last time. Granted, breaking two innocent necks on camera had been more than a little indicative of my sister's turn to the dark side, but I figured there could never be enough clues left behind to back up the idea that Winter Black was a full-fledged criminal.

I tapped out a happy beat on the steering wheel, my grin so wide that my cheeks ached.

God, life was good.

With my sister by my side as an official murderer—her good-girl name now ruined forever—every step of my plan thus far was being carried out to perfection. I was blessed, and all this flawless execution was proof.

The signs were clear. My path was true. Grandpa had always told me I was special. *"Sent to change the land,"* he'd said, *"just as Jesus was sent to save the land."*

The difference between myself and the Savior was that I'd been born to an unholy woman. Jeannette Black was no Mother Mary. Because of that, Grandpa had been forced to cleave me from my filthy human mother's arms and take over my tutelage, ensuring I grew in the light of the truth and fulfilled my true purpose.

In the back of my mind, I could admit that I'd never really felt much like a savior of anything. I often had the sensations of being powerful and in command of a genius intellect, which I enjoyed. And of course, I knew I was a darn handsome son of a gun.

Some things were just straight-up undeniable facts.

But I'd struggled to find that "savior" inside of me. I hadn't shared this inner battle with Grandpa. He didn't take even the teeniest of doubts lightly, and his rage had been even more unpredictable than my own, which was saying a lot.

Damn.

Now, though, I could sense the energy rushing through my marrow, sharpening my purpose and magnifying its steadfast conviction through my brain. Everything was falling into place with ease, and I finally knew that what Grandpa had told me so many times was true.

I was special. A magnificent being. And I had shit to do. Savior shit.

I glanced over my shoulder at Tiny Tim. I now had my own official protégé to bounce on my knee and teach Grandpa's way. Tim would be perfect in helping me accomplish what needed to be done.

That little buttwad didn't realize how lucky he was. He'd thought the joys of life were limited to throwing baseballs and being a proud Hillside Tiger with a crappy haircut. Holy buckets of boring, Batman. I would have *wanted* my family to die if that was the extent of existence they'd provided me with.

Talk about some boring motherbleepers.

Tim was gonna thank me someday. Fall on his itty-bitty knees and praise my name.

The thought of what he would have been…I shuddered. Gross. Pathetic.

My phone buzzed, and I made sure to keep an eye on the road while I checked the text message from my "Greatest Fan." No way in hell was I letting some ridiculous car wreck ruin all this magnificence.

Plus, your insurance rates would shoot through the damn roof, young man.

I grinned. Having all these fans was yet another sign. I planned to call them my followers. Hundreds of people who'd professed and/or demonstrated their allegiance to me even when I was locked up and barely just getting started.

And this new "Greatest Fan," as he or she preferred to called, claimed to have the means and ability to help me in very significant ways.

The current message contained an address outside of Washington, D.C., where my greatest fan promised to have everything ready to set the next stage of my plan into motion.

More than once, I'd offered to pay the mofo in bitcoin, but they'd refused. I wasn't an idiot. The fan wanted *something* in return. I was sure of that. Everyone wanted something. And eventually, he or she would make their request known.

What did I care? If the demand was too ludicrous or even

just some annoying thing I didn't want to deal with, I'd kill him. Or her. Big whoop.

In the meantime, I planned to take full advantage of the arrangement.

Why in the hell wouldn't I?

Winter made a weird noise in her sleep, and I glanced at her. She was so still and so beautiful. With her hair cut short and those crazy red streaks all over the place, she reminded me of a wild animal. A powerful, uncontrollable force just like me.

I'd even noted over the past days we'd spent together —*best killer sibs forever xoxo*—that her vivid blue eyes, which were identical to my own when I didn't have these scratchy-ass, colored contacts in, were taking on a raw, primal glow I hadn't even known she possessed.

My glee bubbled over into a giggle. Given enough time, my sister could become what I was. I no longer had any doubts that Winter had darkness in her.

When she broke Greg's neck, I lost any doubt as to who my sister was. Yeah, yeah, I had a loaded gun, and I'd threat-ened to kill everybody and said all the scary serial killer shit to make her presume she had no other choice…waah waah waah.

No matter how she tried to rationalize her actions, I knew the truth. Millions of people wouldn't have been able to go through with it. A normal person would have pissed themselves and frozen in place, incapable of doing anything at all except watching people die and dying right along with them.

Not *my* sister. Winter had weighed the choices, made the decision, and immediately followed through with the execu-tion. She cut her losses like a damn pro.

Plus, she'd even killed again. She would try to *claim* breaking Andrea's neck had been an act of desperation to save Tiny Tim. I knew that. But there'd been *so* much evidence in favor of me blowing his brains out regardless by that point that I'd been a little shocked by her second act of crickety bone crack.

In fact, I was beginning to think her federal training had, in some unforeseen backfiring way, *helped* in the "make your sis a murderer" arena. She'd learned to make tough calls and make them fast. No second guesses.

As long as we kept activating those cray-cray genetics of hers, that whole Bonnie and Clyde dream had some damn promise. I'd been teasing before. Wishing out loud.

But Winter's moral compass wasn't as strong as she'd convinced herself and everyone else that it was. She had a darkness in there, and if I just took some time to cultivate it...feed and water and care for it...

I could have my sister back.

And what about your damn purpose? What about my plans for you? Do they mean nothing to you when you stack them up against your whore sister?

Grandpa's voice shot through my brain so piercingly loud that I almost screamed. I felt him standing over me. Threatening me with his fists and his desires. Bending me to his will.

I would never dare forget Grandpa's plans or my purpose. Never. I only wondered if I could indoctrinate Winter to walk beside me as I carried them out, given the chance and a little time.

You don't have time, boy.

I slumped in the driver's seat. Grandpa was right. I'd been the lucky man chosen to be raised by The Preacher himself. He'd spent hours and hours telling me that family meant nothing unless a man could pass his knowledge along to someone else.

That was why he'd had no qualms killing my parents or

my sister. And that was why I'd let Tim come along for the current ride. I had to pass the buck to someone. I needed to share my knowledge so that the truth couldn't die with me.

I had to keep Grandpa alive.

But maybe he'd been all wrong about Winter. What if she was reachable? Worthy? Okay, so I didn't have time to hide away in a cabin somewhere and reprogram her brain with all the knowledge I'd accumulated from Grandpa, but maybe that wasn't necessary to gain swift results in my sis.

Winter was further along this path than I'd appreciated. Much further than Grandpa had been able to witness. She might be more open to embracing my purpose than I'd even dared to dream.

Grandpa wouldn't like the idea. I could discern his displeasure hanging over me as I drove. Winter wasn't a part of his plan, and who was I to change that?

"I'm the guy that's breathing air and operating a living human body. I'm the guy that's not six feet underground right now." I snapped the words at the sky and instinctively hunched down, sure some smack or bolt or blow of sorts was coming. But nothing happened.

Another glance at Winter found her just as peaceful and majestic as ever. My sister was a fascinating creature, really. Strong and beautiful...but feral and deadly. A lethal weapon unlike any other.

Grandpa had wanted her dead. I was well aware that he *still* wanted her dead. He whispered, shouted, shrieked the command in my brain all day long.

Kill her, Justin. Kill her now. Kill. Her.

But she *had* been my family once upon a time. Devoted, protective, loyal...and now she was right here, beside me. A bona fide killer who could never go back to her old life.

If she loved me as much as she always professed to, why

wouldn't she choose me over that bullcrap life that was all messed up now anyway?

Those days were over, and she had to know it.

I hummed a happy tune as the car sped down the road, taking us closer and closer to our destination.

I was her brother. Maybe we weren't kids anymore, and I could admit that I'd developed a few new hobbies that were initially off-putting and required an adjustment period of sorts, but we were still family.

Aside from my divine purpose, Winter was all I had left in this stupid world.

And even if she needed some time to accept the truth, she *had* to realize that now...I was all she had left too.

28

Noah poured through the traffic camera footage with Bree at his side. The team had reconvened at the Cherokee Police Department after crime scene techs took over the RV inspection, and he'd wasted no time joining Agent Stafford's surveillance scanning. The sheriff had designated an empty conference room specifically for the FBI's usage.

Walking away from that damn camper had been hard, as it was the closest he'd been to actually finding Winter thus far in their search. He'd had to remind himself that if he ever wanted to touch more than her discarded hair clippings again, he had to keep going.

Finding the Stewarts' car was key, and they'd been able to track the vehicle on a westward route. The car, however, seemed to have vanished at a certain point. All they could do was wait for more traffic footage to be sent to them and scour what they already had.

The rest of the team filed into the room, taking seats and popping open more borrowed laptops to assist the search.

Chris sat at the far end of the table, which Noah thought to be a wise decision.

He still hadn't quite subdued the urge to beat Parker's face in.

Mia took the chair next to Noah, studying him for a moment before speaking. "You doing okay? That offer to talk still stands if you need a sympathetic ear."

The room was small enough that a private conversation was impossible. Autumn and Bree both glanced up at Mia's inquiry, and Noah was aware that this would be a group convo whether he liked it or not.

But what did that really matter anymore? They'd all been openly losing their shit in turns, and his terror over the continued threat to Winter's well-being wasn't a secret. Noah cleared his throat and attempted to keep his voice low. "How did you cope? When your brother was missing, I mean. How did you just...exist...with that godforsaken, relentless panic hammering in your brain?"

Mia considered the question. "Well, I guess with Ned, it was all a bit different. I only had a few hours of what you're experiencing before...before I found out about the accident. But all I could do was cling to hope. Every single minute of that hell, I refused to give up hope."

Noah couldn't avoid thinking that all the hope in the world hadn't helped Ned survive, but he would never say those words to Mia. He regarded her tiny hands tapping away at her laptop keyboard. Agent Logan was small enough to give the impression of being fragile, but anyone who'd survived Quantico was far from breakable.

And he knew that anyone who could experience such a deep loss as Mia had, yet could still speak of the matter willingly and with such *poise* was tough as nails.

She had no reason to dig up the painful memories and was only speaking of her loss to help Noah get through this trying time. Mia might be one of the most selfless people he'd ever met.

"I'll try. I'm trying." Noah swallowed what felt like the weight of the world, nearly making him gag. "To hope, I mean."

"I know you are." Mia rested an assuring hand on his shoulder. "And keep in mind, every available agent is on this case. There are a multitude of great minds at work here, all focused solely on finding Winter. That's a big deal. A huge plus." She offered a small, optimistic smile.

He knew she was right. He also knew that she hadn't had the same comforting thought to hold on to when her brother went missing. No team of experts had been hunting him down, trying to protect him from the danger that had ultimately overtaken the man.

"Thanks, Mia. For checking in. Means a lot." He avoided her dark eyes, unsure if he could handle the wistful sadness in them right now.

"Happy to do it, Agent Dalton." Mia focused on her screen, seeming to understand that he couldn't continue the conversation without breaking down.

Noah thought they'd all underestimated Mia. She was quiet and accommodating enough that no one really gave her much notice, good or bad. The woman had fought her way into the Bureau just like the rest of them, though, and earned herself a spot on the BAU, which was no small feat.

She'd experienced heartbreak that somehow hadn't left the slightest chip on her shoulder. And…she handled Chris like a circus master. Impressive, indeed.

Aiden's phone rang, breaking the silent spell that had settled over the room. All heads whipped his way, and he held up his hand, signaling for quiet while placing the call on speakerphone.

"This is Officer Truman. Sheriff Cagle told me to call you

immediately and keep you apprised of the situation. We've found the Stewart car abandoned off U.S. 74. Parked behind a twenty-four seven diner roughly forty minutes out from Chattanooga. The interior appears to be empty, but my fellow officers are preparing to open the trunk as we speak."

Noah sucked in a sharp breath, noting that Aiden and Autumn did the same in eerie unison. He stood, hands on the table, craning his neck to make out every last word Officer Truman spoke.

There could be valuable clues and answers hidden in that car. There could also be a dead Winter in that trunk.

"Okay. They got the lid up. There's…"

Officer Truman was obviously attempting to identify just what he was dealing with. Meanwhile, Noah was this close to climbing out of his own skin, and every agent in the room was holding their breath.

"A naked woman. Blonde hair. Older. I'd guess early fifties and—"

A scuffle of chaotic excitement blared from the Tennessee end of the conversation.

"Officer?" Aiden pushed, his tone severe.

"She's alive. Holy hell! She's *alive*. But just barely." Truman's breathing became ragged and loud with the discovery.

"Officer Truman, we need her name. If she can speak at all, *get her name now*!" Aiden's eyes were glued to the phone.

Noah nodded, desperate for the information. If they identified the woman, they could hunt down her car, which was almost certainly the vehicle Justin was driving now. That was the break they needed. The information that would allow the team to track that demon down.

Tension crackled through the team as Officer Truman first called for an ambulance. Every second became a century as he tried to rouse the woman.

"Ma'am? Ma'am, can you hear me? My name is Officer Mike Truman with the highway patrol. You're safe now, ma'am. We're gonna take care of you. Can you tell me your name?" Truman's voice was kind and confident as he worked with the victim. "Here. There's a nice, warm blanket for you. We'll get you back to good in no time, ma'am, I promise."

Noah's gut twisted with agony. Truman was a damn good officer, but that didn't make the suspense any easier to handle.

"Agent Parrish? Her eyes are fluttering. She's trying to open them. She's licking her lips. I think she's coming to." The officer stopped speaking, and a raspy, undistinguishable whisper replaced him.

"M-Muh…M-Mar…" She was saying her name. She was still alive and trying to say her name.

Noah rocked back and forth, sure he'd lose his mind to the suspense at any given second.

Come on. You can do it. You can do it. Fight. Stay with us.

More whispering, and then Officer Truman was speaking to them again. "Marjorie Robinson. Her name is Marjorie Robinson. I repeat, *Marjorie Robinson.*"

Aiden pointed at Bree. "Get an APB out on any vehicle registered to Marjorie Robinson with Tennessee or North Carolina plates." He strode toward the conference room door as Bree rushed through it to attack her task. "I'm calling Agent Ming and Sheriff Cagle. The second we have new CCTV coming in, I want every last one of you glued to your damn screens. This could very well be the break we need."

He disappeared into the hallway, and Noah sank back down into his chair, excited but terrified. The chase seemed like a never-ending nightmare. All he wanted was Winter safe in his arms.

Autumn circled the table and approached him, seeming every bit as devastated and exhausted as himself. He stood and hugged her firmly, wishing either of them had a word of true comfort to give the other.

"We'll find her," Autumn whispered.

"From your lips to God's ears." He broke the embrace and sat once again, checking and rechecking that his laptop was fired up and ready the instant new CCTV footage came in.

They were getting closer now. He could sense it. They were nipping at Justin Black's heels. And when they found him…

Noah's fists clenched.

When we find you, you'll never hurt anyone ever, ever again because I'm going to kill you.

He was ready to go. He was *made* for bashing through doors and taking shots at the villains—taking the bad guys down. Noah Dalton was a federal agent and former marine trained for *action*.

Yet all he could do in the current moment to save the woman he loved was stare at a damn computer screen and wait.

AUTUMN COUNTED her inhales and exhales, attempting to retain what was left of her sanity. No one would benefit from her screaming at the top of her lungs, which was fast becoming her strongest urge.

The waiting was unbearable. She knew they'd made progress of sorts in finding Marjorie Robinson alive. A Jane Doe could have taken days to identify, but luck had granted them a living victim and a name. Very soon, they would have the specific vehicle information they needed to hunt Justin down.

And save my best friend.

She took comfort in the fact that Noah didn't seem to

blame her for Winter's disappearance anymore. He blamed himself, which was equally as inaccurate.

But Autumn understood the guilt eating away at his mind and heart. She was enduring the same and likewise blamed herself for not having prevented the situation. Trying to imagine any future where she didn't harbor responsibility for Winter's abduction was impossible.

This was a regret that would follow her throughout the remainder of her life and into the grave. Autumn accepted that truth and told herself that if they found Winter alive, she'd happily carry ten times the weight of her current remorse.

Just let her be okay.

Although, what did "okay" even mean? After what Winter had been through, Autumn knew her friend would be forever changed.

What if they rescued Winter Black, only to find out they'd lost a part of her to the trauma?

"A fax for you, Dr. Trent." Autumn turned in her seat as a female officer handed her a stack of papers. The woman offered a half-hearted smile, which was the best anyone seemed able to manage at the moment.

Autumn returned the same lackluster grin and zeroed in on the information before her. Dr. Carpenter had come through with her promise to deliver the hospital's logs of Justin's visitors. Autumn scanned the pages, anxious to spot a name that set off an alarm of any sort.

Her disappointment rose as she reread the names.

Nothing. No clues to be found there at all.

The scream was back in her throat. She didn't know how long she could hold it in. This was all too much. The fear, the waiting, the remorse—

Too. Much.

And not just for Autumn. While Mia's efforts to comfort

Noah had almost sent Autumn into tears, other agents were at each other's throats. At what point did her team's intermittent emotional outbursts turn into full-blown meltdowns?

She rubbed her neck and tried to refocus on the traffic video before her. Until they had the vehicle information, all they could really do was search for discrepancies in the current footage and possibly catch Justin in a mistake, which would give them an idea of what direction he'd taken after stealing Marjorie Robinson's car.

The laptop glare was beginning to burn her eyes, which had grown gritty from hours spent hyper-focused on the device. Her shoulders ached from the tension she was carrying. Every last muscle, tendon, and cell had been on red alert for far too long now.

Aiden burst through the door, reentering the conference room so abruptly that she jumped in her chair. "I just got the call. Marjorie Robinson drives a black Nissan Rogue, and it's already been tagged going through a toll booth near Washington, D.C."

"D.C.? What in the hell would Black want there?" Chris spoke for the first time since his humiliation by Aiden at the campground.

"And why drive all the way into Tennessee? Did he need to retrieve something first?" Mia added another logical query.

"He could have picked up an accomplice," Bree proposed.

"Doubtful. Even if someone is helping Justin, he wouldn't want to share the limelight with anyone else." Aiden shot the idea down, and Autumn was aware that he did so with many years of dealing with Justin and The Preacher's overlapping cases.

"Narcissistic effing prick." Noah's expression was vicious. Autumn had no doubt that given the opportunity, he'd kill Justin Black, even if excessive force wasn't necessary.

"Regardless of the why, we have the where. I'm going to make a call and charter us a private plane to D.C. Ready yourselves." Aiden left the room yet again, making rapid swipes across his phone screen.

Autumn slapped a palm down on the table. "Distraction. He was just *distracting* us. Making sure he kept his lead."

Bree pushed her chair back from the table. "I think you're right."

Chris snorted. "Well, that didn't work out so well for the little asshole considering we didn't make a grand exodus toward Tennessee. We're closer than he's hoping for."

Even Noah appeared to approve of the comment. He raised an eyebrow and gave Chris a quick nod. Autumn wondered if there was hope for a reconciliation between the two men after all was said and done. And if not reconciliation, then a level of tolerance that enabled their team to continue to function.

They all busied themselves with grabbing bags, coats, and whatever other personal items were necessary so they could leave at a moment's notice.

Minutes later, Aiden stepped into the room, placing his phone in an inner suit pocket. "Wheels leave the ground in an hour. Until then, work with the police on getting any and all CCTV coverage past that damn toll booth."

Hunting for a black Nissan Rogue in a veritable sea of black SUVs. Awesome.

Autumn shook off the pessimism and ordered herself to shut up and get to work.

"We're gonna catch you, motherfucker. We're coming." Noah didn't even seem aware that he'd muttered the words out loud, but that was fine.

He'd articulated the team's sentiment all the same.

29

My Greatest Fan had definitely come through. When I pulled the car up to the isolated cabin waiting for me only an hour or so outside of D.C., I'd instantly known it was the absolute perfect place to rest and regroup for the evening's big event.

A simple little place, really. Two dilapidated but squishy gray couches, an ancient yet comfortable reclining chair that I was testing out now, and an old box television set on a coffee table was all that made up the main room. The kitchen was small, but nothing was falling apart or peeling off the walls. The basin tub sink wasn't rusted, and there was a small, wood-burning oven for cooking and heat.

I'd spotted an outhouse while carrying Tiny Tim inside. That wasn't ideal, but it was better than squatting in the woods.

This was the exact type of place I could raise Tim in. Pass on Grandpa's legacy. Just us and the forest and the truth.

For now, though, I'd focus on gearing up for tonight's occasion.

My first performance as a free man needed to be memorable. I wanted to pull off the type of event that would never be forgotten.

I cranked the handle on the side of the recliner until my shoulders dropped back and a footrest popped out before folding my arms behind my head and gazing up at the wooden ceiling. Being a serial killer was hard. Earning the notoriety was fun and all, but once people comprehended what you were capable of, surprising them became much more difficult.

The random murders along my escape path from the hospital weren't anything special. That crap was exactly what people thought I'd do. And yeah, duh, I enjoyed it. The power I amassed when killing people was always a good time.

But I needed more than the usual horror. I needed astonishment. Awe. The masses had to be kept on their toes where Justin Black was concerned. Rehashing the same old gruesome murders wouldn't do. People would get used to those, and then my name would start to slip from their memories like a bad dream. They'd forget me.

A forgotten man couldn't change the world. A forgotten man was worthless.

I'd thought outside the box for this one. I was stepping foot into a whole new arena, and the epic factor was going to be off the charts.

Phenomenal.

According to social media, a lovely candlelight vigil had been planned for seven this evening in the midst of downtown D.C. Thousands and thousands of mourners had marked their profiles as "Going" on the event's Facebook page, which was about the dumbest freaking thing I'd ever seen anyone do in my life.

They were legit okay with telling the entire world exactly where they'd be and when. Facebook was a serial killer's feasting ground. Dumbasses just lining up and waiting to be targeted.

I was well aware that the average human being was a moron at best, but the abysmal level of intelligence so proudly displayed these days blew my damn mind. Even if I hadn't felt the *need* to kill, I would have killed anyway just because it was so *easy*. And entertaining.

The gathering was planned to "celebrate the life" of some idiot, douchebag boy band member who'd recently died from an accidental overdose.

The ancient leather crackled as I squirmed in the chair too full of disgust to sit still. I had so many problems with the whole memorial debacle, I barely knew where to start. I mean, first of all, boy bands were the worst. Disgusting. A shame to mankind. That kid had done the world a *favor* by leaving it.

Second, what in the serious hell? He'd been on drugs. Hello? Anybody picking up on this? A guy my own age who did drugs to the extent that he actually offed himself *on accident* and parents were letting their teenage children attend this "celebration" instead of giving a crap that their kids worshipped an obvious loser.

Unbelievable.

A freaking drug addict whose only contribution to the world had been some junk-ass, ear-raping songs, and a pretty face. He was nothing. He was *worse* than nothing. He was the scum on the bottom of nothing's shoe.

But the comments went on and on and on, plastering his page with angst and woe and tears. Unbelievable. I was *glad* he was dead. I would have liked to bring him back to life just so I could kill him myself.

I'd do a way better job of it. Much more entertaining.

When I'd sought out an event to showcase my big bang back into society, this perfect little gem had fallen right in my lap. Thousands of completely off-guard nimrods all herded together like cattle, but of their own free will. And what made the opportunity especially sensational was the fact that ninety-five percent of those mourners would be kids.

Stabbing a grown man seventy-two times barely earned you a second glance these days. But look out...kill one kid, and you were the king of the monsters.

The children were our future, after all.

I snorted. If that really was the case, the planet was pretty screwed regardless.

There was a part of me that went nuts knowing the live video of Winter killing the Stewart parents also implied that she'd shot their innocent daughter. Sure, I wanted to convince the world that my sister was just as big of a monster as me, but the price was steep. Sister dearest was getting the credit for the best of the three RV murders. Not fair, when little Nicole had been all me.

Sighing, I returned the chair to the upright position. Kid murders were gold. That was why tonight's event was so genius. I had a special appreciation for the countless dipwads who would be lighting candles this evening for their favorite drughead of a dolt corpse. Those cretins were going to assist me in catapulting my fame to a whole new level of awesome.

Die. They all needed to die. They *deserved* to die.

And lucky for them, I needed a decent-sized group of imbeciles to kill. It worked out for everyone. Beautiful timing.

This would make Grandpa proud. I knew he was mad because I'd debated keeping Winter around, but I was going to make it up to him. He and I would be good again in no time at all.

I couldn't fail the old man. Not after everything he'd

taught me. I had to prove that I appreciated what he'd done for me.

He'd saved me from my family.

He slaughtered your family.

I jumped at the familiar voice, whipping my head toward the squish couch. Winter was still passed out cold. Yet somehow, she was also in my head, trying to poison me.

I clapped my hands over my ears and shook her off.

Grandpa had shown me what love really was.

He raped you. Repeatedly.

A growl formed in my throat. Again with her incessant lies! How was she doing this? What kind of freak power did my sister possess?

Springing to my feet, I stalked over to Winter and glared into her sleeping face. "He gave me a real purpose."

He gave you a sickness.

"Be quiet!" I stomped a foot on the cabin floor. I knew this "other" voice in my head was a consequence of spending so much time around Winter. She was the sole aspect of my life that had changed in recent days.

Winter was the X-Factor.

This is why you have to kill her. She'll infect you before you ever make her accept the light. It's a losing battle, boy.

I pressed my fists to my forehead and rubbed aggressively. Sometimes, there were just too many people talking in there, and they all needed to shut the hell up so I could concentrate on the important matter at hand.

Mass murder.

I glanced at Winter and Tiny Tim still fast asleep on their respective couches. Even with my inadvertent yell, the drugs continued to reign victorious in keeping their cute little noggins in dreamland.

Winter had been somewhat awake when I'd brought her inside. Blinking, she'd groggily scanned our surroundings and tried to figure out where she was. One sweet needle later, and she'd thudded back on the couch like a pile of bricks.

Tim hadn't woken up at all, and if I hadn't painstakingly researched the correct dosage of sedatives to give the little rascal before drugging him, I woulda been worried that Timmy was in coma land. That would be bad, cuz the heck if I knew how to bring someone outta that.

I walked to Winter's couch and checked her arm wound. Her skin was warm and smooth…translucent. My fingers itched to explore the rest of her body and have a little fun. *Really* get to know my sister.

Sadly, there wasn't time for that. I focused on where the bullet had hit her instead. Everything seemed about as fine as it could be. The bleeding had stopped. Nothing was green or leaking pus. I was pretty sure that was a good sign.

I hadn't even intended on shooting her yet, but dang. She'd flat out tried to kill me. She was going to beat me *to death*. I'd read the intent in her eyes. I was almost positive she would have regretted killing me, eventually. She'd been enraged enough to perform the deed but not cold enough to let it slide off her shoulders like no big deal.

Killing me would have haunted her forever. Then again, I seemed to haunt her pretty well alive too. In a way, I was the catch-22 of Winter's entire life.

I put my lips to her ear and sang just above a whisper. "I can't liiive…with or without my sissy…"

She made a slight move, rolling into the couch back. I was sure she was mumbling real words, but there wasn't a translator in the world who could have cracked that code. The meds were wearing off.

That was good. I needed her awake for what came next. And I was about to find out if saving her for this grandiose occasion had been worth the risk that bringing her along had caused me.

I was almost positive I'd made the right move in taking her, but I decided not to dwell on that for fear I'd set Grandpa off again. When he was angry with me, I couldn't focus.

And I *needed* to focus, dammit.

I walked into the kitchen to rifle through the supplies my Greatest Fan had left for me and tore into one of three cardboard boxes. Food, cash, and a change of clothes. Sunglasses and a woolen hat to hide my hair. Had the effing Feds figured out I'd bleached my head by now? Possible. They did usually catch on to vital information like that, albeit long after the discovery mattered.

My beard had grown out a little over the past couple of days, giving me a bit of a shaggy vibe that helped and complimented the horn-rimmed glasses perched on my nose. The last touch was a pair of veneers that changed the shape of my mouth. I popped them in and smiled at myself in the reflection of the stainless steel fridge. Little things like that could make all the difference in the short term. The alteration was real…and I was still stunningly handsome, which only seemed fair.

Long term, I wanted them to look back on the surveillance footage and appreciate how easily they could have stopped me. I wanted them to cry when they observed me just mosey on into that crowd of people right on camera.

There were more cameras in D.C. than anywhere else in the world. Our nation's beloved capital wasn't playing around with lunatics like me. That was great, as far as coverage of my master scheme went.

But the plan wouldn't work at all if I was recognized beforehand.

I shrugged, not especially worried. I'd been scanning the

news all day, and so far, no mention of the latest body or the Stewarts' car. Without that information, the authorities would have no clue where to look next.

They were so far behind me that I was almost embarrassed for them. Federal agents seeking out one of their own, and good god, they were flubbing up the process bad.

That Captain America boyfriend of Winter's was probably losing his rootin' tootin' mind by this point. What was he gonna do without my sister hanging around to use as his own personal whore?

A bolt of rage hit me.

"You're mine, do you hear me? Mine. I'll never give you back to him."

Winter murmured in her sleep but didn't stir.

With one finger, I gently stroked her pale cheek. That asshole had stolen what wasn't his for long enough, turned my sister into an absolute piece of filth. Over my dead body —or hers, whatever was necessary—would he touch Winter Black again.

I bared my teeth at her sleeping form. I would decide how and when she was touched. I controlled her fate. Me.

Mine.

Dear Dr. Trent couldn't be handling all this very well, either. She'd blame herself. *Good.* Maybe if she'd shown up for those meetings with me, she'd have realized what a dumbass idea it was to let Winter keep coming to my room.

"That's what you get for running around doing your redheaded slut stuff instead of saving your best friend's life," I murmured.

Maybe she'd even kill herself at some point down the road.

Or maybe I would kill her.

Beautiful thoughts, but they'd have to wait for later.

I moved to the remaining box on the counter, took off the

lid, and smiled. Fantastic. A maze of wires and C-4 and a nice black vest to hold it all together. Just like Christmas.

There were also a couple of new burner smartphones. Excellent. I had everything I needed. Every. Last. Thing.

Whether or not I had to kill him—or her—later didn't matter one smidge. My Greatest Fan had come through like an Olympic champ.

I was hours away from making history.

30

Winter groaned, the rhythmic taps on her cheeks pulling her from a deep sleep. Waking up was like swimming through a thick, murky lake in search of the surface, only with five-hundred-pound limbs that kept dragging her back down.

The closer she swam to the glittering light, the more weight that settled into her bones, and the more her mind's whispers stoked a growing sense of dread.

Terrible things are waiting up there. Stay down here where it's nice and safe.

"Wakey, wakey, Sissy. We have a very important date, and we can't be late. Obnoxious white rabbit."

She flinched as Justin's voice yanked her from the safe cocoon. "White...rabbit?"

"Yeah, that guy. He was a mess. Like, *get your crap together, dude.* I always hated that damn movie. Not as much as *Fantasia.* That was somebody's straight-up acid trip right there, but still...*Wonderland,* my ass."

Winter struggled to crack open her groggy eyes, squinting when light blazed in. Her head pounded like someone was using her skull like a drum, although the pain didn't seem to bother her much, and the world around her was unsteady. Moving. Where…where were they?

With effort, she rolled her head to the side and spotted a fuzzy person-shaped figure hunched behind a round circle.

She widened her eyes, and the image became a little clearer.

Steering wheel.

Car.

How had that happened? She didn't remember ever leaving the cabin, though she'd barely been aware of the cabin in the first place. Blurry glimpses of rough log walls and little Tim passed out on a couch across from her. A few kerosene lamps illuminating her brother's form as he opened presents.

Winter scrunched up her face to focus, wincing from the exertion. No, not presents. Boxes. They'd gone there for the boxes, she was sure.

The memories slipped away as quickly as they'd materialized, fading like a dream.

Just as Winter began to wonder whether she'd imagined the entire scene, a sudden stop snapped her head back. She gasped and reached for the door to steady herself, but a restraint on her wrist stopped the movement with enough force to wrench her shoulder.

Her hands were tied again. Bound to the bottom of the seat.

Winter blinked, trying to clear her vision. Something was different this time, though.

A few blinks later, and the difference clicked. There were *people* outside. Actual humans, walking right by her window.

She opened her mouth to scream a warning, only her tongue was stuck to the roof of her mouth. Before she could figure out how to unglue it, Justin was shoving a gun barrel into her side.

Winter swallowed several times in a row before her mouth started functioning again. "What...where...?"

He grinned at her, his eyes glazed with insanity. "Not gonna tell ya. I'll show you instead. Soooo much more fun, right?" He giggled. "But I'm warning you once and only once. If you scream or try to run or do any of that stupid heroic crap, I will kill you and everyone around you. I think we've established by now that I don't bluff."

Her foggy brain was still fumbling through Justin's rambling when he gave her chest a light tap. Or more like, he'd tapped whatever thick garment he'd covered her in.

She frowned. She was so used to wearing heavy bullet-proof vests that, until his gesture, she hadn't even registered the extra weight encasing her middle.

Winter instinctively reached out a hand to investigate, but once again, the bindings restricted her motion.

"I really wouldn't touch that, Sis. It's um, what you might call *sensitive*."

His grin widened, and just like that, Winter knew.

A vest. He'd strapped her into an explosive vest. Similar to one designed for law enforcement, only Justin's vest would do the exact opposite.

Destroy lives instead of protect.

Despair engulfed her like a thundercloud. Beneath the vest, her heart smashed against her ribs like it was frantic to escape.

He turned me into a living bomb.

"Believe it or not, Sissy, I did some pretty intense internal wrestling as to what I should do with you. I mean, you'd make a badass sidekick. And we're *family*. I really *should* be able to trust you with anything." Justin's grin dropped, and resentment filled his eyes. "But after some careful consideration and a few reminders from Grandpa, I've accepted that you're just too damn good. The amount of time it would take to deprogram you...I just don't have it, Sis."

Winter's eyes burned with tears. Douglas Kilroy was dead, but he'd never be truly gone. The Preacher would live on forever in Justin's mind and through the atrocities he committed.

"I'm just never going to be able to really, really, *really* trust you. Like, cross my heart and hope to die trust you, ya know? Sucks, but...it is what it is. At least I've found a way for our last moments together to be fun as hell. Way better than jet fighter battles or ditch fishing, I promise."

Justin looked wistful for a split second before his expression went blank, and he held up two burner phones. "One for me, one for you. Mine has the detonator button. *Obviously.*"

Winter jerked her head to one side, followed by the other. *No.* "G-go ahead. Won't get out. You g-go...with me."

She met her brother's narrowed gaze until a sniffle from the back seat shocked her out of the stare-down.

"Oh yeah." Justin waved a hand in the air. "Silly me. I guess I forgot to mention that Tiny Tim came along for the ride. You gonna take out Timmy too, Winter? Be responsible for the murder of an eight-year-old? Jesus. You *monster.*"

For a terrible moment, Winter wanted to say yes. She'd already killed the boy's parents. Justin had blown Nicole's brains out right in front of the child. Tim would never be okay. His happiness had been stolen from him in that RV.

There was a mercy in death that she was sure Tim Stewart would never find in this world.

Besides, how else could she be sure to prevent another Justin from being created? Another Kilroy?

Tim sniffled again, and Winter rejected the thought, her stomach turning. No. She wasn't god or even a fortune teller.

It wasn't within her to make that call, especially not when the street they were parked on was busy, *swarming*, with people.

She turned her head toward the parade of youthful figures streaming outside the passenger window. An even larger crowd walked by on the sidewalk out front. If the car blew up, there was no telling how many innocents the bomb would kill along with her.

Fifty? A hundred? More?

Winter shivered. Whatever the number, it was too many.

Especially when added to the deaths already on her conscience.

"Well, Sissy? Are you gonna blow Tim's brains all over our nation's capital, or behave and do as I ask?"

"Be...have."

If nothing else, she was buying some time for the dregs of her brother's sedative cocktail to wear off, to think and get help. Time to alert innocent bystanders. Escape.

Justin calmly undid her bindings, holding the detonator out of reach. He exited the driver's side and walked around the car, the phone always in Winter's view, just so she didn't accidentally forget that she was a human firework waiting to happen.

Do something.

If only her brain didn't feel as mushy as day-old oatmeal. What had Justin dosed her with this time, and more importantly, how soon until the final effects wore off?

He ushered Tim out of the back seat and helped Winter stand from the passenger's side. Her head spun again, and without thinking, she grabbed onto her brother for support.

With a giant smile, Justin hooked his arms through theirs and led them straight into the heart of the growing crowd.

"Just one little happy family," he declared, winking at her.

Winter was too busy trying to stay upright to waste time replying. When the dizziness subsided enough, she scanned her surroundings. Candles were being passed around, and signs were clutched by hundreds of sorrow-laden kids.

So many teens.

She stumbled, choking on horror as the reality of the situation sank in.

Oh, god. The crowd was almost *entirely* kids.

You should have stayed in the car.

A glance over her shoulder told her that option was long gone. Justin had dragged them too far into the mob.

As he continued ushering them along, the face on all the banners they were passing finally clicked. A famous boy band singer who'd died a few days back. Winter had caught wind of it while flipping through radio stations, shaking her head when she learned the young man had passed from an accidental overdose.

A shame. A shame to lose such a young and promising life.

And now, here she was. Surrounded by young lives and only minutes away from snuffing them all out. If she didn't figure out a way to stop the nightmare, this candlelight vigil would soon be lit by much more than tiny flames.

Tim was sobbing, but many people around them were. It was the perfect cover, and Justin had chosen this event for that precise reason. No one would notice or care if he was leading two distressed individuals through a sea of distressed individuals.

After he'd escorted them deep into the throngs of mourners, Justin halted, handing Winter her phone. A plea rose to her lips, but she'd learned her lesson the hardest way.

If there was any way out of this, it certainly didn't lie in begging her brother for mercy.

Justin Black had none to give.

The depths of his strange brown eyes were tinged with a chaotic mix of sadness and excitement as he leaned in, kissed her cheek, and slipped the backpack he'd been wearing onto her shoulders. "This is the end for us, dear sister."

Winter tensed, and a hollow echo filled her ears. He was going to kill himself too? *That* she hadn't predicted. There was no time now to stop any of this or help anyone or—

He tapped the screen of her phone, and she squeezed her eyes shut, bracing for the excruciating pain that she knew would last for only a moment.

Seconds passed, but no pain came.

She opened her eyes and found him grinning at her, shaking his head. "You silly girl. FaceTime! Besides, I'm the one with the boom-boom button, remember?" He held the phone in front of her eyes. The FaceTime app was up and running and also set to record.

Justin popped a pair of earbuds in her ears and kissed her cheek again…then, before her fuzzy head could decipher his intentions, his wet lips landed on hers. "I am so very, very sorry we can't do more."

She jerked away as bile churned in her stomach, scorching her throat and threatening to spew out. Justin only laughed.

Why did I ever think I could fix you?

"Keep your eyes on the screen, Winter…or else, *kaboom*." He issued the order in a flat tone before grabbing Tim's hand and leading the crying boy away, leaving her alone in a crowd of thousands.

Winter's muscles contracted. She couldn't just stand here, waiting like a lamb for slaughter.

Her gaze swept the tear-streaked faces around her, and her free hand curled into a fist. So many lambs. Too many. There had to be a way to save them.

"Why the sad face, Sissy? You bored? Cheer up. Fun times are on the way."

Justin's voice in her ears jerked her attention back to the

screen. His smiling face took up most of the frame, spiraling her deeper into a pit of despair.

Even as he walked, her brother's eyes never left his phone. He would miss nothing she did. Nothing she said. Unless she came up with a plan, she was stuck.

Her, and every single person within range.

People pressed in on Winter from every side, and yet she'd never felt so desperately alone.

Stop getting distracted, Agent Black. Think.

Except, everything about this scenario was a distraction. The sweat trickling down her back and the horrifying weight of the suicide vest. The drugs that still clouded her mind. The unfamiliar environment and the mobs of people.

She shivered. The entire situation was surreal, like a video game or a bad dream. An adult dotted the crowd here and there, but for the most part, the faces all belonged to teenage girls and boys, huddled into groups and weeping while staring at their candle flames.

"Sissy…"

Remembering Justin's order, Winter jerked her gaze back to the screen, meeting his crazed stare while fighting another wave of nausea. She didn't have to question whether her brother would blow up thousands of people simply because her eyes had strayed too long from the phone.

He would. Of course he would.

Trapped in the middle of that crowd of grieving kids, every minute that ticked by was a living nightmare. Winter's heart beat so frantically, she wondered what would happen if she dropped dead before she could carry out Justin's commands.

Silly question. He'd just blow everyone up anyway.

A silent laugh wracked her body before turning into a muted sob and then back into a giggle that reminded her too much of her brother. Which was ridiculous because nothing about this was remotely funny. She was losing her mind.

Pull yourself together, Agent Black. You were trained better than this. You don't quit until there are no options left.

With effort, Winter pulled herself back from the brink of hysteria. Screw this. She wasn't built to cower like a victim while the world blew up around her. She needed a plan.

Focus, dammit.

She calmed her breathing, pushing through the brain fog to think. She had to break the problem down to its simplest form. What was the first step?

Assess the options.

Right. Options. She could do that.

Winter tuned out the faces, the sobbing. Her fear. Everything except for her heartbeat and the possible courses of action.

Option one, disarm the suicide vest. Since Winter had no idea how to make that happen and Justin would spot her if she even unzipped the jacket to look, she discarded that idea immediately.

Option two: getting people to safety. Also not possible. Justin would hit the detonator within seconds of her yelling "bomb" or screaming at people to run.

That left option three. Get herself to safety, or at least a less populated area.

Panic clawed at her skin. Option three wasn't really an option. Where could she go before Justin knew she was on the move?

Think!

She was desperate, and saving some lives was better than saving none.

She didn't delude herself. Execution would be tricky. There was every chance Justin would catch on right away and punch the button. Odds were high that she'd fail.

There was also a chance, however minuscule, that she could pull it off. If she held the phone close enough, maybe he wouldn't notice the changing background.

The only certainty was if she waited any longer, she was sure to run out of time.

Determination straightened Winter's spine as she began assessing, relying on her peripheral vision as much as possible. No matter which way she looked, the park and streets were crammed full of humans. Her heart squeezed with despair, but she refused to give up.

She'd fight to save these people until the last bit of life was squeezed from her body.

Her drumming pulse urged her to hurry, but Winter kept her head. *Easy does it.*

One wrong move, and it was game over, so she only risked turning an inch at a time. Slow enough to make it difficult for Justin to notice any background shifts.

Hopefully.

Several inches later, her heart lurched into her throat. Rising up in the air, maybe thirty yards away, was some kind of giant statue or sculpture that backed up to trees. With the crowd blocking her view, Winter couldn't be certain the art was set on a concrete base, but there was a decent chance. If she could get over there, she had a shot at ducking for cover at the same time she screamed for everyone to run.

If. Could. Chance. Shot.

Not exactly reassuring, but she was fresh out of options.

Winter set her jaw and began edging in that direction.

Between making sure Justin didn't notice and navigating the crowd, each step was painfully slow. The sweat dripping down her back turned into streams, and after several minutes, she hadn't even made it a quarter of the distance to the statue.

Still, Winter pushed forward, inch by damn inch. Tuning

out the crowd and keeping her eyes trained on the screen at all times.

Just keep moving. You can do this. Slowly and surely wins the—

She froze when Justin's voice blasted her ears. "Lift the phone up so I can see what you're doing."

Her pulse fluttered like a rabbit's, her palm slipping as she lifted the phone high and tilted the screen down. All the while bracing herself for impact.

"Good girl. Now, open the backpack."

When he didn't call her out, the fear constricting Winter's chest eased up a little. *See? He's not omniscient. Just go along with whatever the hell this is so you can buy more time.*

She shrugged the bag from her shoulders and swung it in front of her, wincing as the straps slid across her bullet wound. After fumbling with the zipper, she grasped the metal tab and pulled.

And promptly forgot how to breathe.

Winter stared at her service weapon and ammo while a silent scream exploded through her head.

"I want you to take out the gun and fire a round into the air."

Justin tossed out the order as casually as if he were asking her to toss a Frisbee.

If only you'd killed him when you had the chance. "And if I say no?"

Her brother's laughter flooded Winter's ears. She'd loved that laugh once, but the sound was different now. The most horrible noise in the world.

It was Kilroy's laugh, she realized with a shudder. The devil's laugh.

"Sweet Sissy, if you say no," he sputtered out more chortles, "then...*boom.* Duh."

A voice straight out of Hell.

31

Autumn dug her fingernails into the leather seat of the rented Tahoe as Aiden accelerated into D.C.'s city limits. Noah sat motionless in the front passenger's seat, his shoulders rigid with the same suppressed energy that seemed to surge through all the team members.

The team was closing the gap that separated them from Justin Black, but they were going to need a direction soon.

Very soon.

Since the moment she had learned that Winter was missing along with Justin, the torture had only grown. The weight of anxiety that had settled on her shoulders in the past two days was worse than any fear she'd yet experienced in life.

Marjorie Robinson's Rogue had been spotted at two more toll booths and flying past a bank, seeming to be on a route to downtown D.C. Yet, they had no way of knowing that for sure. Justin could just be playing games with them again.

To make matters worse, Chris sat in the back with her. True, he was primed and ready for action, and there was no doubt the agent was an asset in taking down Justin.

But knowing he believed Winter to be a willing participant in the murder and mayhem filled Autumn with anger every time she glanced his way.

You're wrong, and soon, you're going to feel very stupid.

Of course, that was assuming Parker was capable of self-deprecation, and Autumn had her doubts. Heavy doubts.

Aiden's phone rang. He pounded a finger to the speaker button before the device could ring again. "Agent Parrish. Tell me you've got something for me."

"I do. Winter Black has been spotted in the middle of a memorial service downtown with a gun and wearing what we think is a suicide vest, based on a wire one of my officers saw dangling beneath her jacket. She's shot off a round from what appears to be her service weapon into the air. Corner of Sumner Row and 17th Street Northwest."

Aiden cut the call off, entering the cross streets into the GPS at warp speed while Noah stabbed at his phone to bring up live news coverage.

Autumn's nails gouged the seat as she waited for a visual.

Noah hit another button, and the video popped up. Agent Black stood amidst a giant crowd, screaming at them to "Get down!" and "Don't move!"

She brandished a gun in one hand and a smartphone in the other, but Autumn's attention flew straight to her friend's chest.

Beneath her jacket, Winter's chest definitely appeared padded. Bulky.

The sheriff's words replayed in Autumn's ears. Horror clawed at her throat.

Suicide vest.

This was bad. So very, very bad.

Tears glistened on Noah's cheek as he stared at the woman he loved while a reporter's voice emerged over the footage. *"...and we can now confirm that Agent Winter Black has almost certainly gone rogue from the FBI. She is armed, dangerous, and exhibiting the behavior commonly associated with a mental breakdown."*

"No. No, that isn't true. That cannot be true!" Autumn shook her head in disbelief as she leaned over Noah's seat to get a closer look.

"Well," Chris's smug voice rang out from behind them, "I guess it's safe to say *I told you so* at this point, right? Is this a good time?"

With a roar, Noah twisted and lunged for the back seat. His belt snapped taut, serving as a temporary restraint, and Autumn did her best to push him back the rest of the way. "Noah, no! We don't have time for this. We have to save her!"

Agent Dalton stayed put, but his narrowed eyes promised repercussions at a later date.

Autumn worried that Chris would never live this moment down. Chris might not live in general.

She honestly didn't care much if he didn't.

Winter moved suddenly in the live feed, giving the TV camera a clear shot of the phone in her hand. Autumn spotted Justin's face, animated with laughter and filling the screen of the cell.

"There! He's manipulating her. Justin's on her screen. He's in control of everything." Autumn pointed her finger straight to his face on Winter's screen to prove it was true. Bandaging was wrapped around her friend's upper arm, and what could only be blood was leaking through the white dressing.

"Get me there!" Noah yelled at Aiden, who was already flying through the streets of D.C. at daredevil speeds.

"Four minutes, Dalton! We're only four minutes away. But this damn traffic!" Aiden shouted the words, slowing to a near stop as he approached the cluster of vehicles, no doubt clogging the roads because of Winter.

Noah undid his buckle and threw his door open, leaping to the ground and charging into the crowd.

Aiden cursed under his breath before throwing the SUV into park. The next instant, Autumn, Chris, and Aiden jumped out and followed Noah, their departure accompanied by a chorus of honks from the angry drivers now trapped behind the stationary vehicle.

Autumn weaved her way through the dense crowd, dodging alarmed pedestrians left and right. There were people everywhere. Some of them sobbing, others pushing in wide-eyed fright.

The crowd had already swallowed Noah, but she kept bulldozing forward, aiming in the direction he'd disappeared. As she scanned face after face, she realized most of them were young teenagers, and she pumped her legs faster.

Hurry. They had to hurry, or else they might be too late, and Winter and all these babies would die.

"Down! Stay down! Get out of here!" Chris shouted behind her, attempting to warn hundreds of people who were aware there was a situation but had no idea what was going on or how close to the madness they might be.

Just as a gap in the crowd opened up ahead, Aiden reappeared, pointing at something in the distance. "Noah's headed straight to her!"

Blood roared in Autumn's ears as together they sprinted into the pocket.

Hurry, hurry, hurry.

Autumn's heart leapt when she caught sight of Winter a short distance away, one of the few people standing among a mass of cowering, kneeling teens.

Like she sensed their presence, Winter pivoted toward them a millisecond later. Her face turned stricken, and she started to back away, screaming. "No! Leave! *You have to leave!*"

Noah was the closest, and he only ran faster. So did Aiden and Autumn.

Tears streaked down Winter's cheeks, and her arm trembled as she lifted her hand. Autumn's breath caught. People all around started shrieking.

"Quiet!" At Winter's shout, the shrieking abated, replaced by terrified whimpers. Still sobbing, she pointed the weapon at Noah. "Go! Get out of here!"

"No!" His scream was just one frantic voice amongst thousands.

Autumn's heart seized as he kept pushing forward... straight toward the barrel of Winter's gun. The whimpers gathered in volume until they formed a strange drone, with an occasional shushing and sob breaking through.

A large cluster of teen girls leapt to their feet and made a run for it, crying and pushing to get away, and for a split second, Autumn lost sight of her in the chaos.

When she regained her line of vision, Winter had lowered the gun and was craning her neck, her movements frantic as she scoured the crowd. Autumn darted forward, and their eyes locked. The next moment, Winter angled her phone from her face just long enough to rip something from her ear and hurl it at Autumn.

On instinct, Autumn jumped and snatched the projectile out of the air. Pulse pounding, she opened her hand to reveal a small, round object.

An earbud.

Quick thinking, Agent Black.

Placing the bud on mute, Autumn immediately shoved the device into her own ear, flinching when Justin's wild laughter crackled through.

He sounded further gone than ever. High-pitched and out of control, like he was decompensating.

If his mental state really had deteriorated, then there was

a strong possibility none of them would be making it out of this alive because Justin Black wanted them dead.

All of them. The entire world.

"Okay, Sis, two minutes. Pick somebody and shoot, or you go kaboom. One person or thousands? Make the call, Winter! Make the damn call!" More laughter.

"He's making her choose! Shoot someone, or he detonates the bomb!" Autumn shouted at Bree, Mia, and Miguel, who'd just sprinted up behind her.

"She has to unzip her jacket. We have to know what we're up against." Aiden waved his arms high in the air, catching Winter's attention. He mimicked a downward zip motion across his body, repeating the silent instruction twice.

Winter kept the phone pointed to her face while she lowered the zipper of her jacket with one gentle pull.

Autumn's stomach bottomed out. C-4 cartridges circled Winter's waist, secured in place by a row of pockets attached to the black vest encasing her body. Bright yellow wires connected each cartridge.

She didn't know one bomb from the next, but that contraption appeared nasty.

Aiden's phone was to his ear, summoning the bomb squad he'd already called to the scene. They reached the team within moments, one of them dropping to the ground and crawling toward Winter.

Disguised by the crowd but not nearly enough.

Autumn whirled to Aiden. "Justin's going to spot him if he's watching TV!"

Aiden nodded before swiping at his phone. Seconds later, he was ordering the police to have the media keep filming, but tell all cameras to avoid any footage near the ground.

Autumn bit her cheek so hard she tasted blood. Considering that this was a media holiday as far as sensational news went, she didn't know if the order would do any good. If the tech was spotted, Justin wouldn't hesitate to press that damn button.

His demonic voice hit her eardrums once again. "What in the damn hell? How did they...wow, Sissy. Maybe loverboy *actually loves you.* Yes. I see him, so don't try to deny it." Justin giggled, sending goose bumps crawling across Autumn's skin. "Pressure is off, Sis. I'm picking the first victim for you. Shoot your boyfriend now, or everybody dies!"

"No!" Winter screamed at her brother.

Autumn grabbed Aiden's coat sleeve. "He's ordered her to shoot Noah! Immediately!"

"Do it, Winter! Shoot him now! Shoot him now!" Justin's voice was no longer human.

Winter's hair whipped as she shook her head. "No! Nooo!"

But Noah simply nodded, exuding an eerie calm and thumping his chest.

Oh, god. He was telling her to do it. To shoot him. Widening his stance, he braced for impact.

"He's counting down!" Autumn relayed Justin's words, her heart galloping in her chest. "Five...four..."

Winter's hands shook violently as she trained the gun on Noah, making Justin squeal with delight before he continued to count. "Three! Two! One—"

The roar of gunfire ripped through the air as Noah flew backward, landing in a crumpled heap on his side.

Winter swayed, and her legs shook so hard Autumn feared her friend would collapse. She appeared to catch herself at the last moment, holding her stance as her shoulders shook with sobs.

"What a good little serial killer you're turning out to be, Sissy! I knew it! I knew you had it in you!"

Justin's vile congratulations filled Autumn's ear. She

tuned him out as she willed Noah to move, her nails biting into her palms.

Come on, Agent Dalton. Show us you're okay.

Relief poured through her when he offered a weak thumbs-up. His Kevlar vest had taken the bullet, and though his body would hurt like hell for the next few days, he was alive.

For now.

"Two more minutes, Agent Black! Let's keep this circus roaring!" Justin screamed the order, and Autumn repeated his words to the team.

Bree double-checked her vest and took a deep breath. Before anyone could weigh in on the decision, she'd scurried forward to join a group of huddled civilians on the ground. Autumn watched Winter and Bree lock eyes, and Winter gave an infinitesimal nod of understanding.

Shit. Bree was offering herself up as a target too.

"Thirty seconds left. You'd better hurry!"

"He's counting again!" Autumn's nerves stretched to a breaking point as the bomb tech continued to snip wires from a kneeling position. The tech was slow, methodical, but every time a new wire was cut, Autumn couldn't help but brace for impact.

One wrong wire. That was all it would take to blow them all to dust.

Hang in there, Winter.

If Autumn was this stressed, how panicked must her friend feel, with that awful thing strapped to her? Yet Agent Black endured the storm like the pro she was, filling Autumn's chest with a fierce pride.

The media wouldn't be able to spin the truth this time. Winter was clearly a victim in this situation, and if Autumn had anything to do with it, Winter would be hailed a hero after this was all over.

Special Agent Winter Black *was* a hero.

"Five, four…"

As time ran down, Winter "picked" Bree from the crowd, motioning at the agent with her gun. "You, stand up!"

Bree rose on shaky legs, sending Justin into uncontrolled chortles. "Yes! Go for it! Shoot that bitch! Three! Two!"

Bree burst into tears, begging for her life. "Please! I have a family! No! *Pleeease!*" Autumn had the fleeting thought that Bree had missed her calling as an actress before the bullet struck her vest and blew her backward.

"Yes! Beautiful! *Beautiful!* Do you feel that? Do you understand now? Another! *Pick another!*" Justin demanded, laughing and crying.

"He wants another target," Autumn relayed. More disturbing than anything was that Justin sounded genuinely happy. He wasn't faking or manipulating this time. He was thrilled.

"Me." Chris stepped forward, but Autumn grabbed his arm.

"You look way too much like a Fed."

"She's right. Lose the jacket," Aiden ordered.

Chris ripped off his jacket and tie, rolled up his sleeves, and grabbed a baseball cap off a hunched-down kid. He began crouching his way through the crowd, ready to provide yet another target for Justin's madness.

The bomb tech signaled them, giving a thumbs-up and staying close to the ground.

The vest was disarmed. They'd saved her.

"No bullet for Parker today." Aiden's voice beside her bordered on ironic humor.

Amid a rush of dizzying relief, Autumn couldn't deny that she was a tiny bit disappointed to miss the sight of Chris taking one to the chest. She experienced an immediate pang of guilt for the horrible thought, but none of that mattered when she glimpsed Winter throwing herself into Noah's arms. Agent Dalton winced but held her tightly to him.

Safe. Winter was safe. And so were the thousands of hysterical humans still hunched down in terror. It was going to take a hot minute to spread the word that the threat of imminent danger was gone, but before Autumn could even begin to assist with the crowd, Winter caught her eye and held out an arm, beckoning her.

Tears blurred Autumn's eyes as she hurried over. She'd hugged Winter a million times before, but grabbing hold of her now was different. Heavenly. The affection squeezing her chest caused Autumn actual pain.

Behind them, the rest of the team rushed in, joining their little group as they threw their arms around each other. As the vigil goers began to realize they weren't going to be joining their beloved and ill-fated popstar in the afterlife just yet, people began embracing in droves.

"I wouldn't be so happy if I were you!! You think this is the end? *This isn't the fucking end!* You're all going to get *way worse* than you already had coming for you! You're going to wish you were never born! *I'm going to bleed every single one of you—*" Autumn ripped Justin's voice from her ear, handing the earbud to Aiden.

SSA Parrish gave her a short nod, slipped the bud into his own ear, and began to make his way out of the crowd. The job wasn't over for him.

Or any of them.

Autumn gazed at Aiden's retreating back, remembering that, though they'd saved Winter, they still had a psychopath to catch and an innocent little boy to rescue.

The hunt had only just begun.

32

I leaned back in the leather seat, the airplane engine whirring as the pilot prepared for takeoff. I'd been livid when my plans all went down the crapper right in front of my eyes. I was still technically livid, but self-control was an important part of getting the hell away from D.C. so that I could start over.

Try again.

I rubbed my aching, spinning head. Every damn little thing had worked to perfection right up until the end. I'd lost control of the situation right at the most important part. The big bang.

Where did I go wrong? Had I rushed things, or had I simply fallen prey to bad timing?

Grandpa had been with me, and I'd done exactly what he wanted. I'd even given up my ideas about keeping Winter around. I'd sacrificed her on the damn altar to prove my allegiance to Grandpa's vision.

And I'd sensed his forgiveness. He wasn't mad anymore. He'd stopped screaming in my head.

But maybe I'd had a lesson to learn. The short amount of

time I'd spent considering whether or not I could bend Grandpa's plans to include my sister had irreversibly thrown everything off.

He'd protected me, of course. I was still a free man, and that had to be Grandpa's doing. The unexpected twist I'd faced in D.C. could have very easily ended with my incarceration.

Again.

Instead, I had another chance. And this time, I would do it right.

"No more whores interfering and messing with my brain," I murmured.

Taking Winter along for the ride had been a test, one that I'd almost failed. Winter wasn't my sister. She wasn't family. She was an abomination who happened to have been crapped out of the same filthy woman, and that wasn't *my* fault.

Grandpa had saved me from my "family." He'd given me a real life.

I glanced down at Tiny Tim, fast asleep in the seat beside me. My Greatest Fan had provided a private plane, allowing me and my little buddy a nice, swift getaway. I really did have to hand it to the asshole. The dude had connections.

I refused to believe it was a woman at this point. Any woman with that much power was just disgusting. Impossible to digest.

I stroked Tim's messy hair. This was all too perfect. Poetic, even.

Grandpa had killed my parents so that I could be placed on my correct path, and now I'd killed Tim's parents so that he could begin his new path at my side.

Such a lucky little kid. He just didn't know it yet.

I flipped open the file my Greatest Fan had provided for

me. Tiny Tim and I were about to take on some brand-spanking-new, squeaky-clean identities.

I would become Daniel. The name meant "only God is my judge." Perfect. Cuz every man and woman on this planet could suck it as far as I was concerned.

Tim would become Benjamin, although I planned to call him Ben. His new name meant "son of the right hand."

And I *was* the right hand of God, wasn't I? Grandpa had said as much. He'd told me I was chosen, and there was no doubt left in my entire being that he'd been right.

I'd *felt* it.

I would plan better this time. Much better. I'd go away with Ben and get some things straight in my head. Get some new ideas churning.

Teach Ben what he could be.

This wasn't even a setback. Not really. I'd come out of this more powerful than ever, and my reemergence into the world would be a beautiful sight to see.

A sight no one would ever forget. I'd make sure of that.

The plane made a perfect, smooth takeoff, lifting me above all of the dumbasses who thought they'd be able to lock me up again.

As my stomach dipped, outside the window a series of fireworks burst in the sky over the city. Good ole 'Merica. Always celebrating some meaningless milestone that would never improve their pathetic, miserable lives by one smidge of an iota. I would have liked for my own explosion to have happened today, but that could wait.

"I'll be back, motherfuckers." I closed my eyes and settled back into my seat.

One thing was for sure. I'd be back soon.

※

THE MAN SAT in his car, far enough away from the apartments to not arouse suspicions but close enough to watch. He'd been watching her a lot lately.

And now, on this fine February day, the beautiful redhead was hurrying back and forth from her apartment door, tossing bags into the trunk of her car.

He knew where she was going. He had plenty of contacts to keep him apprised of her schedule.

Autumn Trent was being sent to Quantico for her official FBI training. That meant twenty weeks of not being able to follow or observe her. He wouldn't be able to touch the woman after she disappeared behind those hallowed walls.

He scooted the seat back and stretched his legs. Twenty weeks was a drop in the bucket when you were a patient man, and he could bide his time as well as anyone.

Sure, maybe Autumn would return from that time away a bit more lethal than she'd been going in, but that just upped the entertainment factor. He was more than prepared for an extended fight. In fact, he eagerly anticipated one.

In a battle of wits and wills, he had no doubt who'd emerge victorious.

Strengthen up, sweetheart.

Her absence permitted him five whole months to plan. More than ample time to formulate a strategy, especially for someone of his superior intellect.

A smile stretched across his face as he recalled how he'd helped Justin Black get the upper hand on the FBI. If they'd had just a bit more time to plan, there was no doubt in his mind that the events would have ended on a more successful note.

He chalked the whole thing up as a learning experience, as well as entertainment. Winter Black's abduction had been one hell of a spectacle to ogle. An exhibition that had filled him with great joy.

As a plus, he'd proven his worth to a total psychopath and thus had a nice little leash waiting to be tugged on should he ever need Justin Black in the future. Of course, dealing with that nutjob again would be something he'd have to approach delicately.

But oh, the divine pleasure of being in good with a man who had no moral limitations whatsoever.

He sneezed, and his nose tickled, warning of another one coming on. Cursing cold and flu season, he reached into his glove box for the small pack of tissues he always kept handy but pulled something else out along with them.

A business card. Shadley and Latham. He sneered at the logo, returning his attention to Autumn as she walked back outside, kissed her hideous dog, and handed the four-legged beast off to her neighbor. She waved to the canine and the neighbor woman before getting into her car.

He wrinkled his nose. Waving to a dog? Kissing one? Clearly, she'd formed a deep attachment to the little creature, to the point that she was anthropomorphizing it. Of course, pet owners did that all the time, but Dr. Trent was supposed to know better.

Really, such absurd, distasteful behavior from a psychologist. Logic followed that if something happened to the dog, Autumn would be devastated.

Like, say, something brutal and unexpected.

Autumn's resilience was high enough that he doubted such an act would ruin her life...but starting small was always a good idea.

Eventually, he'd tear her world apart, piece by painful piece. After the way she'd ruined his life, she deserved everything that was coming to her.

The memory of how gleefully she'd destroyed him made his teeth clamp together and his hands clench. He ripped the card to shreds.

After she returned, all full of herself with her new FBI knowledge and her guard totally down, he'd strike again.

He jabbed a button on the door, and the window whirred down. Gathering the shreds of paper in his hand, he tossed them out, letting them flutter in the wind like the ashes that had become his life.

She was going to pay for that. Soon, her life would burn too. He'd make sure of it.

As Autumn's car began to roll away, he pulled onto the road and followed her, staying a few vehicles behind. She came to a light and turned left.

He turned right, imagining those bright green eyes full of terror while he did whatever the hell he wanted to the brazen little bitch.

Anticipation rippled across his skin, and he shivered in delight at the promise of things to come. Delayed gratification often yielded the sweetest of rewards.

"I'll see you soon, Dr. Trent."

The End
To be continued...

Thank you for reading.
All of the Autumn Trent Series books can be found on Amazon.

ACKNOWLEDGMENTS

How does one properly thank everyone involved in taking a dream and making it a reality? Let me try.

In addition to my family, whose unending support provided the foundation for me to find the time and energy to put these thoughts on paper, I want to thank the editors who polished my words and made them shine.

Many thanks to my publisher for risking taking on a newbie and giving me the confidence to become a bona fide author.

More than anyone, I want to thank you, my reader, for clicking on a nobody and sharing your most important asset, your time, with this book. I hope with all my heart I made it worthwhile.

Much love,
Mary

ABOUT THE AUTHOR

Mary Stone lives among the majestic Blue Ridge Mountains of East Tennessee with her two dogs, four cats, a couple of energetic boys, and a very patient husband.

As a young girl, she would go to bed every night, wondering what type of creature might be lurking underneath. It wasn't until she was older that she learned that the creatures she needed to most fear were human.

Today, she creates vivid stories with courageous, strong heroines and dastardly villains. She invites you to enter her world of serial killers, FBI agents but never damsels in distress. Her female characters can handle themselves, going toe-to-toe with any male character, protagonist or antagonist.

Discover more about Mary Stone on her website.
www.authormarystone.com

Connect with Mary Online

f facebook.com/authormarystone
g goodreads.com/AuthorMaryStone
BB bookbub.com/profile/3378576590
p pinterest.com/MaryStoneAuthor

Printed in Great Britain
by Amazon

80804187R00210